the Cottage

Center Point
Large Print

Also by Michael Phillips and available from
Center Point Large Print:

The Secrets of the Shetlands Series
The Inheritance

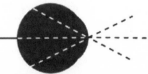

the Cottage

SECRETS *of the* SHETLANDS
VOLUME 2

MICHAEL
PHILLIPS

CENTER POINT LARGE PRINT
THORNDIKE, MAINE

This Center Point Large Print edition
is published in the year 2016 by arrangement with
Bethany House Publishers,
a division of Baker Publishing Group.

The text of this Large Print edition is unabridged.
In other aspects, this book may vary
from the original edition.
Printed in the United States of America
on permanent paper.
Set in 16-point Times New Roman type.

ISBN: 978-1-68324-168-3

Library of Congress Cataloging-in-Publication Data

Names: Phillips, Michael R., 1946– author.
Title: The cottage / Michael Phillips.
Description: Center Point Large Print edition. | Thorndike, Maine :
Center Point Large Print, 2016.
Identifiers: LCCN 2016033917 | ISBN 9781683241683
    (hardcover : alk. paper)
Subjects: LCSH: Large type books. | GSAFD: Christian fiction.
Classification: LCC PS3566.H492 C68 2016b | DDC 813/.54—dc23
LC record available at https://lccn.loc.gov/2016033917

This is a series about generational legacies, those that extend in both directions. As I have written these stories, my thoughts have been filled with influences that have come down to me from my own parents and grandparents and ancestors even further back, including their Quaker heritage. And I am constantly reminded of those who have followed, namely Judy's and my sons and grandchildren, and whatever my life has been and will be capable of passing on to them.

More than two decades ago I dedicated books of a series to our three sons. They were young, and my father's heart was filled with visions of the years ahead we would share together. Now they are grown men. Whatever legacy a father is able to pass on to his sons looks much different to me at today's more mature vantage point from which to assess life's unfolding and progressive journey—both mine and theirs.

Therefore, to our three sons and the men of spiritual stature they have each become, I gratefully and lovingly dedicate the volumes of this series.

---

the Cottage
to
Robin Mark Phillips

CONTENTS

Map of Whales Reef, Shetland Islands   11
Tulloch Clan Family Tree   12

Part 1—July 2006

1. Life Turned Upside Down   19
2. The Visitor   27
3. Tea and Questions   32
4. Ambitions   36
5. The Village   38
6. Baker and Bookseller   49
7. Wave of Past Doubts   57
8. A Fisherman Bearing Gifts   60
9. Two Thoughtful Men   67
10. An Observer   71
11. Memories and Quandaries   74
12. The Journal   78
13. A Legacy Begins—*The Crossing*   83
14. Texan Out of Water   92
15. Snooping Eyes   96
16. Unfinished Business   100
17. Busy Hands   108
18. A Legacy Begins—*The Hotel*   115

Part 2

19. Revelation 125
20. Outburst 134
21. Isobel Matheson 138
22. Fish Supper 149
23. A Different View 157
24. Overheard Threats and Schemes 165
25. Secrets 174
26. The Center 177
27. Sidewalk Meeting 185
28. On the Moor 189
29. Letter Home 198
30. A Legacy Begins—*The Cliffs* 203

Part 3

31. Saturday in Lerwick 219
32. Complex Spiritual Roots 231
33. Where Leads the Quest? 237
34. A Request 241
35. Profession or Calling 245
36. A Legacy Begins—*The Introduction* 254
37. The Price of Obedience 263
38. Sunday at the Parish Kirk 273
39. Decision 278
40. Lerwick Again 282
41. In the Lobby of the Kvelsdro House 290
42. The Mill 298
43. Say It With Fists 302

44. An Invitation   311

45. An Evening at the Auld Hoose   315

46. A Legacy Begins—*The Dinner*   329

47. It Can't Be!   338

48. An Empty Cottage   346

49. A Legacy Begins—*The Silence*   353

50. Above the Atlantic . . . Again   357

Part 4

51. Mother of All Reentries   363

52. High Tea Stateside   367

53. Disconcerting Proposition   381

54. The Green Fields of Home   388

55. The Boulder, the Creek,
    and the Meadow   395

56. An Angry Fisherman   403

57. Stranger in the Meadow   407

58. Who Am I?   416

59. Spiritual Connections   420

60. The Cancer of Spiritual Elitism   425

61. Partners of Necessity   431

62. Fountain of Darkness   435

63. The Rolltop Desk   441

64. Duty and Destiny   450

65. Girl Talk   461

66. Two Are Better Than One   468

67. Clandestine Search   471

Part 5

68. Crisis in Whales Reef   479
69. Aborted Plans   489
70. The Town Square Again   493
71. Confrontation   498
72. Secret Plans   505
73. Falling Out   508
74. The Cliffs   513
75. Guest at the Cottage   516
76. Saturday at the Auld Hoose   523
77. Keeper of the Key   530
78. The Reefs   538
79. Quiet Evening   541
80. Thoughtful Walk   545
81. The Chief's Cave   550
82. Cloudy Future   557
83. The Color of Love   562

CAVE

CLIFFS

PEAT FIELDS

N

MUCKLE HILL

SEA PATH

*W*HALES *R*EEF

AULD HOUSE

GARDEN

BARNS & PENS

ROAD

THE CROFT

THE COTTAGE

HIGH DUNES

CHURCH

FERRY LANDING
TO MAINLAND
SHETLAND

HIGH DUNES

HIGH DUNES

WOOL FACTORY

WHALES FIN INN

HARBOR SQUARE

ROAD

SEA PATH

Whales Reef Tulloch Clan Family Tree
(Descended from Highland Clan Donald)

Donald MacDonald (1749–1810)
Chief of Highland branch of Clan Donald

Ranald MacDonald (1775–1843)
2nd son

Immigrated to Shetlands with portion of clan after Highland
Clearances, commissioned chief of new sept by father

Duncan MacDonald (1805–1862)
Chief of Whales Reef sept of clan Donald

Flora MacDonald (1828–1899)
Only child of Duncan
Cannot inherit chieftainship

Frederick Tulloch   m. (1850)
(1825–1888)
Willed property and
named chief by Duncan

William Tulloch (1851–1915) m. (1874) Esther Walpoole (1853–1921)
Laird and Chief,
Renames clan "Tulloch"

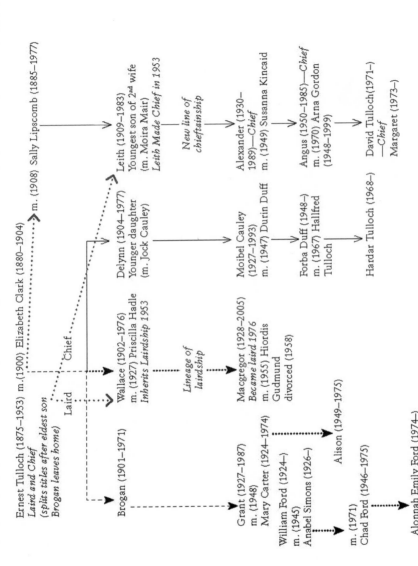

Ernest Tulloch (1875–1953) m.(1900) Elizabeth Clark (1880–1904)
Laird and Chief
(splits titles after eldest son
Brogan leaves home)

m. (1908) Sally Lipscomb (1885–1977)

Laird

Chief

Brogan (1901–1971)

Wallace (1902–1976)
m. (1927) Priscilla Hadle
Inherits Lairdship 1953

Delynn (1904–1977)
Younger daughter
(m. Jock Cauley)

Leith (1909–1983)
Youngest son of 2nd wife
(m. Moira Mair)
Leith Made Chief in 1953

*New line of
chieftainship*

Grant (1927–1987)
m. (1948)
Mary Carter (1924–1974)

*Lineage of
lairdship*

Macgregor (1928–2005)
Became laird 1976
m. (1955) Hiordis
Gudmund
divorced (1958)

Moibel Cauley
(1927–1993)
m. (1947) Durin Duff

Alexander (1930–
1989)—*Chief*
m. (1949) Susanna Kincaid

William Ford (1924–)
m. (1945)
Anabel Simons (1926–)

Alison (1949–1975)

Forba Duff (1948–)
m. (1967) Hallfred
Tulloch

Angus (1950–1985)—*Chief*
m. (1970) Arna Gordon
(1948–1999)

m. (1971)
Chad Ford (1946–1975)

Hardar Tulloch (1968–)

David Tulloch(1971–)
—*Chief*

Margaret (1973–)

Alonnah Emily Ford (1974–)

the Cottage

PART 1

JULY 2006

1
LIFE TURNED UPSIDE DOWN

Whales Reef, Shetland Islands, Scotland

The letter two weeks before had been brief. Less than half a page. Yet in an instant it had turned her life upside down.

Alonnah "Loni" Ford—orphan, athlete, and financial executive in training—was still reeling from the impact of the sudden change to her fortunes.

She pulled the single folded sheet from the pages of the journal in her lap and read it once again.

Dear Miss Ford:

Last year in the small Scottish fishing village of Whales Reef in the Shetland Islands, Mr. Macgregor Tulloch passed away leaving no will and no immediate family. After an exhaustive search in a difficult and controversial probate, we finally have been able to locate your whereabouts and establish contact with you as the closest living heir to Mr. Tulloch's estate. His holdings are sizable, and the estate includes the Cottage which was Mr. Tulloch's lifetime home, as well as most of the acreage and properties of the island of Whales Reef. These will now pass to you.

Unfortunately, time is of the essence in this matter. As it has taken us so long to locate you and, working with attorneys in the U.S., to confirm your identity by certificates of birth and marriage, it is urgent that you sign documents and take possession of the property in person within two weeks. After that time it will pass to the next in line.

If you could email me of your receipt of this letter, and your plans, I would be honoured to establish a time when we could arrange for you to meet me in Lerwick and make plans for you to see the property.

I am,

> Sincerely yours,
> Jason MacNaughton,
> MacNaughton, Dalrymple,
> & MacNaughton
> Lerwick, Scotland
> U.K.

And now two weeks later here she was—on the remote island with the quaint name, in the

Great Room of the so-called *Cottage* spoken of in the letter. She was sitting facing a huge stone fireplace, gazing into a fire she was proud to have made herself, its earthy bricks of peat glowing orange and hot.

Hardly a cottage, Loni thought as she glanced about. Everything Lerwick solicitor Jason MacNaughton had told her about the "manor house" of the former head of the Tulloch clan of Whales Reef had been confirmed the moment she'd walked through the front door.

Not exactly a castle either, she supposed. Yet in spite of its austere stone exterior, it was the nearest thing to a castle she had ever been in.

"Perhaps you are under a misapprehension about the term cottage," MacNaughton had told her. "The word is not always a designation of size. By the standards of the rest of the island, it is a very large dwelling indeed. Mr. Tulloch lived in it alone, however, along with his butler, house-keeper, and gamekeeper."

He was right. The place was huge.

A butler! Loni smiled as she remembered her reaction to the solicitor's list of occupants. She could not help being curious why she hadn't seen these three residents of the Cottage since her arrival. She wondered if the mysterious butler would be wearing a tuxedo and tails.

Her bewilderment over the time warp she had passed through continued as MacNaughton went on to tell her about the island and its clan chief and something called a *laird*.

"Times have changed," he explained. "The two titles—laird and chief—are now separate. But Whales Reef has deep ties to the Highlands of the Scottish mainland. These islanders march to a different drum than most of Shetland. The chief, who is more of a figurehead these days, lives in the other large dwelling on the island. The Old House, it is called. You, of course, as heir, will be the new laird—the traditional Scottish term for lord . . . landlord, if you will. You will basically own the majority of the island. Its tenants will pay you rent."

She still couldn't wrap her head around *that* idea. If she accepted the inheritance, she would be the "laird." A *title* to go with the inheritance, for goodness' sake!

The interview with MacNaughton had taken place two days ago. Loni's brain was still spinning. And if she signed the papers awaiting her back at MacNaughton's office in the Shetland capital, this Cottage where she now sat, and all the land and houses and buildings in the village . . . the entire estate of old Macgregor Tulloch would be *hers*.

She still could not help but think they had the wrong person. Yet MacNaughton repeatedly assured her there was no mistake. She was the long-lost great-great-granddaughter of Ernest Tulloch, the man they called the "Auld Tulloch."

As such she was the closest heir of Ernest's childless grandson, Macgregor Tulloch.

This unbelievable turn of events was all the more unexpected in that she had grown up knowing virtually nothing about her mother's side of the family. From out of the blue that unknown heritage had led her to this out-of-the-way place and a legacy she never knew existed. Her lengthy visit yesterday with retired veterinarian Sandy Innes opened whole new doors into her past. The aging Shetlander was old enough to have been acquainted with the Auld Tulloch, Ernest himself. Listening as he told about the family gathered for Ernest's funeral fifty years before, the heritage of Loni's dead mother gradually came to life. Through the mists of the past emerged an actual genealogy that she was part of.

She had initially not planned to accept the inheritance. She had almost not even answered MacNaughton's letter. But after the urgings of her boss, Madison Swift, back in Washington, D.C., along with a few unexpected tugs at her heart from the unknown past, she had decided to at least check out the situation. She would either sell the property or let it go to the next in line. Two of her distant cousins had been in consideration before she came along, according to MacNaughton, including one of the island's fishermen. Either of them, thought Loni, would deserve the inheritance more than she.

After a day and a half on the remote isle, however, and after her remarkable visit with Sandy Innes, she was viewing her decision through altered eyes. She still planned to be on her way back to the States in what she assumed would be a few more days. Yet everything was beginning to feel much different from when she had arrived.

She didn't know what she would finally decide. All she was sure of was that she had to give it more time. She had temporarily postponed her return flight. How long "a few more days" might be, she had no idea.

Loni folded the fateful letter from MacNaughton and replaced it in the journal on her lap. On the small table beside her sat a second leather-bound volume that had been occupying much of her time since her arrival—the journal she had recently discovered that had belonged to her great-grandmother.

For now she couldn't think about the many implications of the decision before her, whether to accept the inheritance or not. The overwhelming facts were too much to take in, that everything around her—this huge house, its furnishings and antiques and books, the sheep and horses and land, and most of the village she planned to visit this afternoon—by just signing her name, would all *belong* to her.

She had to absorb it slowly. Under most circumstances, she would have talked to Maddy, who was not only her boss but also her best friend. But this was a decision she had to make on her own.

She glanced at her watch. Thinking of Maddy reminded her that she needed to update both her and Hugh on her change of plans.

But she didn't want to telephone. She was enjoying the feeling of isolation. She didn't have an international cellphone anyway, and she didn't want to try to figure out the landline at the Cottage. They would probably try to talk her out of staying. She could already hear Hugh chuckling at the mention of chiefs and lairds. But for some reason Loni wasn't laughing. These people took their traditions too seriously to be made light of.

Maddy might understand, thought Loni. Still, she wasn't in the mood to talk to either her boss *or* her boyfriend just yet. She had to let the silence and peacefulness of this place do its work. Hopefully before too much time passed she would know what she was supposed to do.

She would try to find a fax machine some-where and notify Maddy in writing that she wouldn't be on the plane tomorrow.

Since this morning's breakfast of oatcakes—her supply was already running low—she had been trying to write down what she could remember of yesterday's visit with Sandy Innes, along with reading in her mother's grandmother's journal from ninety-two years before.

An hour later she was still seated with her feet up in front of the fireplace. On the low table beside her sat a large mug of tea, appropriately doctored with milk.

All at once she was startled out of her reverie by the musical chimes of the doorbell. Loni set aside the journal, rose, and walked through the entryway. She opened the door to see a man about her own age, with unruly brown hair falling over his ears and forehead. He was even taller than she was, which was saying something since she stood half an inch short of six feet.

"Good morning!" he said with a smile. "You are, I take it, Miss Ford?"

"Yes, that's right," said Loni, returning his smile. Her eyes flitted to the vase of carnations, chrysanthemums, and American flags she had set outside, a gift from Hugh delivered the previous afternoon.

"I noticed them too," said her visitor with another smile. "Quite a lavish bouquet, I must say . . . and very American. My trifling little offering certainly pales alongside *that!*" he added with a hearty laugh.

He held toward her a small sprig of purple heather tied with a tartan ribbon.

"I picked this for you," he said. "It seems rather a paltry gift now, but it is all I have to offer. I am David Tulloch. I came by to welcome you to Whales Reef."

2
THE VISITOR

Loni stared back at her visitor with a questioning expression.

"Thank you," she said slowly as she took the tiny flowers from his outstretched hand. "*Tulloch* . . . are you—?"

Her voice broke off. She wasn't sure what exactly she had been trying to ask.

Her guest smiled. "Yes," he said, "I am your cousin, if that is what you were wondering . . . a distant one."

"You seem to know something about me, or at least you know that I have Tulloch blood in my ancestry."

"Everybody on the island knows that, Miss Ford," he said, smiling again. "Your reputation, as the saying goes, precedes you . . . or at least your *pedigree,* which is what people around here have been most curious about."

"That's more than I knew about myself two weeks ago. About the Tulloch blood in my veins, I mean. So you and I are related?"

"By the slenderest of threads. Technically we are sort of *half* cousins, if I understand it correctly . . . half *third* cousins, I believe."

"That *is* a distant connection!" said Loni. "The solicitor in Lerwick told me that on the Shetlands, almost everyone was named Tulloch."

Her visitor laughed. "Not so far wrong!"

"Does that make me related to everyone here?"

"It's not quite as bad as that. In our case, you and I both go directly back to the Auld Tulloch, though from different lines."

"Oh, yes—I was told about him," said Loni, nodding. "Ernest was his name, wasn't it?"

"That's right," David said.

"Would you, uh . . . like to come in?" asked Loni.

"Thank you," David replied.

Loni led him through the entry. As they went, unconsciously she lifted the tiny bouquet to her nose.

"Not much fragrance, I'm afraid," said David. "The magic of heather is in its significance and mystery, not its aroma."

"What mystery?" she asked.

"Ah, there you have put your finger on the soul of Scotland," said David. "But it is a magic which has to be discovered for oneself."

"Can you give me a hint?"

"Perhaps that time may come. For now, I will let the heather speak for itself. At the appointed hour it will impart its mystery to you."

"I will have to take your word for it. So, Mr.

Tulloch," said Loni as they walked through into the kitchen, "though it sounds funny to call you that—"

"Why?"

"I don't know. The name has been so mysterious—just like your heather. The letter from the solicitor about all this came to me two weeks ago, addressed to Alonnah *Tulloch* Ford. I thought it was a mistake. Since then my only connection to the name was the man who died. I've thought of him as Mr. Tulloch. Now here I am talking to *another* Mr. Tulloch."

"There are many more besides, believe me," chuckled David. "And your given name is Alonnah?"

Loni nodded.

"It's a lovely name. I've never heard it before."

"Thank you," said Loni with a smile. "Would you like a cup of tea?"

"Yes, that would be nice."

"Actually, I'm a little new to the whole tea thing," she said, glancing about the kitchen with a helpless expression. "I think I'm starting to get the hang of it. But I would feel better if you made tea for us so that it turns out how you like it."

"I'm sure you would do fine, but I'm happy to do the honors if you like."

"Yes, please."

David went to the counter, picked up the water cooker, emptied its contents into the sink, filled it with cold water from the tap, then returned it to its base to boil.

"One of the secrets is to start with fresh cold water. After that, there's nothing to it other than pouring the boiling water over the tea—loose or bags, whichever you prefer. Everyone has to figure out their own brewing time and how strong to make it, how much milk to add—it's all a matter of personal taste. Some only give their tea bags a passing acquaintance with the water. I usually let mine steep three or four minutes. I make my tea strong because I tend to like it with more milk than suits most people. And I always use whole milk, whereas many use nonfat."

As he was talking, David walked to a cupboard, opened it, and took down an unlabeled tin. He removed several tea bags.

"You seem to know your way around," said Loni. "I didn't even know that tea was there."

"Lucky guess!" laughed David. "It looks like a tea cupboard, wouldn't you say?"

"Someone left me a box of tea bags on the counter," said Loni. "And a supply of oatcakes, which I'm nearly out of."

"Mrs. MacNeill at the bakery in the village bakes oatcakes every day. She'll keep you well supplied."

As they chatted, David brought down a blue china teapot from an open shelf above the counter and placed four tea bags inside it. In two or three minutes the water was boiling. He filled the pot with water from the kettle. While waiting for it to brew, he opened another cupboard, took down two large mugs and carried them to the adjoining breakfast room.

"You *do* know your way around this kitchen!" laughed Loni.

"Sorry, I didn't mean to intrude on your space," said David, placing the mugs on the table and returning to the kitchen.

"I don't mind. It isn't as if any of this is actually *mine*. Well, maybe it is . . . I'm still trying to figure out what it all means. I'm just amazed how you seem to know where everything is."

"Don't they say that most kitchens are organized along similar lines?"

"That I don't know, but most men aren't as comfortable in a kitchen as you seem to be."

"I do enjoy myself in a kitchen, and I know how to cook—or at least I can hold my own, I should say." He motioned toward the refrigerator. "I'll let you get milk."

He picked up the teapot and took it into the breakfast room. "I would say our tea should just about be ready," he added as Loni joined him with the carton of milk and what remained of her oatcakes.

3
TEA AND QUESTIONS

"I had been about to ask if you were the designated welcoming committee," said Loni as they sat down.

"I suppose something like that," replied David, adding a generous portion of milk to his cup and pouring a sampling from the pot. Judging its color suitable, he removed the tea bags and waited for Loni to prepare her cup, then filled it before topping off his own. "No one *designated* me with the honor, as you say," David went on. "I am a self-appointed committee of one. Some of the people, I am sorry to say, might not be altogether welcoming, if you know what I mean."

"I halfway expected that," Loni said, sipping at her tea. "Oh, it *is* stronger than I am used to."

"Add more milk if it's too much, or water."

"I think I like it."

"In any event, I apologize in advance if you happen to encounter any unfriendly looks. Our Coira at the bakery, Mrs. MacNeill, for instance, is one whose nose might be in the air when you meet her. She's a lady who speaks her mind. But she's a dear lass—pay her no heed. You mustn't let people like Coira get under your skin. For my part, I am simply a man who thought it would be nice to welcome you on behalf of our Whales Reef community."

"That is very thoughtful of you. As I say, I wasn't really expecting a warm welcome after all the confusion about the inheritance. I'm sure no one is pleased to have an American woman show up like she owns the place."

Loni did not notice the wince that passed briefly over David's face. Nor could she possibly have been aware of the boyhood memories that surfaced momentarily at her words.

"Actually," he said, laughing lightly as he recovered himself, "it would appear that you *do* own the place."

"I didn't mean it like that!" exclaimed Loni in embarrassment. "It was just a figure of speech."

"Of course, I understand. So what are your plans?"

"I don't know—how do you mean?"

"Only that you said that all this has taken you by surprise."

"That's the understatement of the century!"

"So what are you going to do? How long will you stay? Will you move here?"

"That's just what Mr. MacNaughton asked," Loni said. "No, I definitely don't plan to stay. I have a job and life in the States. I haven't even decided whether to accept Mr. Tulloch's inheritance yet."

"Really—why would you not?"

"I don't know . . . there is so much to consider." The thought flitted into her mind that she was being a little too open with this inquisitive stranger. He was a nice, good-looking, friendly man who had an engaging laugh and pleasant smile. But he had as good as told her that most on the island knew all about her. She should probably be more guarded in what she said. Their conversation would likely be spread all around the village before day's end.

"Did you know the man who recently passed away, Macgregor Tulloch?" she asked, changing the subject.

David nodded slowly. "Whales Reef is one of those small villages where, as the saying goes, everybody knows everybody. Yes, in spite of the difference in our ages, Macgregor was a good friend."

"And here I come as a complete stranger whom *nobody* knows to take the inheritance from more deserving relatives." Loni sighed. "I have to admit I have been a little reluctant to go into town. But I don't suppose I can delay it forever. I have to go to the post office, not to mention restock my supply of oatcakes."

"Ah, yes, the all-important oatcakes."

"But despite my reservations, the first two people I have met have been more than gracious. I thank you for making me feel welcome, by the way."

"That's why I came. So I'm not the first?"

"Yesterday I met an elderly man called Sandy Innes."

"Oh yes, Sandy! You couldn't have had a better introduction to the island. He knows its whole history and everybody living here. A dear man."

"Between the two of you, I am beginning to wonder if my fears are groundless."

"I hope that turns out to be the case. But if anyone bothers you, send them to me."

"And why you?" asked Loni. "Are you the mayor or something?"

"The mayor!" laughed David. "That's a good one. No, today I am simply a welcoming committee. David Tulloch at your service."

"Then I will ask you a question," said Loni. "What can you tell me about the two men who were in line to inherit before they located me?"

A curious expression came over David's face. "Only one of the two would have inherited had you not come along," he answered.

"Yes, of course. I think Mr. MacNaughton mentioned a fisherman called Harding, something like that . . . Harding Tulloch?"

"Hardar."

"Oh, right—Hardar Tulloch. He said that he was likely next in line."

The words hit David with the force of a fist in the face. "Uh . . . right, that has been . . . er, the general consensus in the village."

"I believe he is a cousin to me also."

"That is true."

"Then I must be more closely connected to him than you?"

David nodded. "You and he are full cousins, not mere half cousins."

"Which makes you and this Hardar cousins too?"

"Indeed, or as with you, *half* cousins. Hardy and I are probably cousins in some fashion with half the people on the island."

"What can you tell me about him?" asked Loni.

"Probably more than you want to know," chuckled David wryly. "However, I think I should leave it at that."

4

AMBITIONS

It would perhaps be reading more into his preference for strong American espresso to say that it divulged hidden depths to his character of which his American boss was unaware. It was true, however, that its acidity and bitterness mirrored deep currents of frustrated ambition that indeed grated with malevolent and acrid resentment deep in his soul. Yet perhaps his years of playing second clarinet to the blustering big man were soon to pay off.

The quiet Scotsman sipped from the contents of his cup, a triple shot laced with whisky, and continued to peruse the papers that had arrived at the Edinburgh office yesterday. The restructuring of the McLeod company's E.U. division appeared to be progressing as planned. He had been promised a key position at its highest echelons. Possibly he would be put in charge of the whole thing, or, failing that, certainly of McLeod's U.K. interests.

As he continued to scan the files, however, he could find no reference to the troublesome Cayman Island account, flagged last year by the IRS. It was the one skeleton in all their closets that had to be resolved—whether with creative accounting or by paying the money back, though it seemed impossible that much cash could be raised in time—before the tax bloodhounds closed in.

The word *embezzlement* had not actually been used. But once the IRS started sniffing around a major international corporation, hard after what they enigmatically liked to term "irregularities," everyone knew that was what they were thinking. Nor would they stop until *someone* was hanging by his feet from the nearest lamppost.

He would leave that to the company accountants. It was their carelessness that had caused the problem in the first place. Let them sort it out.

He just had to be familiar with every detail of the company's U.K. and E.U. operation, so that when the restructuring came and his appointment was announced, he would be ready.

5

THE VILLAGE

Emerging through the front door of the Cottage about an hour after the departure of her visitor, and seeing the rental car in front of the house, Loni realized she had still not made use of it. Where was there to go? She supposed she might drive into the village. But it was less than a mile away. That would set the locals talking even more than they probably were already—the helpless American who couldn't even walk from the Cottage to the village.

Perhaps one of these days she would take the ferry and drive into Lerwick, or explore some of the rest of the Shetlands.

One of these days . . .

The words reverberated through her brain. What did they mean? How long did she intend to stay anyway—days . . . *weeks?* That was the big question.

For one more day at least, she thought, and she

certainly didn't need the car for what she had to do now. It was time to gather her courage and walk to the village.

She crossed the gravel toward the long driveway leading in the direction of the ocean, then paused. She hadn't locked the house behind her. Come to think of it, she didn't even have a key to any of its doors. Neither solicitor MacNaughton nor taxi driver Sinclair had mentioned keys. The front door was unlocked when they arrived and had remained so ever since. Was this one of those idyllic places where no one ever locked their doors?

She reached the single-track road where she had first seen old Sandy Innes waiting for her arrival, then turned toward town. On the other side of grass-covered dunes to her left she could hear the sea.

It occurred to her that she should have thought to bring more suitable clothes for walking—jeans and her running shoes at the very least. Wherever she was going, she always took workout shoes and trunks. Why hadn't she packed them for this trip? She hadn't thought beyond the professional visit with the lawyer. The dresses, pumps, heels, and sweaters in her suitcase weren't exactly appropriate for exploring an island or a centuries-old fishing village.

Especially these shoes she had on, she thought, doing her best to avoid turning an ankle on the cobblestones. She should have worn the pair of flats she had traveled in. But she wasn't going back for them now.

Gradually a few cottages came into view. A few minutes later she entered the village of Whales Reef. Houses of varying sizes lined both sides of the road, lanes, with narrow gravel cart paths winding in circuitous array between. If some order existed to the placement of the cottages and streets, gardens and fences and animal pens, it was not immediately apparent.

Several women were out, some chatting over low fences, others hanging laundry on clotheslines. A few turned to stare as she passed. She pretended not to notice.

The street gradually widened, and larger buildings replaced the randomly placed cottages. She came to a walkway alongside the street and then the village center Mr. Sinclair had pointed out two days ago. Loni vaguely recognized a few landmarks. But the day had been foggy and her mind was a blur. To her left a wide street led down an incline toward the sea. Across the intersection sat a small freestanding building more modern than the rest, of brick rather than granite, housing a small market. She gazed past it down the street, which came to an end about a hundred yards beyond at a cement quay-enclosed harbor. A couple dozen boats gently bobbed in the tide, the blue of the ocean stretching behind the harbor wall.

Bringing her attention back to the main street,

she saw a small red sign that read *Post*. That would be her first stop. She continued toward it and opened the door.

Three women were standing in line, waiting for a clerk behind a windowed enclosure. Their heads turned as Loni walked inside. She felt every eye scanning her up and down without expression—mostly up, as she was easily eight or nine inches taller than any of them. She smiled and took her place in line. One by one they conducted their business and left the shop.

"Hello," said Loni, stepping up to the window. "Do you have a public fax machine?"

"Nae, mum, we haena the likes o' sich here. Ye'll hae tae gae tae the pub, ye ken?"

"I'm sorry," said Loni with a light laugh. "I didn't understand a word you said. I'm not from around here."

"Oh, aye! I ken that weel enouch. Ye're the American lass." He paused. "I said that we haena a fax here," he went on more slowly. "Ye'll hae tae go tae the inn—the Whales Fin, ken—jist along the street there. Keith's got a machine ye'll be able tae use."

"Thank you . . . the Whales Fin Inn."

"Aye, mum."

When she left the post office, the same three women stood huddled on the sidewalk, talking a mile a minute. They stopped as they saw her and stared in silence.

"Hello again," said Loni. She forced another smile.

There was no reply. Their conversation resumed in low tones as Loni continued on. In spite of the mostly unintelligible accent, she was able to make out snippets of recognizable phrases.

". . . do ye think the chief will say . . ."

". . . tryin' tae take the laird's . . . away frae the chief . . ."

". . . ye ken hoo . . . all on account o' that American . . ."

". . . a'body kens the chief canna bide . . ."

Their voices faded behind her. Loni saw the Whales Fin Inn fifty or sixty yards ahead. She walked through its door a minute later and found herself entering the dimly lit common room of a traditional hotel pub smelling of ale, food, and fishermen, she assumed from their attire, enjoying lunch or beer. Again heads turned and conversations grew subdued.

The tall American, attractive and athletic, would have drawn stares even had there been no inheritance controversy. The men, however, did not seem as eager to discuss her presence as had the women. Loni crossed the floor to the bar as their talk resumed. A smile or two broke out as she hit a wide crack in the ancient wood planking and stumbled briefly in her two-inch pumps. She recovered her balance and continued carefully across the uneven surface. From a strict and conservative religious background, Loni had never been in a bar or tavern in her life. Though the village pub that was such a staple of life in England and Scotland was an altogether different institution than those seedy establishments of the United States with *No one under 21 allowed* emblazoned on their doors, she could not prevent feeling intimidated by her surroundings. The beer and ale taps prominently visible above the counter, and an array of several dozen whisky bottles displayed behind it, added to the slight unnerving of her conscience.

A man in his fifties, washing glasses behind the counter, glanced up as she approached.

"Hello," said Loni. "I'm visiting the island and was told you have a fax machine I might use."

Just then a young woman about Loni's age breezed through an open door behind the counter, balancing a tray filled with several steaming platters and bowls of soup. She smiled at Loni as she walked into the room and began distributing the offerings from the kitchen.

"Ye'll hae tae talk tae my daughter aboot it," mumbled the man, nodding toward the girl delivering lunches to their customers. He caught the girl's eye, cocked his head in Loni's direction, then disappeared through the same door she had come through.

A minute later the girl walked behind the counter.

"Noo, then," she said, "hoo can I help ye, miss?"

"I was asking about the use of a fax machine."

"Oh, aye—if ye'll just let me get Mr. Gordon his pint," she said, holding a large glass under a tap and pulling the decorative handle. She delivered the foamy glass to one of the tables. "Here ye be, Mr. Gordon," she said, and was soon back with Loni.

"Come wi' me, miss," she said. " 'Tis jist in oor wee office in back."

She led Loni through a door at the far end of the public room and into a corridor from which a wide stairway disappeared above. "That's where oor guest rooms are," said the girl, pointing up the stairs. "Jist this way." She continued along the corridor, then opened a door to her right. Loni followed into a small room containing a desk piled high with papers and paraphernalia. A file cabinet and chair were the only other furnishings. "The phone's under this mess," said the young woman with a chuckle. She shoved a few things aside to reveal the fax machine and phone.

"I need to fax a letter to the United States," said Loni. "I hope you don't mind. I'll pay for the call, of course."

The girl laughed. "If ye be who I think ye are, 'tis right comical for ye tae speak o' payin' for the likes o' a telephone call. Ye're likely the owner o' my daddy's whole inn!" she added. "Ye are

44

the lassie frae the States, I take it, who's come tae inherit frae the laird?"

"I suppose so," Loni said with a smile. "I am Alonnah Ford."

"I'm pleased tae know ye, miss. I'm Audney Kerr."

"*Audney*—what an interesting name."

"That's been said many a time!" laughed Audney.

"I know the feeling. It's said to me too. I once knew a girl called Audrey."

"A friend?"

"Not really," replied Loni. "Someone I knew in high school. Was that your father I spoke to a minute ago?"

"Aye."

"He didn't seem too pleased to see me."

"None o' the folk are altogither pleased for a lassie tae inherit," said Audney. "Isna right, in their eyes."

"Is that because I'm a foreigner . . . an American?"

"Somewhat on account o' that, but not mostly."

"What then?"

"Because ye're a woman."

"They don't want a *woman* inheriting?"

"Such a thing's ne'er be heard o' on Whales Reef."

"Hasn't women's liberation reached the Shetlands?"

"Oh, we can vote an' speak oor mind, if that's

what ye mean. But a lassie for a laird . . . that's too much even for the women o' the island."

"Not very modern thinking," said Loni.

"No one would accuse us o' bein' modern, miss."

"I see what you mean," said Loni.

"Some folk may call it bein' behind the times. We would say we love oor traditions."

"What about you? Do *you* agree with the rest of the island?"

"Meanin' no disrespect tae yersel," said Audney, "I hae tae say I do."

"You think the probate courts made a mistake?"

"Oh, I dinna ken aboot that. I jist think it's wrong for a woman an' an outsider tae inherit the laird's property. But 'tis none o' my affair, an' the courts hae made their decision so 'tis up tae us tae make the best o' it, though not everyone thinks so. Most folk are more disgruntled than pleased. Hae ye met the chief yet?"

"I haven't."

"You'll be meetin' him soon, nae doobt."

"You know him, then?"

"Oh, aye. Everyone on the island kens the chief. His daddy an' mine were best friends."

"Were?" repeated Loni.

"Aye. The chief's daddy was lost at sea."

"I'm sorry to hear that."

"Weel," said Audney, pointing to the desk, "here's yer fax machine—do ye ken hoo tae work

46

the contraption? We send maybe one fax a year. I hope the thing still works."

"I'm sure I will manage," said Loni. "Although, come to think of it, I don't know if I remember the codes for the U.S."

"There's a phone book in the drawer," said Audney. "I'll leave ye, if ye dinna mind. Some o' the men'll be wantin' anither pint by noo. An' likely wantin' tae ken what ye said tae me."

"Thank you so much," said Loni. "You've been very kind. I appreciate your honesty, even if you don't like my being here. And really, I don't want your father upset with me—I should pay for the call."

"We'll see what comes o' it," said Audney. "Dinna worry aboot it for noo. Jist come oot an' see me when ye're done."

Left alone, Loni pulled out the letter she had brought from the Cottage and skimmed her brief handwritten message.

To Madison Swift,
Capital Towers, Washington, D.C.
Dear Maddy,
I've decided to stay a few extra days to get my bearings and decide how best to proceed. I've postponed my flight, so no need to pick me up at the airport tomorrow evening.
Would you please call Hugh and let him

know about my change of plans? My cell doesn't work here, but tell him I'll try to get in touch one way or another. The house has a landline, but I don't even know the number. I should get that to you just in case.

Thank you for encouraging me to do this. It's a very interesting place. Still not sure what to do. Much to tell you.

All the best,
Loni

She drew in a deep breath, then set the letter facedown into the machine, entered the codes from the phone book followed by Maddy's office number, then waited for the call to go through.

Three minutes later she returned to the pub. She caught Audney's eye as she was heading back into the kitchen with a tray of empty plates.

"Thank you," she said.

"Nae botha," replied Audney. "Come back when ye can stay for a wee visit."

"Thank you, I will."

6
BAKER AND BOOKSELLER

Loni left the small hotel with much to think about. In spite of what she said about a woman inheriting, the girl had been nice. Who could blame her for being a traditionalist?

There was the bakery across the street. She'd go get more oatcakes.

She walked through the door of the shop accompanied by the sharp ringing of a bell above her. A plump woman, ample midsection encircled by a flour-encrusted white apron, appeared from behind the counter, forehead beaded with perspiration. Her eyes narrowed as she quickly surveyed her fashionably dressed customer.

"Good afternoon," said Loni, suddenly more aware than ever of her American tongue. "I understand you have oatcakes?"

"Aye," said the woman without expression.

"How do you sell them?"

"Any way ye like, mum."

"Then . . . I, uh, I think I would like two dozen. That should do it for a few days."

The woman reached into her case. Her hand made several trips back and forth to a white bag, which she then set on the top shelf of glass.

"And what are those?" asked Loni, pointing beside them.

"Butteries, mum. So ye're the American, then?" she added abruptly. Her voice contained a note of challenge.

"Yes, that's right. I suppose my voice gave me away."

"Yer voice an' everything aboot ye, if ye dinna mind my sayin' so. Ye're no Shetlander, an' that's the truth. One look at ye's enough tae ken that. An' ye got no right tae be takin' auld Macgregor's land an' home fae oor chief." As she spoke, her tone grew heated. "The auld blighter was nae frien' o' mine," she went on, "but the chief's his heir, not yersel'. Ye got nae business here."

Loni stared back, momentarily speechless. "I'm . . . sorry," she said at length. "It is not my intention to hurt anyone or take what belongs to someone else."

"Then what are ye doin' here if ye dinna intend jist that? It doesna belong tae ye, so why did ye come?"

"I . . . uh—"

"Why didna ye jist leave weel enough alone?" the woman shot back.

"I was notified to come to the Shetlands. They, uh . . . they found I was related to someone I had never heard of," replied Loni, fumbling for words. "I knew nothing about it. Believe me, I am just as surprised—"

"Ye come tae git yer hands on what's no yer's," interrupted the woman. "Yer soft words dinna fool me. We ken what Americans is like. 'Tis a' aboot money for the likes o' ye big city folk. The chief doesna take kindly tae Americans, I can tell ye that. Yer kind has caused enough mischief on this island. He's no likely tae want ye interferin' like the woman that was here before. He doesna want ye here an' neither do any o' us. Git on the ferry an' gae back where ye came fae. Ye're no welcome here."

Tears rose in Loni's eyes. "Perhaps I should pay for my oatcakes and go," she said softly.

"I dinna want yer American money."

"I have pounds."

"I dinna want any kind o' yer money. Take yer oatcakes, but dinna darken the door o' my shop again."

Loni turned and stumbled her way out of the shop, the bag of oatcakes still sitting on the case.

Wiping at her eyes, she moved along the sidewalk, hardly conscious which way she was going. Suddenly she was a schoolgirl again, rebuked by Mrs. Schrock for being clumsy and ugly. She hurried through another shop door a minute later, her only thought to get out of sight.

As the door closed behind her, she found herself in a gift shop of some kind. She was relieved to see no one at the counter and no customers. Quickly she made herself inconspicuous between

51

several tall shelves. As she calmed and her eyes came into focus, she saw that she had wandered into what was called the Whales Reef Natural History Museum and Wildlife Shoppe. As her mind cleared, she found the contents and displays fascinating. Not wanting to engage in conversation, she kept to herself when a lady appeared behind the counter.

Fifteen minutes later Loni left the shop with a guidebook to the Shetlands, a dozen colorful postcards, and an assortment of Whales Reef souvenirs—fridge magnets, a mug, a small fishing boat with *Whales Reef* painted on its side, and a key chain. She'd have to get Maddy and Hugh and her grandparents more suitable gifts later, but this was the start of a memory collection. Though after what had just happened, whether she would want to remember her visit here was another question.

Outside again, she glanced back and forth along the street. Getting her bearings, she turned for the Cottage. She just wanted to get out of town without seeing or talking to anyone else.

She began walking briskly back the way she had come. A man was on the sidewalk ahead, arranging books on a small table outside a storefront.

"Good afternoon," he said, turning as she approached. "A pleasant day to be out."

The refined sound of his speech took Loni off guard. It was like nothing she had yet heard on the island. She slowed and stopped.

"You're not from around here," she said.

He smiled and said, "And I would guess that neither are you."

"Is it that obvious?"

"I saw you crossing from the bakery earlier. I guessed who you were. You do stand out. Hearing you just now confirmed my suspicions."

"You're English?"

"London, actually. We are both incomers and foreigners in the eyes of the good people of Whales Reef."

"A dubious honor!"

"Especially for you, I would guess," chuckled the Englishman.

"Why me more than you?"

"They've had several years to get used to me. So they tolerate my presence. But *you,*" he added, "you are at the vortex of a heated local whirlwind of speculation."

Loni sighed. "So I am beginning to discover. Is this your shop?" She glanced at the shop's door, which read, *Antiquarian Books, A. Lamont, prop.*

"Armond Lamont, at your service."

"I am Alonnah Ford." Loni extended her hand. "I am happy to see a friendly face."

"The famous heir of Macgregor Tulloch."

"Or *infamous!*"

"Perhaps not so far wrong. Would you like to come into my humble establishment?"

"Yes, thank you."

"I must say your coming does have the villagers in an uproar," said Lamont as the door closed behind them. "The local scuttlebutt has not escaped my hearing. I am not taken into the confidence of many of the islanders, though my, uh, my friend Miss Gordon keeps me reasonably well informed. I am usually able to put two and two together. All that to say, you are in an unenviable position."

"You don't consider yourself one of the villagers?"

"As I say, I've been here five years. Don't get me wrong. This is my home now and I love it. But with the exception of two or three, in their eyes I will forever be an outsider. In that sense, you and I are on the same side of the fence. Allies you might say."

"After the lady in the bakery, I can use all the friends I can get!"

Lamont laughed. "Yes, Mrs. MacNeill has a reputation for an acid tongue. She was merciless to me when I first arrived."

"How did you win her over?"

"I doubt I ever did. She simply got used to the fact that I was here to stay."

"I'm not sure I can wait that long. I may *not* be here to stay."

"How long are you staying?"

"I don't know . . . a few days."

"And then?"

"That is the big question."

"Well then, just smile a lot is my advice. No one can resist the smile of a beautiful young woman. When sharp tongues like Mrs. MacNeill's speak their minds, I make a point of bending over backwards to be kind, always with a cheerful word at the ready. She can hardly fault me for being nice."

"I shall try to follow your example, Mr. Lamont. That is very good counsel. But did they really all know I was coming and know everything about me?"

"I'm afraid so, to all but the last question. They've been talking about you for a week, though they know nothing about you. But that's the way with gossips, is it not—endless prattle about what they know little about?"

"I suppose you're right."

"On Whales Reef at the minute you are more famous than the queen, though not quite so beloved. But *about* you they know nothing. *Alonnah,*" he added, "it is a very nice name, by the way. It has an old-world flavor that might go down a little more smoothly than some trendy American nickname."

"Thank you for the warning. I will know not to spread around my *Loni*. It's what my friends call me at home."

"Right, stick to the Alonnah. If anything, these people are traditionalists."

"I've been told that. Do you think I could get away with calling myself Alonnah *Tulloch* Ford? It's not technically my middle name, but that's how the letter was addressed when I first heard about Macgregor Tulloch's death."

"The Tulloch name would certainly smooth the way to your reception. Do you have any other connection to the Tullochs?"

"I had a grandfather Tulloch back in the States. It's through him that I am connected to the Mr. Tulloch who died."

"That's a reasonably close connection—your grandfather, you say?"

"Yes, he was my mother's father."

"Then by all means, use the Tulloch," said Lamont. "If anyone asks me, I will say that I met Miss Alonnah *Tulloch* Ford, and a very nice young lady she is . . . in spite of being American!"

"Thank you, Mr. Lamont."

"Be warned, however—my endorsement may not go too far. Londoners are held in no higher repute than Americans."

Loni laughed. "Well, I appreciate it nonetheless. You have been most gracious. It is nice to have another friend in Whales Reef."

"Another?"

"I've met, let me see, three people who have been very kind, though one of them did say she was against the idea of a woman inheriting."

"That, I'm afraid, will be the prevailing view. However, I am confident that you will meet more like her who may not agree with the way things are going but will be kind nonetheless."

"Well . . . you are the fourth. So now the friendly faces outweigh the scowls four to one. Strange how hurtful words go deeper than kind words make up for."

Lamont nodded. "I know something about that myself. But you will find that Scots in general are large-hearted people—more so, in my humble opinion, than my native Englanders."

Loni visited a while longer before resuming her walk home, stopping at the small market near the harbor for a quart of milk, two boxes of packaged oatcakes in lieu of the fresh-baked ones she had hoped for, and some vegetables for her evening's supper.

7

WAVE OF PAST DOUBTS

Loni arrived back at the Cottage.

What should she call the place? she wondered. Was it really her *home?* The stares and whisperings were unnerving. She felt suitably humbled by the chastising she had received from the woman at the bakery. At the same time she was warmed by her exchange with the bookselling Englishman.

She wasn't looking forward to meeting the mysterious chief who bore such antipathy toward Americans. If she had, as many on the island seemed to think, wrested the inheritance from him, in spite of what the girl at the hotel said, he might not want to meet her at all. She could just pass the Cottage and property on to him. Or sell them at a fire-sale price, let Mr. MacNaughton handle everything . . . and get out of Dodge, as they said, before offending anyone else.

She tried to shake off the memory of the brief exchange in the bakery. But it was easier said than done. The woman's biting words replayed themselves in her brain.

"Ye're no Shetlander . . . ye got no right tae be takin' auld Macgregor's land an' home . . . Why didna ye jist leave weel enough alone . . . The chief doesna take kindly tae Americans . . . gae back where ye came fae. Ye're no welcome here." She had the feeling that Mrs. MacNeill probably spoke for most of the island.

She had grown up with whispered comments following her wherever she went, people looking at her with condescending expressions. Doubts and suspicions about her parentage had followed her into adulthood.

Secrets . . . secrets . . . her whole life was a secret. Innuendos, half-truths, strange glances. For as long as she could remember she had endured a cloud of secrecy hanging over her head about her past and her entire identity. Now the oppression of secretiveness was swirling again— the looks from the villagers, the subdued voices, some island secret about the chief and an American who had caused trouble before her.

She had done her best to leave the pain of childhood behind. Now all the old fears and insecurities were being stirred up, throwing her into an emotional tailspin that sent her back to those painful school days. This island was just like the insular community of her upbringing. All her adult life she had been trying to break free from it. Suddenly here she was in another small community being swept into undercurrents just like the ones she had spent so many years trying to escape.

She hated the secrets!

She had left home years ago to get away from the secretiveness of the Fellowship. She had no desire to be part of yet another community where people talked behind backs and where everyone harbored secrets.

Why couldn't people be open and honest and say what they were thinking? *At least Mrs. MacNeill spoke her mind,* Loni thought. *No secrets with a person like her.*

She should just forget about the Shetlands and the inheritance and this Cottage, forget she had ever received a letter postmarked from a solicitor's office in the Shetlands. She should just go upstairs and pack her suitcase, get in the car out front, drive to Lerwick, and fly home.

Let the next in line have it.

8
A FISHERMAN BEARING GIFTS

Loni's thoughts were interrupted by the doorbell.

She opened the door to see a great hulking man with a full crop of black hair, combed down but only partially held in place with some glistening scented substance. His most prominent feature was the girth of his brawny shoulders, which gave way to enormous biceps and a wide barrel chest, though in height he stood an inch or two shorter than Loni. He was wearing what appeared to be work clothes—heavy denim trousers and a thick green wool shirt—clean but probably not his Sunday best . . . unless this *was* his best. In his hand he clutched a bouquet of half-wilted carnations. She had seen several like it for sale at the market. The skin of his clean-shaven face and thick neck appeared as though they had been scrubbed rather harder than they were accustomed to and shone almost pink.

Seemingly taken aback at Loni's height as she opened the door, he quickly recovered himself.

"Good day tae ye, miss!" he said with an effusive smile. "'Tis a pleasure tae welcome ye tae Whales Reef. These are for yersel'." He handed Loni the flowers.

"Thank you," she said. "That is very kind of you. I seem to be drowning in flowers," she added, glancing toward the arrangement of chrysanthemums beside the door.

"I'm Hardy Tulloch," the man said. Having emptied his huge hand of the flowers, he now extended it toward her.

Hearing the name, a pang brought Loni's mind to attention. "*Hardy* . . . that's for Hardar?"

"Aye. Folk on the island call me Hardy. Ye'd be Miss Ford, I take it?"

"That's right," said Loni, nervously shaking his hand. "Come in. I . . . uh, suppose it was time I met you. Mr. MacNaughton in Lerwick told me about you."

"Who's that ye're meanin'?"

"Mr. MacNaughton. The solicitor who contacted me about the estate. He indicated that you were next in line for the inheritance after me."

She led Hardy inside as she spoke, noticing a faint aroma of fish mingled with the hair tonic following him through the door. Her new visitor glanced about uncertainly as he lumbered across the foyer and through the expansive entryway. It was clear that he was not as familiar with these surroundings as her two previous guests.

Having now acted the hostess twice, Loni led the way to the kitchen.

"Would you like tea?" she asked.

"Aye, if ye dinna mind," replied Hardy. "I dinna want tae put ye tae any trouble, mum."

"No trouble. I just came from the market and have a new supply of oatcakes." She filled the kettle with water. "I assume you are the chief I've been hearing about?"

A cloud passed over Hardy's brow. "Dinna say such a thing, mum," he said. "Meaning nae offense, but oor so-called chief isna worth the name. It would be an insult tae be mistaken for him."

At his words, Loni let out a sigh. "Actually, I am relieved to hear you say so. From the little I've heard I haven't been anxious to meet him."

"Nae—I'm no chief, though I hope tae be *Guizer Jarl* o' Shetland one day."

"I've never heard of that—what is it?"

"Somethin' like a Viking chief, miss, an' more worthy o' the honor."

"Then I hope you will be," said Loni. "And I didn't mean to offend you by thinking you were the chief. It's just that I had heard that you would be heir . . . you know, if they hadn't found me, and that the chief doesn't like Americans. I merely assumed that you and the chief were the same person."

"We're as different as any two blokes can be, miss."

"So *you* don't hate Americans, I hope?"

"No fear o' that, Miss Ford. Ye winna find a more acceptin' man than me."

"And is it true that you would be next in line after me?"

"Aye, 'tis true, miss. But why ask ye sich a thing?" said Hardy, attempting to sound nonchalant. "Ye're not thinkin' o' no layin' claim tae what's rightfully yer ain?"

"I don't know, Mr. Tulloch. From the beginning I thought that the estate should more rightfully belong to you than me."

One of Hardy's eyebrows arched slightly.

"Wouldn't you agree?" added Loni.

" 'Tisna my place tae argue wi' the law, mum, or what the courts hae decided," said Hardy.

"I have also been thinking, even if I am technically the heir," Loni went on, "that perhaps you and I could come to some arrangement for transferring the estate, or a portion of it, to you, or if not that, find a way for the two of us to work together. I'm not interested in financial gain, you understand. I am simply trying to decide what would be best to do."

"I will do whate'er ye wish, miss. I'll gie ye my support an' help any way I can. I jist want the best for the poor folk o' the island, ye ken. 'Tis all I want, whether ye're the new laird, or mysel'."

"I am glad to hear that," said Loni with a smile.

She continued with the tea preparations, then set a plate of oatcakes on the table. She and her new acquaintance sat down.

"Any way I can be o' service tae ye, mum," said

Hardy as Loni poured him a cup of tea. "Ye only need say the word. An' if ye need me tae watch o'er yer affairs here when ye're needin' tae return tae the States, ye needna worry aboot a thing. I ken the island an' its folk as weel as any man or woman on Whales Reef. I been here a' my life, ye ken. Jist tell me what I can do for ye."

"Thank you," said Loni. "That is a generous offer and takes a load off my mind."

"'Tis the way it was always done in times past, ye ken—wi' a factor keepin' the laird's affairs in order wi' the folk on his estate, collectin' his rents an' the like."

"Oh . . . a *factor*. Like a business manager."

"Aye, jist the same, mum. Ye'll be too important a lady, I can tell that jist frae lookin' at ye, tae be bothered by little things like one o' the villagers bein' late wi' his rent, or a cottage wi' a leak in its roof. Ye'll be too important for the likes o' sich worries. 'Tis what a factor's for."

"Well, it sounds as if a factor is exactly what I need. And you would seem the perfect choice—*if* I decide to keep the inheritance, of course."

"'Tis yer decision, mum. Like I say, whate'er I can do tae help."

The conversation did not flow so freely as with the two men Loni had entertained previously. Though clearly on his best behavior, the fisherman seemed uncomfortable in his surroundings. Whenever the conversation lagged, however, a few questions about fishing succeeded in boosting it along for another few minutes. Loni judged it best not to bring up the subject of the inheritance again.

"It would be an honor tae take ye oot in my boat," said Hardy enthusiastically as he downed the remaining half cup of his tea in a single swallow. "Ye could see hoo the men o' Whales Reef earn their livin'. Though ye'd had tae wear somethin' less posh, ye ken. The fishin's a wet an' dirty business."

Loni laughed. "I would definitely try to dress accordingly!"

"So do ye want tae try it then, mum?"

"I'm not much of a sailor. What if I get seasick?"

"I'll take personal care o' ye, mum. Dinna ye worry. I'd keep a steady rudder an' no take ye oot unless the seas are calm. We canna hae any harm come tae the most important lassie on the island."

"Well, I will think about it," laughed Loni again. "It would certainly be a new experience."

"In the meantime, mum," said Hardy, rising from the table, "my crew's waitin' for me doon at the harbor."

"You're going fishing this afternoon?"

"Aye. We're bound up til the waters off the coast o' Unst. We'll be oot most o' the night. If ye'd join us, I'd take ye for a wee sail an' bring ye back safe an' sound afore we set off for the deep water."

"Maybe next time."

"Weel then, I need tae be sayin' good day tae ye, miss. But if ye'd do me the honor o' haein' supper wi' me when I return, I'd like tae treat ye tae a catch o' my ain fish tomorrow night."

"Won't you be too tired after a night of fishing?"

"I'll git cleaned up an' hae a wee nappie first. Dinna ye worry aboot me, miss. It would gie us the chance tae talk more, like ye say, aboot hoo the two o' us can work together for the good o' the people o' the island."

"Thank you, Mr. Tulloch. That sounds delightful. I accept your invitation."

"Then I'll keep the best cod or haddock for oor supper."

"I will look forward to it. Would you prefer to come here?"

"That is very kind o' ye, miss. It might be more pleasant for ye at that. My bit hoosie is a mite fishy, if ye ken my meanin'. If ye'd care tae hae me, I'd be pleased tae bring oor supper."

"When should I expect you?"

"Right aroun' six, mum."

"I will look for you then."

"That sounds right fine."

Loni rose and they walked slowly to the door.

"Are ye sure ye winna come oot wi' us today?" asked Hardy. "I'd be pleased tae wait for ye."

"To be honest, I don't have any grubbies, as we call work clothes," said Loni. "And I have to say that the idea of going out on a fishing boat still frightens me a little."

"Naethin' tae worry aboot, mum. I'll let ye come aboard the *Hardy Fire* while she's still moored tae the harbor wall."

"Now that I can do!" laughed Loni. "Maybe in another day or so I will be ready to try it. And thank you again for the flowers."

9

TWO THOUGHTFUL MEN

About the same time as Hardy was walking into the village market for his purchase of carnations, his cousin set out from the Auld Hoose, faithful sheepdog bounding ahead of him. With his visit to the American Miss Ford fresh in his mind, David Tulloch could not erase from his mind the revelation that Hardy was considered next in line for the inheritance. Jason MacNaughton had not divulged even to him that the probate inquiry had progressed so far in Hardy's favor.

Walking up the gradually increasing slope of the Muckle Hill in the north center of the island a while later, he pushed his reflections aside as he recognized a familiar figure ahead. He quickened his pace.

"Reverend Yates!" he called as he drew near.

The minister turned and greeted David with a smile.

"Hello, David," he said. "I did not expect to find anyone else out on these wild moors."

"Nor I," laughed David. "But they are hardly so wild—I am usually out with my sheep on most days. I rarely meet anyone but the gamekeeper. I must say it is a surprise running into you."

"I admit, I am not a great walker," rejoined Yates. "However, I have had a number of, shall we say, consequential matters on my mind of late, including an important decision looming on my personal horizon. I felt the need for a solitary walk."

"Well, you couldn't do better than the Muckle Hill. There is something about high places that clears the brain and offers a broader perspective. It is one of my favorite places on the island. Have you not been here before?"

"A time or two, though not often."

The two men continued to chat as they made their way up the steepening slope, David's dog running ahead and behind and circling them before running off again with boundless energy.

"Tell me about the monument," said Yates, pointing to the slab of high stone rising out of the earth several hundred yards ahead of them.

"The Muckle Stane—not much to tell. It is reportedly of ancient date, Pictish or druidic in origin, though some say the Vikings erected it."

"And the symbols and inscriptions?"

"Their meanings have been lost to time. I tend to read into it what I want to."

"A universal human trait," said Yates. "Don't we all interpret meanings and events, not to mention history, people, and ourselves, according to our own experiences and biases?"

David nodded. "An apt observation. Yes, we do exactly that. At least I for one would plead guilty."

"So you have aroused my curiosity. What do *you* read into the stone?"

"I opened myself up for that," said David with a smile.

"You did indeed," laughed Yates.

"Actually, its meaning comes not so much from what I read into the inscriptions on the stone, but that it reminds me of the past, of the heritage left us by our ancestors, and of the charge upon my shoulders as chief to do my best for our people. I draw from the stone the reminder of the human quest to know our Creator. I realize I am probably reading more into it than may have been the reality. But that is what the stone means to me. Thus I often come here to pray."

"A noble meaning to give it, I must say. In my opinion, we never go wrong by investing life with high and eternal significance. If we err, at least we do so on God's side of the thing rather than man's—looking for higher meanings rather than lower."

"A profound insight," agreed David. "I will remember what you say."

They reached the peak of the hill and stood a moment gazing at the stone.

"So what kinds of things does the stone inspire you to pray?" asked Yates. "I ask because my present predicament, as you allude to, involves how best to serve the people of Whales Reef. I suppose in my own way I am in a similar position to yours, feeling the responsibility of my position to do my best for them. I am not sure I am doing so effectively. There are a few precious souls who seem to respond to my preaching, though mostly I feel that I am still a stranger here even after three years. I would like to discuss the matter with you in more depth if the opportunity arises."

"I will look forward to that."

"Today, however, I would very much like to know how you perceive *your* role. Perhaps that is the same as asking what you pray."

David took in the words seriously. He led them to a large, flat stone. The two sat down, and the dog, ready for a rest, settled at their feet.

"My father brought me here often as a boy," he began thoughtfully. "From him I learned what is called the Chief's Prayer."

"I would like to hear it."

David remained thoughtful a minute. "I pray," he said at length, "that the people would know God as I tend to think people of old were striving to know Him and reach toward Him with their obelisks and monuments. Essentially I pray that God would keep and protect the people of the island in His care and love and come to know Him as their Father, as Jesus knew Him. And I pray that I would be His faithful and obedient son."

It grew quiet for some time.

"A beautiful prayer," said Yates, nodding. "Now I know why I was led out onto the moor this afternoon—I needed to hear those words. It will help me focus my own thoughts about what I am to do."

"It would seem we are both a bit pensive today," said David. "I will leave you to your prayers. May God give you wisdom."

"And you, David. I am glad we ran into one another. I hope we have the chance to visit again soon."

10

AN OBSERVER

As the two men parted, David glanced southward and saw Hardy approaching the Cottage in the distance, flowers in hand.

In spite of the prayer he and the minister had just been discussing, the sight sent the young chief into an emotional tailspin. He thought he had resolved his inner conflicts, wrestled with his demon-angel, and placed both past and future into God's care. It became apparent that he had not laid the matter of the inheritance and his own future to rest as thoroughly as he had assumed.

It was on a day just like this a year ago, having completed a long and peaceful walk out on the moors of this beloved island, that he had discovered the dead body of the cousin he called his uncle Macgregor, lying cold in his bed in the Cottage.

He could not possibly have envisioned the complications that would arise from his kinsman's failure to leave a will. Everyone had assumed as a matter of course that David would inherit both estate and title of the aging clan patriarch. No one had foreseen that the heir hunter employed by the courts would discover more potential legitimacy to Hardy's claim than first met the eye, and then find an even closer heir no one had ever heard of in America. Nor did anyone suspect that unscrupulous oil interests had for some time been greedily eyeing the prime location of Whales Reef for their own ends.

The future of the island had been hopelessly complicated by the freezing of Macgregor Tulloch's assets pending resolution of the probate investigation. Unknown to anyone on Whales Reef, the laird's secret benevolence had for decades provided for many on the island through the subsidizing of the Whales Reef woolen mill. Suddenly that financial support had been turned off. Now a year later the future of the factory and its various enterprises was in more doubt than ever.

David watched as Hardy disappeared into the Cottage. The entire chain of events flew through his brain like an arctic nor'easter. A flurry of conflicting thoughts surged within him as he relived the year of ups and downs in the controversy over his distant cousin's inheritance.

He knew exactly what Hardy was doing. He had been watching his cousin charm unsuspecting young women since they were both teenagers. It was not difficult for David to imagine how Hardy was subtly wooing her trust. Most girls came to their senses soon enough. In this case, however, Hardy needed to succeed only long enough to persuade the innocent Miss Ford to relinquish control of the island's property to him. She might conceivably fly back to the States without realizing what she had done.

The moment his two cousins were inside, David strode down the far slope of the hill toward the North Cliffs.

As Hardy Tulloch and Loni Ford sat down to tea and oatcakes in the Cottage, and while David Tulloch was traipsing over the spongy moor of the island, a large black Range Rover came bounding along the single-track road of mainland Shetland. Seeing the road coming to an end ahead of him, the driver ground the big SUV to a stop a few yards in front of the small wharf.

He swore at the sight.

Patience was not a virtue he had cultivated in his personal or business life. He let out an exasperated sigh. This was not an inconvenience he had budgeted for. However, there was nothing he could do but cool his heels and await th arrival of the ferry that would take him across the channel to Whales Reef. He had no choice but to sit and wait.

He removed a silver flask from the pocket of his coat. Good thing he'd filled it to the brim with single malt before leaving the hotel in Lerwick.

11

MEMORIES AND QUANDARIES

His mind full of many thoughts, David reached the North Cliffs. He eased himself onto the thick sea grass a short distance from the edge and gazed out to sea. Sensing his master's mood, the sheepdog tucked in beside him.

For all his soul-searching and benevolent words to the islanders about making the American woman feel welcome and giving her their support, watching Hardy disappear into the Cottage tied a knot in David's stomach. Long-dormant resentments rose within him—toward Hardy's father and toward the American man and woman who had divided the people of Whales Reef. Their toxic religious fanaticism had created such self-righteousness between friends that it cost the life of three villagers, including his best friend.

Now another American was in the Cottage at Hardy's mercy.

The irony was so thick he could cut it with a knife. A tall American woman . . . returning to Whales Reef as heir to everything on the island. How could fate play such a cruel joke on him?

Unbidden memories washed over him from out of the past.

———

A ten-year-old boy, book of drawings in his hand, sprinted away from the village school, terrified at the touch of Sister Grace's hand as she tried to coerce him to repent of his sins. His flight cost him a whipping from his father, though he had chosen that over the humiliation of returning to the school and lying to Miss Barton and Sister Grace by saying he was sorry for what he had done.

Two years later that same boy stood on the harbor wall staring out to sea, a terrific storm howling around him, giant waves pounding the shore like thunder, the wind tearing the tips off incoming whitecaps in a frenzy. Behind him a dozen men of the village, including his cousin Hardy's father, stood stoically watching the desperate attempt to return to land by one of their fellow fishermen who had been caught off guard by the sudden storm. So deep had the exclusivity of the Fountain of Light defiled their souls that they would lift no finger to help one of their own, because he had not "seen the light." With tears in his eyes, the boy watched the laboring *Bountiful* in the distance, with his friend Armund aboard, slowly sink into the deep.

The boyhood calamities that had shaped him seemed to assault his life every two years. As a young teen he stood looking out over the same water on the opposite side of the island. His tears on that fateful day had already been spent in the hour since learning that the sea had claimed another life from among the fishermen of Whales Reef. The victim this time was Angus Tulloch, the chief himself. As the youth stood gazing at the expanse of gray-green water, a cold, eerie calm descended upon the son as he contemplated throwing himself over the precipice and joining his dead father.

The fourteen-year-old, now heir apparent to the chieftainship, had not done so. But the reality and strength of the primordial urge forever reminded him that life was both precious and fleeting. In an environment as hostile as the Shetlands, nothing could be taken for granted.

———

David's thoughts returned to the present. He had weathered those youthful storms. Though the pain of loss remained, he hoped he had become stronger from them. He had learned that God was to be found in neither prophets nor churches, but in the depths of the heart yielded to its Maker. He had lost a father, but he had discovered a *Father*. For that he was eternally grateful.

However, he was still a mortal man. A man with emotions, weaknesses, ambitions, dreams . . . and perhaps fears.

Now he was facing a new crisis. He found himself reliving the same question that had haunted him since the uncertainty and controversy over his uncle's inheritance had changed the fortunes of Whales Reef: *What was the right thing to do?*

The American heiress seemed like a pleasant young woman. But she was utterly ignorant of all that was at stake. Hardy knew that fact as well as he did, and was not above exploiting it.

Alonnah Ford had admitted to coming to the Shetlands for the purpose of getting the property off her hands. A terrible feeling in David's gut feared that Hardy would be the beneficiary of her unwitting generosity.

She had no way of knowing who Hardy really was. Was it his place to speak up? To do so would make him look worse than Hardy—low, grasping, greedy. The very idea was more than distasteful.

What action was demanded by *right* and *truth* when the only way to make that truth known was to divulge someone else's evil intent?

Was silence *always* the right course?

When did it serve the greater good to do that which, in other circumstances, might be wrong?

How well did he really know this American called Alonnah Ford? He might tell her everything and she laugh in his face.

One fact was borne upon him with devastating clarity. The coming of Alonnah Ford to the island had complicated the dilemma of the inheritance all the more.

12

THE JOURNAL

After Hardy's departure Loni drew in a deep breath and glanced around her. There was so much to think about—chiefs and fishermen, cousins and bakers, antagonistic women and friendly English booksellers. And still the great question hanging over her, *what to do?*

Her eyes fell on the journal beside the chair in front of the fireplace. Somehow she had the feeling that the answers she sought—about her past and perhaps her future as well—were waiting to be discovered in that nine-decades-old mysterious volume that had lain buried so many years in a drawer in her grandfather's desk back in a barn in rural Pennsylvania.

Slowly she walked toward it, hesitated a moment, then picked up the book, grabbed her sweater from the couch, slipped on the flats that were certainly better than heels or pumps for exploring the island, and set out for the fresh air and open spaces.

She wasn't quite sure what to make of the big man who had just left. It was hard to imagine him as her cousin . . . even a *third* cousin. Unconsciously her nose twitched as she walked through the foyer. The hint of fish still lingered.

He seemed nice enough. She couldn't hold being a fisherman against him. Fishing was obviously the lifeblood of the island and an honorable profession. He seemed genuinely willing to help. And as she herself said, if he was a more deserving heir than she, it was only logical that she rely on him.

She walked toward the shore, then along the sandy stretch of beach between the Cottage and the cliffs.

As she went, the island's solitude gathered around her. The stretch of beach came to an end, and difficult rocky bluffs rose ahead of her. Loni turned inland, away from the coastline, and struck out across the heathery moorland.

Where was it, she wondered, *that the youngster Sandy Innes was sitting with the dying sparrow so many years ago, with the two who had shared the poignant moments with him?*

She would discover soon enough that the book she was carrying in her hand would give her another perspective of that same encounter through the young woman's eyes.

Had her steps taken her inland and north as she left the Cottage, she would have met her other and more introspective cousin on his return from the North Cliffs to the Auld Hoose. As it was, the two passed within three hundred yards of each other like proverbial ships in the night.

Hardy left the Cottage in rare spirits and walked back to the village with a jaunty step. If his appeal of the probate decision failed, he was confident that he could win over the American girl until she was putty in his hands.

The crew of the *Hardy Fire* was standing by to shove off the moment he reached the harbor.

"Cast off, lads!" he cried, jumping aboard from the quay.

"Ow, Hardy—ye smell like a woman!" exclaimed Rufus Wood.

"Nae for long, Rufus!"

"And just look at you," put in Gordo Ross. "I've never seen you so turned out in my life."

"Canna be any explanation than that a woman's caught yer fancy," added Wood.

"Ye winna be far wrong," said Hardy, a twinkle in his eye. "An' a bonnier one than anyone's seen on this island, an' wi' money besides unless I'm no the judge o' character I think I am," he added with a grin.

"Are ye goin' tae marry her, Hardy?" asked young Ian Hay.

"Gie me time, Ian . . . jist gie me time!"

Ten minutes later they had passed the harbor wall and were steadily picking up speed as the next ferry left the Shetland side for its twelve-minute crossing to Whales Reef. Plowing through the water, the *Hardy Fire* sent a turbulent wake toward it.

At the bow of the ferry, observing the fishing vessel disappear in the distance, stood a big man sporting a white ten-gallon hat. He had no idea that the skipper of the well-appointed craft that had sent the ferry rocking was the very man his people had been negotiating with for almost a year in an attempt to gain control of the island he was now approaching.

Even before they docked, the Texan was scanning the shoreline toward the site his engineers had earmarked for the oil refinery he intended to build here.

The ferry bumped against the wood planking of the dock a few minutes later. The newest visitor to Whales Reef strode back and climbed into his rented Range Rover, glancing one last time at the red fishing boat disappearing around the coastline of the island.

Wandering inland from the sea, Loni spied ahead a large flat rock—the topmost third of a boulder mostly buried in the earth. It was set into the barren landscape, inviting occasional passersby to pause a moment in whatever business brought them here.

Loni approached, sat down, and set the brown leather journal on her lap. She looked about in every direction. She was completely alone. Quietly, peacefully, she drew in several long draughts of the refreshing sea air.

She pulled her sweater more tightly around her shoulders and opened the volume recounting her great-grandmother's first visit to this very place, and the voyage across the Atlantic that brought her here.

The Journal of Emily Hanson, she read in a careful hand inside the cover.

Loni turned to the first page. There were the same words with which she had begun the tale yesterday:

I am so excited! A month ago I learned of an opportunity to travel as a lady's companion to the Shetland Islands of Scotland.

When Dean Wilson told me why she wanted to talk to me, I couldn't believe my good fortune! She explained that her aunt needed a traveling companion for an excursion to the Shetland Islands.

At first, Daddy objected to my going. But after meeting Mrs. Barnes, who was so nice and full of enthusiasm about my accompanying her, Mama made it almost impossible for him to say no. As it turned out, Grandma Hanson was the most enthusiastic of all about the trip. She told Daddy that I was going and that was all there was to it. . . .

13

A LEGACY BEGINS— *THE CROSSING*

New York Harbor, The United States, 1924

A young woman of twenty-two stood at the rail of the Norwegian ocean liner *Viking Queen* bound from New York to Glasgow. She was certainly no world traveler, yet here she was embarking on the most unforeseen adventure imaginable.

She was on her way to the British Isles!

As she stood gazing over the side of the massive vessel, Emily Hanson's brain was quivering with excitement.

It had all begun a month before. Returning to her boardinghouse after morning classes, her landlady handed her an envelope that had come by messenger. It bore the stamp of the Dean of Women for Wilmington College. Would Emily come to her office at her earliest convenience?

"Hello, Emily," Dean Wilson had said when they were alone. "I asked you here to inform you of an opportunity that has come up. I am aware of the topic for your senior thesis. I think you would be well-suited for what I have in mind."

Dean Wilson paused briefly. "My fifty-eight-year-old aunt was widowed three years go," the dean went on. "She is scheduled to embark shortly on a trip to Great Britain. There she will join a Northern Adventure Tour to the Shetland Islands. My aunt is hoping to find a personable young woman to make the trip with her, at her expense of course. With your major in biology, and knowing of your interest in naturalist studies, I thought of you. I have told my aunt about you. She is very anxious to meet you."

"What would I have to do?" Emily asked.

"Simply be my aunt's companion, share her

accommodations, take meals with her, help her pack. My aunt is healthy and self-sufficient, but she needs someone with her, to talk to—a friend to share the trip with. You would not be a maid but a companion."

All the arrangements were quickly made. Emily's parents took her to New York. Now here she was about to set sail across the Atlantic toward whatever unknown destiny fate had marked out for her.

One of Emily's hands clutched the rail so tightly her knuckles turned white. The other waved to her mother and father on the quay below. Emily could tell that her mother was crying.

Beside her, Miles Hanson stood stoic, the brim of his black hat hiding whatever emotion he may have been feeling to watch his youngest daughter embark for worlds unknown. Of seven or eight generations of faithful Friends, Miles Hanson traced his spiritual lineage to George Fox and the beginnings of the Quaker movement in seventeenth-century England. Quakers in general were socially ahead of their time. Yet in spite of what he judged his progressive outlook on life, these were strange new times for men like Miles Hanson. Quaker women were growing accustomed to making their own decisions. Getting the vote was but the beginning.

Notwithstanding his objections, therefore, his wife and daughter made the necessary arrangements for Emily's adventure on their own. While they sought his blessing, in the final analysis Miles Hanson had had very little to say about it.

A deep resonant blast sounded from the ship's horn. Emily felt a tremor beneath her. The *Viking Queen* slowly moved away from the dock and picked up speed. With the skyscrapers of New York's skyline looming behind them, gradually her parents faded from Emily's view.

Though they were still surrounded by land, a wave of aloneness swept through her. Yet it was bracing, like a dash of ice water in the face. It was a good aloneness—challenging and stimulating.

A few minutes later they steamed by the Statue of Liberty. As she gazed up at the famous monument, a feeling of pride in her native land rose in Emily's heart. For the first time in her life, she would be leaving American soil. Lady Liberty's strong, stoic, resolute, almost heroic face seemed to invite the question: *What did it mean to call oneself an American?*

True, Emily thought, it was English blood that ran in her veins. When did one cease being English and become an American? Maybe she was not leaving at all, but returning . . . returning to the land of her roots, where her Woolman and Borton ancestors had come aboard *The Shield* in 1678. That shipload of intrepid Quaker immigrants were but the beginning. Quakers poured into the middle colonies of the United States for generations afterward. Led by William Penn's vision of peace, equality, and justice, they had established the most balanced and equitable colonial societies anywhere in the vast British Empire.

Yes, thought Emily, she would call herself an American. She was not only proud to be an American, she was proud to call herself a Quaker.

A voice intruded into Emily's thoughts.

"Oh, there you are, Emily dear."

Emily turned. "Hello, Mrs. Barnes," she said. "I didn't mean to desert you. I was so caught up in waving to my parents as the ship left the harbor, I'm afraid I drifted along the rail and forgot you were beside me."

"Think nothing of it," rejoined Mrs. Barnes. "While you were waving down to your father and mother, I went to our stateroom for my hat. And there is someone I want you to meet . . . a young man! He is one of the assistant stewards on our deck. He is very handsome in his white uniform. I told him all about you."

Inwardly Emily sighed. It had already become obvious that one of her hostess's objectives was to bring romance into Emily's life. How could she make Mrs. Barnes understand that romance was the last thing she was interested in?

Three hours later, after their first shipboard meal, Emily stood at the front of the ship, looking out on open sea. Mrs. Barnes sat in a reclining deck chair behind her. No land was visible. The gentle swaying of the ship under the ocean's swell gave further evidence that they were well on their way.

When Mrs. Barnes awoke, Emily was seated at her side, writing in a leather-bound book.

"Oh, good heavens," said Mrs. Barnes sleepily. "I must have dozed off. What is that you are writing?"

"My journal," replied Emily. "My grandmother gave it to me for the trip. She told me not to open it until land was out of sight. She said that it was now my turn to follow the Quaker tradition of journaling and write about my adventure."

"Why do Quakers keep journals?" asked Mrs. Barnes.

"I don't know. George Fox, the founder of the Quakers, kept a journal. So did John Woolman, the famous American Quaker. He is my great-great-something grandfather. For Quakers, the inner spiritual life is very important, how God speaks to your heart. Keeping a journal of thoughts and feelings and prayers is a way to record your life with God."

"I suppose I should know all about that. My husband's family was Quaker, though he didn't practice religion much."

"There are many branches of Quakerism," said Emily. "For some, Quakerism is becoming more secular than spiritual. But there are also ultra-conservative Quaker communities that are almost like the Amish in trying to remain separate from the world."

"Is your family like that?" asked Mrs. Barnes.

"No. I suppose we are somewhere in the middle. My parents are spiritually devout, but we dress and go to school and drive a car and live like everyone else. We value the spiritual roots of Quakerism. But my father is a banker."

The rest of their first day at sea passed leisurely. That night, in spite of the gentle swaying of the ship, Emily slept for nine hours and awoke to sunlight streaming into the stateroom.

Twelve hours later, on her second evening on the *Viking Queen*, most of the guests on the pleasure liner were just warming to the after-dinner revels. By nine o'clock the majority of those aboard were having a gay time of it.

In her stateroom, Emily sat with pencil in hand, reading a thick volume entitled *Bird Species of the British Isles*. These were more luxurious quarters than her spartan accommodations at Wilmington College in Ohio.

The door opened and Mrs. Barnes breezed in.

"Have you still got your nose in that book of yours, Emily?" she said. "You are coming to the ballroom?"

"I would rather not, Mrs. Barnes," replied Emily, glancing up with a smile. "I have two other books I need to finish before we arrive. I want to make the most of my time on the islands."

"This is no time for studies, my dear. Being on board an ocean liner is a chance for fun, adventure, romance!"

Emily laughed. "Didn't I tell you when we met that I'm not the adventurous type, Mrs. Barnes? You are the world traveler—I will leave the adventure to you."

"Come, come, Emily—the whole ship has turned out. This is the first big celebration of the voyage. The band is warming up. Dancing will be under way before we get back. And remember the steward boy I introduced you to? He will be there, and he is very good-looking, don't you think?"

"I suppose. But honestly I don't notice such things," said Emily. "People don't accuse us Quakers of being romantics."

"Well then, I shall see if I can make one of you. Now come—put on that lovely green-and-yellow dress I saw you unpack."

"Do I have to, Mrs. Barnes?" said Emily slowly. "I will if you insist."

The older woman smiled a motherly smile. "No, my dear. You have done your duty by me for this evening at dinner. The whole table was taken with your humor and wit. You are more knowledgeable about politics and world affairs than I am. Some of the men around the table were astonished later when I told them that you will be in your final year of college next year and are traveling to the

Shetlands to research your thesis. Men don't expect pretty young women to be intellectuals as well as articulate conversationalists."

After donning a different pair of diamond earrings and adding another necklace to the two already hanging from her neck, the woman who had made this trip possible left the room with a smile and wave. Emily realized that she had grown fond of Mrs. Barnes in the short time they had known each other.

Yet the two traveling companions were clearly from different worlds. According to Dean Wilson, her aunt had cut a wide swath through the glittering social circles of New York and Philadelphia during the Gay Nineties. Emily, on the other hand, came from as straitlaced an environment as could be imagined. The most wicked event that haunted Emily's past was sneaking a drink from her father's coffee cup at seven, knowing full well that coffee was bad for children and would cause them not to grow properly. Now in her twenties, she still stood but two inches above five feet. This fact, she was convinced, was directly attributable to the secret sin of her childhood. Not even her collegiate studies in biology and human physiology had yet managed to persuade her otherwise.

14
TEXAN OUT OF WATER

As it rumbled off the ferry, Jimmy Joe McLeod accelerated the Range Rover onto the landing and turned right toward the village of Whales Reef.

The rough single-track road was not much wider than his rented SUV. Stares followed as he sped toward the disorderly array of stone buildings of diverse sizes and shapes.

He eased back on the accelerator, glancing to the right and left as the vehicle slowed. *Quaint* was not the expression this particular newcomer would have used to describe the place. A backward dump was more like it. The best thing he could do for these people was level these ramshackle huts and put the place to better use by extracting and refining oil.

He scanned the shop signs as he rolled slowly by. Now that he was actually here, he wasn't quite sure what to do. How would he find the woman?

The post office . . . one of these two-bit stores . . . *somebody* was bound to know where she was. His eyes strayed to the largest sign he had yet seen. *Whales Fin Inn*, he read. He knew the look of such places. A good old-fashioned pub. Just what he needed.

Best beer in the Shetlands, the sign boasted.

That was good enough for him. Where better to get an earful of the local scuttlebutt? She might even be staying there, for all he knew.

He pulled to a stop next to the narrow walkway, though the huge SUV blocked the street from allowing any other vehicle to pass, and walked inside. The clomping of his oversized alligator boots echoed across the wood floor as heads turned to see the massive Texan striding across it. Most of those present had never observed such a spectacle in their lives. Whether a genuine beaver hat had ever been on the island was doubtful. The man was straight out of a John Wayne movie.

"How do, partner!" bellowed Jimmy Joe as he approached the bar. "That's some claim outside about your beer."

"Most folk on the island are partial tae my great-grandfather's special," replied the man behind the counter.

"Well, that's good enough for me. Pour me a glass and I'll give your ol' granddaddy's brew a try."

Keith Kerr held a pint glass under the tap. Jimmy Joe watched the frothing amber liquid fill it to the rim. Keith set it on the counter in front of his colorful customer, who took a long and satisfying swallow.

"Well, dang if your granddaddy didn't know what he was about!" he exclaimed. "That's right fine indeed. I might have to wrangle the Texas rights to this brew out of you."

"I'm afraid the recipe for our special blend is not for sale."

"That's been said to me before, partner. But when Jimmy Joe talks business, ain't too many who can say no. Money talks, and when I want something I let the money swing the deal. But the reason I'm here is that I'm looking for a gal by the name of Ford, an American. Got anybody like that staying here?"

"I'm afraid not, sir."

"She's around someplace. Word is, she's tangled up in this inheritance business of yours since the old fella died a year ago. You must have heard of her."

"I have," said Keith. He did not care for this big man's bluster. With the exception of his two quirky regulars, the MacFarlane sisters, the hotel owner's prejudice against the laird's so-called heir spread to all Americans.

"Know where I'd find her?"

"Can't say as I do."

"Daddy, why don't you tell the man?" said a feminine voice as Keith's daughter came out from the kitchen. "She's at the Cottage. A'body kens that."

Jimmy Joe turned toward the newcomer standing in the kitchen doorway. "Hey there, little lady. Sounds like you're the one I need to be talking to, if you wouldn't mind repeating yourself, that is. Whatever you said blew past me faster than a tumbleweed in front of a West Texas gale."

"I was jist sayin' that the new laird's bidin' at what's called the Cottage," replied Audney. " 'Tis the laird's hoose, ye ken."

"Don't sound too imposing. What's that you call her—*laird?*"

"Aye. She's the new laird on account o' bein' Macgregor Tulloch's heir."

"An' ye're bein' a mite too free wi' yer tongue tae a stranger, lassie," put in Keith.

"Hold on there, partner," said Jimmy Joe. "No Texan's a stranger for long. The name's Jimmy Joe McLeod, and I hope you'll give me your hand!" He held his great paw across the bar.

With obvious reluctance, Keith took it. Jimmy Joe gave his hand a vigorous shake.

"Now that's more like it! And what's your name, little lady?"

"I'm Audney . . . Audney Kerr. This is my daddy, Keith."

"Well, I'm right pleased to know you both," said Jimmy Joe. "So where's this here place you're telling me about? I came to your town to have a little talk with this Ford gal."

"You don't know her?" asked Audney.

"Never met her in my life."

"Weel, the Cottage is jist oot o' the village aboot

95

a mile or so. 'Tis the biggest hoose on the island. Jist drive on the way ye're goin' if ye came fae the ferry, an' keep on till ye see it on yer left. Ye canna miss it."

"I'm much obliged to you, miss," said Jimmy Joe. "I reckon I'll be seeing you again."

15

SNOOPING EYES

Dougal Erskine had been keeping his eye on the Cottage for two days, doing his best to follow the chief's wishes, to stay out of sight and not bother the American woman until she had grown accustomed to her surroundings. He had not yet met the new so-called laird face-to-face. That she was an American was bad enough. In his opinion she had no right to the old laird's inheritance. But if anything, Dougal Erskine was loyal to his chief. David had told him to treat the young lady with respect, to keep watch over her interests, and to do his best for her.

He and the two Mathesons had slept at the Auld Hoose the first night. Saxe and Isobel were still there, along with the laird's dogs, but he had come over to his own quarters last night. Keeping to himself and staying out of sight, he had managed a few chores around the barn and stables and had tended to the animals while the lady was in the village. He was well aware of Hardy's visit and came out of hiding again the moment Loni disappeared behind the high dunes toward the beach.

He heard the engine of an approaching vehicle long before it rumbled down the long drive and wheeled to an unceremonious stop in front of the Cottage. He paid it little heed, however. Whoever was driving had not come to pay *him* a visit.

Muttering to himself about Americans and loud cars ruining the peace of the island, he continued toward the chicken coop to gather the day's eggs for Isobel. A few minutes later his attention was drawn by the figure of a massive man sporting a big white hat, walking around from the front of the Cottage, peering in the windows, knocking on the kitchen door, then continuing around the east wing.

Whoever this interloper was, he had no business prowling around the laird's Cottage, *whoever* might be the rightful laird.

The next instant he was on his way to intercept the stranger.

"An' what might it be that I can help ye wi?" he said, approaching from behind.

Startled by the gruff voice at his back, Jimmy Joe spun around.

Not often at a loss for words, the sight that met his eyes was entirely unexpected. He stood gaping at the apparition that seemed to have appeared out of thin air. The man's full salt-and-pepper beard and crop of wild bushy hair would have been enough to startle anyone. The bright plaid jacket, dirty wool cap, manure-encrusted boots and corduroy trousers, and the tall shepherd's staff in his hand—which Dougal had grabbed from the side of the barn just in case the fellow tried any funny business—completed the incongruous image.

"That is," Dougal added, "if ye dinna mind my askin' what ye're doin' poking aboot where ye got nae business?"

The fire in the man's eyes, and his thick menacing accent, were enough to jolt Jimmy Joe's senses back to reality. He broke into a great laugh.

"Where'd you come from, partner?" he said. "Dang if you ain't a picture! But I'm right glad to see somebody's about the place—tried the bell but I couldn't raise nobody."

"I asked ye a question," growled Dougal. "Do ye intend tae gie me an answer?"

"Musta plumb slipped by me. Your accent's a mite thick. What was it you're wanting to know?"

"What ye're doin' pokin' aboot. Looks like trespassin' tae me."

"Whoa, laddie—don't get your dander up."

"I ain't yer laddie, ken, nor anybody's laddie. So I'll jist thank ye tae be takin' yersel' off the laird's property."

"Hey, I don't mean no harm. I just came paying a friendly visit to the lady of the house."

"The new laird's nae home, ken. Ye'll hae tae come back later."

"When will she be back?"

"I dinna ken."

"Sorry, I don't follow you. Who in the heck's Ken?"

"I said I canna say when she'll be back."

"Where is she, then?"

"I canna say," answered Dougal, by now more determined to be obstreperous than he was protective of his new mistress.

"She can't have gone far. Is that her car out front?"

"It's nae her's," replied Dougal, truthfully enough, though conveying just the opposite.

"Will she be back today?"

"I canna say," said Dougal a third time.

Frustrated, but thinking better of alienating this local yokel whose support he might need, Jimmy Joe decided on retreat as his best option.

"Well then, partner," he said, "you tell her I'll be back to see her. McLeod's the name."

"I dinna ken when I'll be seein' her."

"Don't you work for her?"

"I'm the laird's gamekeeper. But I keep tae mysel', an' she keeps tae hersel'."

More confused than ever, and himself by now as irritated as the grumpy bearded fellow, Jimmy Joe returned to his car. He had a good mind just to sit where he was and wait, though he might sit all day. For all he knew, the woman had gone to the city. He didn't like the idea of being stymied by this cranky coot, but he didn't know what else he could do without riling the old cowpoke even more.

He started the engine, turned around, and slowly made his way back toward the village while considering his options.

By the time he reached the village he had decided to have something to eat at that pub—and another glass of what he had to admit was the best beer he'd ever tasted—then book a room in the place for a few hours. He'd catch a little shut-eye and try to knock out his jet lag. Then he'd drive out to the big house again in a couple of hours.

Hopefully by then the lady would be back and her meddling gamekeeper would be off somewhere with his sheep or cows.

16

UNFINISHED BUSINESS

Loni came to herself and realized she was cold. She had been sitting on this rock, reading for an hour, maybe two, and had completely lost track of the time.

Unconsciously she glanced at her wrist. She

wasn't even wearing her watch. It was so unlike her. She, Loni Ford, executive assistant to Madison Swift, whose every minute was packed with productivity and phone calls and reports and appointments . . . wandering about a remote island not even knowing what time it was.

Loni shivered briefly, then rose, clutching the journal that had absorbed her attention for however long she had been reading, and looked about. She had even lost her sense of direction.

She had come from the shore, and there over a rise in the moor she saw the roofline of the Cottage—*her* Cottage, she thought with a smile . . . *if* she decided to claim it.

Making her way back, she was not thinking of tea but of hot chocolate. She wondered if she would be successful in finding anything suitable in the well-stocked kitchen cupboard. Hot chocolate in front of the fireplace sounded like a perfect way to warm up.

The doorbell chimes an hour later roused Loni from an uneasy sleep. She had dozed off after her walk. She glanced beside her. The half-completed cup of chocolate on the low table next to the chair was now cold.

She drew in a breath and stood. Trying to shake away the remnants of her nap, she gathered her wits and walked to the front door. She half expected to see some familiar face come for a return engagement, though which of her former visitors might be calling again she had no idea. The sight that met her when she opened the door, however, took her breath away.

A huge man stood towering above her, easily six-foot-four and 240 pounds. If she hadn't known him for a Texan from the cowboy hat and alligator-skin boots, the first words out of his mouth would have confirmed the fact quickly enough. Her two island cousins, the one muscular, the other tall by Shetland standards, would have been dwarfed beside him.

"How do," he said in a booming drawl. "I reckon you'd be Miss Ford."

Loni stood gaping, trying to absorb the incongruous sight. "I'm sorry . . . you'll have to excuse me," she said after a moment. "I just woke from a nap and . . . I confess, I am a little bewildered. Am I still in the Shetlands . . . or did I somehow get transported to Dallas?"

The big man roared with a sound as gregarious as the rest of his manner.

"You're still out in the middle of nowhere," he said, still laughing, "you can take it from me!"

"I must admit, it's nice to hear someone I can understand for a change, although your accent is noticeable enough."

"You know what us Texans say—we don't speak with an accent, it's the rest of the country that talks funny!"

"If you say so," laughed Loni. "At least I can understand you. But what in the world are you doing here? I thought I was the only American for miles."

"There's a bushel of us 'round about these oil fields up here."

"Of course. I should have thought of that. I suppose you look like an oilman at that."

"Jimmy Joe McLeod, ma'am," said Jimmy Joe, removing his hat and extending a hand. "I'm right pleased to make your acquaintance."

A quizzical expression passed over Loni's face as she took in the stranger's name, but she couldn't immediately place it. With the sound of America in her ears, not even realizing it, the *Loni* came forward to replace the persona of *Alonnah*.

"As you surmised," she said as she shook the offered hand, "I am Loni Ford. I still don't know what you're doing here, but would you like to come in?"

"Don't mind if I do, ma'am."

Loni led the way into the house. Jimmy Joe glanced about with obvious surprise as he crossed the expansive entry hall and followed her into the Great Room.

"This is mighty plush. Wouldn't know this island had a place like this. Looks like the lounge of a five-star hotel."

He eased his large frame down and nearly filled the couch.

"They tell me it is what they call a manor house," said Loni. "I've only been here a couple days myself. From what I understand, this has been the home of the laird for more than a century."

"The laird—that's what they call their head honcho?"

Loni smiled. "Something like that."

"Well, they got their own way of doing things, that's for sure."

"I've noticed that too," she replied.

It was silent a few seconds. Loni was still wondering to what she owed the pleasure of this unexpected visit. Her visitor seemed to sense her unspoken question.

"What I'm doing here," said Jimmy Joe, "is that you and I got a little business to tend to, though you might not have been told about it yet. You are the new owner of all this?" he added, gesturing around the room. "I got the right Ford, ain't I? You are the lady that inherited old Macgregor Tulloch's land?"

"That's right," answered Loni. "Though I haven't actually signed the papers to accept the inheritance yet."

"I didn't know that," said Jimmy Joe with more interest than he allowed himself to reveal. "Well . . . don't reckon that changes things. Once you do, then we'll get down to business."

"What kind of business, Mr. McLeod? I didn't

realize that the late Mr. Tulloch had business interests in Texas."

"Wasn't nothing in Texas. It's his property here he and I were negotiating about."

"Negotiating . . . in what way?"

"He was planning to sell me the island, that's what," replied Jimmy Joe. "Best thing we coulda done for these folks."

"Nobody told me anything about it," said Loni, clearly taken aback.

"I ain't surprised. We were talking in private, keeping the thing under wraps, know what I mean? Didn't want folks getting all riled up. You know how these kind of folks are."

"But what could you possibly want with all this?"

"Investment, that's what. Ain't that your game—investments? Done a little investigating about you. That's why I figure you and me's cut outta the same cloth. Property up here in oil country's gonna skyrocket one of these days."

"I thought it already had."

"I mean *really* take off. I figure why not get in on it, and in the meantime do these poor folks some good."

"How would your buying the island do that?" asked Loni.

"The money, what else? I was fixing to split the profits sixty-forty with the old Tulloch fellow, so that he could pass on the island's good fortune to his people. I could make them all rich and still come away with a little profit for myself."

"What exactly would have been the terms of the split?"

"The island folks and their laird would get the sixty, of course. I ain't no greedy man."

Loni sighed. "I can hardly believe this. The lawyer handling the estate mentioned nothing about it."

"He didn't know. Like I said, it was just between the old laird fellow and me."

"You and Macgregor Tulloch had actually struck a deal about his selling the property on the island?"

"Yes, ma'am. My people were arranging everything. But then the poor old geezer up and died before we could close the deal. That's why I'm here, so you and I can get the thing finished."

Loni gazed out the window, trying to take in this sudden rush of new information. "Well, I must say," she said after another pause, "this takes me quite by surprise. I will have to think about everything you've said."

"You don't want to be thinking too long, ma'am. We need to get moving on this thing."

"Surely there's no urgency."

"You know what they say, a good investment waits for no man . . . or woman neither."

Words she had heard from her grandfather many times rushed back into Loni's memory. *God is never in a hurry.* Not only were their sentiments on haste versus caution complete opposites, so too, thought Loni, was everything about the two men.

"Still," she said, "I need to think about it."

"Don't mean to rush you," added Jimmy Joe. "I'll be in Lerwick another couple days. Why don't you come into the city and you and I'll have dinner and we'll hammer out the details? 'Course you gotta sign them papers first," Jimmy Joe went on as if everything had been decided. "You got a solicitor handling all that . . . London, Edinburgh?"

"The man handling the estate is in Lerwick."

"So much the better! You come into the city—how 'bout the day after tomorrow? That'll give you all the time you need to think things over. You and I'll go see this feller of yours, then we'll have dinner and see what we can do."

Jimmy Joe rose. Still reeling, Loni followed him to the door.

"I'm fixing to make you a rich little lady, Miss Ford," said Jimmy Joe. "Get ready for your life to change."

And as abruptly as he had appeared on her doorstep, the big Texan was gone, leaving Loni staring at his retreating Range Rover from the open door of the Cottage with his last words still ringing in her ears.

My life's already changed about as much as I can handle for one week, she said to herself. *I'm not sure I can handle much more.*

17
BUSY HANDS

For the rest of the afternoon and evening, Loni tried to read. But she was too distracted by the events of the day to concentrate. Finally she put aside her great-grandmother's journal and wrote for an hour in her own.

She was in bed by 8:30 with *The Scent of Water* by English novelist Elizabeth Goudge, a book she had discovered on one of the bookshelves in the Great Room. It hardly seemed the kind of fare Macgregor Tulloch would have appreciated, although she really had no idea what sort of man he was or what might have been his taste in books.

The next morning, Loni went out again. Her brain was still on a roller coaster after yesterday's visit with the big Texan. She was hardly planning her steps but found herself on a path leading west from the Cottage. When a few buildings and chimneys became visible, she struck out over the springy turf in the direction of the village.

Approaching Whales Reef fifteen or twenty minutes later from the north, Loni came to a narrow lane that led between the cottages at the edge of town. Full of thoughts of the past, aware that she could well be retracing her great-grandmother's very steps, she hardly noticed the stares that followed her tall blond form.

She came out on the main street of the village and glanced to her right and left. She was on the opposite side of the inn and square where she had walked yesterday. She turned away from them and soon found herself on her way out of town westward in the direction of the ferry landing.

Where was the great hotel that had once attracted so many visitors to Whales Reef? Had it been torn down in the years since her great-grandmother was here?

She looked up the hill to her right. There was the church with its tall steeple looming as a silent monument to the spiritual tradition of the island. Closer at hand, she saw another large rectangular building and a wide drive leading up toward it. Envisioning the island during her great-grandmother's time, it seemed the hotel where she had stayed must have been near this very spot.

She walked up the long drive. The building in front of her was by far the largest she had seen on the island, of two stories and, though run down, with surprisingly ornate touches of design that spoke of better times. At first glance it almost appeared abandoned except for a red van parked in front. The lights on in the windows also indicated human activity. She approached and tentatively tried the front door. The handle turned, and the door swung open. She walked inside.

The sight that met Loni's eyes was as unexpected as seeing Jimmy Joe McLeod at her door the previous afternoon. She found herself gazing into a huge room where fifteen or twenty women of varying ages were engaged in the most extraordinary activities. Some sat at spinning wheels. A small group to her right sat in a circle knitting. At the far end of the room several large looms were busy weaving some colorful pattern of cloth.

The moment she walked in, the buzz of conversation accompanying the hum of the spinning wheels instantly ceased. Fingers stilled. Looms stopped. Every eye turned toward her.

Loni smiled nervously at a woman near the door at one of the spinning wheels.

"Hello," she said. "I, uh . . . I was just out for a walk and I—"

"Ye'll be wantin' tae see Mr. MacBean, I'm thinkin'," said the woman without waiting for Loni to finish. "Rakel," she called across the floor, "gae up an' tell Mr. MacBean that the American lass is here tae see him."

A young woman about her own age at the far side of the room jumped to her feet and bounded up a flight of stairs against the opposite wall.

Loni waited awkwardly in the heavy silence. A moment later a man emerged from an upstairs office. He descended the stairs and came toward her.

"You would be Miss Ford, I take it," he said, extending his hand. "I am Murdoc MacBean, the factory manager."

Loni smiled and shook his hand.

"Yes, I'm Alonnah Ford . . . er, Alonnah *Tulloch* Ford. I'm sorry to interrupt. I was out for a walk and just happened in. I don't mean to inconvenience you, but I didn't actually come to see you. I was looking about, wondering where the old Whales Reef Hotel used to be."

"This is the hotel, or was many years ago," replied MacBean, doing his best to speak in understandable English.

"*This* building?"

"Yes, ma'am. It fell into disrepair after the hotel closed. Then laird Wallace, one of your own great-uncles, I'm thinking—folks are saying that you are descended from Wallace's older brother, as I understand it."

"I admit to being confused about all the connections myself," said Loni.

"What I was saying was that when Wallace was laird, he undertook to save the auld hotel, which was in a bad state and near collapse, they say. He modernized it and converted the place into a woolen mill, as you see it now."

"How wonderful. It would have been a shame for it to be lost."

"Aye. It has been a boon for the island's folk, especially the auld women and fisher wives."

"Oh . . . how is that?"

"Giving them paid work, ma'am. The mill sustains the island's economy, along with the fishing of course. We sell our wool products all over Britain."

"I see." Loni scanned the large room. "Yes, it certainly seems full of productivity," she said, though at the moment all activity had stopped. Every eye remained glued on the American newcomer. Every ear was straining to hear the conversation in progress near the front door.

"We're not so busy at the moment," said MacBean. "What you see is less than half our normal staff. Times have been difficult, you might say."

"Are orders for your products down?"

"Not a bit, ma'am. We have more orders than we can fill. 'Tis the financial complications of the inheritance, you see, all the waiting and with the mill's bank account suspended, though no doubt you know all about that. We haven't had the capital to operate. We had to cut hours and staff."

"Actually I know nothing about it," said Loni. "What does the inheritance have to do with the mill's finances?"

"Laird Macgregor—Mr. Tulloch, that is—he owned the mill. The building, the business, like the rest of the island, are all the laird's. When he died, the money stopped flowing on account of the confusion about his heir, you know—folk thinking his heir was the chief but then finding out about yourself. You should talk to the chief about it. He understands more than I do with the solicitors and bank and all."

"I didn't know about all that. I only learned of the inheritance two weeks ago. And all this time your mill has been without capital?"

"That's about it, ma'am. It has been a difficult year, especially for the women without other livelihoods. These women you see working today most of them haven't been paid in three months. They're hoping for better times now that you're here."

"Why with me here?"

"You're the laird, ma'am. 'Tis *your* mill now. These ladies work for you. With you here, the accounts will be unfrozen and we'll have capital to operate again. At least that's what we're hoping. Like I say, you'll have to talk to the chief. He knows the details."

"I was given to understand that the chief wouldn't have inherited anyway."

"Oh, aye—some said that Hardy would inherit. But it doesn't matter now that you are here."

Loni's brain was doing its best to absorb the flood of information. Suddenly this inheritance that had dropped into her lap was bigger than just a house. Here was a once-thriving business whose future depended on the outcome of the inheritance. No wonder people were anxious about what she would decide.

She was beginning to understand the looks and stares and whispered comments. It was not merely her taking the inheritance away from their chief or the fisherman Hardar. There was more at stake. And a flamboyant Texan was waiting in the wings to buy it all and, if he was right, make her and all these people wealthy. Yet apparently none of them knew a thing about it.

She smiled again at the mill manager, a pensive smile. "Well, thank you for the information, Mr. MacBean. I suppose I will continue my walk."

"Would you like a tour of the factory, ma'am?" asked Murdoc.

"Yes, I would," replied Loni softly. "But I think another time."

"At your convenience, ma'am."

Loni walked toward the door. Behind her the buzz of activity gradually resumed.

She glanced back one last time. The hum of several spinning wheels made music in her brain. As the hubbub rose, gradually out of the mists of the past came faint echoes of an orchestra and a ballroom filled with dancers, waiters scurrying between tables, festive merrymakers enjoying an exotic adventure to the northernmost reaches of the British Isles.

She had envisioned the setting as she had read of it in her great-grandmother's hand. Now it all seemed to come to life in her mind's eye.

18
A Legacy Begins—
The Hotel

Whales Reef, 1924

A freelance journalist turned from the bar where he had just ordered a thick pint of dark stout and surveyed his surroundings.

This has to be the most incongruous scene I have ever laid eyes on, thought Robert Glendenning.

Filled with the music of a live orchestra, the expansive ballroom of the Whales Reef Hotel might have been set in the middle of Mayfair or Kensington. The wide oak dance floor, the glittering chandeliers, the period furnishings of Georgian vintage, all combined to exude an atmosphere of regal luxury.

What could a glamorous party of Londoners—the women with dresses designed in Paris, ears and necks and wrists bedecked in jewels and lavish finery, the men in tuxedos and sporting silk cravats and gold cuff links—be doing in such a remote place?

To many Englanders the very word *Scotland* struck horror at thoughts of the untamed north. Savages brandishing claymores, forsooth! Half-naked men traipsing over snow-covered mountains in kilts. Yet indeed, it was to the wilds of Scotland's Shetland Islands that this evening's merrymakers had come.

The courageous expedition to these outlying islands could only be undertaken by ship, traveling so far north into the arctic expanse of the Atlantic that icebergs were not uncommon during the winter months. With the *Titanic* still green in the memory, such an excursion to Britain's farthest limits was not to be undertaken lightly.

And yet the scene was somehow fitting for 1924. These were the rollicking postwar years when not only dance steps, dress lengths, and hairdos were pushing the boundaries of culture beyond what had been seen before, so too was the appetite for travel among England's elite. African safaris, treks to Egypt's pyramids, and excursions throughout the Greek islands were all the rage among those who could afford it.

"So, Mr. Glendenning," said a voice at his elbow, "you appear lost in reflection."

The journalist turned to see a youth striding toward him.

"What do you think of our fair little isle in the middle of the North Atlantic?" the young man added.

The Londoner's journalistic instincts quickly took in the newcomer. Good-looking, dressed fashionably in an expensive brown suit of the latest cut, bearing himself with culture and breeding, he appeared in his early twenties. His obvious polish and sophistication, however, clashed with the thickly accented timbre of his tongue.

"You have me at a disadvantage," said Glendenning. "You seem to know me, but I confess I have no idea who you might be. I detect an unmistakable Shetland accent. And by laying claim to this island I assume you a resident. Yet your speech bears scant resemblance to what I have heard since my arrival."

"I'm not sure how I should take that!" said the young man. "However, I am a native. In that you are correct. And though I did not think of laying personal claim to it, as you say, when I approached a moment ago, this is in fact, or will one day be, my island."

"How so?"

"I am Brogan Tulloch."

"Ah yes, Tulloch. I know the name. I am pleased to meet you. I am, as you already knew, Robert Glendenning."

The two men shook hands to formally acknowledge their acquaintance.

"Your name is one of importance in these parts, I believe," said Glendenning.

"My father is the laird," said Tulloch. "He is the landlord, the owner of most of the property on the island. Hence laird."

"And you, I take it, if you will one day inherit, must be his eldest son."

"I congratulate your powers of deduction! I am indeed a son of privilege who is doing his best to enjoy my inheritance while I am young enough to make the most of it. What are you drinking? From the looks of that black mud and its foam in your glass, Guinness I would say."

"I must admit, I downed half of it in a single swallow. I was so cold when I came in half an hour ago following an after-dinner stroll that my fingers and toes are still frozen."

"You'll warm up when we get another couple of pints in you. Craig," the young scion of Whales Reef called to the man behind the bar, "another Guinness for Mr. Glendenning and a Laphroaig single malt for me. Put both on my tab."

"You have a tab here?" asked the London journalist after his Shetland friend had ordered the drinks.

"A very active tab," laughed Tulloch. "And a larger one than my father would like. But one is only young once, as they say!"

"And your father?"

"He is a good soul. He pays my tab with an occasional fatherly admonition. He doesn't think my habits become the son of the laird."

"It's not just his son he is concerned about, I take it, but the future laird?"

Tulloch nodded. "You are correct. The lairdship

will pass to me, as well as the chieftainship."

"I'm afraid you've lost me there," said Glendenning. "What do you mean, the chieftainship?"

"As well as being laird, my father is also chief."

"I thought chiefs went out with Culloden and the Highland Clearances. The only chiefs I know of in these modern times wear headdresses in American Wild West shows."

Again Tulloch laughed. "An old-fashioned custom, perhaps. Believe it or not the chieftainship does persist here. We are but a small island clan, and the title is mostly honorary. Yet the people consider it of great importance. Tradition and all that. So tell me, Mr. Glendenning," he added, "what are you doing here? What kind of story are you planning to write about your sojourn in the Shetlands?"

"I haven't decided yet. I came on this excursion ostensibly to write about the kinds of people who are interested in nature and wildlife. I've written about safaris to the upper Nile and cruises down the Amazon and the natives of jungle tribes. But what sort of people are bird watchers and whale chasers? I thought it would make an interesting article. After being here a week, however, I'm wondering if the real story might be the people of Whales Reef rather than the tourists who come and go."

"Not so intriguing if you ask me. As far as I'm

concerned, Whales Reef is the end of the world. It just happens to be my misfortune to be heir to an island of birds and fishermen."

"What will you do when you inherit, then? You do not sound altogether enthusiastic about your prospects."

"I cannot envision living my whole life in this godforsaken place. But don't tell my father that."

"Do you attend the soirees for all the groups that come to grace your fair island?"

"It's the only entertainment and culture available here," replied Tulloch. "Most of the tours that come sell themselves as offering a blend between luxury and outdoorsy naturalism, with a bit of danger thrown in. It's all in the publicity. Bring your gowns and tuxedos, but don't forget to pack your boots, binoculars, and rain gear, goes one sales pitch. The rich from London tromping around on a Scottish moor or along a desolate crag above a wild sea . . . they convince themselves they are communing with the great universe and its flora and fauna. Then they retire to the hotel, dress for dinner, sit around a warm fireplace with drinks in hand and all the comforts of home. The hotel and tour managers have devised a wonderfully elaborate scheme."

"Who does own the hotel?" asked Glendenning.

"Actually, it belongs to my father."

"From the little you've told me, he doesn't strike me as the type."

"He's not," said Tulloch. "The celebration, the drinking, the finery—it's not for him. He loves this island for its own sake. He disdains the fact that it has been turned into a tourist destination."

"How, then, did such a hotel come to be here?"

"My grandfather was an entrepreneur and businessman. He built the Whales Reef Hotel and developed it into a tourist destination before the war. After his death, and when the war was over, my father leased it to a London firm. They manage everything. My father rarely shows his face. Instead he wanders about the island lost in his spiritual reflections. Bit of a mystic, my father, I suppose you might say."

"And you?"

Tulloch laughed and raised his glass. "I play the rôle of unofficial host to the proceedings, adding local color and charm, as it were—the son of the chief." He drained the contents of his glass and signaled to his friend behind the bar to pour him another. "I come for dinner most evenings and grace the visitors with my presence. I never miss the first and last evening, when the hotel's guests all dress to the nines, with live music and dancing and celebration. A new tour usually arrives every week or two. It's fairly constant through the summer months. The hotel's owners do their marketing well."

"And does romance with any of the young female

guests occasionally result?" asked Glendenning with a smile, his gaze sweeping across the dance floor.

"One never knows," rejoined Tulloch. "Every tour brings new possibilities."

PART 2

19

REVELATION

Loni closed the door of the wool factory behind her and slowly walked away.

Instead of returning down the long drive, she left the mill and cut overland in the direction of the church. She walked around the building a few minutes later, then found her way through the gate and into the enclosed cemetery in back. Passing through the gravestones, some of whose markers were worn so smooth as to be illegible, she came to the Tulloch family plot. She wandered among the graves, reading names she now recognized from Sandy Innes's story two evenings before.

There was the grave of Ernest Tulloch, whose memory and funeral had prompted Sandy's reminiscences, and then other names caught her attention: Elizabeth, Sally, Wallace, Leith. Brogan Tulloch, however, was conspicuously missing. At length she came to a grave whose covering grass was greener and the headstone clearly newer than the rest. "Macgregor Tulloch," she murmured, the man whose death a year ago had thrown her life and the future of this island into such uncertainty.

Were these actually her relatives, her mother's family? Had she at last discovered the roots she had never known, the *home* of her maternal ancestors?

Beyond the plot of Tulloch graves, as she continued to wander about, her eyes fell on many Scottish and Shetlandic names, some of which she recognized—Innes, Gordon, Legge, MacNeill, Mair, Kerr, Munro, MacPherson, Ewen, MacDonald, as well as many more Tullochs scattered among the stones.

Did this cemetery represent what she had come to the Shetlands to find without even knowing it . . . roots, posterity, family, belonging?

When she left the cemetery a few minutes later, a man emerged from the back door of the church. He smiled in greeting.

"Good morning," he said. "I am Stirling Yates, the minister here. Is there anything I can help you with?"

"No, but thank you," replied Loni. "I was just having a look around the cemetery."

"American . . . you wouldn't by chance be the new laird that has the community all abuzz."

"Guilty," laughed Loni lightly. "I am Alonnah Ford."

"I am happy to meet you," said Yates, offering his hand. "If there is any way I may be of service to you, please do not hesitate to call on me."

"I appreciate that, though I do not anticipate being here long."

A thoughtful expression flitted across the

minister's face. "I know the feeling," he said cryptically. "But however ambiguous our mutual futures may be, my offer stands."

"Thank you."

They parted and Loni returned around to the front of the church, then left the grounds by the drive back to the main road down the hill. She came out a minute or two later near the ferry landing. She paused, debating whether she wanted to walk through the village again. A figure came striding toward her along the road from beyond the landing. She recognized her second visitor to the Cottage from two days earlier. He lifted his hand in friendly greeting.

"Hello again, Miss Ford," he said with a smile as he approached.

"Good morning, Mr. Tulloch," said Loni.

"Getting the lay of the land of your new estate?"

"I don't know about that—just out for a walk. It was a nice day. Besides, nothing is mine *yet*."

"Soon will be, I should have said."

"There are still many decisions to be made."

"I understand. Which direction are you headed?"

"Nowhere in particular. I was trying to decide which way to take back to the Cottage. What about you?"

"I live back over there, along the western road," David replied. "I was on my way into town. Care to join me?"

Loni nodded and they fell into step beside each other.

"You were visiting our small parish church just now?" said David.

"I stopped at the mill a few minutes ago," said Loni, pointing up the hill to her left. "Then I made my way over to the church and the fascinating cemetery. I am discovering that my decision about what to do is more complicated than I had imagined."

"In what way?" asked David.

"I had no idea there was such a thriving business on the island, or what *had* been thriving before the confusion over the inheritance. I met the mill's manager . . . I'm afraid I've already forgotten his name—"

"Murdoc MacBean—another of your distant relatives."

"He explained about the financial strain they have been under."

David nodded thoughtfully.

"It seems the future of the mill, at least in the immediate future, is up to me. All I can wonder is if I am going to be the cause of *another* business that has been going for generations having to close its doors."

"I'm afraid I don't follow you."

A wistful smile came over Loni's face. "I was raised by my grandparents," she said after a moment. "My parents died when I was an infant."

"I didn't know that. I am sorry. That must have been difficult."

"Being an orphan has challenges, I will say that. That's one of the reasons my family roots were mostly as unknown to me as I was to people over here. Everything about my past was shrouded in secrets. I never seemed to know who I was. My grandfather—both my grandfathers, actually—was a furniture maker. My father was an only son. When he died, and then when I didn't want to continue the business, a year ago my grandfather retired and closed the doors of his showroom. I can't help feeling guilty."

"You had other plans?"

"Nothing specific. But when I left home for college I think they always hoped I would come back to the family business. I had learned it from the ground up when I was young and enjoyed many aspects of it. But it wasn't a life I could have been happy in."

"I can see that it would be hard. What is it you do now, if you don't mind my asking?"

"I am assistant to an investment executive in Washington, D.C."

"What does that entail?"

"We coordinate investments, mostly for corporate clients and a few individuals with sizable portfolios—stocks, bonds, mutual funds, real estate, commodities . . . that sort of thing."

"Sounds pretty high finance."

"I suppose it is."

"And you like it?"

"I do. It's exciting, challenging. There's always something new on the horizon."

"Do I detect a *But* in your tone?"

"There's that lurking feeling in the background of having disappointed my grandparents, not following in their footsteps."

"I know something about that," said David. "I have a number of relatives, one aunt in particular, whom I will never please as long as I live."

"Now it seems the mill here is in the same boat, waiting for me to decide on its future."

"But you wouldn't . . . I mean, when you say another business having to close its doors," David went on in a more serious tone, "you're not thinking of shutting down the mill?"

"I didn't mean that. I was only referring to the uncertainty and that its future seems to be up to me, and that I still don't know what I should do . . . about everything."

"I see."

"You have to understand—as much as this inheritance situation has changed things for all of you on this island, I am still trying to get used to the shock of it. The first I heard of it was two weeks ago. Before that, I had no idea of any connection to the Shetlands. I'm just a girl from a simple, hardworking family. I have, I think, about twelve hundred dollars in the bank," she laughed.

130

"Now I'm told I own all this property, and people are calling me laird. This is an enormous change. My head has been spinning for two weeks."

They walked on in thoughtful silence.

As they reached the outskirts of the village, from out of a lane to their left between several stone cottages, Audney Kerr bounded into the street.

Imperceptibly David caught his breath in surprise and turned away. But Audney walked straight forward and greeted them.

"Hoo are ye, Miss Ford?" she said with a bright smile.

"Fine," replied Loni. "Hello again."

"An' good day tae yersel', David," Audney added.

"Hello, Audney," said David. He lowered his voice. "If I could jist hae a word wi' ye in private," he said softly. "Will you excuse us a minute, Miss Ford?"

He motioned to Audney and led her a few steps across the street. She looked back over her shoulder. "I'm glad tae see ye finally found the chief," she called back to Loni.

The word slammed into Loni's brain with such force she felt her knees buckle. She scarcely heard the next words that passed between them.

"What was it ye wanted tae speak wi' me aboot, David?" Audney was saying.

"Nothing," he said with a smile of irony. "It won't matter now."

131

Loni was staring at the two as if through a blurry haze. But her thoughts were years and many miles away.

———

A gangly teenager walked into school, her books in a canvas bag over her shoulder. She stood a head taller than any other girl in the small Quaker high school of twenty-seven students. But her height and awkwardness weren't the worst of it. It was the whispered comments constantly swirling around her . . . stares, giggling when she walked by, people talking behind her back. No one ever shared a secret with her . . . the secrets were only about her. She was always on the outside.

She started along the corridor toward her first class, then hesitated. She saw three girls down the hallway. They stopped as they saw her coming, stared at her, then put their heads together and began whispering and giggling.

She felt her face redden. She could not turn and run. That would only make them laugh all the more. Keeping her eyes on the floor and hugging the wall, she continued on.

At the far end of the hall, a good-looking boy of sixteen came around the corner. The three girls scurried toward him.

"Hello, Davis," purred one of the three in a flirtatious voice.

"Oh . . . hi, Audrey," he said. Then he drew her away from the others. "Could I just have a word with you alone, Audrey?" he said softly, leading her a few steps away along the hall.

The girl called Audrey glanced at her two friends with a mischievous grin, then followed.

The tall girl tried to hurry past while the two were distracted by the popular Davis Jackson probably making a date with equally popular Audrey Stanton.

A voice sounded behind her.

"You're not one of us, you know," said one of the girls. "You never were. You don't belong here. Why don't you just go back to where you came from?"

Blinking hard, she reached the classroom and tried to hurry inside.

"She can't," said the other loudly. "She doesn't know where she came from. No one does! She's an o-r-p-h-a-n. Ha, ha, ha!"

The sound of their laughter echoed in her ears as she closed the door and hurried to her desk at the back of the room, trying desperately to stop the rush of tears flooding her eyes.

———

20
OUTBURST

As if coming out of a thick fog into the light of day, Loni's eyes came back into focus. There stood David with a sheepish expression on his face.

"You . . . *you're* the chief!" exclaimed Loni.

"I'm afraid so," replied David, trying to smile.

"Why didn't you tell me?"

"It never seemed to fit into the conversation," answered David apologetically.

"You didn't think I had a right to know?"

"Of course, I just didn't—"

"Didn't *what?*" interrupted Loni.

"I didn't want to add to your pressure right now."

"How would it have done that?"

"Because of the confusion about the inheritance. When I came to the Cottage, I simply wanted to extend my welcome as a resident of the island, not someone you might somehow consider . . . well, a threat."

"You should have considered the *truth*. Whatever I might have thought about you would have been better than hiding it."

"Please, Miss Ford," said Audney as she came

forward. "I shouldna hae opened my big mouth. 'Tis my fault. I'm sorry tae hae said—"

"It's not your fault, Audrey."

"*Audney,* miss."

"Whatever. It's not your fault that this . . . Mr. Tulloch . . . this *chief* of yours tried to hide the truth from me. He wasn't honest. I've lived with secrets all my life and I hate them." She turned and walked away.

"Miss Ford," said David, taking several quick steps after her, "honestly I meant no harm. If we could just talk—"

Loni spun around. Her face was flushed.

"I do not want to talk about it!" she said. "Just leave me alone. I need to think. Maybe I should go home and just let the big fisherman have the inheritance. I don't want it. I never wanted it. I don't know why I even came here."

"Ye canna, miss," implored Audney, hurrying after them. "Ye canna gie it tae Hardy."

"If I am the heir, why can't I do what I please?"

"But ye canna do that. 'Tis the *worst* thing ye could do."

"So it could go to your chief instead?"

"Aye, he's the rightful heir. A'body on the island kens it."

"Apparently the court doesn't agree," said Loni. "The lawyer in Lerwick told me that Mr. *Hardar* Tulloch would be next in line after me."

"That canna be, miss. Tell her, David . . . why winna ye tell her?"

Loni turned again to David, her eyes flashing. "Yes, Mr. Tulloch, what do you have to say for yourself? No doubt you think *you* deserve the inheritance?"

The silence that followed was awkward. David did not answer.

"Tell me, Mr. Tulloch," repeated Loni. "Should the inheritance rightfully be yours?"

"That is not for me to say, Miss Ford," he replied. "Legalities decide such things, not what you or I or Hardy or even Audney or anyone on the island may think."

"I'm asking what *you* think."

David drew in a sigh, then spoke in a cautious and measured tone. "Then I would say that it would be wise for you to be very careful. I would suggest that you go slowly and make no rash decisions. Everyone you meet may not be what they appear."

"And it would seem that you are the perfect example."

David did not reply.

"Are you going to tell me what you think about the inheritance?" persisted Loni.

"I would rather not."

"You insist on being secretive again?"

David said nothing.

"You keep being chief from me, and now you

won't answer a simple question. Well, it doesn't matter anyway. I'm sure the other Mr. Tulloch will do his best for the people of the island. And *he* doesn't keep secrets from me."

"Ye canna think that, miss," said Audney, again her voice urgent. "Ye dinna ken him the way I do. Tell her, David. Tell her what Hardy is."

Again David remained silent.

"And it just so happens that he and I are having dinner tonight," Loni added. "It will give me a chance to discuss plans for the island."

Loni walked quickly away, back in the direction she and David had come from. Audney and David stared after her in stunned silence.

"I'm sorry aboot blurtin' oot aboot ye bein' chief, David," said Audney at length. "I didna ken ye hadna told her. When I saw the two o' ye together, I jist—"

"No bother, Audney—forget it," said David. "Miss Ford knows who I am now."

"But why wouldna ye tell her aboot Hardy?"

"It's not my place, Audney. I won't speak against the man."

"Then what are we goin' tae do? Ye heard what she said."

"I don't see that there's anything we can do about it. If Miss Ford declines the inheritance, then we will be back where we were before and the court will have to decide."

21
Isobel Matheson

Overwrought and paying little heed to where she was going other than vaguely trying to find her way back to the Cottage, Loni walked through the precincts of the Auld Hoose, having no idea who lived in the place, before striking eastward across the island.

Confused and still angry, she walked inside the Cottage and threw herself onto the couch. A few tears came and went. She tried to read but to no avail. Finally she went upstairs, flopped onto the bed, and mercifully fell asleep.

Shortly after lunch, sitting in the living room thumbing absently through one of the guidebooks she had bought in the village, she heard an outside door open in the kitchen, then close. Soft footsteps followed across the floor, then the faint creak of a cupboard door.

She rose to investigate. Walking into the kitchen, she saw a woman who appeared to be in her late fifties. Her unknown visitor was as startled as Loni was.

"Oh my . . . excuse me, miss!" exclaimed the woman, noticeably flustered. "I didn't know you were home. I didn't mean to intrude. I was just bringing over a few things for you."

"Bringing me . . . from where?" said Loni.

"From the Auld Hoose, miss. I'm your house-keeper, you see . . . I am Isobel Matheson."

"I am happy to meet you, Mrs. Matheson. I am Alonnah Ford."

"It's *miss,* miss. Neither my brother nor myself are married. Though when folks call me missus, I usually say nothing. It keeps them from feeling sorry for me, if you know what I mean. But I thought you should know how things stand."

"I see. Are you the one I have wanted to thank for the nicely stocked kitchen when I arrived?"

"Mostly the chief, miss."

Loni bristled but ignored the reference.

"He told me what to bring," the housekeeper went on. "He wanted you to be comfortable and feel at home."

"You say you are my housekeeper . . . you worked for the former laird, then?"

"Aye, miss."

"Where do you stay? I mean, do you live here?"

"Aye, miss—that is, we did, my brother and myself—in the west wing."

"Why have I not seen you about?"

"We've been at the Auld Hoose, miss. You know, the chief's house across the island."

"Why there?"

"The chief thought it best at first, miss."

"Were you under the impression I would not want your services?"

"We didn't know, you being the new laird and all, and an American with your own way of doing things. The chief didn't want us to be in your way. He thought it best for us to stay with him until you were settled and decided what you wanted."

"About you and your brother, you mean?"

"Aye, and Mr. Dougal—he's the laird's game-keeper. He tends the laird's animals—your animals now, as it would seem—though he took some of them, and the dogs, to the Auld Hoose when we heard you were coming."

"Why was that?"

"The chief didn't want them in your way, miss. Dogs can be a nuisance, you know, barking and running about. And you know how it is with dogs having to get used to strangers. So he thought it best if they weren't here. Not everyone wants dogs sniffing and licking and bothering like dogs do. The chief was trying to think of what he could do to make it pleasant for you when you arrived."

"And the food in the kitchen—that was the chief's idea too?"

"Aye, miss."

Loni drew in a thoughtful breath and exhaled slowly. "Well, I have no idea what I should do either," she said. "I don't suppose there are job descriptions for new lairds."

"I wouldn't know about that, miss."

"One thing is certain," said Loni with a light laugh, "I've never had a maid before."

"I'm a housekeeper and cook, miss."

"Oh, of course . . . I'm sorry."

"Will you be wanting our services, miss?"

"I don't even know how long I will be staying myself. I don't suppose I can answer your question yet. I will not be living here. I'm not sure how much there would be for you to do after I return to the States."

"What will become of the Cottage, miss?"

"I honestly have not thought about the implications. Everything's happened so fast. But . . . would you like to have tea? I would like to know more about what you and your brother did for the laird."

"Shall I fix you a pot, then, miss?"

"That sounds nice. I am still very much an amateur when it comes to making tea."

"Very good, miss," said the housekeeper, happy to have a familiar job to occupy her hands. She moved quickly to the counter and filled the water boiler. "Shall I bring it to you in the breakfast room?" she asked.

"Perhaps you misunderstood—I thought we would have tea together."

"Together, miss?"

"Yes. Let's sit in the Great Room."

"You want me to have tea . . . *with* you, miss?"

"Is there something unusual about that?"

"My brother and I never had tea with Mr. Tulloch. He was the laird, you see. We would never have taken tea in the Great Room."

"The old British feudal spirit. Well, you shall have tea with me, Miss Matheson, and we will have it in the Great Room."

Five minutes later, sheepish yet with the hint of a pleased smile, Isobel Matheson entered the Great Room bearing a tray lavishly outfitted with tea and an assortment of biscuits and cake from the refrigerator.

"That looks lovely," said Loni.

The housekeeper set the tray down and poured out a cup for Loni. She glanced about uncertainly.

"Pour yourself a cup, Miss Matheson," said Loni. "Please, sit down and be comfortable."

"Where would you like me to sit, miss?"

"Wherever you like. This is more your house than mine."

"Don't say such a thing, miss. You are the laird now. You have to be mindful of your station, if you take no offense at me speaking my mind. You're not the same as other folk now."

"If you say so!" laughed Loni. "I can see I have more to get used to than I realized."

As they drank their tea and nibbled at digestive biscuits, Loni found her eyes scanning the book-shelves of the large room.

"By the way," she said, "another thing I have

wanted to ask is where the Elizabeth Goudge books came from?"

An embarrassed expression came over Isobel's face. "I'm afraid they are mine, miss. I hope you don't mind. I can take them away if you like."

"No, of course not. I don't mind at all. I'm enjoying one myself at the moment."

"The laird let me keep some of my books on his bookshelves—on *your* bookshelves, I mean. He thought they looked nice with the others."

"They do look nice. Are all these in the bookcases yours?"

"No, miss. Just a few. Some of the others are old and very rare, as I understand it. They came with the Great Tulloch's wife from England in the 1800s, along with much of the china and silver and Delftware and porcelain you see in the cabinets over on the far wall. She was a wealthy lady, they say."

"This room is certainly full of very beautiful things," said Loni, "as is the whole house. I find Chippendale and Georgian and Victorian cabinets and chairs and sideboards and desks everywhere I turn. It is all very exquisite. In its own way this house is a museum, not to mention the paintings and tapestries and vases . . . and of course the books. So do you keep all your books here in the Great Room?"

"Oh no, miss. I have more in my own room."

"What other authors do you read?"

"I'm also keen on Mrs. Oliphant and O. Douglas and Diana Mullock and Silas Hawking. And of course Edna Lyall and George MacDonald."

"I hope you don't mind if I sample some of your books while I am here."

"I would be honored, miss. There's nothing better than sharing a favorite book."

"Perhaps you will show me the rest of your collection one day. Was your boss . . . the laird, I mean—Mr. Tulloch—a reader?"

"Not that I saw, miss. He valued the books for their learning and such like, but I do not think he was a great reader. They say the Auld Tulloch was terribly fond of books. I think many of the books are his, the MacDonald stories mostly, though I'm told he kept most of his library in the room at the top of the stairs, before it was locked and . . ." Isobel stopped and glanced away.

"You were about to say something, Miss Matheson?" said Loni.

"Nothing, miss."

Loni smiled. "I believe you are right about the Auld Tulloch, as you call him, being fond of books," she said. "It is easy to tell that from his study upstairs. It is lined with books from floor to ceiling."

"The locked room, miss?"

"Yes," said Loni, smiling again.

"You've been inside it, miss!" exclaimed the housekeeper.

Loni nodded.

"How?"

"I brought the key from America."

"Was there . . . ?" began Isobel, her face whitening.

"A dead body?"

"Aye."

"No," laughed Loni. "Just books, as you suspected, and everything you would assume a learned man's study should contain—probably exactly like it was fifty years ago. I understand it has been locked ever since Ernest Tulloch's funeral."

"Aye, never opened that I know of."

"Would you like to see it, Miss Matheson?"

"Oh, I don't know if I should," replied the housekeeper nervously. Her tone, however, betrayed eagerness.

"I don't know why not. Come," said Loni, rising.

Tentatively Isobel followed her out into the foyer and up the stairs. A minute later she was standing in the mysterious study, gazing about in wonder.

"What a lot of books," she said softly. "It is a shame Mr. Macgregor wasn't able to use it himself."

"And all these years the key lay hidden in a desk exactly like this one," said Loni.

"Where was that?"

"In the back of my grandfather's barn—recently,

that is. Before seventeen or eighteen years ago, I don't know where it was."

"No one knew what became of it, miss," said Isobel. "That means you are the Keeper of the Key."

"I'm afraid I don't understand."

"It's an old family legend about the locked room being the Bard's Chamber and its key being held by the Keeper of the Key."

As she spoke, Loni recalled Sandy's story of Ernest Tulloch's funeral.

"And now the key is back home," she said, "and here we are in the mystery room—the Bard's Chamber, as you say."

They looked about a few more minutes, then returned downstairs to their tea.

"I notice that you speak clear English," said Loni when they were again seated. "Are you from the Shetlands, Miss Matheson?"

"Aye. My brother and I have cousins on mainland Scotland. But we also have American roots. Our mother prided herself in teaching us proper English."

"How interesting. How did that come about? Most people trace their roots from America to Britain or Europe, not the other way around."

"Aye, miss. Our mother was a genealogist—she was interested in such things. She was fascinated with America and knew of Lady Margaret's story, about her going to America and her daughter marrying a Matheson, just as my mother had herself."

"I'm sorry—who is Lady Margaret?"

"She was from an old Scottish family with an estate called Stonewycke just inland from a village on the northeast coast called Port Strathy."

"*Stonewycke* . . . what an interesting name. What does it mean?"

"I couldn't say, miss, though I think it goes back to Viking times. Our mother took my brother and me to visit Lady Joanna at Stonewycke when we were young."

"Lady Joanna?" said Loni, growing more confused by the minute.

"Aye, Lady Margaret's granddaughter. She was from the United States like yourself, Lady Joanna that is. She came to Scotland just like you, not knowing her family roots. She married Alec MacNeill of the Port Strathy MacNeills, but we were related to her through her American father. She was Joanna Matheson, you see. But on her mother's side she descended from the Stonewycke Ramseys and Duncans through her grandmother Maggie Ramsey Duncan—that's Lady Margaret. So our connection with Lady Joanna was a distant one, which our mother discovered by tracing our genealogy. Lady Joanna treated us as if we were closer than mere distant cousins. She found it wonderful that we were related to her American father. I think it pleased her that our mother had discovered our American roots, and that the connections went in both directions, if you know what I mean."

"Is Lady Joanna still living?" asked Loni.

"She died when I was a young woman, miss—1971, I believe it was. But her daughter, Allison—"

"Her daughter was named Allison?"

"Aye, miss."

"That was my mother's name!"

"Was it now? That is a coincidence. Lady Joanna's Allison was married to the well-known MP Logan Macintyre. They're both gone now too, though Lady Allison only died six or seven years ago. We were privileged to meet them as well. The Stonewycke estate is now in the hands of Lady Allison and Sir Logan's daughter, Hilary, and her husband, Ashley Jameson. Perhaps you will visit them at Stonewycke."

"I'm not related to them like you are."

"They would welcome you just the same, especially knowing how similar your story is to Lady Joanna's. I would be honored to contact them on your behalf, miss."

"Well, we shall see," said Loni with an appreciative smile.

The conversation drifted into other channels. The two women parted twenty minutes later on friendly terms. No more was said about what might be Loni's plans for the housekeeper and her brother.

22
FISH SUPPER

When Hardy Tulloch walked into the Whales Fin Inn a little before six o'clock late that afternoon, he was greeted by the half dozen or so fishermen with whistles and catcalls. He was cleaner than any of them had ever seen him, hair slicked down and wearing what appeared to be a new shirt and new trousers. And sporting a tie. Who in Whales Reef would have guessed that Hardy Tulloch even owned a tie?

"Ow, jist luik at the dandy!" called out one of Hardy's cohorts.

"An' a tie!" chimed in another. "What's become o' oor Hardy?"

"He'll soon be too posh for the likes o' us."

"Ow, ye reek o' one o' them ladies' shops in Aberdeen, Hardy!"

"It's nae perfume ye're smellin', but the fragrance o' a man's cologne."

The room burst into laughter. "An' where'd ye find it?" someone shouted.

"Never ye mind where I got my hands on it. I hae mair friends o' the female persuasion who owe Hardy a thing or two for past favors, than ye'll ever hae yersel', if ye ken what I'm talkin' aboot."

"Ow, aye—we a' ken yer reputation wi' the ladies, Hardy."

"What's next for ye, bubble bath after a night wi' the fish? Ha, ha!"

"What's next'll be none o' yer business," retorted Hardy, giving the man a slap on the shoulder. "Let's jist say that afore ye next set eyes on me, the fortunes o' this island'll rest wi' me. But noo I got mair business that requires my attention than tae waste my time wi' the likes o' yersel's."

He strode to the counter, followed by more good-natured jibes, where Keith was waiting. As was common practice among the island's fishermen, Hardy had left one of the choicest fish of his recent catch with Keith a few hours earlier, gutted and cleaned, to be filleted, battered, deep-fried, and with instructions to have it steaming and ready just before six.

Hardy left the inn a minute later carrying a large plastic bag, casting a final grin toward his fellows as he walked through the door with unbounded confidence. Though the use of it was felt rarely on the island, Hardy did own an automobile. He loaded his two ample fish suppers into the passenger seat and was soon on the way to his rendezvous with destiny. If he played his cards right, he would be sitting pretty by the end of this night.

As she awaited her evening's guest, in spite of her pleasant visit with Isobel Matheson, the emotional ups and downs of the day had left Loni with a single overriding desire—she wanted to go home.

She sat down in the Great Room, trying to unravel her tangled thoughts. She had come to Scotland, she had done her duty to her ancestors and whomever else might care, but she was not cut out for life in this place. She was an outsider. It was time to face that fact. She was anxious to get back to her real life and put this little fairy tale about long-lost inheritances behind her.

Obviously, however, she could not simply walk away. She had to come to some decision about what to do and how to handle this complicated situation she had landed in the middle of. The future of this island was in her hands. Like it or not, she had inherited this Cottage and everything that went with it. She had to deal with it.

And despite her nonchalant remarks to Maddy and Jason MacNaughton about caring nothing for it and letting the inheritance go to the next in line, she was businesswoman enough and practical enough to realize that it would be irresponsible simply to walk away. Her short time here had at least had the effect of revealing that she must handle the thing responsibly and professionally. In spite of saying that the inheritance meant nothing to her, after more level-headed reflection she could not deny that it would be a blessing not to have to worry about finances and be able to provide for her grandparents should they ever need financial help.

There were others to consider as well—namely the people of this island, especially the women whose livelihoods depended on the mill. Much was at stake for *many* people.

She needed to get a thorough assessment of what was involved. Tax implications would come into it too. She had heard that estate taxes were worse in the U.K. than in the States, which accounted for so much of the aristocracy losing their property in the past century. She needed to find out more on that score from Jason MacNaughton.

She would also have to make arrangements for whatever might be necessary in her absence. About one thing she hadn't changed her mind— she certainly had no intention of living here.

Her thoughts were interrupted by the sound of the doorbell. She rose and set her quandaries on the shelf for the time being.

"Evenin' tae ye, Miss Ford," said Hardy as Loni opened the door.

"Hello, Mr. Tulloch," said Loni with a smile. "Did you have a successful night fishing since I last saw you?"

"Aye, mum, an' I hae the fruit o' my labor in the bag here—a nice fresh cod for oor supper."

Loni's first thought was the fear that they would have to clean and cook Hardy's catch, though the smell of what seemed like French fries coming from the bag was promising. She led him inside. The pungent aroma of aftershave followed him, mingled with whatever was in the bag. Loni could not help smiling to herself. The man was trying hard, she had to say that for him, even if the role of country squire did not seem altogether natural to him.

"So . . . do we need to cook your fish?" she asked as they entered the kitchen.

"Oh no, mum. I took it to Keith at the hotel an' he fried it in his batter, along wi' plenty o' chips for us. I brought a bottle o' wine tae gae wi' oor fish an' chips. All ye need is tae set us plates and glasses an' supper'll be served."

"That should be easily arranged," said Loni, taking two plates and wineglasses from the cupboard. "How nice—fish and chips."

"As fresh as can be had," rejoined Hardy. "This lad was swimmin' aboot in the sea this time yesterday."

Loni laughed. "Then it will definitely be the freshest fish I have ever partaken of in my life. Come to think of it," she added, "my grandfather used to take me fly-fishing for trout. We always ate what we caught the same day. So what I said is not quite true but close."

Five minutes later they were seated opposite each other in what was called the breakfast room, adjacent to the kitchen. Loni had still not had a meal in the formal dining room. It did not seem fitting for two people to sit down to a supper of fish and chips from a plastic bag and wrapped in newspaper at a formal dining room table that would seat twenty.

Hardy poured out generous portions of wine into each of their glasses, then lifted his glass in a toast. "Tae oor future together," he said, "an' tae a happy an' prosperous future for yersel' as the new laird o' Whales Reef."

"Thank you," said Loni, taking a sip as Hardy downed half the contents of his.

He then turned his attention to the main course.

"Dinna be shy, Miss Ford," he said, breaking off a large chunk of fish and lifting it to his mouth with his fingers. "I hope ye dinna mind, but 'tis the only way tae eat fish an' chips."

Loni laughed and followed suit. "I will take your word for it," she said, tearing off an edge of fish and picking it up with her fingers. "Oh, this is delicious!"

"Glad ye like it, mum."

"I have to say, these are enormous portions. And you brought enough chips to feed a small army."

"I didna want ye tae go hungry, mum."

"No danger of that. Do fishermen ever tire of fish?"

"I ne'er heard o' sich a thing. Wi'oot fish, folk wouldna long survive in the Shetlands."

"I suppose you're right. Though now there is the oil."

"A body canna eat oil."

"There is money in it."

"No for the likes o' us on Whales Reef."

"What if there was?" asked Loni.

"I dinna think I follow yer meanin', Miss Ford."

"I had a visit yesterday—after you left, late in the afternoon—from a man named McLeod, a Texan."

Hardy took in the information with more interest than he allowed himself to divulge.

"He said that he and Macgregor Tulloch had arranged for Mr. McLeod to buy his property on the island," Loni went on. "Do you know anything about that?"

"I heard somethin' aboot it," replied Hardy guardedly. "When it was known that I would inherit—that is, afore they found yersel', ye ken—McLeod's solicitors were speakin' tae me aboot it."

"Had you been intending to go forward with the deal?" asked Loni.

"I, uh, hadn't altogether decided, mum. It seemed tae need a bit more lookin' into."

"After his visit," said Loni, "I found myself thinking more seriously about what you mentioned when we talked before, about the possibility of your helping me oversee a few things."

"Whatever I can do for ye, Miss Ford."

"And you would be willing, as you said, perhaps

to act as my factor when I return to the States? I would pay you, of course."

"Aye, I would, mum, if that's what ye want. I'm nae concerned aboot bein' paid. I make a good livin' wi' the fishin'. I jist want what's best for the folk o' Whales Reef."

"I am relieved to hear that."

"An' if ye decide tae sell tae the Texan, if ye like, I could handle the transaction for ye, like we talked aboot afore, especially as I know some o' McLeod's folks already."

"That makes sense."

"Ye can leave it tae me. Ye jist tell me what tae do an' I'll make sure tae do the best for the folk o' the island."

"That is very kind of you, Mr. Tulloch. I will have whatever papers are necessary drawn up to name you as my agent, and have Mr. MacNaughton in Lerwick contact you and arrange the particulars. I will want you to leave me all your information as well, so that you and I can be in regular contact."

As Hardy walked from the door of the Cottage to his car some time later, his brain was spinning. In spite of his effort to remain calm and sound matter-of-fact, he was inwardly fuming to learn of the Texan's double-dealing. After all their smooth talking and paying for his attorney fees and planning for him to sell when he became laird, it sounded like McLeod was trying to cut him out.

Meanwhile, in the house behind him, Loni was also revolving many things in her mind. By the time she went to bed that night, she had reached a decision. She would make arrangements tomorrow to fly back to the States. And if she hoped to get a new reservation on such short notice, she would need Maddy's help.

She could call from the house phone. But hearing Maddy's voice would jar on her thoughtful mood. She didn't want to get into a *discussion* about everything. Plenty of time for that later.

She would walk into the village and fax her first thing in the morning.

23

A DIFFERENT VIEW

Though she would not put him forward as representing the ideal man to spend an evening with—Loni smiled at the idea of comparing him with the Husband List at the back of her journal—the time with Hardy Tulloch had helped solidify her resolve regarding what to do.

Yet in spite of having reached a decision, all through the night her subconscious was ill at ease. And she knew why.

She awoke about seven and tried to put the gnawing unrest out of her mind. After what had become a daily morning fare of oatcakes and jam—she was going to miss the oatcakes—Loni returned upstairs to the master bedroom, took her suitcase from the closet, and flopped it on the bed. She opened it and stared at it a few seconds.

Might as well get started, she thought. By this time tomorrow, or the next day at the latest, she would be on a plane heading home.

The thought sent her mind straight toward the source of her discomfort. She couldn't leave without apologizing to David Tulloch, the "chief." She had behaved badly and knew it. Eating crow was never pleasant, but it had to be done.

And if she was going to send a fax to Maddy from the hotel, she could not do so without seeing Audney. What a nincompoop to confuse her with Audrey Stanton! She had to apologize to Audney too.

Bundling in her thickest sweater and then throwing her green scarf around her neck, Loni left the house two hours later. Taking the same path she had discovered yesterday, she followed a course directly west from the Cottage. Continuing past the point where she had turned toward the village before, she soon came upon a sizable stone cottage surrounded by diverse animal pens and several small outbuildings. She also saw sheep, several cattle, and a corral enclosing six Shetland ponies. Even as the place came into view, three or four dogs bounded toward her, barking and raising such a ruckus that her first instinct was to turn and run.

But they were so friendly and boisterous that she soon realized she had nothing to fear. Coming from the direction of the small house she now saw a familiar figure ambling toward her.

"'Tis a blessing tae see ye again, lassie!" said Sandy Innes.

"And likewise to see you, Sandy," rejoined Loni.

The old man embraced Loni, then reached as high as he was able and planted a kiss on her cheek.

"'Tis an honor tae welcome ye at last tae the Croft, my own humble bit hoosie," he said, stepping back. "An' hoo are ye farin' on the island o' yer kith an' kin?"

Loni smiled. "Just fine, Sandy. I have met some interesting people, taken a lot of walks, and I think am beginning to understand why you love your island so much."

"I am delighted tae hear it. Can ye come intil the hoosie for a drap o' tea wi' mysel' an' the two ladies?"

"I'm afraid I need to run an errand in town," replied Loni. "Unfortunately, my time here is about up. I am on my way to the hotel to send a fax home about my return arrangements. I had hoped to see you to say good-bye. I had a feeling you lived over here somewhere."

"Then on yer return til the Cottage perhaps. Oor wee croft is a plain enough place, but we'd be honored tae share oor table wi' ye. Ah, here come the ladies noo," he added with a glance toward the house behind them. "They were on their way intil the bakery."

Loni saw two ladies walking toward them, one as old as Sandy himself, the other somewhat younger.

"Look who's here, lassies," said Sandy. " 'Tis the lass I was tellin' ye aboot, oor new laird hersel'."

The two ladies smiled a little shyly as they came.

"Miss Ford, meet my sister, Eldora, an' my daughter, Odara. These are the two who take sich good care o' me."

"I am delighted to know you both," said Loni, reaching out a hand to the elder of the two. The next instant, she was swallowed in an affectionate embrace. It was followed by a second from the younger. Neither of their white heads reached even to her shoulders. She was reminded of trying to embrace her tiny grandmother back in Pennsylvania.

"Oh my!" she exclaimed. "That is quite a welcome for a stranger."

"Ye're no stranger tae us," said Eldora. "Ye're family tae a' the island noo . . . an' oor laird besides."

"Ye canna know hoo happy we are that ye've come, lassie . . . I mean *laird*," said Odara.

"I'm not laird yet," laughed Loni.

"What for no?" said Sandy.

"I still have to sign the papers and make legal arrangements. Nothing is final until all the *i*'s are dotted and the *t*'s crossed, as we say."

"But ye will soon enough, an' we're right glad."

"Aye we are, lassie," added Eldora.

"I must admit I am surprised to hear you say that," said Loni. "Although knowing that you are Sandy's sister and daughter, I suppose I shouldn't be. No one has made me feel more welcome than Sandy. I am fortunate that he was the first person I met here. But I don't believe *everyone* is glad."

"Only them that doesna understand," said Eldora. "If it hadna been for yersel', rumors were runnin' wild that Hardy would shut up the mill. We've been worried sick aboot it. Noo that ye're here, Sandy told us what a nice lassie ye are. We ken that ye'll put everythin' back the way it was."

"I'm certain that Hardy would not have shut down the mill," said Loni. "He seems genuinely concerned for the welfare of the island."

The *humph* that sounded from Eldora's lips could hardly be mistaken.

"Ye've met him then, I take it?" asked Sandy.

"Twice in fact."

"Don't be fooled by the blackguard, lassie," said Eldora. "He's a connivin' rascal, jist like his father."

Loni looked at Sandy with an expression of bewilderment.

"Ye'll hae tae excuse my sister," he chuckled. "She's a lassie that speaks her mind."

"Is what she says true?"

"'Tis always two sides tae any dispute or question," replied Sandy. "I wouldna be quick tae speak ill o' any man. But 'tis the truth that there hae been things said o' auld Hallfred, Hardy's papa, that I would rather die than hae said o' me, an' it grieves me tae say that by a' accounts the son's headin' doon that same road, if that tells ye anythin'. But I would ne'er give up on what the Lord might be able tae do wi' any man, even Hardy Tulloch, an' he's in my prayers. What Hardy would do in the matter o' the mill, I canna say an' I wouldna speculate. Such speculations are generally more relished in by the women o' the species, if ye winna take offense o' my sayin' so."

"Papa, hoo can ye say such a thing?" said Odara.

"Forgive me, lassie, but ye ken 'tis true as weel as me."

"It may be true, but ye shouldna say it, Papa. Women must be allowed their gossip, ye ken."

"I'm surprised at ye, lassie, after a' the mischief o' lawless tongues against one ye care aboot. If anyone kens the evil o' a loose tongue, it's yersel'."

"Aye, ye're right, Papa. What am I thinkin'? Forgive me for speakin' against ye."

Sandy laughed, gave his daughter an affectionate hug, and turned again to Loni. "Ye see

162

hoo it is, Miss Ford. There's been considerable dispute an' uncertainty aboot what was tae become o' things afore ye came, wi' Hardy an' the chief swirlin' in the middle o' the talk."

"But we ken noo that everythin' will work oot for the best," added Eldora. "We're jist relieved that Hardy winna be able tae do any mischief. He canna bide the chief," she added, not so willing to let go of her grievances as her niece, "an' would close the mill jist tae spite him if he could. Oh, but lassie," she exclaimed, coming close again and squinting at the scarf around Loni's neck. "Hoo could I not hae seen it! Yer scarf . . . how did ye come by it?"

"I bought it in Aberdeen on my way here," replied Loni.

" 'Tis one o' oors, isna it, Odara—jist look!"

Loni removed the pale green scarf from her neck and handed it to Eldora. The elderly woman turned it over with gentle fingers, examining its weave, then looked for the label.

"Aye, jist as I thought—Whales Weave. 'Tis from oor own mill."

"I can't believe it!" said Loni.

"Aye, an' I mind this very scarf . . . ye see, there it is, the wee stray whitey bit amongst the green, jist where I remember it. I knit it mysel'."

"You made it!" exclaimed Loni.

"Aye, lassie."

"The wool's fae one o' Daddy's own sheep,"

said Odara. "Ye mind, Daddy, 'tis the sheep wi' the bits on his wool that winna take the dye."

"Aye," said Sandy. His sister pointed out the tiny strands of white scattered through the green weave. "Lassie," he said to Loni, "if ye'll come wi' me I'll introduce ye tae the very laddie yer scarf came from."

Loni followed Sandy toward a flock of sheep grazing on the far side of the cottage. They scampered toward their master as he approached, heedless of the stranger at his side. Sandy seemed to know every one, mumbling in some unintelligible language as he made his way among them. Gradually they all returned to their grazing until but one was left who, to all appearances, had recognized his name from among the rest.

"Here he is, lassie," said Sandy. "This is the laddie who grew the hair for yer scarf."

Timidly Loni reached down and ran her hand along the furry back.

"He hasna much on him noo on account o' the recent shearin'. In six or eight months ye'll hardly recognize him. But ye can see some o' the tiny hairs whiter than the rest, jist like on yer scarf. They winna take the color, we dinna ken why."

"It is a lovely thing, to know the very sheep it came from," said Loni. "I will treasure this scarf all the more."

Sandy returned her smile, then glanced back to

where his daughter and sister stood watching. "I think the lassies are waitin' for ye."

"Did ye see the whitey bits, lassie?" asked Eldora as the two returned.

"I did indeed," said Loni. "I will not soon forget the sight. And to think that I bought it before I knew any of you, before I had been to the Shetlands, having no idea what Whales Weave even meant."

Sandy laughed with delight at her obvious pleasure.

Ten minutes later, flanked by the two older women talking back and forth as if she were their own long-lost granddaughter, Loni resumed her walk into the village.

24

OVERHEARD THREATS AND SCHEMES

Loni left her two companions at the door of the bakery and continued toward the Whales Fin Inn. With her suitcase half packed back at the Cottage and the decision made to go home, she walked through the door of the hotel not exactly brimming with confidence, but at least knowing her adventure to the Shetlands would be over soon.

She entered the dimly lit common room and walked to the bar. A lady she did not recognize was working behind it.

"Hello," said Loni. "Is Audney here?"

"Wait jist a minute, miss," replied the woman without expression. She turned and disappeared into the kitchen.

Two or three minutes later, Loni heard voices from behind the closed door. A moment later Audney appeared.

Her eyes darted away momentarily when she saw Loni. Then she came and stood behind the bar.

"I, uh . . . I have to apologize for yesterday," began Loni. "I was dreadfully rude to you both. I don't know what came over me. I am very sorry." She forced an awkward smile.

Audney's countenance instantly brightened.

"Oh, dinna bother yersel' aboot it, Miss Ford," she said. "We all hae oor bad days. We'll say nae mair aboot it."

"Thank you," said Loni. "That is very kind of you."

She hesitated, then smiled with an embarrassed expression. "I really would like to talk to you sometime," she added. "I meant what I said. I am truly sorry for my behavior. I didn't just come in because I need a favor, but . . . would it be possible to use your fax again?"

"Aye, miss. Ye ken where it is. Jist go back intil the office an' help yersel'."

"Thank you."

"Uh, oh—I think I hear Hardy's voice comin' along ootside."

"Then I will be off," said Loni. "I'd prefer not to talk to him."

"Did ye hae yer supper wi' him?"

Loni nodded. "We had fish and chips. He said your father fried it for us. It was a new experience for me—eating supper with my fingers. I enjoyed it, actually. But I would just rather not see him again so soon."

"I understand. He's a bit bigger than life . . . an' louder! When ye're finished wi' yer business, then, ye might want tae leave by the back door," Audney said. "Noo scoot, Miss Ford, afore he sees ye."

Loni hurried through the door into the rear corridor of the hotel. She heard Hardy's loud voice as he came in from the street with two of his friends.

She stepped softly toward the small office, wanting to take no chance of Hardy catching a glimpse through the door swinging closed behind her. But she could not keep from making out everything he said as the voice Audney had once likened to a foghorn bellowed into the room.

"Three pints for me an' my frien's, Audney!" he boomed.

"A mite early for ye, isna it, Hardy?" she heard Audney reply.

"We're nae headin' oot till the afternoon tide."

"An' Hardy's celebratin', aren't ye, Hardy?" said a youthfully enthusiastic voice Loni did not know.

"Shush, Ian!" growled Hardy. "Sometimes ye dinna ken when tae keep that loose tongue in yer fat mouth."

"What are ye celebratin', Hardy?" asked Audney.

Loni heard Hardy's feet crossing the floor to the bar. When he spoke, it was in a softer tone. Her curiosity getting the best of her, Loni tiptoed back toward the door she had just come through and strained to listen.

"Jist that yer lookin' at the new laird o' Whales Reef," said Hardy.

Loni's ears perked up at the words. She was as surprised as Audney.

"What are ye bletherin' aboot, Hardy?" said Audney. "A'body kens that the American lassie Miss Ford's the new laird. Ye're nae mair laird than I am."

"Aye, that's as weel as may be, but"—and here he lowered his voice yet further—"ye're speakin' tae her new factor."

"What!"

"Ye heard me weel enouch," said Hardy. " 'Tis a' arranged. The Ford lassie's made me her factor, tae watch o'or her affairs when she gaes back til the States. That's as good as makes me *actin'* laird, if no laird in actual title."

"I dinna believe a word o' it."

"Ye can ask the lassie hersel'. An' if ye dinna speak mair kindly tae me, like I told ye afore, I may find it necessary tae raise yer daddy's rent."

Loni's eyes shot wide as she listened.

"Ye wouldna dare," retorted Audney.

"Once the lassie's gone, I'll do whate'er I like," Hardy shot back. "I'll be handlin' her money, an' I'll send her what she's expectin' an' she'll be none the wiser. I'll hae the power tae act on the laird's behalf on the island. She'll do whate'er I tell her."

"An' what aboot the mill?"

"I'll hae tae decide when the time comes. I may jist sell it."

"Ye wouldna dare," said Audney again. "Miss Ford'd fire ye."

"Who's tae say she'd ken a thing aboot it?"

Loni listened in speechless astonishment.

"She'd find oot," said Audney.

"She wouldna be bothered if I made her a hand-some profit. Ye ken Americans—a' they want is money. She winna ken an' winna care. What cares a lassie the likes o' her for a mill sae far away anyway?"

"What good would it do ye tae sell it? The money is still hers."

"As long as she git's what she's expectin' I'll keep the rest. So ye see, yer daddy's rent will be up tae me. But like I told ye afore, when ye're my wife, I'll nae doobt find it in my hert tae go easy on yer daddy—him being the father-in-law o' the factor, ye ken."

"An' I'll tell ye what I told ye afore too—that I wouldna marry ye if ye was the last man in the Shetlands."

By now Loni's ears were burning with indignation. Her first instinct was to march out and put an end to Hardy's plans once and for all.

A brief scuffle from the common room, however, kept her rooted to the spot. It was followed by a cry from Audney. "Ouch, Hardy, let go o' me, I tell ye!"

Hardy's only reply was a great laugh. It was unwise, for the next sound Loni heard was a woman's hand whacking Hardy across the cheek.

"How dare ye, Audney!" he yelled. "Ye'll think better o'—"

He stopped abruptly. The outside door opened again. More footsteps and voices came into the pub.

Hardy apparently thought better of pursuing the heated conversation with an audience made up of more than his own cohorts.

"Ho, Noak, my friend!" he called out. He turned from the bar and strode back across the floor. "Hoo's the fish runnin' for ye?"

"Nae so good at the minute, Hardy."

"Come an' join me an' the lads for a pint."

"Thank ye, Hardy."

Noak Muir sat down with Hardy and his friends.

The other newcomers found a table across the room.

"Bring Noak a pint, Audney!" brayed Hardy. "So, Noak," he went on when he was seated, "I'm ready wi' the cash as soon as ye say the word."

Their voices softened, and Loni heard nothing further. Still outraged, she tried to calm herself. She needed to think.

She turned again for the office, sat down on the room's one small chair, and tried to decide what to do, glancing again over the letter she had been about to fax to Maddy. She had been on the verge, as Hardy said, of making him her agent, with authority to act on her behalf. She had assumed that she might come back to check on things, perhaps after a year. If all was well, she would arrange matters so that she and her grandparents were well provided for. Then, as had been her first inclination, observing all legalities and seeing to potential tax issues, to turn ownership of the property over to Hardy.

Hardy's words to Audney changed everything. Such a plan was clearly out of the question now. Audney's warnings and the cautions of Sandy and his sister echoed in her ears.

Lost in thought, Loni did not hear several more men enter the hotel. Any thought of confronting Hardy then and there was put to rest a minute later when the door between the corridor and common room swung open. Two men walked through, then stood quietly talking beside the banister leading upstairs. The first voice she recognized well enough.

". . . wanted tae speak tae ye in private, Noak," David was saying. "Sounded tae me like I heard ye an' Hardy makin' plans for him tae buy yer boat."

"Ye ken times is hard, David," said the other man.

"Aye, but ye canna sell tae Hardy."

" 'Tis the medical bills, David. They're threatenin' tae take me tae court if I dinna pay."

Loni held her breath, hoping nothing would give away her presence so close by in the open office.

"But, Noak," said David, "ye ken that Hardy is tryin' tae take control o' a' the fishing on the island. Look at Gundar an' Iver. They sold him their boats an' noo are in worse straits than before."

"I ken, David. I ken he's nae wantin' tae git his hands on my boat oot o' the goodness o' his hert. He's only offerin' half what it's worth."

"Aye, he's a sly one. I shudder tae think what would hae happened wi' him as laird."

"What else can I do, David?"

"Jist gie me a little more time, Noak. I promise I'll find some way tae help ye wi' yer bills. I dinna ken what. I'll contract for another book an' ask for an advance. I'll do somethin'. I winna turn my back on ye."

"I ken you winna, David. Ye're a faithful chief

an' a good friend tae every man, woman, an' child on the island. But my bills are desperate."

"Jist gie me a little more time, Noak. We'll find a way wi'oot yer sellin' tae Hardy."

When they were gone, Loni shook her head in disbelief. She was furious, though at the same time confused. How could she so thoroughly have mistaken what was going on? A moment's reflection also brought a wave of relief to have discovered the truth in time.

She could definitely not leave the island yet. She had to rethink her plans, especially her intent to turn over her affairs to what now appeared to be her less-than-scrupulous third cousin *Hardar*.

And what about the Texan?

She turned the sheet of paper over and wrote out a new message:

Dear Maddy,

I was all set to head for home. I thought I had reached a resolution about what to do. All of a sudden a monkey wrench slammed into the middle of my plans. So I need to stay a while longer, hopefully only a few more days. In the meantime, I need you to do something, if you don't mind, which is to find out everything you can on one James Joseph ("Jimmy Joe") McLeod, an oilman presumably from Texas, though I have my doubts he was born there. I know you're busy, and I hate to ask, but this is important and I have no way to investigate here on the island.

Thank you.

Loni

25

SECRETS

Loni walked back to the Cottage along the sea.

From when she had set out an hour earlier, her plans were turned upside down yet again. As if her three days here had not already been tumultuous enough—now this.

She considered herself good with people, level-headed, a reasonably shrewd judge of character. How could she have been so gullible as to believe Hardy's snow job? She felt like an idiot.

Unbelievable! Hardy had planned to embezzle from her. Had she really been so easy to con?

The realization was shattering. If such a blow-hard was able to bamboozle her, not exactly with his charms—no one was likely to accuse Hardy Tulloch of being *charming*—how well-equipped was she, Husband List notwithstanding, to be wise in choosing a lifetime mate?

She would have to put that question on hold. She had more pressing things on her mind.

Apparently she had misjudged her other third cousin just as badly in the opposite direction. She had not only been rude to him, she had made judgments about his motives and character that were completely wrong. Just as she had heard Hardy's duplicity with her own ears, she had also heard David being kind and understanding, pledging to help a fisherman who was down on his luck.

Loni reached the Cottage, made herself a cup of tea, and sat down in the breakfast room. Through the window she could see about a third of the barn. Beyond it lay the open moor of the island. It really was a peaceful setting, she thought. Beautiful in its own way—stark, plain, rugged.

There was no logical explanation other than Audney's name sending her back to childhood— afraid, lonely, insecure, and a girl named *Audrey* and her friends with their cutting remarks. Back then she had taken solace alone with her tears. All at once as an adult, she had struck out. She had never spoken in such a caustic tone to anyone in her life. What had come over her?

The irony was that she, of all people, had no business getting angry about secrets. She had spent the last dozen years keeping her past carefully guarded. Not even Maddy, her best friend, knew much about her upbringing.

Didn't the psychologists say that you were most critical of the faults in others that were actually your *own* most glaring weaknesses? She appeared to be living proof of that theory. Her accusations against David were really accusations against herself. For all she knew, David might not be a secretive man at all.

She, on the other hand . . . her whole life was a succession of secrets. Whatever had taken place with her father and mother, how they had met, why they had left the Fellowship . . . she knew nothing about it.

She had perpetuated the secretiveness. When she left home for junior college, then later at the university, followed by her friendship with Maddy, she never let anyone all the way inside.

She was secretive toward Hugh too. She sometimes complained that she didn't really know him, that he did not open up and share his feelings.

Who was she to talk? She didn't either. She had done exactly the same to Hugh as she had accused David of doing to her. Secretiveness was as intrinsic to her being as her DNA. She maintained her protective shell thick and intact.

Her angry outburst played itself over and over in her mind. What had she expected, for a perfect stranger to show up at her door and announce, *Hi, I'm David. I'm the chief*?

Unpleasant as it was to face, she was a bold-faced hypocrite. There was nothing else to call it. She had expected a level of openness from David that she had never given to anyone.

26
THE CENTER

Loni rose, left the breakfast room, and wandered about the Cottage with her mug of tea in hand. A few minutes later she found herself slowly climbing the stairs and walking into the private office and sanctuary of Macgregor's grandfather, her own great-great-grandfather Ernest Tulloch, the room about which so many morbid legends had swirled through the community.

Seeing it like this, sensing the spirit of the man who had occupied it, much of what Sandy had told her stole back into Loni's memory.

Pervading the room were subtle scents that reminded her fondly of her own childhood—oak, varnish, and leather mingled with the faint aroma of books, dust, paper, ink, and hints of wool from the Persian rugs on the floor.

She sat down at the rolltop desk, such an exquisite twin of the one in storage back in Pennsylvania. It was piled with books and papers, Bibles and notebooks, much the same, she assumed, as it had been when Ernest's widow had sealed the room after his death. The ink in two glass inkwells had evaporated, leaving behind only dry, cracked reminders of earlier times when writing was done with real ink. Beside them lay three fountain pens. She picked one up tenderly, removed its cap, and examined its gold nib for a moment, wondering what words or thoughts Ernest had written with it.

Two Bibles lay in front of her. A large King James with the Greek text beside it was open to Philippians, chapter 4. Her eyes went immediately to the verse underlined on the page. The words were familiar, yet suddenly alive with meaning, as if Ernest rather than the Apostle Paul were speaking them:

"Finally, brethren, whatsoever things are honest, whatsoever things are just, whatsoever things are pure, whatsoever things are lovely, whatsoever things are of good report; if there be any virtue, and if there be any praise, think on these things."

Her eyes strayed to the small Testament beside it. From the heading on the page she saw that it was a translation by a man named Moffatt. The significance of the passage from Second Timothy 4 could hardly be mistaken—again, as if Ernest himself were speaking from decades long past:

"My time to go has come. I have fought in the good fight; I have run my course: I have kept the faith. Now the crown of a good life awaits me."

What a statement for a man to make as he sensed his earthly life coming to an end—whether a first-century Jew named Paul or a twentieth-century Scotsman named Ernest.

Though he had been gone for more than fifty years, mused Loni, Ernest Tulloch was still here. The room had been locked for half a century. Yet sitting here now, no time had passed. He might as well have been shuffling through these papers a few days ago, reading in these books one last time, putting things in order, writing in one of several notebooks or reading these two poignant passages as he reflected on his own life.

She was experiencing yet another time warp, not this time out of her fast-paced city life but into the heart and mind of her great-great-grandfather.

What truths and secrets did the life of Ernest Tulloch have to reveal?

Absently she opened a few drawers of the desk, exactly as she had when poring through the one in the barn back home. How different were the contents. Yet in another way, how much the same, for they each told a similar story of the passage of time. Here she found no mysterious key or necklace, though by now her appetite was sufficiently whetted to hope that Ernest had somewhere left writings she might discover.

The thought had scarcely passed through her brain when her hands fell on a thick packet bound by a drawstring labeled *Letters to and from Brogan*. Here indeed was a treasure trove—letters from her great-grandfather to his father.

Almost reverently she opened the folder and withdrew several of the envelopes. The postmarks were American. She scanned several that were obvious carbon copies of letters Ernest had written his son. One in particular brought tears to her eyes as she read the affectionate outpouring of a father's love. Keeping out that single touching letter, she replaced the rest, refastened the packet, and set it back on Ernest's desk.

A row of books stood between two bookends on the top shelf of the desk. Loni recognized several as among her own grandfather's favorite devotional writings: *The Journal of John Woolman*, Kelly's *Testament of Devotion* and what appeared to be its German counterpart, *Heiliger Gehorsam*. Then next to them, *The Imitation of Christ* and *The Collected Works of Henry Drummond*. Two were the exact same editions she had brought from the desk in Pennsylvania, abundantly underlined and annotated, twin copies of the same books. Several other German titles completed the small collection: *Das Leben Am Zentrum*, *Wahre Spiritualität*, and *Die Große Sache in Der Welt*.

She did not think the Whales Reef Tullochs were Quaker, yet here were several of the same books so highly regarded by her own grandfather. Along with these were three volumes, each bearing the same odd title, *Unspoken Sermons* by the man MacDonald. Was this preacher MacDonald the same novelist Isobel Matheson had spoken of?

A photograph album on the desk full of family pictures and small portraits also bore further investigation. A thick notebook beside it drew her eye, lying partially obscured by papers and files behind the two Bibles. She withdrew it from its hiding place. Its cover, in large handwritten script, displayed the words *Germany Letters*. Intrigued, she opened it. Inside the cover she read, *Letters from Pomerania, 1897–98, Ernest Tulloch.* A few moments' perusal revealed it as a collection of transcripts of letters, apparently written by young Ernest to his parents.

Loni turned to the first entry. *Dear Mother and Father,* she read, *I have so much to tell you after only a few days here on the farm. Herr von Dortmann is an amazing man. He is not a mere farmer but a true philosopher and a man of depth and wisdom. Already he treats me like a son, though he loves his own young son, Heinrich, with an affection wonderful to behold. I can tell that I will learn much from this man. . . .*

Loni leafed through the volume, pausing here and there to read snatches of Ernest's reflections from his time working on a farm on the Continent.

Herr von Dortmann has given me a book that he says changed his life. It is called Das Leben Am Zentrum, *or* Life at the Center. *It is in German, of course, and though I can dig out most of the meaning, my German is not so perfect that I am not greatly anticipating obtaining an English translation when I return home. . . .*

Loni set the notebook of letters aside. Her eyes again scanned the books on the desk. There was the very book mentioned in the letters, along with its English translation. She took down the German edition—its binding old and loose, the pages yellowing. The inscription inside the cover revealed it as the very book given to Ernest by the German farmer with the date 1897, so worn and with tiny English translations sandwiched in the margins that it must have been read a dozen times.

She replaced it and now took down the volume beside it, the devotional Testament her grandfather in Pennsylvania was so fond of and a copy of which she had discovered in the matching desk in the barn. She could only surmise that Ernest had passed on his personal copy to Brogan at some point and replaced it here in his study with this newer one.

Loni opened it to the first page. Even as her eyes fell on the words, she could hear her grandfather's voice reading them aloud to her and his dear Anabel:

> Deep within us all there is an amazing inner sanctuary of the soul, a holy place, a Divine Center, a speaking Voice, to which we may continuously return. Eternity is at

our hearts calling us home unto Itself. It is a dynamic center, a creative Life, a Light Within which illuminates the face of God and casts new shadows and new glories upon the face of men.

What an amazing thing, thought Loni, that this same book, which had in such a short time become a classic of Quaker literature, would find its way into her life from three different sources.

As she continued to gaze about, Loni's eyes took in a dozen or more framed photographs—all the family, she assumed, of Ernest Tulloch, though they were unlabeled. The older couple must be Ernest's parents, two wedding photographs, no doubt, of Ernest as a younger man with his first wife, Elizabeth, then with his second wife, Sally, and a number of photos of Ernest with three young men, obviously his three sons, and their sister. A quotation, also framed, hung on the wall among the photographs, written out on parchment in an ornate script. Slowly Loni read the words:

I went up to my study. The familiar faces of my books welcomed me. I threw myself in my reading-chair, and gazed around me with pleasure. I felt it so homely here. All my old friends present there in the spirit ready to talk with me any moment when I was in the mood, making no claim upon my attention when I was not! I felt as if I should like, when the hour should come, to die in that chair, and pass into the society of the witnesses in the presence of the tokens they had left behind them.

—George MacDonald

How wonderful to imagine that perhaps Ernest Tulloch *had* indeed died in his favorite reading chair.

Loni's spirit grew yet more peaceful. Something was here, something deep, powerful, unknown . . . something that to know would be worth any price, something that to know would be the greatest treasure in the world.

This was no mere office, but a chamber of reflection, a sanctuary of communion with God. What was it Isobel Matheson had called it— The Bard's Chamber? Just as Sandy Innes had also said. Every inch revealed the character of the man who had occupied it. She realized that she had entered the inner sanctum and prayer closet of Ernest Tulloch's soul.

Had this study been preserved, perhaps not only for her but nevertheless specifically *for* her, its life and spirit kept hidden but alive, dormant, awaiting the appointed season for its renewal and rebirth into a new generation?

If so, her first duty was to awaken it within herself. Loni began to pray.

God, what does it all mean? Open my eyes and heart to comprehend the legacy that is here. What would You speak to me through the memory of this man I never knew yet whose blood flows in my veins? Breathe wisdom into me through this chamber of solace that links the past and the present, and perhaps the future as well. Breathe into me the life that inhabits this sanctuary. And make clear to me what you want me to do about this island and its future . . . and about my own?

Her heart was full . . . of what she could not have put into words.

She smiled at the reminder of the rumor of the dead body. One thing that was certainly *not* here was death. This study contained more life than any room she had ever been in.

27

SIDEWALK MEETING

Washington, D.C.

"Maddy . . . hey, Maddy!" called a familiar voice from across the street.

With an inward groan, Madison Swift turned from the door into Capital Towers in Washington's business district. A sharply dressed man about her own age dashed toward her through the morning traffic.

There were only three people she allowed to address her by the informal "Maddy"—her mother, her sister, and her friend and assistant Loni Ford.

That Loni's boyfriend, Hugh Norman, was *not* one of that select circle, however, did not prevent his presuming on his relationship with Loni to carry himself more casually toward Maddy than she liked. The liberties he took extended beyond mere conventions of address. He came by to visit Loni unannounced and expected her to drop whatever she was doing for as long as he was inclined to stay. He made himself at home in her office like he owned the place. He considered himself entitled to special privileges throughout the entire floor, using the staff restrooms and lounge and lunch area whenever he liked. He had gone so far as to open Maddy's closed door and barge into her office without waiting for an answer to his knock when she and Loni were in conference.

What annoyed Maddy most about Hugh was the unspoken condescension he conveyed toward their profession as a whole. The obvious superiority he felt as a congressional aide over the likes of mere businesswomen was palpable. He didn't try to hide his view that his work was more important than theirs. This was Washington. Politics defined the capital. He was of the elite who ran this town. Why shouldn't he come and go anywhere in it he pleased?

Maddy knew she possessed a cynical streak. Hugh was probably not really such a bad guy, as political types went. But she had met so many exactly like him that whatever tolerance she had left had worn thin.

A host of such thoughts flitted through her brain in a second or two as she waited. It would be useless to pretend she hadn't seen him. Hugh would just follow her inside and up to her office. She would rather deal with him on the sidewalk.

"Hey, Maddy . . . glad I caught you," said Hugh as he ran up.

"You're out early," said Maddy. "I thought you congressional aides kept cushier hours."

"Had a breakfast meeting with some donors."

"The life of the mover and shaker, eh?" said Maddy. Her sarcasm was altogether lost on her audience. "What's on your mind, Hugh? I need to get to work. Or was this just a chance *hello* on the street?"

"Not entirely. I need to talk to Loni. Any word when she'll be back?"

"Just what I've told you three times already—I don't know. She will be back when she's ready. She has a lot on her plate."

"I've tried to call several times, but I keep getting her voice mail."

"And you won't get through. She doesn't have an international cell."

"I really want to talk to her. Some opportunities have come up this week, big developments and a major turning point in my future . . . *our* future. She and I need to make plans. Say, I just had a thought. I'll go up with you and try to call from your office. You must have a number for her."

"Why don't you call from your own office?"

"I can't do that."

"Why not?"

"A personal international call on the congress-man's dime just wouldn't be kosher."

"But it would be okay from mine?"

"Well . . . sure—it's different."

"How so?"

"You're not a congressman."

"You're right. But I do have work to do." Maddy moved toward the door.

"So could I use your phone to call Loni?"

Maddy turned back to face him.

"No, Hugh. It's my office. It's where I work. And all this is beside the point anyway. I don't have the number for Loni's house there. I'll see you later."

Maddy walked into the building, leaving Hugh on the sidewalk gazing after her with a bewildered expression.

Maddy took the elevator to the seventh floor. She arrived at her office at twenty minutes before eight o'clock. A glance toward her fax machine revealed a single sheet that had come through during the night.

She picked it up and read the brief message, then smiled.

Stay as long as you like, girl! she said to herself. *Not that I don't miss you, but what Hugh doesn't know won't hurt him.*

And as far as the big lout of a Texan was concerned, thought Maddy, nothing would please her more than to uncover some dirt on him.

28

ON THE MOOR

Whales Reef, Shetland Islands

Loni went out about two o'clock, her great-grandmother's journal again in hand, along with one of Ernest Tulloch's books she wanted to peruse. After the swings of emotions of the last twenty-four hours, she hoped some words of wisdom from the venerable upstairs study would give her some perspective and remind her of her purpose here.

She sought the same stone where she had read earlier. Twenty or thirty minutes later she was again engrossed in the story from the previous century.

Gradually Loni lost track of time. At length a faint *baa*-ing interrupted her reading. Glancing up she saw fifteen or twenty sheep scampering toward her.

She laid the journal on the stone and rose. Within seconds the small horde had surrounded her and were bumping and jostling against her legs. They were more rambunctious than Sandy's flock.

"Hey!" she laughed as she stooped over to pet a few woolly backs. "What's all this?"

Whether they sensed that she was a new object for their affection or they were merely curious, they clustered and bumped more closely than was comfortable. From the uneven footing, and the surprising strength of some of the larger rams against her, Loni lost her balance.

With a cry she toppled over several of them, sending the flock scurrying out of harm's way.

The next thing she heard was footsteps running toward her.

"Miss Ford!" cried David, hurrying down the incline behind his sheep. "Are you all right?"

Loni half lifted herself around to face him. "You came just in time to see me at my undignified worst," she said. "I'm fine, I think—taken by surprise mostly."

"Are you hurt?" asked David, stooping beside her.

"I don't think so," said Loni, trying to stand.

"Let me just . . . Ouch! I must have twisted my ankle. Your sheep are friendlier than I expected."

"I am sorry. I should have—"

"It was my own fault. I'm really not always a klutz like this. I should have stayed where I was sitting."

"I'm afraid they do tend to be curious and overly friendly."

"Even toward strangers?"

"Especially toward strangers."

Loni stood on one leg, then tentatively shifted her weight to the other.

"How is it?" asked David.

"Tender. I definitely came down awkwardly. But I don't think it's sprained. I'll get ice on it and it should be okay. Would you help me back to the stone?"

Leaning on David and hobbling on one leg, Loni returned to her makeshift bench. David eased her to a sitting position.

"That's better," said Loni. "Thank you. I'll be fine now."

"I think I had better help you back to the Cottage. In fact, I should fetch my cart and drive you home. My house is less than a mile away, just over that ridge there."

"Please don't bother. I'll be okay. I just need to rest a minute."

"If you say so. But I'm not leaving until we're sure."

David walked a short distance away and sat down. "What are the books you were reading before my lads and lassies interrupted you?" he asked.

"The one is an old journal, my great-grandmother's. I discovered it among some family mementos back in the States. She came to Whales Reef in 1924."

"How fascinating. And the other?"

"It's one of Ernest's, the Auld Tulloch I believe you call him. I borrowed it from his study upstairs."

"The locked study?" said David in surprise.

"Yes—that's right, you don't know. It turns out I have had the key to the room all along, or one of my grandfathers in America did. I ran across it recently, along with the journal, but had no idea what it was for. I brought it with me and it turns out that it opened the study door."

"That's fantastic!" exclaimed David. "I can't wait to see it." He then hesitated. "I mean, if you don't mind, that is . . . if you would want to show it to me."

"Of course. You have a right to see it. You are, after all, the *chief*."

The heavy significance of the word hung in the air.

"Speaking of which," Loni went on, "I really have to apologize for all those things I said yesterday."

"Please don't worry about it," said David. "Nothing to apologize for."

"Are you kidding? I have twenty things to apologize for! I was rude, arrogant, and entirely hypocritical."

David began to laugh. "I assure you, it isn't so bad as that," he said. "Seriously, I took no offence. I understand the awkwardness of your situation here, and the pressure you are under. There's really no need—"

"Please, Mr. Tulloch," persisted Loni. "I feel terrible about my behavior. I was a complete idiot. I realize how I was wrong about you. I misjudged you terribly and . . ."

Tears filled her eyes and she turned away.

"I am *so* sorry," said Loni softly. "I don't know what came over me. You probably think me a ridiculous emotional female. Believe it or not," she said, struggling to regain her composure, "I'm usually more or less . . . well, halfway rational at least. But secretiveness has always been hard for me. I grew up around secrets. You had every right not to tell me you were the chief. I completely overreacted. It was stupid. I hope you can forgive me."

"Of course," said David, gazing at Loni with a tender smile. "All is forgiven."

"It was as if all the years of pent-up frustration burst out all at once, and I took it out on you. I'm sure you were trying to be kind. Maybe some-time I will be able to tell you about it."

"I will look forward to that."

"But not today!" said Loni, trying to laugh. "For now I just want to forget it. I don't want to feel any guiltier than I already do."

"Fair enough," said David. He rose and walked to where Loni sat on the stone. He extended his hand. "So, Miss Ford, shall we start over again as friends?"

Loni smiled and took his hand. "Yes, *Chief* Tulloch . . . friends."

"I would prefer *David* to chief."

"I'll see what I can do. And if we are going to be on a first-name basis, maybe it's time—" she paused, a smile spreading across her face—"I think it's time you called me *Alonnah*."

"A positively beautiful name it is. Well then, Alonnah Ford, look at you. You fell over some dirty sheep onto the wet ground. If you don't mind my saying so, your posh clothes are a mess. I'm afraid I even see some . . . organic matter on those expensive shoes."

"Organic matter?"

"Actually, we call it manure."

Loni burst into laughter. "That's what we call it too. I grew up in farm country. A little organic matter doesn't gross me out *too* much."

"In any event, you definitely need some new duds—especially walking shoes. I'm surprised your feet aren't covered in scrapes and sores wearing those flimsy little things about the island," he said, pointing to Loni's feet.

"Actually, I do have one or two blisters."

"Then what do you say to me taking you into Lerwick tomorrow to get you outfitted in some more suitable Shetland attire?"

Loni smiled. "I would like that."

"And I think we also ought to get you back to the Cottage. If your ankle does need ice, the sooner the better. Here, take my hand again."

Once more David helped Loni to her feet.

"What's the verdict?" he asked.

"If you don't mind my leaning on you, I can make it. It's not sprained. I've had enough experience with injuries to be sure of that. But you're right—I should get ice on it."

"This isn't your first, then?"

"Not by any means. I swam and ran competitively in college and have done quite a bit of running and some racquetball since. Twisted ankles are part of the game."

"Then let's be off—don't forget your books. What was your great-grandmother doing on Whales Reef?" he asked.

"She came as a lady's companion to a wealthy widow. Apparently this was quite the tourist destination."

"I've heard that," rejoined David. "Times have certainly changed. Although," he added as a slow grin came to his lips, "we do have two American sisters who seem determined to revive that tradition."

"How so?"

"They come at least once a year to attend one of my tours. I will just say they are an interesting pair!" he said with a light laugh. "But their hearts are in the right place, and they dearly love the Shetlands."

"One thing I would like to know," said Loni as they went. "Tell me about the financial struggles of the man called Noak, I think his name is."

"Noak Muir. How do you know about that?"

Loni's face flushed as she realized her blunder. "Do you mind if I don't tell you just yet?"

"More secrets?" suggested David with a twinkle in his eye.

"I'm afraid so. It would appear that you have caught me."

"Not my intention."

"I know. I will tell you, I promise. I just want to think of the best *way* to tell you."

"Fair enough."

David went on to explain about the kidney problems with Noak's daughter that had compelled them to use private medical services rather than the National Health Service and the bills that had resulted. He concluded by telling her about Hardy's offer to buy the *Bonnie Muir.*

"I take it you do not consider the offer in Mr. Muir's best interest?"

"You seem to know more about this than you are letting on," chuckled David. "But you're right,

I do not. It is the worst thing he could possibly do."

Loni took in the information but asked no more questions.

By the time they reached the Cottage, Loni was hobbling reasonably well. She stopped at the kitchen door and turned before going inside. "Thank you for seeing me safely home," she said. "And again, I am extremely sorry for yesterday."

"Forget it, remember?" said David. "Over and done with. If you have something else to wear, I would like to take your shoes with me and clean them up."

"Really, there's no need."

"My sheep caused the mess. Besides, dealing with such things is not women's work. I'm a sheepherder. It goes with the territory. I would feel better if you let me handle it. I will bring them back sparkling and fresh."

"Okay—that's very chivalrous of you."

"Let's just call it neighborliness," laughed David.

Leaning against the side of the door, Loni removed her shoes. David bent down to pick them up, then hurried off to rejoin his flock.

As Loni watched him go, a smile spread over her lips. Hugh would not be caught dead doing such a thing.

29
LETTER HOME

Loni spent that evening composing a letter to her grandparents. It was full of memories, reflections, and nostalgic outpourings, with a poignant tone of affection, ensuring, when they received it, that both William and Anabel Ford would read their granddaughter's words through eyes swimming in tears.

Dear Grandma and Grandpa,

I have more to tell you than a letter possibly can. But I will try.

I am in the middle of nowhere, as I would have judged it a few days ago—200 miles from Scotland's oil capital of Aberdeen and about 250 from the coast of Norway.

Yet in a sense I feel cozily at home. This is the greatest surprise of all. How could I feel at home in the middle of the ocean so far from my "real" life?

I had planned by this time to be on my way back to the States. I had not antici-pated that being here would stir so many things awake in me. My perceptions began to change even before I set foot on the island. I felt it even as I stood in the fog on the ferry that took me across to the island.

I have embarked on an adventure of discovering where I came from, and maybe discovering at long last who I really am. That's not to say there haven't been some hard things. Not everyone has welcomed me with open arms, but most of the people have been very accepting.

You will scarcely believe this, but I am sitting in the former study of my great-great-grandfather, a man called Ernest Tulloch. I am writing from his writing table, using one of his fountain pens I had to wash and clean and find fresh ink to fill it with. This is just one of many new experiences—writing a letter in longhand with an old fountain pen!

There are Quaker connections all around me. Many books in this room you would recognize as among your favorites, Grandpa. There is so much that you and Ernest Tulloch had in common. I am realizing how deeply my life has been doubly enriched by my heritage from both sides of my ancestry, my father's and my mother's. Being here has made me hungry to learn more about my Ford and Simons ancestries too. You've probably told me much that I have forgotten. I suppose young people don't value their ancestry until they are older. I will probably be pestering you with questions for years!

The small island of Whales Reef—I cannot believe I am saying this!—that I have apparently inherited most of, is about four miles by two miles, with a village of what I would guess to be a few hundred people. It is only accessible by ferry. There are a few shops, a hotel and pub, a bakery and post office and gift shop, a small market, and a church. Fishing and sheep are the main sources of income. There is a woolen mill that employs a number of the village women. If I accept the inheritance, I will be what they call the "laird" of the island. I have actually been called that a few times! It will take time to get used to.

In some ways Whales Reef is a community like ours at home, where everybody knows everybody, where gossip abounds, and where there are hearts of gold and other hearts not quite as pure. I have been so lonely at times that I have longed for your arms to hold me, Grandma, protecting me from the pain of the world, soothing me and telling me that everything will be okay like you used to do.

So many memories fill my heart of the rich life you gave me. It was a priceless heritage that I am beginning to appreciate for what it truly is.

I wish you could be here with me, Grandpa. There are so many books here that you would know. Ernest was a man of God just like you. On the shelves and desks here are several open Bibles which he must have been reading right up until he died. I feel surrounded by learning and wisdom.

Though I have had bouts of loneliness in the last week, I have found something here that I suppose I needed. I needed to know where my mother came from. Knowing more about both my Quaker roots and my Shetland roots gives me a feeling of completeness. It makes me all the more thankful for the spiritual heritage the two of you gave me.

My time here has forced me to do considerable soul-searching. I know if I brought this up to you in person that you would both be gracious and tell me I have nothing to apologize for. However, I feel I need to apologize to you for not taking the Quaker heritage of my upbringing as seriously as perhaps I should have. I realize that I have been drifting spiritually since leaving home for college. I am sorry for that, and for other ways I have hurt you. Being here has turned me back toward my roots—including my Quaker roots with you and in the Fellowship, which, believe it or not, I do treasure in spite of the pain I had to endure at school.

I thank you again for the life and love you poured into me. You were not only the best grandparents in the world, you were actually my parents too, and I am so grateful for you.

I haven't made any definite plans, but I should be home in a few more days, a week at most. I have many decisions to make. I want to talk to you when I get home and get your advice about all this. Please pray for me, as I know you do, that I will have wisdom and will be able to hear God's voice.

There is so much more . . . but it is late and I will write again soon, I promise.

I love you both so much!
Loni

Loni set the letter aside and retired to her bedroom. It had been an emotional day. She was dead on her feet.

Twenty minutes later, curled up under the thick duvet and with two pillows behind her, Loni was ready to end the day with a few more minutes in her great-grandmother's journal. As she read, she was reminded again of the striking parallel to her own story—two young American women transported halfway around the world to this small remote island.

How much has it changed in ninety years? she wondered. When her great-grandmother went out for the memorable walk on her first day here and encountered three individuals destined to change her life forever, did everything look much the same as it did now? Did she perhaps use the same flat stone for a bench that Loni had been sitting on earlier that day when interrupted by the chief's flock of rambunctious sheep?

30

A LEGACY BEGINS— *THE CLIFFS*

Whales Reef, 1924

Making its first appearance of the day shortly after three in the morning, the sun had already risen high over the North Atlantic. A moist chill, however, still clung to the ground. June had come to the Shetland island of Whales Reef. That did not necessarily mean balmy days of shirtsleeve warmth. Today the mercury would probably reach about fifty-two degrees on the Fahrenheit scale. Though well-bundled in a thick navy-blue wool overcoat, the walker making his way with uneven steps along a sandy stretch of isolated shoreline shivered as he went.

The tide was out and the sea calm. Even so, the tiny wavelets whose gentle splashing rhythm would have been music to the ears of most reverberated like sledgehammers inside his brain. He had thought the sea air might act as an antidote to his monstrous hangover. It was obviously not helping.

He turned irritably inland, across the upper portion of the beach, and crossed a patch of small rocks. The crunch of his feet exploded in his ears like machine-gun fire. Cresting the dune that ran parallel to the water, he arrived at last on the open moor. The grassy peat provided soft padding for his steps. With a sigh of relief, he struck out across it.

What had brought him out at this ungodly hour of the morning, with a hangover and a sour disposition, Brogan Tulloch could not have said. He hated mornings, especially after a binge. But he could not lie in bed a moment longer. So he had climbed into his boots, thrown on his coat, and gone out into the morning.

A new gaggle of sightseers had checked into the hotel the previous afternoon. Two full busloads from Lerwick had come over on the four o'clock ferry. Brogan always made a point of being on hand to have a scrutinizing look at the newcomers, especially those of the female persuasion who appeared between eighteen and twenty-five. But his initial assessment of this particular assortment of prospects had not been encouraging. Most appeared more studious than aristocratic. Old women and balding men and student types carrying textbooks—not the sort that drew his eye. Along with the adventure seekers from London's social register, colleges and universities also sponsored junkets to these out-of-the-way locales, often in conjunction with summer academic programs. This tour had obviously been infiltrated with more bookworms than he preferred.

The night of their arrival, too, had proved a disappointment. Rather than the usual merry-making, after dinner those from the Glasgow University group had attended a lecture, of all things, by a professor of naturalist studies on the origins of the Shetland pony, the effect of the Highland Clearances on life in the Shetlands, as well as a status report concerning several endangered species of Shetland sheep. A more boring evening Brogan could not have imagined. He hoped the rest of the week proved more eventful.

He had no destination in mind. He was just walking in hopes that somehow last night's whisky would pass through his system more quickly than usual.

Whenever he was on this part of the island, however—which was not often these days—his steps unconsciously fell into old habits. The legs of boyhood usually led in the direction of the cave. His fondest memories of childhood were of his adventures with his brother, many of them among the dangerous bluffs at the far end of the island.

Twenty minutes later, the pain from his hangover subsiding by degrees, he approached the bluff. Even now a slight tingle in his knees and hollow feeling in his stomach gave evidence to the breathtaking suddenness with which the bluff gave way to what he and Wallace years ago dubbed the Great Cliff. The view from the edge of the precipice was truly awe-inspiring. On a clear day from the northernmost cliffs of the island you could see the entire outline of Yell and through Codgrove Sound to the southern outline of Unst.

The most terrifying sight of all was straight down two hundred feet of sheer drop to the rocky shoals of the sea. It was the most dangerous place on the island. Tales abounded of murders and suicides and lovers leaping into the abyss of death rather than marry someone other than their true love. Whether or not any of the stories were true, they fueled the terrified imagination of one generation after another of Whales Reef youngsters, every one of whom had been forbidden more times than they could count from venturing to the island's northern reaches.

As Ernest Tulloch's eldest son continued aimlessly on his way, ahead he spied a figure seated on the ground nearly at the edge of the Great Cliff. It appeared to be a girl or young woman with binoculars around her neck. Her back was turned, but she had a sketchbook in her lap and pen in hand. It wasn't unusual to see tourists wandering around the island. The place was a blasted breeding ground for tourists. But he had never seen one here.

Good heavens, what was she thinking? The goose was seated with her legs dangling over the side of the cliff!

Aware of her danger, Brogan broke into an unsteady run.

His effort at haste was brief. His pulsing head swayed and his knees buckled. In his present condition, he would not dare get within yards of the drop-off!

He tried to focus his throbbing brain. He had to warn the girl of the danger . . . but without startling her.

He began walking again, whistling softly and kicking at an occasional stone, trying to make just enough noise to alert her of his presence.

Her head turned. His plan had obviously worked. She was a small wisp of a thing—

couldn't be more than a teenager. Through her dark-rimmed glasses, the girl looked at him with an expression of annoyance.

"Ho, I say there!" said Brogan, though the effort at speech was difficult. "I didn't expect to see anyone out so early."

A sudden flurry of orange, black, and white erupted a few feet to the girl's right. Several brightly colored puffins flapped into the air and out from the cliff toward the sea.

"Now look what you've done!" cried the girl. "You scared them off!"

"It's only a few puffins!" laughed Brogan, wincing from the echo between his temples. "There are thousands more where those came from," he added. "This ruddy island is full of them."

"Not so close as those! I have been sitting here an hour coaxing them closer."

"Well, you obviously had a nice look at them. Now it's time to come away from that cliff."

"But I hadn't finished my drawing."

"You'll have to finish it another time. You need to come back from the brink there. It's not safe."

The girl seemed unconcerned with his warnings. "Why did you come barging up and yelling like that?" she persisted. "It may take days to get another such opportunity."

"I was hardly yelling," said Brogan, moving

slowly toward her. "I was worried that you were so close to the edge."

"I was managing just fine until you came along."

"You really need to get back. It's very dangerous."

Several feet away, Brogan stopped. The girl said no more but sat looking out over the expanse of watery blue below. He stood staring at the back of her head of brown shoulder-length hair.

"Is this the highest point on the island?" she asked after a moment, still without turning to face him.

"It's the highest bluff along the shore," answered Brogan. "There is a higher hill inland."

Again it was quiet.

"You're American," said Brogan. "Staying at the hotel, I take it—with the tour that just arrived."

"Very good. How could you tell?" she said, at last turning toward him.

"Your accent, obviously. It reminds me of the proverbial chalkboard. How you people can so thoroughly butcher the English language is beyond me."

"What about you? I can hardly understand a word you say."

"There—your perky air gives you away. Where are your parents, anyway? What are they doing letting you wander out alone at such an ungodly hour of the morning?"

"My parents!" laughed the girl. "My parents happen to be five thousand miles away."

"Wherever they are, they didn't teach you to do as you're told."

"I am old enough not to need people telling me what to do."

"As old as that, are you?" quipped Brogan.

"I am. As for the time, I've been up for hours. I don't happen to be one who sleeps away the best part of the day. Why can't you let me enjoy the peace and quiet of the view?"

"Even without your precious ruddy birds to keep you company?" said Brogan sarcastically.

"I would certainly like to try."

"At least let me see your drawing before I go," said Brogan, trying one final tactic to get the stubborn girl away from the cliff.

"I will keep my drawing to myself, if you don't mind. I cannot imagine that you are really interested in the pelagic species of the auk family of seabird, *Fratercula arctica*."

Brogan laughed, though a little contemptuously. "A walking encyclopedia, are we? Well, have it your way, then. If you wind up down on the rocks, don't come to me for sympathy. I try to give you a little friendly help and get rudeness in return. I suppose what should I expect from an American?"

At last the girl pulled her legs back up from the edge of the cliff and stood facing the man who had intruded so abruptly into her morning.

"The rudeness is all on your side, sir," she said. "I take it from your accent that you are a native here. Is this your customary way of treating guests to your island?"

"Trying to help them not kill themselves by falling into the ocean, you mean?" retorted Brogan. "Yes, I would like to think we are helpful and considerate hosts," he added with a wry smile.

"Well, then, thank you for your consideration," rejoined the girl with equal sarcasm.

She walked away along the edge of the bluff.

Annoyed yet further by the impertinence of her turning her back on him, Brogan took several steps after her.

"Hey, lassie, I suggest you mind your manners. Do you have any idea who you are talking to?"

"No, and I don't care."

"You had better care or I may have you thrown off my land."

"Your land!"

"Yes, my land."

"I don't believe a word of it. Whoever you are, you should be more polite to visitors."

She stopped and turned and stared at him a moment. "Besides all that, I think you are drunk. Your eyes are bloodshot and puffy. You are unshaven and unkempt. If you were really the owner of this land, you would not go about in public looking like that. Good day, sir!" she said, then tromped off.

Brogan stared after her, by now so angry that, had his head not been splitting, he would have continued the heated exchange until he was on the winning side of it. As things stood, he decided to let it go. Besides, she was walking away so fast he doubted he could keep pace with her.

An uncharacteristic pang smote him. He didn't like being put in his place by a pip-squeak of a girl, and an American at that. But maybe she was right. He probably did look a mess. Even without a mirror, he could feel the puffiness in his eyes. They were no doubt red as two beets.

What he really needed, thought Brogan, was a drink. But out here there was nothing to be had but fresh air . . . and ruddy puffins!

He turned and wandered back the way he had come.

After her unceremonious morning encounter, the American newcomer to Whales Reef was anxious to get back out for another walk. The tour's first full day on the island had taken up the rest of the morning and most of the afternoon. Finally she decided to skip the optional afternoon session, tracing Norwegian influence on Shetland customs, and again seek the barren moor north of the village.

The exchange near the cliffs that morning had unnerved her. She knew she had behaved badly. She needed to make peace with God about it.

She hoped she might somehow run into the young man again to apologize to him as well.

From all she had been told to expect about the Shetland weather, it was a surprisingly warm day. It was after four when she left the hotel, though the sun was so high in the sky it might as well have been noon. She struck out with no destination in mind other than to be alone. Vaguely praying as she went, the light sea breeze on her face, the sight of sheep grazing in the distance, and the faint cry of gulls above the shoreline to her right all combined to soothe her troubled spirit.

She made her way over the uneven heathery terrain and gradually walked north and east from the center of the island in the direction of the sea. After going about two miles, ahead she saw a small lad who looked to be five or six, hair of bright orange, seated on a stone and staring down at the ground. Beside him sat a man. They were not speaking.

As she came near she saw that their thoughts were occupied by an injured bird on the ground between them. A black-and-white sheepdog lay motionless behind the boy. She sat down a few feet away. It remained quiet for several minutes. None of the three were compelled to disturb the tranquility of the afternoon.

"We are helping this little bird die in peace," said the man at length. His voice was soft and serene.

The girl smiled and nodded. She sensed that this was no time for words.

After perhaps twenty minutes, the dog stirred and lifted its head. The boy's attention was riveted on the tiny form on the grass. A slight flutter and the next moment it was over. He stared down for another few seconds, blinked hard, then stood.

The man reached into his pocket and dug out a small coin. He reached up and handed it to the boy.

"This is for ye tae remember the day, Sandy," he said. " 'Tis a wee token tae keep. I want ye tae tell me one day when ye ken what it means."

The boy took the coin, looked at it a moment where it lay on his palm, then pocketed it. He turned and walked away across the moor, sheep-dog bounding after him.

Man and girl were left alone, each remaining quiet.

Finally she rose and left the scene. With her journal in hand, she wandered back in the direction of the village from which she had come. After a short time she turned inland and spied a flat boulder ahead, walked to it, and seated herself comfortably on its surface, reflecting on the boy and man she just left.

She placed the leather journal in her lap and removed a pen from her bag. She thought for a moment, then methodically began to draw. Soon a remarkably lifelike sketch of the bird on the ground and the boy on stone beside it emerged on the blank page. After a quarter of an hour, when she was satisfied with the image, above the sketch in an artistic script she wrote, *A Boy and a Bird.*

She paused, trying to remember every word of the conversation she had heard. She wrote for twenty or thirty minutes. She had long since lost track of the time when a crisp gust brought her senses awake. She realized that the afternoon was waning and that Mrs. Barnes would expect her back for dinner. After their first full day on the island, tonight would be a festive evening and Mrs. Barnes was probably already wondering where she was.

She rose and began the walk back to the hotel.

PART 3

31
SATURDAY IN LERWICK

Loni Ford and David Tulloch walked through the door of Shetland Outfitters to an array of clothes, shoes, hats, boots, and hunting and fishing and all manner of outdoor apparel and supplies. Binoculars, compasses, knives, flashlights, tents, backpacks, nature books, even rubber rafts—all assaulting their senses, along with racks and displays throughout the store of every kind of outdoor clothing imaginable.

"Oh, look!" exclaimed Loni, lifting a small pewter ram displayed along with glassware and tartans, which no self-respecting store of its kind in Scotland would be without. "I will buy some small gifts here to take back with me."

"This is one of my favorite places in Lerwick," said David. "It's not high fashion, but you will find a good pair of hiking boots and perhaps a warm vest. I might also recommend a work shirt and denim trousers."

"I have all that at home," said Loni. "Seems a shame to buy a new wardrobe for another day or two."

"Is that your schedule—you'll be leaving so soon?"

"I had planned to leave two days ago. Then I thought today. I was half packed. Actually, my suitcase is open beside my bed back in the Cottage. Then the truth finally dawned on me about Hardy. I'm embarrassed to say that I had intended to place my affairs in his hands."

"I take it you changed your mind."

Loni nodded.

"I would be less than honest if I did not confess to profound relief," said David. "Though not from any supposed advantage to myself."

"I think I understand that now too," said Loni. "And that brings me to what I didn't tell you yesterday. I suppose now is as good a time as any to come clean." Loni hesitated and glanced away briefly. "The reason I knew about Mr. Muir's financial trouble, as well as your offer to help, not to mention the few things you said about Hardy, was that . . . I was eavesdropping. I heard the whole conversation."

Momentarily perplexed, a slow grin spread over David's face. "That's actually quite funny!" he said.

"Not intentionally," added Loni. "I was in the back office sending a fax. Audney's let me do that a couple times. Suddenly the two of you came through the door and I was trapped with no way to get away without being seen."

"You were in a predicament for sure," he chuckled. "But no harm done, other than my own embarrassment at your hearing me speak candidly about Hardy. I would be loath to criticize him to your face."

"You have already demonstrated your honorability in that regard. And I respect you for it, though it made me mad at first. But I was wrong and I know it."

"No more on that—remember."

"You wouldn't have needed to tell me anything anyway, because I got an earful from Hardy himself before you and Mr. Muir came in. Now that *did* make me angry!"

"What did he say?" asked David. "He wasn't rude to you or hurt you in any way?"

"Nothing like that. I was already in the back of the hotel. He had no idea I was listening. But his voice carries, if you know what I mean. He was boasting that he would be running my affairs when I left the island, saying terrible things to Audney too. He may have grabbed her, but I think she took care of him with a slap across the face."

"Audney can hold her own," said David with a smile. "But it concerns me that Hardy thought he could worm his way into your affairs."

"It's my own fault. I implied that I would put him in charge during my absence. I assumed he was next in line for the inheritance. He was so confident about it, to be honest I never doubted him. And I had been angry at you, and . . . well, it was stupid of me, but that's what happened."

"You and he haven't put anything in writing?"

"No. And after what I heard him saying, I will watch my step around him in the future. I misread him, I misread you, I misread the whole situation. But as you say, that is behind us. So to answer your question, I don't know how much longer I will be here. I suppose some more rugged clothes would be a good idea."

"Then here is a good place to start," said David, indicating a rack of rain gear. "I don't know if you've noticed, but it rains in Scotland."

Loni laughed and lifted a yellow rain slicker. "I'll look like one of the fishermen!"

"If it were winter, I would recommend one of these heavier jackets with insulation to keep out the cold. As it is, I think . . . let me see, this rack over here. I have a windbreaker from this company. It's perfect for summer rainy weather." He pulled a navy-blue windbreaker from the rack.

"I can see from looking that it's ten sizes too big."

Loni perused the rack, trying on several, finding her size and a style she liked. At length she pulled out a light misty-green jacket with hood and abundant pockets.

"Perfect," said David. "Try it on."

Loni handed David her bag and slipped the windbreaker over her head.

"That's it," said David with a nod. "It exactly matches your green eyes."

"Now you are a fashion expert too?" laughed Loni.

"Let's just say from what little I know about the feminine species that they consider it important to look good as well as coordinate the colors of the wardrobe even when being utilitarian."

"Who told you that?"

"If a man intends to survive in this world, he had better be paying attention."

"Well, you are right," rejoined Loni, inspecting her selection in a nearby mirror. "Of course everything has to match. How most men can be clueless about such a fundamental principle I have never understood."

"I hope you won't lump me into that large mass of *most men* whom women consider clueless."

Loni laughed good-naturedly. "I am coming to see that perhaps you are a little different. Actually, I *do* love this green. I'll take it."

"Good . . . okay next, gloves and boots."

"I have gloves."

"I mean *Shetland* gloves—warm, waterproof, rugged. I doubt you will want your dress gloves getting messy grabbing a handful of sheep's wool or rubbing down the back of a Shetland pony after a rainstorm."

"You think I will be rubbing down horses?"

"One never knows. Give me time. And you've

already seen how rambunctious the sheep can be. You are the laird, after all. A laird gives attention to his flocks and herds as well as his people, as the Bible says."

"If you say so!" laughed Loni. "Speaking of my encounter with your sheep, thank you for cleaning my shoes. How did you get them smelling so fresh? There was no trace of . . . well, you know what they had on them."

David laughed. "We farmers and shepherds have our tricks of the trade to deal with the smellier aspects of our work."

"I will have to learn your secret. Anyway, I appreciate it. I had about written those shoes off."

She removed the green windbreaker and began wandering about. "Oh, fleece!" she said, stopping at another display of outerwear. "I love fleece, and everything on this rack is on sale."

"So which is more important, color or price?" asked David.

"Color, no contest. But price is a close second. I would never pay a hundred dollars for a fleece vest no matter how beautiful, but neither would I buy an orange one that was on sale for ten."

"Very complicated!" laughed David.

"Shopping for clothes is a science," said Loni.

"I am beginning to see that. As much as I may have observed certain things, I have to say this is a first for me."

"What?"

"Accompanying a woman on a shopping spree?"

"I hope it won't go so far as a *spree*. Oh, but I do like some of these vests. Hmm, what do you think of this one?" said Loni, pulling out a fleece on its hanger and holding it up.

"Pink?" said David. "I didn't take you for pink."

"Why not?"

"I don't know. I know pink is sort of the ultimate feminine color, but you are . . ." David stopped. "Something tells me I should quit while I'm ahead!" he added.

"A wise man knoweth when he has contracted foot-in-mouth disease."

David roared, attracting glances from throughout the store. "Very perceptive!" he said.

"Pink is admittedly a tricky color," said Loni. "Some pinks are awful. But when it hints of lavender, then lovely subtleties emerge."

"Ah, now you are speaking my language—the subtle pinkish hues of heather and its mystery."

"Maybe that's why I like it. And look—this pink goes exquisitely with the windbreaker."

"I'm not sure it will be the right thing when you're wrestling a mud-splattered sheep to the ground."

"You insist on making a rustic of me!"

"Like I said, give me time," said David, adding the fleece to the windbreaker he was holding. "All right then, a rain hat, boots . . . oh, here are rubber mackintoshes and not in yellow. If you showed up in the village wearing one of these, with wellies on your feet, you would instantly be accepted by the entire fishing community."

"They would laugh at me!"

"Okay, maybe that's a bad idea. Still, humor me—try one on. And the boots."

"All right, but just for fun."

With an armload of rain gear, Loni walked toward the dressing rooms. A few minutes later David heard giggling coming from inside. Soon Loni appeared wearing knee-length wellies and a rubber rain hat and a huge raincoat that extended down over the tops of the boots.

"You insisted!" she said. "But you have to admit, this is a little over the top."

David could not help but laugh. "I'm sorry," he said. "But this really is a picture worth a thousand words."

"No one is going to take me for a fisherman! Do you have your camera?"

"I'm never without it."

"Then we have to get a picture. Maddy will crack up."

After suitable posing and much laughter, David managed to capture the spirit of the moment.

"Now let me get out of these things!" said Loni.

"I don't know," said David. "It's growing on me. I could see you on the deck of a fishing boat, rain in your face, shouting out orders to your crew."

"That's not going to happen!"

They left the store an hour later, Loni outfitted in her new waterproof angle-high hiking boots, thick warm pink fleece vest, and light green Gore-Tex windbreaker, along with a pair of tough warm leather gloves and a wide-brimmed rain hat, a pair of jeans, and carrying a bag of a few additional items.

"You will definitely be the most color-coordinated and attractive young lady on Whales Reef," said David as they emerged onto the sidewalk.

"That was fun," said Loni. "You make me laugh."

"I hope that is a good thing."

"A very good thing. I didn't laugh much as a girl. It always feels good."

"How about a cup of coffee or tea?" said David. "Then I'll show you around the city. Just down the street is one of my haunts when I'm here—The Cappuccino Club."

"*Cappuccino* . . . really? In the Shetlands? I would love a peppermint latte."

David laughed. "Don't let the sign on the door fool you. Somebody probably thought the name sounded clever. Mostly it's a tea shop."

"Do they serve coffee?"

"Sure. But I doubt it will be up to your standards."

"I'm game to try it."

They dropped off Loni's purchases at David's car, then walked to the coffee shop. Loni ordered a latte but was surprised how quickly it came.

They found a table and sat down. Loni took a sip from her cup.

"Ugh!" she exclaimed.

"Not good?"

"Whatever it is, this is definitely not a latte!" she said with a grimace. "This is just bad coffee with skim milk in it."

"That's what they think latte means—regular coffee with cold milk."

"Not espresso?"

"They have no idea what the word even means."

"But that's what cappuccino is. And *skim* milk—nobody puts skim milk in coffee. I wish I could make you a true latte—it's strong *espresso* coffee—really strong but full of flavor, with steamed milk or half-and-half. Absolutely delicious if done right. By the way, are you responsible for the bag of Starbucks at the Cottage?"

David nodded. "I had to order it. It arrived the day before you did."

"That was incredibly thoughtful. I have to say, Starbucks brews a richly flavorful cup of coffee. But I have been trying to get used to tea as well."

As they left the shop thirty minutes later, Loni recognized a taxi parked on the street. She peered through the window. The man sitting at the wheel was out of the car in an instant.

"Lassie, lassie!" he said, embracing her with a warm hug. "Ye're the last person I expected tae see!"

"Hello, Mr. Sinclair," exclaimed Loni, "how wonderful to see you again."

"Ye're lookin' bright an' cheery since I last saw ye."

"I am feeling much better about life," said Loni. "I was pretty gloomy that day."

"I wouldna call it gloomy, lass—ye jist had a lot on yer mind an' wasna sure what would be expected o' ye. I'm glad tae see that the answers tae oor prayers are makin' themselves known."

Glancing back and forth between the two, David hardly knew what to make of Loni's greeting and conversation with a man who seemed an old friend.

"Mr. Sinclair," she said, "I would like you to meet David Tulloch, chief of Whales Reef. David, this is Rev. Richard Sinclair."

"I'm happy tae meet ye, sir," he said, holding out a hand. "I've heard o' ye—I hae yer two books at home. 'Tis an honor tae meet ye."

"Thank you, Rev. Sinclair."

"If ye're a friend o' the lassie's, it'll just be *Dickie,* if ye please. An' that goes for yersel' as weel, lassie," he said to Loni.

"Thank you," said David.

"An' are yer island folk takin' good care o' oor Miss Ford?"

David smiled and glanced briefly at Loni.

"They are indeed . . . Dickie," she said, answering for him. "I am learning many things about the Tullochs, and about myself."

"I'm happy for ye indeed, for that's the most important kind o' learning o' a'. If a body's learnin' aboot himsel', everything else will fall into place. Oh, here's my fare noo. Best o' the day tae ye both. I'm right pleased tae make yer acquaintance, Chief. I hope I might be privileged tae see ye again."

Loni and David resumed their walk along the sidewalk.

"A personable man," said David. "A minister and a taxi driver—an intriguing combination."

"Not half so interesting as a chief and shepherd who writes books," said Loni.

David smiled sheepishly.

"Why didn't you tell me you were an author too?"

"It's not the kind of thing you go around talking about."

"I would think you would be proud. Writing a book is an enormous accomplishment. And you've written *two*."

"Actually I'm in the process of putting the finishing touches on a third. My publisher is expecting it soon."

"Wow. That's what I mean—what an accomplishment. Now that I think about it, I did notice your name when I was in the Wildlife Shoppe in the village. The name didn't register at the time. Why keep the fact that you are an author secret?"

"I don't necessarily try to keep it a secret. Sure, I am proud of my work. But you don't go around telling people, 'Hey, I write books!'"

"Hardy probably would."

David smiled at the thought. "That is a very humorous image," he said, chuckling. "Yes, he probably would at that."

32

COMPLEX SPIRITUAL ROOTS

"It was obvious that your taxi-driving friend cares deeply for you," said David as they left the city to begin the return drive to Whales Reef. "How did you come to know him?"

"He met me at the airport with his taxi and took me to Mr. MacNaughton's office, and then to Whales Reef," replied Loni. "He was the first Shetlander I met."

"From the sound of it, you could not have done better."

"When he and I were on the ferry on the way over to Whales Reef, I was so nervous and feeling alone that I asked him to pray for me. I'd never done anything like that in my life, though I know my grandparents prayed for me. In those few moments I knew that he sensed what I was going through. Then later when we parted at the Cottage, he gave me such a tender and loving look, almost like . . ." Loni stopped as an unexpected lump rose in her throat. "Sorry, wha

I was going to say was that it was almost like the look of a father. I'm an orphan, you know. I never knew my father or mother."

"Right—you told me that earlier," said David softly. "You said your grandparents raised you?"

Loni nodded.

"And they were Christians?"

"We were Quakers . . . or *are* Quakers. They are very devout. What I am, I don't know. I suppose that's another thing I am trying to figure out. I consider myself a Christian. But as to labels, I wouldn't know what to call myself. I haven't been active in church since leaving home. I have no denominational ties, except of course to the Quaker community where I grew up. But I haven't been to church with my grandparents in fifteen years."

"I don't mean to pry," said David, "or intrude where you don't want me. I know you value your privacy and—"

"No, it's fine," interrupted Loni. "Say whatever you were going to say. If I expect you not to keep secrets from me, I need to take my own medicine."

"What I was going to say is that I know very little about the Quaker faith. I've read about George Fox during the tumultuous 1600s and know that most of his followers immigrated to the American colonies. As to what Quakers actually believe, I am woefully ignorant."

"I don't know that I am a very reliable source," said Loni. "I grew up in a small conservative Quaker community—not representative of modern Quakerism as a whole. The Society of Friends, as it is called, has evolved into a liberal and socially active movement. Though they are a tiny minority, a few pockets of conservative Quaker churches hold to deep spiritual foundations closely tied to its historic roots."

"Fellowships like that of your grandparents?"
Loni nodded.

"What do they believe, then?"

"Mostly, I suppose, along similar lines to the historic ideas and doctrines of Protestantism. Most fundamentalist Quakers would probably consider themselves in the mainstream of conservative Christian thinking. They do not differ significantly in doctrine from Baptists or Presbyterians or Anglicans or whatever. I think it's mostly a difference of emphasis. Quakers focus on individual and personal response to God, which every man or woman has to discover in their own hearts. I'm probably not saying it like my grandfather would. But that's my perception. The church and the Bible are important, of course, but for Quakers not as foundational as the personal and inner revelation of God's Spirit."

"Interesting. Catholics rely on the church and its tradition. Protestants base truth on the Bible. And Quakers come along with an emphasis on individual faith."

"Maybe something like that. Quakers use the term the *Light Within*. For Quakers, responding to God's inner Voice is at the foundation of faith. But I am no expert. The people in the Fellowship back home consider me a backslider. I was always a black sheep."

"Why?"

"Long story. I'm not altogether sure. Someday I hope to get to the bottom of it. I think it had to do with my father leaving the Fellowship too. But after he and my mother were killed, my grandparents didn't talk much about the past. I don't know the details."

"Secrets, huh?"

"Something like that."

"So you're the backslider of the community?"

"Imagine me coming home for a visit, dressed modern, driving my red Mustang through the farm country, weaving in and out of horse-drawn Amish buggies—our Quaker community is in the middle of Amish country. Yes, I'm afraid I raised a few eyebrows. Now I feel bad for the grief I caused my poor grandparents."

"You actually drove a red Mustang?"

"A convertible—I forgot to mention that."

David laughed. "A Mustang convertible and sharing the road with horses and buggies. That is hilarious!"

"My grandparents didn't think so. I learned to visit them at night and keep out of sight." Loni sighed thoughtfully. "That's what makes all this so complicated. It's about more than an inheritance. The very fact of my being here stirs up the unknown of my past. Who were my parents, who was my mother, where did she come from? Suddenly here I am in the very place where my mother's grandfather was born. Trying to put that into the perspective of my American Quaker heritage, and then figure out what I believe as a Christian myself . . . I'm not sure what to think."

"I am beginning to see that your coming here has more far-reaching personal significance than simply inheriting a house and some land."

"Much more!" rejoined Loni. "And what should I also discover but that there are Quaker connections to the Auld Tulloch. You should see the books in his study. They could belong to a Quaker minister."

"I had no idea," said David. "I am not aware of Quaker affiliations in our family."

"In a way it is all coming full circle. In Ernest

Tulloch's study I am connecting with the very tradition my grandparents instilled in me."

"Amazing when you think about it."

Again Loni grew thoughtful.

"When I was young," she said after a moment, "I was fond of a book about two girls. One of them had a special meadow where she would go to be alone. It seemed so quiet and peaceful. About a mile from our house, there was a stream where my grandfather took me fishing. I would sit up high on a big rock and watch him. When I got a little older I started going there myself. Exploring one day I discovered a tiny clearing in the middle of the woods. I thought I was in heaven. It became my own special place just like in the book, an oasis of peace where I could go after school when the other children had been cruel to me and where I could cry and think and dream. I kept going there for years. Sometimes I would see animals. But mostly it was just to be by myself."

"What did you think about?" asked David.

"I don't know, girl things, who I was and where I had come from."

Again Loni was quiet.

"The woman I work for professes herself an atheist," she continued after another minute. "For the first time I find myself wondering how comfortable I should be with that. If I am going to call myself a Christian, do I need to take it more seriously? Should my faith play a more significant role in my relationships? I have never asked such questions." She drew in a deep breath. "This is embarrassing to be talking so much about myself. I've never done this with anyone. You already know more about me than Maddy and Hugh or anybody."

"Maddy—your boss?"

Loni nodded. "Madison Swift."

"And Hugh . . . your boyfriend?"

"Something like that."

"Then I consider myself privileged to have been the recipient of your openness. Please, no cause for embarrassment."

They reached the end of the road and stopped to wait for the ferry.

33

WHERE LEADS THE QUEST?

"Do you mind if I ask a favor?" said Loni as they waited.

"Of course not," answered David.

"After all this talk about church and faith and God . . . I think I would like to go to church tomorrow. I'm afraid I would be too self-conscious to go alone. Would you go with me?"

A grin spread over David's face.

"What?"

"I was just thinking how that would set people talking."

"Why?"

"I'm not an every Sunday churchman sort of guy, not to mention the fact of the chief and new laird arriving together—that would be note-worthy in many eyes."

"I'm a little surprised by what you say—about yourself, I mean."

"To borrow what you said a minute ago, a long story."

"My curiosity grows."

It took David several moments to respond.

"My spiritual journey, like yours, contains pain," he said at length. "I don't talk about it because it's private. I've grown as you have, but some pains never completely go away. It still hurts to remember."

"I know what you mean."

"The short explanation, I suppose, is simply to say that journey toward truth, if you want to call it that, was sidetracked and dealt a serious blow when I was a boy. I have not told you about the American couple who was here for a time, teaching a corrupt form of experientialism that created much havoc in our community. My best friend died as a result of the divisiveness they caused."

"That's awful. I had no idea."

"It still hurts to remember," said David with a

sigh. "The church here was directly involved. Because of that, for many years I refused to have anything to do with organized Christianity. But over the years God softened my heart and turned me toward Him rather than any teaching *about* Him. Thus, as I grew into manhood my spiritual quest has not involved the doctrine of any man or church, or any system of dogma, though I hope I have been receptive along the way to the quiet influences of honorable men who have pointed to truth. And with that has come a love for the church—the *true* church, God's people. Mine has been a quest to discover who God is and how He works in human hearts, free from the corruptions which man seems often to bring into it."

David paused. The ferry was approaching the landing.

"You are obviously a man at peace," said Loni. "Wherever and however you found it, your quest for truth must have borne fruit. Have you found, as you say, who God is and how He works?"

David smiled. "The quest continues, of course. But I think I have discovered a few things."

"In a nutshell?"

"That's a difficult question to answer. If you asked me I could go on for an hour about Scotland's religious history. But reducing the results of my own spiritual odyssey to twenty-five words or less—that is a greater challenge."

"How about if I give you fifty words?" said Loni. "I might even agree to a hundred."

David smiled. "Very open-minded of you. All right, let me see . . . I think I would say that God is a good Father whom we can know through His Son Jesus—by listening to what He said about God and obeying His commands. I would say that we learn about God, and come to understand Him, by living His principles. Fatherhood is the greatest truth in the universe. We understand God's Fatherhood by being His obedient children. How's that?"

"Well done!"

"I'm probably pushing my luck and going over the hundred words, but I would also add that in some ways my spiritual outlook is summarized by a prayer I try to live by from Kempis's *Imitation of Christ*."

"There is a copy of that in Ernest's study."

"I am not surprised."

"I would like to hear it."

David paused and glanced away.

" 'Thou knowest what is expedient for my spiritual growth,' " he said in a quiet voice. " 'Let Thy will be mine, and let my will ever follow Thine. Breathe knowledge of your will into my spirit, and give me courage, humility, and good cheer to do it. Make me your pure, dutiful, and humble disciple and your obedient son.' "

"It is a beautiful prayer," said Loni. "My grandfather would like you. You and he are amazingly alike. He might even make a Quaker of you."

"No labels or affiliations for me!" laughed David. "I am simply a man who is trying to be a faithful follower of Jesus Christ. Anyway, to answer your question," he added as they drove off the ferry onto the landing of Whales Reef, "I would be pleased to go to church with you tomorrow."

They parted a few minutes later, agreeing that David would come by the Cottage at ten o'clock the following morning.

34

A REQUEST

David walked into the Auld Hoose about four o'clock. Isobel was in the kitchen preparing supper for the small household.

"Did you have a pleasant time in da toon, Mr. David?" she asked.

"Very nice, Isobel. Our Miss Ford has big decisions to make. But I sense that the islands are beginning to work their magic on her."

"Will she stay, Mr. David?"

"I don't know, Isobel," replied David thoughtfully. "There is more to her than people realize. She will fit in here nicely. About the future, who can say? But I believe she enjoyed herself today."

"Rev. Yates came by when you were gone.

He asked if you would telephone or go by the parsonage when you returned. He said he needed to talk to you today."

Fifteen minutes later David knocked on the door of the manse, which sat across the road near the western edge of the village.

"Hello, David," said Rev. Yates, opening the door. "Thank you for coming. Please come in. Tea? The kettle is already on."

"Actually, that does sound good," said David. "I only just returned from the city."

They chatted easily during tea preparations.

When the two men were seated a few minutes later, the minister began in a serious vein. "Do you recall when we met on the Muckle Hill and you told me of the chief's prayer?" he said.

David nodded.

"Your words lodged powerfully in my mind. I have been praying a similar prayer myself—that as their minister, I will know what is best for the people of this island."

Yates paused a moment.

"I have what may strike you as an unusual request," he went on. "I am facing a big decision. I suppose it would not be going too far to call it a personal crisis, though that may convey an erroneous impression. I am not dying of cancer or anything like that. I might even call it a *good crisis*. Yet it is one I do not want to face alone. And truth be told, in the short time I have been on

Whales Reef, I have made no close friends. A minister is looked upon differently than others. It can be difficult to get *close* to people. You and I have enjoyed occasional stimulating conversations, but mostly a minister's pulpit seems to be a barrier to getting close to his people.

"Therefore, what I want to ask is this," Yates said. "I would like to submit the decision before me to the guidance of God's Spirit. Obviously I have already done so. But we are told when two or three are gathered together in His name, that the Lord is in the midst of them. I would like to ask you to pray with me, and further if you know of another man or two of prayer who could join us who you trust and who could seek the Lord with you on my behalf. I would like to pray with other men of faith to be certain I am hearing from God. I am thinking of Alexander Innes as one. I know from conversations he and I have had that he understands God's ways."

"I would be happy to," said David. "But if you do not mind my asking, why me? We have not spent a great deal of time together."

"I think I may know you better than you may suspect," Yates said. "It is more than clear to me that you are a man of faith."

"I hope you are right," David said, smiling. "However, I do not equate churchgoing with practical essential Christianity, so how much help I can be in a decision involving the church,

I don't know, although one in your profession witnesses evidence of that dichotomy every week in your congregation."

Yates laughed lightly. "Sad but insightful," he said. "You are closer to hitting the nail on the head than you have any idea—as I hope I will have the opportunity to explain later. I would love to hear the story of your spiritual journey?"

"And I would love to share it," rejoined David. "However, it is not something I am quick to divulge. One must be careful to whom one opens one's heart. Timing is as important as receptivity. And as you called this particular meeting, I defer to *your* agenda today."

"I see I did not misjudge my man!" Yates laughed again. "You are kind as well as sensitive. And you are right. As interested as I am in your story, I did have my own reasons for asking you here."

"What about the church people, your elders?"

"I am not as close to them as I might like. Most of them tend to see spirituality through the lens of church services and functions. I need a small circle of advisors, as it were, from outside the church leadership."

"Then as I say, I would be honored," said David. "And yes, I have just the man. He is one who has been purified by fire, as they say, and has been through some spiritual crises of his own. I know he would be honored to pray with you."

35
PROFESSION OR CALLING

About eight o'clock that same evening, David returned to the parsonage with Noak Muir. Stirling Yates had no idea of the history that existed between the two men. He had received scattered and inconclusive reports about the Fountain of Light and the turmoil it had caused. About Noak Muir's involvement, and the subsequent reconciliation between himself and his younger chief, he knew nothing. Sandy Innes, who of course knew the story well, was already on hand with the minister.

Tea prepared, the four men sat down in the small sitting room. A comfortable peat fire blazed away in the fireplace. They were soon talking freely and openly.

"The crux of my quandary," said Rev. Yates after a few minutes, "bluntly put, is whether I am to continue in the church."

If the men listening were shocked by his statement, they showed no sign of it. All three took in his words thoughtfully and seriously.

"By that, I'm sure you understand, I mean specifically the *ministry,*" Yates went on. "Of course, we are all part of the church universal, the body of Christ. I am speaking of the organized church, the outward form, the administrative infrastructure, the buildings and services and bureaucracy that make up the Church of Scotland. It is not a question of losing my faith, or even of losing my belief in the veracity and importance of the visible church. I love the Church of Scotland. But am I to continue as one of its clergymen? That is the question before me for which I covet your prayers.

"I am a relatively young man—forty-four to be exact. However, I am approaching the age where, to wait many more years, would make it difficult to alter life directions. If a change is on my horizon, I need to make it. If I am to remain serving God's people in my present capacity, then I need confirmation that such is indeed the case."

Yates paused. His three companions felt no need to fill the silence with their thoughts. Their responsibility was to listen with prayerful attentiveness. They waited patiently.

"In order that you will be able to pray with understanding," the minister went on, "I would like to give you a brief summary of my spiritual history."

He drew in a deep breath, then began again.

"I come from several generations of ministers," Yates said. "Strange as it may sound, the pulpit or clergy or ministry—however you want to describe it—has been our family business, so to speak. My father, my grandfather, and my great-grandfather were all ministers, curates, rectors, vicars, and the like, along with one brother, two uncles, and a cousin or two that I know of. I'm not sure why this blessing, or blight, was visited upon my family, but I grew up from the cradle knowing that the ministry was expected of me. I was set early on a course that would land me squarely in the pulpit.

"One more singularly unequipped for the ministry it would be difficult to imagine. I had no depth of faith. The ministry was a profession not a calling, which must certainly be one of the most grievous things that could be said of any man in any profession. Honestly, I do not know if I was a Christian at all.

"But I dutifully learned my trade, learned to conduct business meetings and call on the sick and administer communion and dish out platitudes. Most vital to the profession, I learned to write socially relevant but spiritually useless sermons that did no one an ounce of good, and certainly turned no hearts in humble obedience to God. But I became a good minister. I was sent to several churches in succession, each larger than the previous.

"I continued to hone and refine my secularly religious craft. With much practice, I began to be seen as one of Edinburgh's up-and-coming young clergymen—a man to watch, as they say. Yet I was completely void of spiritual *life* in my soul. No more perfect image of the blind leading the blind could be found than to watch me in action every Sunday morning as I solemnly, humorously, energetically, and with such imagined wisdom intoned the empty words of my faithless religiosity."

Yates turned away and wiped his eyes. Sandy reached over and laid a gentle arm on his arm. David and Noak waited as he regained his composure.

He drew a steadying breath. "I tell you these things with a heart full of shame. Yet it is my story, and I do not shrink from it. Only a handful of individuals know parts of it. Not even my own parents, God bless them, know the depths of my struggle."

He paused again, breathing deeply for a few moments.

"Then began an altogether unexpected series of events," he went on. "My grandfather, the retired vicar, died. Among his possessions was a file of old sermons and notes and personal journals and several Bibles from *his* grandfather, who had also been a minister in the south of England around the turn of the last century. Some stain existed on this man's reputation. I knew nothing about it other than that he was looked upon as the clerical black sheep of the family tradition.

"In any event, his papers had come down through the family. Nobody wanted them, but neither did they want to simply toss the man's life's work on the fire. In going through my grandfather's effects, his widow, my grandmother, asked if I would like the box from mysterious old Grandfather Diggorsfeld.

"Why not avail myself of some fresh sermon material? I thought. If they were any good, resurrecting them would save me countless hours of work. No one would know them to be recycled from a century earlier before the First World War, especially from so far away as Devon. I would spruce up the language and contemporize the anecdotes and have a ready supply of sermons at my disposal for years to come. So I took them.

"As I began to go through the papers, however, I was met with a discovery that was the last thing I expected. These were like no sermons I had ever read, and certainly like nothing I had ever preached or heard preached. They were *personal* . . . heartfelt expressions in which the honesty was palpable. The man poured out the depths of his soul to his listeners.

"What kind of man preaches personal sermons and exposes his questions and struggles and doubts to his congregation? I asked myself. To do so broke every convention of the ministerial *art,* as we were taught to preach in seminary. A minister must never admit doubt, never question the sacred doctrinal tenets of the church, never speak of personal quandaries in matters of theology or belief.

"I put aside the first selection and tried another. It was the same. Then another . . . and another, all with the same result. My first instinct was to close up the box and be done with it. But I could not help being intrigued by this man who had been my own great-great-grandfather and his deep quest for truth as revealed in his sermons.

"It did not take me long to realize that I was reading the heart cries of as intellectually honest a man as I had ever encountered, a man on a quest to personalize his faith. At root it was a quest to understand the heart of God.

"It was all new to me. More than merely new, it was *revolutionary*. I had never confronted the idea of an individual and personal spiritual quest, nor the notion that it might be my responsibility to ask if what I believed was actually true. Or, to take it even further, to look in the mirror and ask if I believed anything at all. Christianity, as I had always thought of it, meant a system of ideas. Preparation for the ministry in seminary was simply a series of exercises in training prospective clergymen to do four things: disseminate that orthodox system of ideas, proselytize on the basis of those ideas, keep people sufficiently interested so that they kept coming from week to week, and stimulate financial giving.

"The concept of anything *personal* in it was

utterly foreign. The idea of *searching* for truth, of *hungering* to understand God, and especially of *questioning* the accepted system of dogma . . . such concepts were utterly off the radar of ministerial training. It was a foreign spiritual language.

"Once begun, such uncomfortable thoughts could not be controlled. I hadn't planned to ask if I was really a Christian. The question simply *came*. I could not keep it away.

"My well-ordered and socially acceptable world began to crumble. The first Sunday after my discovery of the box of sermons wasn't so bad. I put together one of my standard meaningless messages and delivered it without incident and received the warm handshakes and predictably commonplace comments of, 'Nice sermon, Reverend,' when it was over.

"The week after that proved more difficult. My words sounded hollow in my ears. Between Sundays I was reading sermon after sermon of my great-great-grandfather's and was finding them food for my hungry soul. By the third week I was struggling mightily.

"A few more Sundays went by. Increasingly I heard my own voice from the pulpit, preaching as if it were not me at all but an automaton spouting learned maxims and platitudes. My voice sounded like a machine, complete with humor and anecdotes and all the inflectionary gimmicks designed to keep a congregation engaged. Yet I saw myself for what I had always been, an empty spiritual shell.

"I knew I could not continue. I manufactured some excuse and told my congregation that I needed to be gone for two weeks. I drove down to Devon, where I visited the church in the village of Milverscombe, where old Grandfather Diggorsfeld had preached. I holed up in a bed-and-breakfast with nothing to keep me company but the memory of my great-great-grandfather—his writings and journals and papers and two of his Bibles. I read and read, then walked the streets and country lanes and haunted that old church in the early-morning hours.

"In the box of his effects I had also discovered an illuminating correspondence with one of his parishioners named Charles Rutherford of Heathersleigh Hall, kinsman of the well-known Samuel Rutherford. I gathered from my reading that Charles was a man of some importance in England in the years leading up to the war.

"By then I was aware that my great-great-grandfather's quest for truth involved a quandary over certain theological issues fundamental in what I have called his quest to understand the heart of God. There was much discussion of these matters in the correspondence with Rutherford, and they found their way into more than one of his sermons as well. The result was that he was eventually charged with heresy and removed from his pulpit.

"My own great-great-grandfather became for me a mentor out of the past. I realized I needed to follow his example of courage to ask hard questions of his faith and of himself. I knew I needed to search for truth in my heart. I needed to know God, know who He was, know how He worked. I needed to *seek* God, and *find* Him. I needed to discover whether or not I truly believed.

"It was a fearsome thing. It meant letting go of the comfortable existence I had known. It meant relinquishing the past and venturing into the unknown. It might mean, as it had for my great-great-grandfather, criticism and rejection and false judgments against me. Part of me was terrified, not knowing where my steps would lead.

"But there could be no turning back. The quest had taken hold of me. I could not stop it. Nor did I want to.

"Eventually one afternoon, walking along an isolated stretch of the shoreline, I fell to the sand on my knees, surely the most unwilling, chastised, humbled, and sore-hearted man in Devonshire, and admitted two things. I admitted to God that I had indeed been an unbeliever, no true Christian, and therefore a hypocrite in the full sense of the word. Secondly, I admitted to myself that I *wanted* to know Him. I *wanted* to believe. I *wanted* to be a true and honorable Christian man.

"I closed my eyes then and there, eyes full of tears, and I prayed perhaps for the first time in my life—really prayed, *God, if you are real, reveal yourself to me, show me who you truly are, and show me what you want me to do.*

"When I rose, I felt no different. But I knew I had crossed a great divide—the divide between a system of ideas and true belief, the divide between church and faith. I cannot say I suddenly *believed* or had *faith* in that moment, but I *began* to believe in that moment. And that was enough."

As the night closed in around the four prayerful men of God in the manse, across the island in the Cottage, Loni lay in her bed, reading in the journal whose story had by now thoroughly begun to captivate her.

36

A LEGACY BEGINS—
THE INTRODUCTION

Whales Reef, 1924

By the evening of his unnerving morning walk on the moor, Brogan Tulloch had recovered from his hangover. He had shaved, taken a cold bath, enjoyed an invigorating breakfast about noon, then listlessly whiled away the afternoon with that random lack of purpose so well cultivated in those who do not have to labor after their daily bread.

He strode into the hotel about eight o'clock, dressed and dapper, once again in fine fettle.

Though its heyday was past, the luxurious Whales Reef Hotel was still probably the finest hotel in the Shetlands. By some miracle the great hotel had not put the more humble Whales Fin Inn out of business. Most of the locals still preferred to drink their ale and enjoy their fish and chips in the smaller pub at the center of the village. To Brogan, however, the large hotel on the hill was almost a second home. Word had reached him through his sources that a second tour group had arrived in the afternoon, and that a soiree was planned for the evening.

He made straight for the ballroom. Music there was already in swing. Brogan made a beeline for the bar.

"A Caffreys, Craig," he said. "Just something to wet the tonsils. We won't count this one on my quota for the evening."

"Very good, Mr. Tulloch."

"Any word on the hotel's new guests?" asked Brogan.

"Mostly Londoners, I believe, sir. From what I could observe in the dining room a short time ago, society types I would say."

"Any unattached young women?" said Brogan, arching one eyebrow.

"One or two, I believe, Mr. Tulloch," said the tender of libations, setting down a pint glass in front of him.

"Perhaps my fortunes are looking up. That busload that came in yesterday was not exactly what I had in mind, if you catch my meaning."

"A bit too scholarly for your taste, Mr. Tulloch?"

"I think, Craig, that you have captured the essence of it to perfection!" laughed Brogan.

He took a satisfying sip of the amber brew. With glass in hand, as was his custom on such occasions, he surveyed the room with a probing eye. As he did, he kept observant watch on the wide stairway that descended from the first floor, where most of the guest rooms were located. He allowed his gaze also to drift toward the corridor from the lobby and the doors to the dining room and several smaller lounges.

"No more journalists like that fellow who was here last week?"

"Not that I have been apprised of, sir."

"Ah, well, too bad. A personable chap. I rather enjoyed visiting with him. But I suppose the Shetlands are of limited interest to the press."

Gradually more of the hotel's newest guests appeared, in ones and twos and small groups, all dressed for the occasion. It was not difficult for Brogan's experienced eye to distinguish between those from London's society and the earlier arrivals, about whom, as Craig had noted, clung the air of academia.

An hour later the ballroom was nearly full. A few guests were dancing to the lively music of the band from Lerwick. Most, however, were clustered in small groups or seated at tables. Craig at the bar and his two assistants moving about the room with trays in their hands were busy keeping the company well supplied. By now Brogan was mingling freely among the company as if he personally were the host of the evening's fête, greeting newcomers, introducing himself, and regaling the ladies with stories of local color guaranteed from much experience to charm, fascinate, and amuse.

Meandering across the floor, a young woman at the bar arrested his attention. He paused and took her in briefly. Though so short that at first glance she might be taken for a teen, she carried herself with a bearing and demeanor of one older. He took her for the early twenties. The dress she wore was a little long to be entirely fashionable in these times of risqué hemlines, extending a full six inches below the knees. It hung gracefully, however, and ideally suited her well-proportioned and shapely body. Though he was observing her in profile and from his vantage point could only see half of it, her face drew him. He would not, at first glance, have called it a beautiful face. He would reserve judgment until after having a closer look.

But it was an engaging face . . . captivating assuredly, mysterious perhaps.

He turned and sauntered toward the diminutive mystery girl. He approached as Craig handed her two glasses.

"Here you are, miss—two sparkling waters."

"Might I perhaps interest you in something a bit more festive?" said Brogan with a jaunty air. "Craig here has several excellent local single malt whiskys I can personally recommend. It will be my treat, if you would care to join me."

Hearing his voice, the girl turned and cast on Brogan a curious expression of surprise. She seemed about to speak, then hesitated. Slowly her visage melted into a humorously amused smile. The effect on Brogan, especially in that she uttered not a word, was bewitching.

She turned, glasses in hand, still saying nothing, and walked away.

He stared after her hardly knowing what to make of the one-sided exchange. Coming to himself, he strode after her. He was not one to be turned away by a single rebuff. She was just sitting down next to a white-haired woman.

"I hope I did not offend you," he said, flashing the smile that had worked its magic so many times in the past. "I did not mean to be forward. I only wanted to ask if you would like to join me for a drink. I am Brogan Tulloch, by the way, son of the chief and laird of Whales Reef."

The girl looked up from where she sat. Again her lips broke into the same enchanting smile with a touch of the roguish in it. She seemed about to speak, yet still hesitated.

"I confess myself somewhat confused," she said after a lengthy pause, smiling impishly. "Why such an important man as the son of the chief would want to have a drink with a brash and outspoken American whose grating voice reminds him of fingernails on a chalkboard."

At her words, recognition dawned. Brogan's jaw dropped. He stared blankly at the face that seemed—without glasses and seen clearly rather than through the blurred vision of a hangover—so transformed from that morning.

"You!" he stammered. For one of the few times in his life, Brogan Tulloch found himself at a loss for words.

"It is, indeed," rejoined the girl. She was obviously enjoying his discomposure. "I must say, it is nice to know your name at last, and why you take such a personal interest in visitors to your island. Mrs. Barnes," she went on, turning to the woman beside her, who was taking in the exchange with great interest, "may I present Mr. Tulloch. Mr. Tulloch, this is Mrs. Harriett Barnes. But I must warn you, she is American too."

Quickly recovering himself, Brogan smiled. "A pleasure, Mrs. Barnes," he said, taking her hand. "May I welcome you to Whales Reef. And perhaps I might take the liberty of making a request of you."

"Uh, why yes . . . yes, of course."

"Would you be so kind as to introduce me to this charming, and I must say witty, young lady beside you?"

"But I . . . that is, I assumed the two of you were already acquainted," said Mrs. Barnes. She stared back and forth in confusion between the two young people.

"We encountered one another on the moor this morning," replied Brogan. "Unfortunately, our meeting occurred before I was altogether myself. We did not have the chance to exchange names."

"Oh, I see," said Mrs. Barnes. "Then, Mr. Tulloch, may I present my traveling companion, Miss Emily Hanson."

"Miss Hanson," said Brogan, dripping with aplomb, "it is a pleasure to meet you officially at last. And now that I am in my right mind, I hope you will accept my sincere apology for my lack of gentlemanly comportment this morning."

Before Emily could reply, the party of three was interrupted by the approach of a man several inches shorter than Brogan, to all appearances in his early thirties. His rumpled hair spilled down over wire spectacles, and he was draped in an ill-fitting and well-worn wool suit. He glanced back and forth between Emily and Mrs. Barnes.

"Excuse me, Miss Hanson," he said nervously, his voice betraying thick Glaswegian. "They are finally playing a waltz—I'm afraid it's the only dance I know. Would you perhaps care to join me?" he added, his eyes flitting briefly toward Brogan.

"I would be delighted, Dr. MacDonald," replied Emily. "It is the only dance I know as well. My father won't allow me to dance to anything modern."

She stood and walked in the direction of the band. The man hurried after her, seemingly as surprised as he was pleased.

Brogan stared after them as they made their way toward the dance floor, then turned to Mrs. Barnes. "And who might that be?" he asked. "The fellow is obviously not English."

"That is Dr. MacDonald—professor of natural history from Glasgow University," replied Mrs. Barnes. "He is the guest lecturer for our tour."

"He will be with you all week?"

"I believe so. We will travel throughout the islands. He will be speaking to us all about the wildlife and history of the Shetlands. Perhaps you will join us for some of our lectures, Mr. Tulloch."

"Ah, right—we shall see, Mrs. Barnes. To tell you the truth, I had about all of that sort of thing I want at the university. How long will you be here on Whales Reef?"

"One more day—tomorrow and tomorrow

night. Then we return to the main island, what do you call it?"

"Shetland. Just Shetland."

"Oh, and then we take a bus north to the other two big islands."

"Yell and Unst."

"Yes, and travel about . . . I think we spend a night on each of them. Then we shall be back for our last three nights here again."

"By then you should know every inch of our little island."

"Emily certainly will. She's more interested in the wildlife and birds and whales and plants than I am. I lost my husband three years ago, you see."

"I am sorry to hear that, Mrs. Barnes."

"One learns to fill the time. And he left me more money than any woman has a right to, and I have no children. I consider it my duty to spend as much of it as I can!" she added, laughing. "Since I enjoy traveling, I join tours to out-of-the-way places. Emily is working on some sort of college paper—that's why she is with me."

"A scholar, is she?" said Brogan. He was amused at the thought.

"I suppose something like that. That's probably why Dr. MacDonald was taken with her from the start. Not exactly the sort of man I might have chosen for her, but who am I to stick my nose in?"

"You and she are not related? I assumed you her grandmother or aunt or something?"

"I have only known Emily a month. My niece is dean of the college where Emily is enrolled. She thought we would get along nicely."

"And has that been the case?" asked Brogan.

"Very much. She is a most pleasant girl, though not very social."

Brogan nodded. After a few parting pleasantries, he moved away to pursue his lighthearted fraternizations elsewhere.

37

THE PRICE OF OBEDIENCE

Though most in the village of Whales Reef were by then in their beds, at the manse the parish minister was completing his story to his audience of three.

"I continued to read the writings of my great-great-grandfather," Rev. Yates was explaining. "Gradually by his example my reading began to change. I saw that it now became imperative that I go to the source.

"For the first time in my life I began to read the New Testament—I mean *really* read it. I started with the Gospels. If my quest was to know God, then where else was I to begin but with the account of the Man who said He knew God, and said He came to show men that God was their

Father? I saw that I must take up the New Testament as if I had never seen it before.

"The account, as biographies of the world's great men go, was scanty and incomplete. But it was enough to reveal what kind of man Jesus was—the principles by which He lived, His ways of looking at things, how He conducted himself with people, and His thoughts about God and His brothers and sisters of humanity.

"I began to read the four Gospels with an eagerness it would be impossible to describe, as a starving man seeking food. They were no longer mere weekly readings from the prayer book. The words came alive off the page. I saw that Jesus taught no doctrinal system. He told people how to behave and think. Suddenly it was all so simple. Jesus told His followers what to *do*. Our job was to obey His instructions and commands. Nothing more, nothing less.

"To explain all that followed would take hours, and I fear I am already taking up too much of your time."

"Please," said Noak, "think nothin' o' that, sir. Ye canna ken hoo much I am enjoyin' yer story. 'Tis touchin' my hert where I hae had my own hypocrisies tae deal wi' as David kens better than any man alive. Please, jist tell us a' if we're here till midnight!"

Yates chuckled. "I hope I shall not keep you that long, Mr. Muir. Well then, suffice it to say that from that moment on I became a student of the New Testament. Before many days had passed I knew that in the man Jesus Christ I was also coming to know His Father, the being we call God. The more I read of Christ's words, the more I realized that I wanted to *do* what the words said. I wanted to obey Him, think like Him, treat others as He treated them. I *wanted* to call myself a Christian.

"But how was I to do that? How was I to begin *being* a true Christian when all my years in the church, all my so-called religious training, had only succeeded in leading me down a blind alley toward spiritual emptiness? The answer was startlingly simple. It was the great truth to be found literally in every verse of the Gospels—by doing what Jesus said.

"I would begin by *obeying* the first thing that came across my path where I could do something that Jesus told His disciples to do, whether it be to pray for one who had hurt me or turn the other cheek or help one who was less fortunate or give to the poor or express gratitude or trust God for my tomorrow. That's when I first said to myself, I *am* a Christian. I *will* do these things. I *am* a follower of Jesus Christ. I will obey what He tells me to do.

"By then I had been a minister for eighteen years. But I had only been a true Christian, a follower, a *doer* of what Jesus said a few days—

or I should say, an *attempted* doer. What an infant I was! I had read the New Testament in prayer-book readings many times, yet I was now reading it for the first time as my life's guidebook, to receive my marching orders for each day. More than all the rest I devoured the red letters of the Gospels. I needed to know what Jesus told His disciples to do before I could do it.

"The first thing that came across my path to do," said Yates with a smile, "was so small and insignificant it is almost embarrassing to mention it. Yet for me it was a revelation, because it was the first thing I had ever done in my life where consciously, as a *choice,* I tried to obey something Jesus told His followers to do."

"I would like to hear about it," said David.

Again Yates smiled at the memory. "I was in the market in Devonshire where I had been staying. It was late in the day and the aisles were crowded. I was distracted, standing looking at the cans of soup on the shelf. A man bumped me from behind, pretty hard. I nearly lost my balance. As I recovered myself, I was shocked when he spoke rudely to me. 'Why don't you watch what you're doing!' he snapped. Then just as quickly the words I had read that morning rose in my mind, *Return evil with good.* Though my natural reaction might have been to scowl at the man to make sure he received a full dose of my annoyance, I turned and smiled and said, 'I'm so sorry. That was careless of me.'

"And that was it. The man strode off without a word or acknowledgment of my apology. For me, however, in that moment my life started down a new road. I saw what an easy, immediate, practical, moment-by-moment thing obedience to Jesus really was. I had done something—tiny though it was—because Jesus *told* me to. It was a stunning revelation. Suddenly being a Christian was filled with worlds of practical immediacy. I have not been the same since. I don't claim to obey His commands very well. But at least I now know what it means to be a Christian. It means to be a follower of Jesus in the small moments of every day, to do what He said—not so very complicated at all."

"An amazing story," said David.

"Imagine what went through my mind as I envisioned returning to my congregation. What would I say to them, 'I have been preaching to you as a non-Christian'? What would my staid elders do with me? No doubt report me to the session!" Yates chuckled.

"I saw my personal duty plainly enough," he went on, growing serious again, "to study and acquaint myself with Jesus and His teachings, then to put those teachings into practice. But how could I carry out such a lofty mission, recognizing myself as but a babe in the high realms of spiritual truth, while continuing in my position as minister? Now that my eyes were opened to my prior hypocrisy, it seemed the only responsible thing to do was resign.

"Indeed, I gave long and prayerful thought to precisely that possibility. But I could gain no assurance one way or another that it was the right course. I did not reach a decision in the matter until my drive home from Devon.

"Gradually my way became clear—at least for the immediate future. I would follow my great-great-grandfather's example. I would bring my congregation into my quest. While perhaps not divulging every aspect of the spiritual doubts and quandaries that had led me to it, I would be open with them in a way I never had been before. I would do my best to encourage them to accompany me in new discoveries of truth, in the quest to know God more deeply, and to do what Jesus said. I assumed they would eagerly join in with me.

"I scarcely remember what I said from the pulpit my first Sunday back in Edinburgh. I do know that it was the first time in all my years in the pastorate that I had stood behind the pulpit without notes and simply shared from my heart. I tried not to say too much. I didn't want to shock them. I was, however, honest in saying that I had been reevaluating many things in my life and faith, which over the coming weeks I hoped to share in more detail. Then I spoke simply about Jesus and His commands and what I was beginning to see that being a Christian meant.

"The reactions were understandably mixed. Some were unnerved. Some seemed to respect my honesty. Others had not the slightest idea what I was talking about. I could see the varied looks and expressions in their eyes as they filed out after the service. Actually, I found it humorous.

"In the coming weeks, as I continued in much the same vein, there began to be *talk*—and the word was laden with dark significance—that found its way to church headquarters. Conflicting reports reached church leaders about a change in my methods. Some of the influential members of my congregation had expressed 'concern.' The elders were mindful of the flock. Doubts must not be allowed to fester. At the outset I knew nothing of these reports. Many of my people were actually beginning to understand what I was talking about and were, like me, reading their Bibles with new enthusiasm. But as is always the case, the powerful are threatened by change.

"A day came when I received a polite but stiff visit from two members of the regional committee on church discipline, accompanied by one of my church elders and the wealthiest contributor in our congregation. None of them wore smiles. The call was formal and less than cordial. They put the question to me bluntly: Was I losing my faith?

"I could not help laughing. 'My faith has never been stronger,' I replied. 'That is not the impression of some of your parishioners' was their answer. 'We are concerned that division not be permitted to develop,' they said. Therefore, they concluded, they must insist that I cease preaching in the same vein that had been my custom in recent weeks, and return to more traditional methods and topics.

"I was stunned. Though I knew some were not interested in pursuing practicalities of faith, I never expected such a reaction. But those of the powerful clique were indignant that their pulpit should be degraded by such low practices as the raising of questions, thus destroying the solemnity of the weekly homily.

"Yet still I did not perceive the danger. I tried somewhat to modify my approach. However, I continued to urge courageous thought, personal application, and self-examination. I continued naïvely to assume that eventually the truth would win out. I had no idea how intransigent was the opposition to my 'new preaching,' as it was called.

"Unbeknownst to me, the criticism became especially acute when I hinted at certain long-held ideas which, as my great-great-grandfather had discovered, bore deeper looking into. A faction in the church developed, led by the wealthy elder I mentioned who, unknown to me, began setting about to find a pretext to have me removed.

"Eventually I was called before the session to face an inquisition of sorts. I was yet the more astonished that my quest to understand the heart of God, and my urgings upon my congregation to live in obedience to Jesus Christ, were being labeled as divisive and heretical.

"I see in retrospect that I had been far too outspoken. But the damage was done. I found myself put in a position where I could deny neither my convictions nor my conscience. I had to answer the charges humbly and honestly, which I did. Even at the eleventh hour, I assumed that my openness would demonstrate that they had nothing to fear from me but the truth.

"My naïveté continued. In disbelief I listened to their decision: I must either step down from the pulpit and resign my office or submit to the discipline of being sent to some obscure parish where I could continue to serve without doing too much damage, though they phrased it differently. If I chose the latter, it was their hope that I would come to see the error of my ways and could, in time, gradually reinstate myself in their good graces and regain my standing.

"I chose the latter option and was sent here, as far away as they could send me. I suppose they did not consider the good people of Whales Reef worthy of being protected from my heretical ideas."

Rev. Yates let out a long sigh, and the room fell silent. The fire in his hearth had long since grown cold. "And now," he went on, "I find myself at a new crossroads. The question has grown upon me in recent months whether I do indeed belong in the church at all.

"Nothing specific has caused this reevaluation. It has been a slowly deepening thought root. I have grown to love this little church and the people of your community. But I am loath to do or say anything that might have the effect of causing division again, here or anywhere. And I find myself questioning whether one such as myself, who has come to hold many perspectives that lie outside the mainstream of orthodox church thinking, will not inevitably cause division of one kind or another. Even if it is nothing more than my continual challenge that Christians learn to think for themselves, that danger seems ever present."

He paused again and looked at the three men.

"I am sorry for going into such detail. But I wanted you to know why I asked you here. I would simply like us to pray, as four men seeking God together, knowing that His Spirit is with us, asking Him to make His will clear to me."

"I would be honored to pray with you," said David. "And please, as my friend said a few minutes ago, do not apologize for the time. I too have been moved by your story. May I seek God with the humble heart you have demonstrated and be as willing as you to be the Lord's obedient disciple."

He glanced toward Noak.

"Aye, I'd be privileged tae pray wi' ye, Reverend,"

said Noak. "I ken somethin' aboot doubts, an' I've had tae struggle wi' what my own faith means, as ye say, for no bein' the man I thought I was. I honor ye for yer honesty, an' for a' ye've brought tae oor community."

Again it fell silent. The eyes of the three turned toward Sandy. He was already in prayer. They bowed their heads and joined him.

It was indeed nearly midnight when Noak, Sandy, and David left the parsonage and parted on the road outside to return to their homes.

38

SUNDAY AT THE PARISH KIRK

As churches went in a secular age, the Whales Reef Parish Kirk was probably more widely attended per capita than most throughout the United Kingdom. In a village as small as Whales Reef, that eighty or a hundred men and women gathered for worship when the bell in the steeple rang out over the island at 10:30 every Sunday morning might seem remarkable. Its Sunday school usually boasted an additional fifteen or twenty youngsters, who were taken to a small room off the vestry during the sermon for hand-crafts, games, digestive biscuits, and Bible stories. The fact that eighty percent or more of the population may *not* have been on hand in no wise lessened the influence the kirk exercised over the island, nor the general sense of quiet that pervaded the village on the day of worship. The Whales Fin Inn served no alcohol all day. Even the children seemed more well behaved on Sundays.

The Sabbath, however, placed no restraint on conversation, nor on its dark counterpart. Neither the free airing of opinion nor the whispering prattle of idle tongues were considered sins, either on Whales Reef or anywhere in Christendom. And as gossip could be spread without inflicting *visible* injury, it was the favorite Sunday pastime for most of the island's women, and not a few of the men as they gathered at the square, the harbor, or at the pub for whatever teetotaling fare was their preferred substitute for Keith's special brew.

The morning's service in the church on the hill served as the weekly engine to stoke the fires of discourse and information. There was always *something* to report. Even those disinclined to endure getting dressed up in their finest clothes and standing through six verses of every hymn, then sitting in stiff-backed, uncomfortable pews through sermons they had little interest in were nonetheless curious about who told whom about what, and what so-and-so said about such-and-such.

Sunday was *news* day. What was there to report? What was going on?

Everyone on the island had his or her own sources within the intricate verbal network by which information circulated. The only question was whether they wanted it fresh off the press, in which case they must be at the service, or whether they were content to wait for it to circulate through normal channels until it came within hearing of their own itching ears.

The first news broke upon Whales Reef well before the toll of the morning church bells. Dressed in suit and tie and looking every inch the country gentleman he was, David Tulloch appeared at the Cottage shortly after ten. He and Loni had agreed that, weather permitting, they would walk overland to the kirk. As a downpour had erupted at 9:30, David appeared at Loni's door with umbrella in hand and his car waiting. Their drive through the village was noticed by a few, as was his curious stop at the Muir home to pick up the man of the house, equally displayed in his finery.

When the three got out in front of the church and walked inside together, wide-eyed Grizel Gordon did not even wait for the service to be over. She turned on her heels and waddled back to town, heedless of the rain, her tongue eager to tell anyone she could find that "The chief an' the American lassie's at the kirk t'gither!"

Inside the church, all eyes were riveted on the second pew from the front where their new laird sat tall and upright between David Tulloch and Noak Muir. The significance was lost on no one of such a display of unity as symbolized by David and Noak in church together—Noak one of the Fountainite fishermen responsible for the loss of the *Bountiful*. Neither man was often seen in church. What were they doing here on this day, and *together?*

As eager as tongues were to wag about Loni and David, and likewise to resurrect the old Fountain controversy in which Noak Muir had played such a prominent role, never having been through the door of the church since, they were provided yet further fuel for their gossip by the Rev. Stirling Yates himself.

By now most of his weekly listeners had accustomed themselves to his unorthodox style of preaching without a memorized text, and his habit of sharing out of his own experience, even if they did not fully grasp the heterodox implications suggested by some of his observations. Thus it was not until he was halfway through his message that ears began to perk up with the sense that his tone was different today, with gradual hints that something big was in the wind.

Yates began with an abbreviated version of his personal story as recounted the previous evening to Sandy and the two men flanking Loni. As rumors had been circulating on the island since his arrival that he had been sent to Whales Reef under a cloud, interest grew as his story unfolded. Loni, who had never heard anything like it in her life, sat enthralled.

None in the building, however, not even David or Noak, was prepared for the announcement with which he concluded his message.

"I have thoroughly enjoyed my time here on Whales Reef," he said. "I came to you as a stranger, as the Lord said, and you took me in. I came, in a sense, as a prisoner in exile, and you visited me with your kindness and your open-heartedness. I was sick of heart, and you ministered your goodness to me. My time here has rejuvenated my spirit and I thank you one and all.

"However, in one sense I realize that perhaps I did not sufficiently value unity in the body of Christ. The result caused confusion in my former congregation. And as I look to the future I know I cannot abandon my views nor my conscience nor my belief in God's infinite Fatherhood. Thus I cannot guarantee that disunity might not result again from something I might say. I have therefore been seeking the leading of God's Spirit about my suitability for the pastorate. I have prayed with friends that God would make His will for my future known. I did not expect a quick answer. Most prayers are answered slowly. However, in this case, the answer was almost immediate. I awoke at four in the morning from a sound sleep. I knew instantly that the answer had come. I went out in the stormy morning—though thankfully the rain had not yet begun—and walked the length and breadth of your beloved island, praying for you all, as personally and individually as I possibly could."

Yates paused and drew in a deep breath.

"In closing . . . I have decided to leave the pastorate and to resign as your minister. Whether this change will be permanent, I do not know. I covet your prayers, that in the months and years to come I will know God's will, and will have the strength, courage, and humility to do it. I will contact church headquarters in Edinburgh tomorrow to begin the process of finding a replacement. I will, of course, stay on until one can be found.

"God bless you all."

Rev. Stirling Yates walked from the pulpit, as was his custom, accompanied by the singing of the final hymn.

39

DECISION

Reverend Stirling Yates's very personal message exercised an unexpectedly powerful impact on at least one of his listeners. Self-conscious as the service began, Loni knew that all eyes were probably glued to her back. She and David were sitting beside each other in the second row, and stood a head taller than most everyone in the building when they rose for each hymn. As the minister began to speak, however, she found herself so caught up in his story that she forgot her surroundings entirely.

She had never heard so honest and intimate an account of a personal spiritual quest from a minister. His story reminded her of David's recent narrative about his own inner journey. Rev. Yates's candor in speaking of his weaknesses and doubts, especially, and his search to find truth in unexpected places, his willingness to be criticized and disciplined by the church, and his love for God's people all touched her deeply.

He had paid a price for his faith. Now he was willing to pay an even greater price by walking away from a job he had come to love in order not to cause dissension.

After the service, as people milled about, David introduced Loni to what must have been twenty or thirty men and women. They were friendly and obviously glad to see him in church. Sandy, Eldora, and Odara stood beaming with pride in their new laird. Then Loni, David, and Noak dashed through the rain to David's car.

"Everyone seemed as glad to see you in church as they were probably curious about me," said Loni as they drove away.

"I'm certain the village tongues are wagging!"

David laughed. "Believe me, you and I will be the subject of many conversations today."

"Not Rev. Yates's announcement?"

"That will be talked about too. I must say, it was a shock, though Noak and I had some inclination from talking with him yesterday evening. But I did not expect a decision so soon."

They dropped Noak off in the village, then continued on to the Cottage. David jumped out and hurried around to the passenger side with his umbrella, then escorted Loni to the door, doing his best to keep her as dry as the blustery rain would allow.

"Thank you for going with me, David," said Loni.

"Of course. I'm glad I was there for Rev. Yates's announcement. It was good for people to see you out in the community."

Rain squalls continued all day. Even with the hiking boots and other attire from her purchases in Lerwick, Loni was not tempted to brave the tempest. The rain came down in sheets, battering the windows ahead of thirty- to forty-mile-per-hour wind gusts. She built a fire in the Great Room and was happy to remain where she was.

It was a good day to be alone. She needed time to think. She felt Rev. Yates had been speaking to her alone. Nothing he said bore specifically on her life. She was simply struck by the idea of personal growth, change, that one's spiritual life was meant to be, as he said, a flowing river and not a stagnant pool, a river whose course you could not always predict in advance. Spirituality was moving and growing. Faith meant more than filling one's mind with ideas and beliefs you were taught while remaining stagnant in those ideas. Faith meant growth into a new and deeper and expanding knowledge of God.

Maybe growth was intrinsic to the Quaker tradition. But she did not remember hearing it emphasized so personally, especially from one in the midst of quandaries and uncertainties. It was Yates's example that moved Loni. She had been filled with doubts and questions too. But she could grow and learn. She, too, could be a flowing river of growth.

If Rev. Yates had the courage to make such a difficult decision as to step away from his profession because of his principles, why was she being so wishy-washy about the decision facing her about Macgregor Tulloch's inheritance?

Any normal person would die for such a fairy tale to drop in their lap. *What am I so afraid of?*

It was time to make up her mind.

When evening came, she had reached the decision to return to Lerwick first thing in the morning. She would delay no longer.

That evening she made two phone calls. She left a message on Jason MacNaughton's voice mail, asking him to call her when he got in Monday morning. She would like to see him and the estate accountant tomorrow. The second call was to David, asking if he would accompany her into the city.

40

LERWICK AGAIN

Jason MacNaughton arranged his schedule to meet with Loni at eleven o'clock the following morning.

"Will you be joining us, David?" he asked as he shook hands with his two visitors.

"I would like to speak with you and the accountant myself," said Loni, "and go over the details about Mr. Tulloch's estate. I asked David to accompany me in case I need to ask his advice about something. I hope that's still all right, David," she said, turning to David.

"Of course. I brought work with me," he replied. "I'll be at the Cappuccino Club. Call me if you want me to come up."

He left them, and MacNaughton led Loni into his office, where the accountant was waiting.

"Miss Ford, may I introduce Mrs. Bemiss, who has acted as Mr. Tulloch's accountant for years."

"Thank you for coming, Mrs. Bemiss," said Loni as she sat down.

"So, Miss Ford," said the attorney when they were alone, "zero hour approaches. Have you reached a decision?"

"First," said Loni, "I want to thank you for your consideration in trying to make me comfortable at the Cottage."

"David saw to most of it," said MacNaughton.

"I gathered that. Still, I wanted to express my gratitude. I have been very comfortable."

"I am glad to hear it. I am happy to have been of service."

"Also, I have been thinking long and hard about your admonition a week ago about duty. Your words did not fall on deaf ears, as you may have thought at the time. I still have no idea what I will do long term. I do not plan to move here and uproot my life. But I realize I have a responsibility to the people of Whales Reef that I cannot take lightly. So, in your words, I am prepared to acknowledge and carry out my duty, as it were."

"I am delighted to hear it."

"In terms of the practicalities, however, I have several questions."

"Of course."

"Please, do not think me being frivolous, but I must have a direct answer to this question: What will happen if I do *not* sign the papers, if I simply walk away and go home?"

"I'm sorry, I understood that you—"

"Please, Mr. MacNaughton. I need you to answer me directly."

"All right. I believe the matter of the inheritance would revert again to the probate court, and they would decide the matter."

"But you do not know what would be their decision?"

"That's correct. I'm not sure that is known at this point. Once you were located, investigation into the other parties concerned stopped."

"But either David or Hardy would inherit in place of me?"

"Presumably yes."

"With Hardy appearing at present as the leading candidate?"

"That was my reading of the situation."

"So in a sense, if I walked away, I would have no assurance one way or the other how it would turn out?"

MacNaughton nodded.

"With the former laird's finances still frozen and the woolen mill still without operating capital?"

"Correct."

Loni nodded and drew in a thoughtful breath.

"I see. Thank you for the information. That is how I assessed the situation as well. Neither of those uncertainties are ones I am willing to live with. If I could be assured that David would inherit, I might indeed walk away. But since I cannot, I really have no alternative. So, Mr. MacNaughton, I will accept Macgregor Tulloch's inheritance. I will sign whatever papers are necessary to set in motion what needs to be done."

"Ah, good—that is brilliant news and will be a relief to many, I'm sure." The lawyer immediately opened a thick file that lay on his desk, preparing to dive into the paper work.

"I have a second question," said Loni, "equally important before I actually put my name on the dotted line."

Somewhat crestfallen, MacNaughton waited.

"I need to get some idea of the tax implications facing the estate," said Loni, now addressing herself to the accountant. "Mr. MacNaughton told me before that Mr. Tulloch's holdings were sizable. I still have no inkling what that means. As I look over the property on the island, most of it old and in various stages of disrepair, I cannot imagine the total value to be in excess of a million dollars. There may be liens or mortgages and other debt. I really have no clue what is involved. I need to know exactly what will happen the moment I sign. I want no surprises about taxes. I don't want to find a noose around my neck where I inherit property worth a million dollars, which comes with indebtedness of six hundred thousand and then find the government coming after me for estate taxes of another six hundred thousand, leaving me having to sell off the whole island and then declare bankruptcy. How would that do the people of the island any good?"

MacNaughton laughed. "You seem to have a fairly clear grasp of certain unfortunate financial realities that do indeed face many children and grandchildren of our time."

"I am acquainted with cases involving some of our own clients back home. It is a much too frequent occurrence. The government has long and grasping fingers."

"In your case, fortunately in the process of the probate proceedings, an evaluation of the estate was carried out. So we can have a pretty clear idea where things stand, don't you think, Mrs. Bemiss?"

The accountant nodded. "I do not think the situation is as dire as you outlined, Miss Ford," she said, "though there will be sizable estate taxes to consider. I believe the estate will be able to absorb them. Let me just . . . I have some figures here." She opened one of the files she was holding and scanned several papers. "The current threshold for zero tax is two hundred eighty-five thousand pounds, or something under half a million dollars. Above that, you will be liable for taxes at a rate of forty percent."

"Wow—that is criminally high!"

"We are a socialist state, Miss Ford. Wealthy capitalists and landowners are the enemy of socialism. The government will take all it can get to eliminate family wealth and distribute it to the lower classes. As you say, long and grasping fingers."

"Then if my assessment of the island's value is correct, I would face taxes between one hundred fifty and two hundred thousand dollars. Maybe I need to rethink what I said and let Hardy have it. He can pay the taxes!"

MacNaughton laughed.

"I will not minimize the magnitude of your dilemma. And in one sense, the problem is greater than you may realize."

"How so?"

The solicitor glanced toward the accountant.

"Macgregor Tulloch's estate is probably worth closer to six million pounds, or in dollars something like ten million," said Mrs. Bemiss.

"Ten million!" exclaimed Loni.

"Leaving you facing three and a half to four million dollars in inheritance taxes."

Loni stared back with an expression of stunned disbelief. "Oh my, this is far worse than I imagined!"

"There would be some who would not use the word *worse* to describe suddenly finding yourself a millionaire."

"I'll hardly be a millionaire if I go bankrupt in the process!"

"The good news," rejoined Mrs. Bemiss, "is that there is virtually no outstanding debt.

Additionally, Mr. Tulloch had something in excess of three million pounds in stocks, bonds, and securities. Of course, those holdings are subject to the forty-percent tax as well, but that is included in the valuation. Those assets are liquid and will be sufficient to relieve most of the tax debt."

MacNaughton said, "In everything he did, the late Mr. Tulloch was an astute manager of his finances. He knew his death would trigger a major tax event. Rather than life insurance, he began investing years ago in safe securities that would, when the time came, cover the tax burden to his heirs. Going back to the years when my father helped him manage his affairs, he was always thinking of David. It would seem that his plan succeeded admirably, though he obviously did not anticipate *your* being its recipient. The property you would have to sell off to raise the balance needed for taxes would be minimal."

He glanced at Mrs. Bemiss again.

She nodded and added, "Given the oil leases, it would be easily accomplished."

Loni's brain was spinning to take everything in. "I suppose the bottom line is, would the homes and mill on the island be in jeopardy?" she asked.

"Not in the least," replied Mrs. Bemiss. "You will be left without much cash if you use the liquid assets to pay the taxes. But the bulk of the estate would remain intact except what you chose

288

to sell, which I assume would all be on mainland Shetland. Whales Reef should be unaffected."

"And if and when I need to return to the States," said Loni, turning again to MacNaughton, "I assume there would be an easy legal means to put my affairs into your hands, with David acting as my representative so that everything resumed as before—the mill, finances and salaries flowing, income coming in, accounts payable being paid . . . no glitches or problems."

"Certainly. After you are legally in possession of the estate and assets, you can set up matters any way you please."

"I see," said Loni. "One more question. I realize that legalities take time. However, once I sign the papers, how long would it be before the mill's account can be unfrozen?"

"That is a good question. I will have to look into it. Having worked on several probate situations in the past, I am ninety-five percent confident we will be able to effect that almost immediately. I would say a matter of days at the most."

"All right," she said. "I want to talk to David now and lay it out before him. Could we come back in an hour or so?"

MacNaughton nodded. "Why don't we take an early lunch and meet back here at one?"

41

IN THE LOBBY OF THE KVELSDRO HOUSE

After lunch, with David at her side, Loni, Jason MacNaughton, and Mrs. Bemiss examined every entry in the complex balance sheet of Macgregor Tulloch's estate, projecting future taxes and every imaginable contingency that could be connected to the estate and its future. By the end of their meeting, confident in the counsel of both professionals that, with the sale of one or two oil leases, she would have more than enough to cover all inheritance taxes, Loni signed the preliminary papers to initiate legalities toward the transfer of Macgregor Tulloch's assets into her name.

Having already made several calls and received firm assurances, Jason reiterated that arrangements could begin within the week to unfreeze the woolen mill's bank account. He had that morning personally visited Douglas Creighton at the bank, apprising him of the situation. The two men had, he said, already set things in motion.

Leaving MacNaughton's office, their next stop was the bank, where Creighton was waiting for them with appropriate documentation ready for Loni's signatures.

Half an hour later, David Tulloch and Alonnah Ford left the bank and walked to Loni's rental car.

"You drive," said Loni, opening the passenger door.

"You have to learn to navigate our roads sometime," said David.

"Maybe. Just not today. Once we leave the city, most of Shetland's roads are one lane anyway—left, right . . . there's no difference."

"Point taken!" laughed David as he slid in behind the steering wheel.

"There is one stop I need to make," said Loni while David pulled into traffic. "The Kvelsdro House Hotel. There's someone I need to see—the Texan I told you about. Seeing him is the last thing I *want* to do, but I have to make contact and tell him, *No deal*. Otherwise he will show up on my doorstep again."

They walked into the lobby five minutes later.

"I'll write him a brief message and slip it under his door."

"Do you know what room he's in?" asked David.

"No."

"They won't give you the room number."

"I didn't think of that. I really don't want to see him. I have reasons."

"Then write your note and I'll deliver it. What are knights in shining armor for? Besides, how bad can it be?"

"He's big and intimidating."

"So is Hardy!" laughed David. "I'm sure he will be more well-behaved than our mutual cousin."

"I guess I will take you up on it, then."

They went to the front desk. Loni wrote out a brief message on a sheet of hotel stationery:

Mr. McLeod,

After much thought, I have reached a decision not to sell any portion of Whales Reef. I will have far too much to occupy my attention as the estate is transferred into my name to entertain any major changes at this time. If my plans should change, I will contact you. If you would be so kind as to telephone this number when you return to the States and leave a message with your contact information, I will keep your name and number on file in case my plans change—777-555-1372. Please do not call on me again. Thank you for your interest in Whales Reef.

Sincerely yours,
Alonnah Ford

"Here it is," she said, folding the paper and handing it to David.

"All right," replied David, "I'll have the desk clerk ring him. He'll either invite me up or come down to the lobby."

He returned from the desk a minute later.

"Your friend Mr. McLeod is on his way down."

"Oh no—I've got to hide!"

"Make it quick. I happen to know these elevators move quickly."

Frantically Loni glanced about.

"Step into the restaurant over there," said David. "I'll keep him facing the opposite direction. How will I know him?"

Loni smiled. "Believe me, you'll know." She ran across the lobby just as the bell sounded announcing the arrival of the elevator.

Behind her she heard the echo of boots across the floor, followed by David's voice.

"Mr. McLeod, I am David Tulloch."

"How do, partner!" boomed Jimmy Joe. "Tulloch . . . mighty common name in these parts. You any relation to that old feller who died a year ago on the island called Whale Something?"

"He was a distant cousin."

"Then I'm right pleased to know you, son!" said Jimmy Joe. "What in the heck can I do for you?"

"I have a letter to deliver to you, Mr. McLeod. It is from the American, Miss Ford."

He handed Jimmy Joe the folded sheet.

A cloud crossed the Texan's brow. He seemed to suspect that good news would not be delivered through a third party. He quickly scanned Loni's message.

"What's this about?" he demanded, eying David carefully.

"I really could not say, sir."

"Why didn't she come see me herself?"

"She did not explain her reasons. She simply gave me this note to deliver."

"She's handing me the brush-off and I don't like it. No, I don't like it one dang bit. And you're telling me you know nothing about it? You mixed up in this in some way?"

David did not reply.

"Just what do you know, son?"

"I'm sorry, Mr. McLeod. I am simply a messenger boy. Whatever your business is with Miss Ford, you will have to take it up with her."

David turned and began walking toward the exit.

"Hey, wait one dang minute, boy," Jimmy Joe called after him. "I ain't done with you. I got questions, and I want some answers."

David paused and looked behind him, then took several slow steps back toward the large man. He gazed straight up into the Texan's eyes.

"Mr. McLeod," he said, "I have told you what I know. I have given you Miss Ford's letter. Please do not order me around. Do not follow me or badger me further. And I strongly recommend that you do not harass Miss Ford in like manner. Do I make myself clear?"

He turned again and strode across the lobby and

through the hotel door, leaving Jimmy Joe staring speechless after him.

From where she was hiding behind a wooden screen, Loni had heard every word. Her eyes widened as she saw David walk out of the hotel, leaving her stranded.

She prayed the big man would not take it into his head to come into the restaurant about now. A moment later she heard his boots moving back across the lobby away from her.

The instant the elevator doors closed, she sprinted for the front door and toward the parking lot. She found David in the driver's seat, waiting for her.

"Thanks a lot!" she laughed, scrambling in. "What was the big idea leaving me inside with him?"

"Sorry about that," said David. "I had to figure out how to make an exit while hopefully discouraging him from following."

"I'm not sure I like your plan. What if he'd seen me?"

"You could have handled him," laughed David.

"I don't know about that!"

"It was a calculated risk. I knew you'd follow when the coast was clear. It worked, didn't it?"

"I suppose. But I about lost my breakfast when I saw you walk out, and there I was with Jimmy Joe muttering under his breath twenty feet away." Loni began to laugh softly.

"What?" said David.

"A messenger boy!" she said as they drove away from the hotel.

"It's the best I could think of on the spur of the moment."

"You could have told him you were the chief."

"Right! Can you imagine his reaction to that? 'The chief? What's that y'all's talking about, boy?'" said David, doing his best to imitate the Texan. "'What in the heck's a chief got to do with it?'"

By now Loni was in hysterics.

"That is unbelievably good," she said. "You could actually pass for a Texan."

"Please! I'd sooner try to pass for an Englishman."

Soon they were on their way back to Whales Reef.

"So, after a week of indecision," said David, "it appears I would now be correct in addressing you officially as laird."

"I suppose," answered Loni sheepishly. "And you *are* willing to oversee things when I return to the States?"

"I would be privileged to help, though I hope that won't be real soon."

Loni smiled but did not reply.

"And then," she said, "with all this decided, I have to figure out some way to tell Hardy I have changed my mind, and that he will *not* be serving as my factor. Though maybe for the present I should let him assume whatever he wants. We'll have to find the right way to break the news that you will be in charge in my absence, not him."

"When that time comes, you leave Hardy to me. I will tell him."

"What if he doesn't believe you?"

"I'll tell him to call Jason."

"Knowing Hardy," said Loni, "he will come straight to me. I'll have to face him sooner or later."

"My mobile number is programmed into the phone at the Cottage. If Hardy shows up at the door, or the Texan for that matter, you call me. Don't even answer the door. I will be there in less than five minutes. However, I don't think Hardy will get physical with you."

"I heard him getting rough with Audney."

"True, but there's too much familiarity there. I have the feeling he would be cautious around you. Still, I would rather be on hand."

"I don't want him getting rough with you either."

"Neither do I!" said David. "Believe me, neither do I."

42
THE MILL

As they continued the drive back to Whales Reef, gradually it became quiet. With the signing of her name, they were both aware that everything had changed. The speculation and uncertainty, for the moment, had been put to rest. How everything would work out in practice over time remained as uncertain as ever. But the papers had been signed. The deed was done.

Waiting for the ferry, David at last broke the silence. "What would you think of us driving to the factory right now and telling the people that the mill will shortly be on firm footing again?"

"I would like that very much," replied Loni.

They drove onto the ferry. She got out of the car and walked to the bow. She was still standing there ten minutes later as the ferry approached the dock. She could hardly believe how timid and afraid she had been when she first crossed these waters, with Dickie Sinclair quietly praying for her.

Now here she was, if Jason MacNaughton was right, though she could hardly bring herself to think it . . . a *millionaire,* a laird, owner of an entire island. Behind her in the car sat her third cousin, or half-third cousin, the chief of the small clan.

How could she possibly explain all this to Maddy . . . or Hugh? How could she convey the range of emotions, the ups and downs, the tears and the laughter, everything she had been through this week? Would they understand? *Could* they understand?

She returned to the car as the ferry bumped against the landing on the Whales Reef side.

"We may not have the luxury of waiting and hoping for the best with Hardy," said Loni as they drove toward the mill. "If we make a public announcement, he's bound to find out and cause a fuss."

"We won't divulge anything that he should find threatening."

"The mere fact of your being with me when we tell the ladies will probably annoy him."

"I'm sure it will," said David. "Why don't you go to the mill alone, then?"

"That isn't what I meant. I want you with me. I'm still . . . you know, nervous about what people think."

"I understand. I'm happy to stand with you. We will worry about Hardy when the time comes. Just remember what I said. You call me the instant he tries to talk to you about anything, whether on the phone or in person. And it would appear we have arrived," he said, pulling up in front of the former hotel. "This should be fun!"

The moment they walked inside together, all work ceased. Every eye turned toward them, faces expressionless.

A twinkle in his eye, David cast Loni a wink, then stared back into the large room with no more expression on his face than those twenty or so greeting him. He allowed the silence to go on almost uncomfortably long.

"Hey, ladies!" he exclaimed at last, breaking into his characteristic smile. "Why so glum? Your new laird brings news. Where is Mr. MacBean?"

"I'm here, David," replied Murdoc. Hearing the sudden pall of silence, he had emerged from his office onto the landing at the top of the stairs.

"Good—everyone present and accounted for," said David loudly. "Now, for those who have not had the pleasure, let me introduce Miss Alonnah Ford, great-great-granddaughter of the Auld Tulloch, my own third cousin, I am proud to say, and the new official laird of Whales Reef as of about two hours ago. Miss Ford," he added, sweeping his arm toward Loni.

"Hello again," said Loni, smiling but obviously nervous, every eye still glued to her face. "As David said, I have some news about the mill, which I hope will put your minds to rest and relieve some of the uncertainty that I know has been plaguing you."

She paused and smiled again, glancing over their faces.

"David and I have just returned from Lerwick, where I met with our solicitor, accountant, and banker. I assured them all that it is my intention for the Whales Reef Woolen Mill and Factory to continue in business stronger than ever. We have set in motion everything necessary for the mill's bank accounts to be unfrozen. Your manager," she added glancing up the stairs, "should have funds available in a day or two to pay all your back salaries and reinstate the mill's staff to full strength. I hope—"

Whatever else Loni had been about to say was instantly drowned out by shouts and cries of joy and clapping and such a ruckus as had not been witnessed in that room in over a year. As Murdoc MacBean came bounding down the stairs two at a time, hardly able to contain his shouts of ecstasy, every chair in the place emptied.

Aging Eldora Gordon hurried toward Loni. Her warm embrace, followed by an equally affectionate hug from Odara Innes, told the rest of the ladies all they needed to know. A swarming human tide engulfed her. Every woman wanted to thank Loni and congratulate her and touch her, even kiss her.

The hubbub seemed in no hurry to settle down after fifteen minutes. Gradually it quieted. As if by common consent, again all eyes came to rest on Loni.

"With Mr. MacBean's permission," said Loni, "if there are no urgent orders pending, I would like to invite you all to take the rest of the day off . . . at your full salaries, of course. And on your way home, I want each of you to stop by the market for a bouquet of flowers—if their supply holds out—which will serve as a small token of my appreciation for your hard work in keeping the mill going through very difficult times. I will tell the shopkeeper to bill the flowers to the Cottage. It is a small thing, but is all I can think of at the moment. I will show my gratitude to you all more fully later. Mr. MacBean, your flowers are for your wife for putting up with what I'm sure have been many sleepless nights on your part."

Laughter and more clapping followed as Loni waved, then turned to follow David out the door.

43

SAY IT WITH FISTS

"That was great," said David, laughing as he and Loni left the mill. "You won over the entire island in one fell swoop. Telling them to go home early, and the flowers—a masterful stroke. And you nailed Murdoc with the sleepless nights. He has been a worrywart all through this. Well done, Alonnah!"

Loni laughed. "Thank you, but we had better stop by the market and alert them that they are soon to have a run on cut flowers."

Ten minutes later David and Loni got out of Loni's rental car in front of the Cottage.

"I'm beat," sighed Loni. "A long and emotional couple of days."

"You can relax now. Your decisions have been made."

"I think I will take a long hot bath and read for the rest of the day. Do you want to take the car? You can bring it to me tomorrow."

"No, I'll walk."

"Are you sure?"

"I'm sure."

"I will see you later, then. And thank you again for everything, David. I don't know if I could have gotten through all this without you."

"Don't mention it. But don't sell yourself short—you are stronger than you think."

"If you say so!" laughed Loni. "By the way, it's probably time that the Mathesons and Mr. Erskine stopped camping out at your place. They can come home if they like. I still don't know what I will do with a butler and housekeeper, but they ought to be able to stay in their own quarters. That is unless they are a help to you."

"They are all wonderful, but it is a bit much having people underfoot all the time."

"Then tell them they can come home whenever

they want. But tell Miss Matheson not to wait on me."

Loni walked inside and flopped onto the couch in the Great Room. She wasn't sure she could even summon the energy to climb the stairs and get ready for a bath. She was spared the decision whether to fall asleep where she lay or take a bath when the doorbell startled her upright.

She rose and walked into the foyer. The unmistakable shadow of Hardy Tulloch's massive form against the curtain over the window next to the door sent her hurrying to the phone in the kitchen. Seconds later, David answered.

"David, it's Loni. He's here."

"Hardy?"

"At the front door."

"That didn't take long. I wonder how he found out so soon—or maybe it's just a social call."

"I doubt that. Please come."

"I'll be there in three minutes."

Even as Loni hung up the phone, the chimes rang again. Trying to remain calm, she walked slowly toward the door.

That Hardy could already have heard what had transpired at the mill, though perhaps incredible, was susceptible of a ready explanation. When Rakel Gordon appeared at home two hours before the mill's closing time, with a bouquet of flowers in her hand, her mother was all eyes and full of questions. Either the mill had finally been forced to close its doors or Rakel's none-too-secret romance with bookseller Armond Lamont had taken a more serious turn. Grizel instantly peppered her daughter with questions, with the result that she was flying along the street toward the bakery within minutes. To be the first with news was a point of honor between Grizel Gordon and Coira MacNeill. On this day, if no one had yet been into the bakery, Grizel held the winning hand.

Just back from a long night and most of the day at sea, trudging his way up from the harbor toward the inn, Hardy saw Grizel disappear into the bakery. The look on her face told the story. He only had to wait two or three minutes before hearing everything, with embellishments, first-hand. He ran home, threw on a clean shirt, and was on his way to the Cottage within minutes.

Seeing Hardy peering through the curtain, Loni opened the door and tried to smile casually.

"Hardy," she said.

"Good day tae ye, Miss Ford," said Hardy, taking little notice of her use of his given name for the first time. "Word's aboot town that ye've been tae the mill wi' plans an' promises an' the like."

"I went to the mill, yes," said Loni calmly.

"I was o' the opinion that ye wanted me tae handle yer affairs on the island, mum."

"I believe we were talking about when I return to the States."

"Aye, t'was part o' it. But I thought we had an agreement, mum."

"You think I should not have spoken to the ladies at the mill?"

"I'm jist sayin', mum, 'tis the traditional role o' the factor tae see tae sich things."

"I'm sorry you misunderstood me," said Loni, smiling again. "But I saw no reason to keep the ladies in suspense any longer than necessary. I had been into the city and had seen our solicitor. I signed the papers to remove any remaining doubts about the inheritance. I thought it advisable to tell the mill's employees that their jobs are secure."

"I understand David was wi' ye, mum."

"That's right."

"Why was David wi' ye an' no yer factor?"

"He is the chief."

Hardy's fingers twitched, and the back of his neck reddened. "Like I told ye the first time we met, he's no worth the name. An' why didna ye let yer factor make the announcement at the mill as would hae been proper?"

"Meaning you, I assume?"

"Aye."

"You're not my factor yet."

"Ye gae me yer word, mum."

"That was before I overheard you in the hotel

treating Audney the way no gentleman should treat a lady."

"Audney an' me's got an understandin'. I dinna expect ye tae ken aboot sich things yersel', no bein' fae here."

"None of my business, is that it?"

"What's atween a man an' his woman's atween them alone."

"Then is it my business when you boast about your plan to embezzle from me when I returned to the States?"

Whatever rejoinder Hardy might have thought to make to Loni's starkly accurate charge was forestalled when David's mud-splattered ATV came speeding around the corner of the Cottage from the direction of the moor. It skidded to a stop on the entryway gravel. David leapt off and strode quickly toward the front door.

Hardy turned toward him like an enraged bear.

"I should had kenned ye were at the bottom o' this deception!" he snarled. "What lies hae ye been spreadin' aboot me, David?"

"I've uttered not a word against you, Hardy. Whatever Miss Ford has learned about either of us, she has discovered on her own."

As he spoke, David came forward and subtly insinuated himself in front of Loni. The symbolism of the gesture was not lost on Hardy.

"Thinkin' tae protect the lady, are ye?" he sneered.

"I hope that will not be necessary," replied David.

"Please, Hardy," said Loni, stepping alongside David, "I think it would be best if you go."

"Ye an' me's no finished wi' oor business, Miss Ford."

"I think we are for today, Hardy. I will not discuss whatever we may need to while you are in such an emotional state."

Clearly furious, Hardy glanced back and forth between them. He took a step forward. David met him with arms outstretched. Loni quickly stepped behind David again.

"Git yer hands off me, David!" growled Hardy.

"Gladly. Just step away."

"No for yersel' or any ither man."

"I believe Miss Ford asked you to go."

"I'll hear it fae her, no yersel'."

"Please go, Hardy," said Loni firmly.

Hardy stood his ground. David's hands still rested against his great chest.

"Git yer hands off me, David!" repeated Hardy.

Whatever David would have done would never be known. Hardy did not give him the chance. The next instant he threw David's outstretched hands aside with his left arm. With almost the same movement his huge right fist slammed into David's cheek just below the eye.

Loni screamed as David staggered back. He managed to keep his footing, but his knees wobbled from the blow. He rushed at Hardy, fists clenched, and threw several blows to his midsection before Hardy sent him sprawling away, this time to the ground.

Hardy came forward and kicked David several times with his booted feet.

"Stop!" shrieked Loni. She rushed headlong at him. "Hardy, stop! Stop it, please!" She reached around his shoulders and tried to pull him away from David, but she might as well have been trying to budge an elephant.

With the back of his arm, Hardy threw Loni aside as if she weighed no more than a fly. She fell to the ground with a cry.

It was fortunate that David lay dazed and did not see it. Otherwise he would have attacked Hardy in a fury. It would have been all the pretext Hardy needed to hold nothing back, in which case he might have killed David. Instead, hearing Loni's cry and realizing what he had done, he thought better of pursuing the thing further. He knew about Americans and lawsuits. If she was the new laird, he did not want whatever legal action he decided upon jeopardized by a countersuit charging him with assault.

He stormed away, leaving Loni lying on the gravel with a bruised knee and bleeding forearm, with David on the ground a few feet away.

She managed to pick herself up, limped into the house, and returned a minute later with a saucepan of water from the kitchen and a towel. Terrified that David might be seriously injured, she stooped down as best she could and dabbed at his face and neck and forehead. He had no visible injuries other than one eye and cheek already swelling from Hardy's fist.

Gradually David came to himself.

"Oiee," he groaned as he tried to open his eyes. "I feel like I've been run over by the Flying Scotsman."

"Not so far wrong," said Loni. "But it was your cousin."

"I vaguely remember."

"Do you think anything's broken?"

David struggled to sit up. "I don't think so. Did I land anything? Does he even have a scratch?"

Loni smiled sheepishly. "Sorry . . . I don't think so."

David began to laugh. "Well, no matter. I don't know that I've ever landed much of a blow on Hardy. Ouch, that hurts! I may have some bruised ribs—hopefully nothing is broken."

"Do you think you can stand up and get into the house?"

"Help me to my feet," he said, reaching for Loni's hand.

"You can rest a bit, then I will drive you home. You'll have to leave your cart or Jeep or whatever kind of contraption it is here."

"I'll send Dougal for it."

"It appears that you may not get rid of Miss Matheson so soon after all," said Loni. "I'm sure she will want to nursemaid you."

"What happened to you?" he said, now noticing her bleeding arm. "Did Hardy do that?"

"It's nothing, really. I fell down trying to pull him off you."

"Well, thank you for that."

"Let's get you inside, cleaned up, and home."

44

AN INVITATION

As Loni had predicted, Isobel Matheson would not hear of leaving the Auld Hoose with David laid up. Nor did her brother or Dougal, with a single woman now in residence, think it fitting to return to the Cottage without her. They would wait until David was back on his feet.

Dougal Erskine made his appearance an hour after Loni had delivered David home, introducing himself and explaining how things stood, telling her that David was resting comfortably and that Isobel was babying him something dreadful.

"I thought that might happen," laughed Loni.

"Aye, mum. She's a good-herted soul, bless her, but tends tae be a bit o' a mother hen, if ye ken my meanin'."

"I think I do," said Loni. "I'm glad David is in good hands."

"Aye, we'll take care o' the laddie, dinna ye worry about that. One o' us'll be seein' ye in the morn tae gie ye a report on the chief."

Loni had her bath, which was more painful than she had anticipated but was good for her spirits as well as her wounds, which she dressed and bandaged. She spent the evening trying to write of the events of the last several days in her journal. So much had happened, the task was daunting.

It was in fact David himself who appeared at the door of the Cottage about eleven the following morning.

"You!" exclaimed Loni when she answered the door. "You're supposed to be resting in bed."

"As you can see, I no more need to be in bed than you do," he said cheerfully.

"No offense, but your eye looks terrible. It's turned blue."

"Honestly, I'm okay—bruised ribs but nothing broken."

"What about that eye? Should you see someone?"

"You know men—we hate to go to the doctor. I have to admit, I do have a fierce headache. But ibuprofen helps. So, I wanted to update you on the situation. Isobel is insisting on staying to look after me. It looks like it will be another day or two before your staff returns."

"Totally fine."

"I also said that I wanted to have you over for dinner but did not want her waiting on us. I did, however, ask her to do a little baking first, though I will handle most of the preparations. That brings me to my question—would you do me the honor of dining with your chief tonight at the Auld Hoose?"

"Are you sure you are up to it?"

"Absolutely. I will be heartbroken and utterly shattered if you do not accept."

Loni laughed. "I don't know that I believe you. But as I told you before, you make me laugh, and maybe that is worth a little white lie upon occasion."

"I would never lie to you," said David.

"I know you wouldn't. I was kidding, and I accept your invitation."

"I would offer to come get you, but I will be tenderly watching one of my specialties where timing is critical. I cannot leave the kitchen. If you don't mind driving yourself over . . . seven sound okay?"

"How will I know where to go?"

"Drive through the village, past the ferry landing. About a half mile farther you will see a driveway to the right. The Auld Hoose is the only dwelling beyond the landing."

"Then I will be there at six fifty-five. I would not want to miss the unveiling of your soufflé or whatever it is."

"It will remain a surprise. It's a date then. I will see you tonight."

When Loni came downstairs that evening, she was surprised to find Miss Matheson in the kitchen.

"Isobel . . . hello," she said. "Did you change your mind and decide to return to the Cottage today?"

"No, miss," replied the housekeeper, looking up from the counter as Loni came into the room. "Oh my, you are a picture! What a lovely red dress, miss."

"Thank you," said Loni.

"You are certain to turn the chief's head, miss, if you haven't already. You're beautiful, if you don't mind my saying."

"That is very kind of you."

"I was about to say that, with your permission, we will remain at the Auld Hoose until the chief is himself. But he was out of nutmeg, for his custard, you see. I told him I had plenty. If you wouldn't mind taking it over, miss."

"Of course not. Did you walk over?"

"Aye, miss."

"Would you like to ride back with me?"

"Oh, no, miss. This is your evening alone with the chief. You don't want an old lady like me tagging along. I would rather walk."

Loni laughed. "I would be happy to give you a

ride, but I understand. And you are welcome here whenever you want to return."

"We will be glad to be home, miss, and hope to be of service to you. For tonight at the Auld Hoose we will keep out of sight and be as quiet as church mice. We don't want to disturb you and the chief."

45

An Evening at the Auld Hoose

At six minutes before seven, Loni parked in front of the Auld Hoose, the laird's residence in former centuries and that of the chief ever since. She walked to the door and lifted the intricate old black iron knocker.

When the door opened, the sight nearly took her breath away.

There stood David in full kilt and Highland regalia in the tartan of his clan, sword at his waist, bonnet on his head from which his brown curls spilled in profusion.

A gasp escaped her lips. He had stepped straight out of *Braveheart*!

"You look absolutely lovely, Alonnah," he said with a quiet smile. "Beautiful and radiant."

Loni's heart gave a flutter. "What about you?" she said, her voice momentarily husky. "You look like a painting off the wall of a castle. Though your black eye does somewhat tarnish the image of the conquering hero."

David began to laugh, then winced as his hand went to his chest. "I am happy to provide a moment of amusement. So with that concluded, I welcome you, my lady, to my humble abode—an actual *cottage*. Won't you come in?"

"Here is your nutmeg, compliments of Miss Matheson," said Loni, handing him the small container.

"Ah, yes, the garnish for my dessert. Thank you very much." David offered her his arm. Loni took it, and he led her inside.

"I realize that Miss Matheson is probably on her way back across the moor," said Loni. "Where are your other two houseguests?"

"Off in their own corners, occupying themselves for the evening. Actually the Auld Hoose is not a great deal smaller than the Cottage, just older and not as posh, as we say."

He led Loni into the great room. It was neither so large nor imposing as the room that went by the same name at the Cottage, but it was equally breathtaking. A peat fire burned brightly in the fireplace.

Loni gazed about in wonder. Exquisite bookcases were filled from floor to ceiling with volumes passed down through the decades. The family library had been divided equally between the two houses, and she was beholding the poor man's version of what she had already seen in the Cottage.

The room also held sideboards and several glass cases of china, silver, and glassware. Between windows, the walls were accented with traditional Scottish memorabilia—faded tartans, a variety of swords, dirks and sgian-dubhs, a ram's head, two antlered stag heads, a coat of mail, a shield, and an ornately painted Tulloch family crest. From two large hooks hung an ancient set of decaying bagpipes. Loni saw a harp standing in one corner. Soft Scottish music came from a sound system somewhere in the room.

"I am enchanted by the music," said Loni. "Even before I knew anything about all this, I was haunted by Celtic music. And the swords and tartans!"

"Most of what you see came from the Highlands of mainland Scotland with old Ranald MacDonald in the early 1800s," said David. "Probably nothing here is of great value. Still, it is beautiful if you like antiquities, which I do. I treasure every inch of this place."

"It is spectacular."

"And now, my lady," said David, again offering his arm, "if I may escort you to the dining room, I believe our table is waiting."

He led Loni through a central hall and into a long but narrow room of subdued light, ornately paneled with oak that appeared to be two hundred years old. Stretching nearly its entire length was a massive oak table, surrounded by at least twenty high-backed chairs. At the far end, two place settings sat opposite each other, with silver and goblets and platters and a vase of roses between them. David led Loni to one of the chairs, slid it out, and assisted her into it.

From the center of the table he lifted a salad bowl and its two long salad tongs. He handed the bowl to Loni, then walked around and took the chair opposite her.

"For your dining repast this evening," he said, "the chef presents a garden salad of lettuce, kale, scallions, spinach, and chopped Brussels sprouts topped with roasted almonds, hazelnuts, walnuts, and grated Parmesan cheese."

"It looks delicious," said Loni, serving herself, then handing the bowl to David.

"An entrée will follow," continued David, "featuring succulent steaks of fresh North Atlantic salmon, thinly filleted and slow-cooked in a mouth-watering bath of butter and the chef's special blend of herbs. Accenting the entrée we have a vegetable dish of broccoli, chopped onions, and cashews, stir-fried to perfection, and, for the discriminating palate, thin chips of sliced yellow sweet potato delicately fried to the hint of crispness in olive oil and pepper."

Loni could not help laughing. "It sounds like a feast!"

"I hope you will say so an hour from now."

"I know I will. Did you prepare everything yourself?"

"What chef would do otherwise? I confess, I did ask Isobel to bake the lemon cake and raisin tarts. She is a master of desserts."

"Oh my—two desserts!"

"No, *three*. We must never skimp on dessert. The *pièce de résistance* will be a rice pudding with rum sauce, my own masterpiece that I would trust to no one else."

"This is amazing. You are a chef as well as an author of renown, tour leader, speaker, and chief no less."

"And shepherd," added David. "Perhaps, in light of eternity, my most important calling of all."

"Yet more humble than the others."

"All the more reason that it may be considered greater in God's kingdom."

Two hours later they were seated in the great room, a new supply of peats blazing away in the hearth, talking freely.

"I must say, your rice pudding was like nothing I have ever tasted," said Loni. "It was light as a soufflé, rich as custard, with a wonderfully mysterious combination of tastes."

"That is the secret, the richness of crème brûlée, the body of rice, with raisins caramelized through-out the mixture as the eggs and sugar and cream work their magic. Though some might object, I confess I do use double cream. If one intends to fashion a decadent dessert, why skimp on the cream is my opinion. The final secret is to stir the browned crust gently into the custard so that the rich amber layer is mixed throughout the entire pudding. Timing, of course, at each stage, as with all truly exquisite recipes, is everything."

"You do sound like a master chef," laughed Loni. "It was absolutely delicious. I am afraid I ate too much!"

"I may have too."

"Do you play the harp?" asked Loni as her eyes drifted to the silent instrument across the room.

"I wish I did," replied David. "It was my great-grandmother's, I am told. I am afraid I am not very musical."

"I would like to know about her," said Loni. "Though I suppose I'm not technically related to your side of the family tree, am I? But I am curious about it all. I came here knowing nothing about my mother's side of the family. Now I am eager to know everything. Tell me why the family traces its roots to mainland Scotland."

"That's why we consider ourselves Scots more than Norsemen . . . with the exception of Hardy, of course! Those Viking warriors do capture his fancy."

"I get that!"

"To understand our family's history, you have

to go back to the Highland clearances of the late 1700s and 1800s. Do you know anything about it?"

"Not a thing."

"In brief, the large landowners in the Scottish Highlands discovered that they could make more money raising sheep than renting out their land to poor crofters. So they evicted hundreds of thousands of families. They simply told them they had to leave. Thus the Highlands were mostly cleared of people to make room for sheep to graze."

"That sounds cruel."

"It was. It created a great migration of high-landers to wherever they could go—Canada, the Scottish lowlands, England. And some came to the Shetlands. Also involved was that uniquely British dilemma, unknown to you Americans, of what to do with younger sons of the aristocracy. This inheritance situation involving you and me has roots centuries earlier when eldest sons inherited everything, often leaving younger sons with no visible means of support. Everything has changed now, of course. Modernism is all about fairness. But it was not so two hundred years ago. Thus it was in the early 1800s, during he Highland clearances, that one Ranald MacDonald, second son of Highland chief Donald MacDonald, without much to call his own but his good name, was sent to the Shetlands by his father with just enough to purchase a small tract of land for a new and smaller branch, or sept, of the family clan. He settled on Whales Reef. His son, Duncan, had no sons, and his daughter, Flora, could not inherit the chieftainship. Duncan therefore named her husband, his son-in-law, Frederick Tulloch, chief as well as laird. Frederick's son, William, inheriting the mantle of both titles, changed the name of the clan to 'Tulloch,' and thus our small clan, a smaller stream flowing out of the historic Clan Donald, came into being.

"In the final years of the nineteenth century, William Tulloch turned the Tulloch name on Whales Reef into a dynasty. He raised the lairdship and chieftainship from the lower middle class into wealth and distinction. He was Ernest's father—Ernest being our most recent common ancestor. Though not a titled lord of aristocratic standing, Ernest's father, William, was one of Scotland's *nouveau riche* and well-known on mainland Scotland and England. He married a London socialite, Esther Walpoole, who, as the rumor has it, wanted the prestige of a title but hated the Shetlands.

"William used the industrial revolution, the investment opportunities of the expanding British Empire, even the continuing Highland clearances, all to his advantage and died a wealthy man. He modernized the Whales Reef harbor so that as he prospered, so too did the local fishermen, enabling them to pay higher rents, and as a result the whole island thrived. He came to be known as the Great Tulloch."

"Let me get this straight," said Loni. "He would be your and my great-great . . . let me see, our great-great-great-grandfather?"

"I believe that is it," replied David. "He was born and raised in this very house, but then he designed and built the new manor house that is now your home."

"And why was it called the Cottage?" asked Loni.

"The story is that the name arose among some of the builders and stone masons during construction, and it stuck. William moved his family from here across the island in 1882. The laird's former home, where we are now sitting, became the Auld Hoose. There William's parents, Frederick and Flora Tulloch, lived until their death. Thereafter for a time the Auld Hoose served as home to William's factor and, as his entrepreneurial vision expanded, his business manager. Eventually it went to the youngest of Ernest's three sons, Leith, my own great-grandfather."

"But not mine?"

"Right, not yours."

"What about the hotel—the big hotel, I mean—where the mill is now?"

"In the Gay Nineties, William continued his

improvements to Whales Reef with the construction of a lavish hotel on the island. He then went on a public relations campaign to market Whales Reef and its new luxury hotel to the burgeoning Victorian elite in the south. It was the perfect holiday resort in the remote, mysterious far north, full of interest for naturalist studies, which, in the aftermath of Darwinism, were all the rage. It perfectly fed the appetite at that time, fueled by interest in Africa and unknown regions of the globe, the world of Teddy Roosevelt and safaris and David Livingstone's explorations.

"As an interesting footnote, one of Ernest's cousins was an American explorer by the name of Leonodis Hubbard, who died in 1903 exploring the wilds of Labrador. In any event, the hotel sponsored more than mere bird-watching expeditions, but rather high-society adventures, with balls and parties and excursions on great pleasure boats in waters farther north than any English lords and ladies had ever been, where they could view whales and dolphins, perhaps even a distant iceberg. The hint of danger combined with a little science, a little history, a little evolutionary theory with an occasional lecture on Shetland's indigenous species and walks along lonely moors and to isolated sea caves, all contributed to making the Whales Reef Hotel and its Shetland Naturalist Adventure Excursions highly lucrative and successful."

David stood to stoke the fire and then returned to his place across from Loni.

"World War I put an abrupt end to most activity at the hotel," David went on, "which coincided with William's death in 1915. His son, Ernest, inheriting the small island empire his father had built, was different from old William in almost every way. His passion was the land and its people, not the money or his father's investments."

"Reminds me of someone I have met recently," said Loni.

"Stop interrupting my story, and please don't crack any jokes. It hurts to laugh. My ribs, remember!"

"Sorry. Go on."

"Okay, then . . . as much as he disliked the hotel, old Ernest recognized the good his father had done for the people and the fishermen. He also recognized the economic benefit to the island the hotel provided. He hoped that in the long run its emphasis on Shetland's natural wonders would outweigh the social glamour for which it had been known during the nineties and early years of the twentieth century. Ernest enjoyed being a laird more than a businessman, making sure homes and buildings and fences and the harbor were in good repair, improving the roads and so forth. He built a new ferry landing and helped finance increased service to and from the mainland. He also devoted his attention to developing flocks of sheep on the island, finding markets for their wool, and being the best landlord possible to the people of the island.

"He married Shetlander Elizabeth Clark of an old Lerwick family. They had three children—two sons, Brogan and Wallace, and a daughter, Delynn, whose birth in 1904 cost Elizabeth her life. And obviously this is where you come into the story.

"Ernest was devastated by Elizabeth's death. But he remained a devoted father. As Brogan, Wallace, and Delynn grew, though he tried to instill his values into them, one of his sons, as the story goes, could not but be enamored by the social goings-on of the hotel."

"I take it that you are speaking of Brogan?"

David nodded. "The glamour of the groups that came and went was intoxicating to Ernest's young heir."

"So how does his second wife, Sally, whom everyone speaks so fondly of, come into it?" asked Loni.

"Ernest knew that his children needed a mother. He traveled throughout the Shetlands, believing that the family name and legacy must be of Shetland blood. Eventually he met Sally Lipscomb, ten years younger, daughter of a landowner on the island of Yell. Rumors circulated on Whales Reef that their widower laird was smitten. No one knew any details other than that

Ernest increasingly disappeared for days, sometimes weeks, at a time. After one such period away from his young family for three weeks in 1908, he returned with, it was presumed, a new bride on his arm. That was Sally, whom the villagers, the staff at the Cottage, and Ernest's young family all took to their hearts. She is, of course, my great-great-grandmother through the son of their marriage, Ernest's third and youngest son, Leith."

David paused and drew in a deep breath.

"And there you have a thumbnail sketch of the Tullochs of Whales Reef," he said.

"Amazing," said Loni. "Thank you. I am happy to know all that, though I will probably only remember a fraction of what you've told me. This family of mine about which I knew absolutely nothing two weeks ago has quite a history."

"I suppose all families do, if you can discover them in the vaults of the past. There are legends, too, of pirates and scoundrels and murderers in our family's history—smugglers and criminals and duels and sword fights, knights in shining armor and damsels in distress, along with cads and blackguards and thieves."

"I want to hear all about all those too!" said Loni excitedly.

They continued to talk late into the night. By the time David realized that Loni's eyelids were beginning to sag, it was after midnight.

"I think it is time I take you home," he said.

Loni smiled dreamily. It had been a magical evening.

A moment later David was standing before her, if possible even more handsome than he had seemed when he had opened the door to her knock six hours before.

"Up," he said, offering his hand. "I cannot have you falling asleep on my couch. People would talk."

Loni sighed, reached for his hand, and rose to her feet. A few minutes later they were in her car, David at the wheel, creeping slowly through the quiet village. Neither seemed anxious for the evening to end. No words were spoken during the short drive.

They arrived at the Cottage, David stepped out, walked around to the passenger side, opened the door, offered his hand, and helped Loni from the car. The moment she was standing, he released her hand and the two walked to the front of the Cottage. Never had the island seemed so still and quiet.

They reached the door. David faced her, caught Loni's gaze for the merest instant, smiled, then turned without a word and a moment later disappeared around the stone wall of the great house on his way back over the moor toward his own.

Not even a "good night," thought Loni. The meeting of eyes had been enough.

She walked inside and up the stairs to the master bedroom. She went to the window. By now it was close to one o'clock. The pink at the northern horizon could have been either from the sunset just past or the coming sunrise. In the distance through the dusk, Loni watched the kilt-clad chief disappearing through the gloaming.

She stood motionless at the window until he was out of sight.

46

A LEGACY BEGINS— *THE DINNER*

Whales Reef, 1924

Brogan Tulloch sauntered into the hotel dining room on the evening following his brief introduction to Mrs. Barnes's traveling companion. He knew the tour group sat down to dinner every evening at seven. It was now six forty-five. He was famished but had other things on his mind than food. There was one individual he particularly hoped to see.

Across the room, his spirits picked up the moment he spotted the young American at a table alone. He strode toward her. She glanced up as he approached, her expression impossible to read.

"Good evening, uh . . . Miss Hanson," said Brogan with an uncharacteristically nervous smile.

"Mr. Tulloch," she said, nodding slightly. The silence as he stood in front of her was surprisingly more awkward for him than it appeared to be for her. "Would you care to sit down?" Emily said, yielding to what he obviously expected.

"Thank you," replied Brogan. He pulled out the chair beside her and eased himself into it. "I hope you will permit me . . . that is, I would like to apologize again for my behavior yesterday morning."

"Really, there is no need, Mr. Tulloch. You apologized. I accept your apology. No need for either of us to belabor the point."

"I just hoped that there might be something I could do to make it up to you."

"I assure you, there is no need."

"You are very kind. So . . . how, uh, were your day's explorations and adventures?" His effort at conversation came off a little cumbersome yet sincere. "The lectures were stimulating, I trust?"

"Yes, very good. Dr. MacDonald's talk this afternoon had little to do with wildlife as such. He mostly gave a thumbnail overview of Scotland's history and of the Shetlands in particular. It was fascinating. I had no idea the Shetlands used to be part of Norway."

"Yes, I seem to recall something along those lines, now you mention it," said Brogan.

"You are a Shetlander and that comes as news to you?"

"History was never my strength in school."

"What was?"

"Hmm . . . a good question. I'm not sure I had a strong subject."

"At least you are honest about it."

"What was yours?"

"Actually, I got A's in most everything. Not creative writing, however."

"Really, why is that?"

"I don't know, I just wasn't very good at it. But except for two or three subjects, school was easy for me."

"Somehow I am not surprised."

"Why do you say that?"

"I don't know—I suppose because you are the scholarly type, conducting research for a paper of some kind. Isn't that what Mrs. Barnes said?"

"Do I detect a hint of mockery in your tone for my scholarly pursuits?"

"No, no—please, I meant nothing like that," rejoined Brogan quickly. "I am dreadfully sorry if I conveyed anything other than respect. The last thing I want to do is put my foot in my mouth again. Honestly . . . forgive me."

Emily could not help but smile at the earnestness of his appeal. "Maybe I'm the one who should apologize," she said. "I didn't mean to cause you uneasiness. I said what I did half in jest. I didn't really think you were mocking me. I shouldn't have teased you."

"That is a relief. Truly, I meant nothing by it."

"I realize that."

"So, changing the subject, tell me something new and exciting you learned today?"

"I already told you about the Shetlands and Norway."

"Something else, then."

"Are you really interested, Mr. Tulloch? You're not just toying with me?"

"No, honestly. Don't tell me I have done it again with my foot in my mouth!"

Emily broke out in a high musical laugh. "Goodness. I will have to watch myself to make sure you don't think you are offending me with every other word. I'm really more thick-skinned than that. I fear I did overreact to you out on the bluff. I was rude and I too am sorry. But to answer your question, besides the intriguing connection between the Shetlands and Norway, maybe what I would say is more a conjecture on my part than something I learned. I am thinking that what Dr. MacDonald told us may explain the odd dialect I have noticed here—English, with Scots, Norwegian, and hints of German all thrown in together."

"Is that what I sound like?" laughed Brogan.

"Your speech is more refined than most. But when walking about the village and listening to people talking amongst themselves, supposedly it's English, but I can't make out a word they say."

"Sometimes neither can I, and I grew up here."

An effusive voice interrupted the conversation. They had been so engrossed they had not seen the twosome approaching.

"Mr. Tulloch," said Mrs. Barnes, "how wonderful to see you again!"

Brogan and Emily glanced up to see Mrs. Barnes and Professor MacDonald standing beside the table.

"Hello, Mrs. Barnes," said Brogan, rising. "I seem to have barged in on your table. My apologies. Here—I yield the seat back to you."

He held the chair for Emily's guardian. The older woman sat down, beaming to have a gentleman seat her with such flourish, and one, as she thought, from the British aristocracy.

Brogan turned to the professor. "Dr. MacDonald, good evening," he said and offered his hand. The two men shook hands. "Miss Hanson has been raving about what she is learning from your lectures."

"I am glad to hear it," replied MacDonald, shuffling his feet and adjusting his glasses. "One does one's best, of course. But sometimes one cannot tell—with tour groups, you know— how technical one should make one's remarks."

"Judging from Miss Hanson's comments, I would say you have struck exactly the right chord. Well, I will leave you all to your dinner. It was a pleasure to visit with you, Miss Hanson. I hope you all enjoy the remainder of your tour." He turned to leave.

"Oh, don't go, Mr. Tulloch," Mrs. Barnes called eagerly after him. "Won't you join us?"

"I wouldn't want to intrude—"

"Nonsense. There are four chairs and only three of us. Do join us."

Brogan glanced at the other two. Emily smiled and nodded. Though her expression was still difficult to read, she seemed to assent to the invitation.

"If you're certain you don't mind," said Brogan. "I would enjoy that very much. Thank you," he added. "I will just tell Carl to add another dinner to your table and put it on my tab."

He hurried off and returned a minute later. By the time he sat down, Emily and Dr. MacDonald were engaged in brisk dialog. Most of the dinner they spent in conversation about the subject of the day's lecture.

Meanwhile, Mrs. Barnes entertained Brogan with continuous chatter about everything that came into her head. Though he would have preferred that his and the professor's roles were reversed, he remained witty and charming and in every respect a perfect gentleman. He did his best, with limited success, to keep an ear open to the conversation across the table, managing to pick up snatches here and there.

"I don't know if you are familiar with newts, Miss Hanson," the professor was saying. "They are something of a hobby of mine."

"My knowledge of salamanders and small amphibians is rather limited, I'm afraid," replied Emily.

"Yes, right—perhaps I should clarify. While newts are indeed aquatic amphibians of Salamandridae, belonging to the subfamily Pleurodelinae, as I am sure you are aware, not all aquatic salamanders are considered newts. Newts differ from salamanders in the shape of the tail. They are a very special breed, most of whose species display a marked sexual dimorphism."

At the peculiar direction of the conversation, Brogan glanced back and forth between Emily and the professor. Mrs. Barnes's voice faded to a murmur in the background.

"I hope you won't think me terribly naughty," Dr. MacDonald went on, "but it is by their breeding habits that so much of the animal kingdom displays its individuality. Take newts, for instance. As the season approaches they live mostly in water, sustaining themselves on tadpoles, insect larvae, and crustaceans. Eventually they make their way to land, where worms and slugs become the preferred diet. During the courting season the male newt becomes brilliantly colored, then makes his affections known, as it were, by standing in front of the female newt and vibrating his tail and bending himself into a semicircle. A most unusual display, though I confess I have never actually witnessed the mating spectacle firsthand."

He paused and allowed a brief smile to play at his lips. "One wonders," he said, "if Darwin noted similar behavior in the larger reptiles and amphibians of the Galapagos."

The quirky direction of the professor's zoology lesson struck Brogan as fraught with humor. Unable to prevent a smile, he looked down at his plate, hoping his expression would not be noticed.

A moment later, unconsciously he glanced at Emily. Her gaze flitted toward him. Their eyes met. Emily's lips parted with a subtle smile of her own. Just as quickly she returned her attention to the professor, who was chuckling lightly as he added a few more remarks about the distinction between crested and palmated varieties of the newts in question.

Brogan did his best to refocus his attention on the story Mrs. Barnes had begun several minutes earlier. Both Emily and Brogan knew better than to glance toward each other again for fear of what might be the result.

As they finished their cake, ice cream, and coffee, Dr. MacDonald had risen, cup in hand, and was engaged in conversation with a group of tour members at the next table.

Mrs. Barnes also hoisted herself to her feet. "Would you excuse me?" she said. "I need to freshen up."

Brogan quickly stood, offered his hand. A moment later he and Emily were left alone. Still standing, Brogan glanced across the table. "Would you like to go outside for a walk?" he asked.

Emily smiled. "Yes, that would be nice. Will it be cold? Shall I go up to the room and get a coat?"

"It could be nippy," replied Brogan. "But we'll explore the hotel gardens briefly. If it is too much, we'll return inside." He did not add that he was not eager for Emily to encounter Mrs. Barnes just now, or the proposed walk was likely to become a threesome.

He stepped around the table, helped Emily to her feet, and led the way out of the dining room to the lobby and through the front doors.

They returned some thirty minutes later after a pleasant conversation that had occasionally become more probing than Brogan would have anticipated.

"It has been very nice visiting with you, Mr. Tulloch," said Emily before they parted.

"That sounds rather final!" laughed Brogan.

"Remember, we're leaving Whales Reef in the morning."

47
IT CAN'T BE!

Dreamily Loni woke up the following morning to happy memories of Celtic ballads, kilts, tartans, and swords, with legends of pirates and kings, murderers and lairds, chiefs and harpists dancing in her head.

She rolled over and sighed contentedly. *What an evening.* David was a perfect gentleman—erudite, polished, gracious, well-spoken, kind . . . an author, historian, naturalist, respected by everyone on the island.

She glanced at the clock. *Eight-fifty.* She had expected to sleep until ten or eleven.

She rose, feeling surprisingly rested after only six or seven hours of sleep, and glanced about the bedroom. The red dress, such a hit with Isobel Matheson, was draped where she had tossed it over the back of a chair. Her two-inch black patent leather heels lay on their sides beneath it.

Today she would try out her new Shetland jeans and wool fleece and hiking boots. The sun was shining . . . a perfect day to explore the island again for the first time knowing that it was *her* island.

The thought was still unbelievable. Strike that about it being *hers,* she said to herself. She couldn't think that way. She didn't *want* to think that way. Whatever duty had fallen to her, whatever windfall had dropped into her lap, she would never forget that this island could not be possessed by any man or woman. It belonged to the people of Whales Reef, belonged to them because they loved it. She would simply walk the island and enjoy it because it was Whales Reef, and for no other reason than that she was learning to love it as they did.

After tea and oatcakes, she set out from the house. Her steps took her toward the village. She was ready to meet people, to hold her head high, to look her new role in the eye and not shrink from it. She still didn't know what she would do in the long term. She would talk to Maddy and her grandparents and get their advice. Jason MacNaughton and David would obviously be part of that conversation too. She would need wise input from many people.

For now, however, she would enjoy the moment. The mill was on solid footing again—or soon would be. She had weathered her initial doubts, endured caustic remarks from disgruntled villagers, tried to ignore suspicious glances, and seen through Hardy's little con game to get control of the island. She wasn't sure whether she had entirely put the Jimmy Joe McLeod situation behind her, but like Scarlett O'Hara, she would worry about that another day.

She entered the village, walking with a jaunty step. Dressed in her colorful heather-pink vest, heads now turned toward her with smiles and greetings.

"Mornin' tae ye, laird," said a woman Loni had never seen before, pausing to smile and curtsey slightly as she passed.

"Good day, Miss Ford," nodded a man, whose wife at his side smiled shyly.

Loni crossed the street and entered the market.

"Mornin' tae ye, Miss Ford," beamed the lady behind the counter.

"I see you have a fresh supply of flowers," said Loni.

"Aye, mum. An' quite a stir it was yer buyin' flo'ers for the folk at the mill. They're grateful for a' ye've done."

"Flowers was the least I could do," said Loni with a smile.

"I hear ye had supper wi' the chief," said the woman.

"People know about that, do they?"

"Aye, miss. The whole village kens it."

"Well, it was very nice. David explained how the Tulloch family came from the Highlands—it is all so interesting. Yes, I enjoyed myself very much."

She left the market and continued into the center

of town. Cheerfully she greeted the women and an occasional fisherman walking toward the harbor. Everyone seemed to know of her speech at the mill and her evening with David.

Let them talk! thought Loni. She would do her best for them. But she wouldn't try to hide it like old Macgregor. She would win them over with kindness. And what better time to begin than the present? She would see if she could coax a smile out of Mrs. MacNeill.

With eager step she headed for the bakery. Walking briskly, she came up behind two ladies engaged in animated dialog. She intended to fall into step with them. But with soft-soled shoes on her feet, the ladies did not hear her approach behind them. As fragments of their conversation caught her ear, Loni slowed.

"Oh, aye, but what is poor Audney thinkin'?" one was saying.

". . . naethin' o' it, I tell ye," rejoined the other, "means naethin' . . . chief was jist bein' neighborly . . ."

"Think ye that's a' . . . way I hear it, the lassie was at the Auld Hoose maist o' the night."

". . . dinna believe a word o' it! The chief wouldna . . . a thing no man o' dignity would dare . . ."

". . . jist tellin' ye what I heard . . . an' wearin' a skimpy red dress, the way I hear . . . nae doobt what was on *her* mind."

Loni gasped as she fell back.

"Jist gossip, I tell ye . . . ye ken the chief . . . has tae be civil tae the lassie . . ."

"Aye . . . but he's proposed tae Audney . . . shouldna be carryin' on wi' the American lassie . . ."

"Oh aye . . . a'body kens Audney's still in love wi' him. But after . . . at the Auld Hoose . . . chief still in love wi' her?"

Loni's steps froze. She turned away, face flushed, lungs struggling for air.

A moment later she was hurrying back the way she had come. She had to get away. This was awful! Did they really think she was trying to seduce their chief?

David was too good and pure and honorable. How dare they associate him with such low rumors! Did they really think she was a Jezebel?

By now she was half running past the market, eyes stinging, face hot, hurrying desperately to get out of the village.

And David . . . engaged to Audney!

That was the most stunning blow of all.

Engaged.

It was suddenly obvious. She should have seen it a mile away.

Loni hurried past several outlying houses and turned from the road toward the sea. A few minutes later, turbulent emotions overwhelming her, she was walking along the beach.

It had been years since she had had to endure the humiliation of being gossiped about . . . of suspicious glances and cruel whisperings.

Proposed . . . The word seared her brain like a hot knife.

"He's proposed tae Audney . . . shouldna be carryin' on wi' the American lassie . . . Oh aye . . . a'body kens Audney's still in love wi' him."

Over and over their words rang in Loni's ear.

"Proposed tae Audney . . . Audney's still in love wi' him . . ."

Why should it rattle her? Audney and David had their lives to live. It was none of her business. She had no reason to get flustered. Why, then, could she not stop the words she had heard, and why—?

Loni's eyes went wide. She shook her head in disbelief. No, it couldn't be *that!*

Then why did the blue of his eyes, even if one of them was swollen, take her breath away?

There were a million reasons! *Why shouldn't it?* she argued with herself. She was only human after all. They were just friends, nothing more. Why shouldn't his laughter make her smile? Friends enjoyed each other's company, didn't they? Why shouldn't she notice his eyes and laugh with him? Women paid attention to things like that all the time.

Why did the vision of David's smile make her heart flutter? Why had the sight of him in his kilt at the door of the Cottage sent a rush of heat up the back of her neck?

She shook her head as if to banish the outrageous notion. The idea was preposterous . . . unthinkable.

She was practically engaged to Hugh. David was engaged to Audney!

No one owed her an explanation. Then why did learning of their engagement upset her? She *wasn't* upset. She refused to be upset!

She was just . . . *surprised,* that's all. She hadn't known . . . hadn't expected it.

Yes, that was it. She was just surprised.

Why shouldn't David have one more secret? She had no claim on him. She couldn't expect him to divulge every detail of his life.

So he was engaged . . . so what? What did she care? It changed nothing.

Actually, this was good news. Audney was a sweet girl. She deserved someone like David rather than the oaf Hardy.

Yet all the rationalizations in the world could not still the storm in Loni's heart. She turned from the beach and was soon walking across the moor along the bluffs that led to the North Cliffs.

Confusion inundated her like a tidal wave. Emotions assaulted from all sides, hammering against her skull like a thousand voices yelling at once. David was engaged . . . *engaged!* He was off-limits!

Besides, she loved her life in Washington. She wasn't about to jeopardize everything she had worked for with some overseas schoolgirl crush. Her first instincts had been right. She should never have come here, never become involved in the whole sordid mess.

What if someone found out how she felt? What if a look or glance betrayed her? It would be impossible for them to work together.

Good heavens—laird and chief. Suddenly the quaint arrangement sounded like a relational straitjacket.

More secrets. It was always secrets!

She possessed the secret of all time, and one she could positively not divulge to a soul so long as she remained on the island.

And David. David must *never* know!

Loni came to the cliffs, then turned inland and south again across the moor. Slowly the turmoil of her feverish brain calmed. She began to breathe more easily. The chilly air against her hot cheeks woke her to the untenable reality of her presence on the island.

By degrees the convulsive earthquake that had rocked Loni's brain settled into quiet resolve. She knew what she had to do.

48
AN EMPTY COTTAGE

After his memorable evening with Loni, David slept long into the morning. Now a day and a half after his encounter with Hardy, the full effects of the pummeling he had received were at last being felt over every inch of his body. He had hardly been able to shift in bed during the night without waking himself in pain. When morning came, the eye, which had functioned more or less normally the previous evening, was nearly swollen shut.

By ten-thirty David was coming groggily awake and feeling miserable. The ordeal of getting out of bed seemed unthinkable. Though equally odious was the idea of helplessness, he submitted to the inevitable and reached for the bell Isobel Matheson had placed at his bedside with the stern injunction to use it if he needed anything.

The faithful housekeeper, now pressed into service as nurse, knocked and entered the room a minute later.

"How are you this morning, Mr. David?" she asked.

"I've been better, Isobel," groaned David. "To tell you the truth, I'm feeling rather poorly."

"Did you and the lassie have a nice evening?"

"Very nice. We talked until after midnight. She is intelligent, witty, and has a delightful sense of humor. Yes, I enjoyed myself. However, now I have to figure out how to get out of bed."

"You stay where you are, Mr. David. I will bring you tea, and you rest until you feel better."

"Make that coffee, and strong," said David.

"Would you like anything to eat?"

"Not yet. But a couple ibuprofen, if you would be so kind."

"Very good, Mr. David. I will see to everything."

David remained in bed the rest of the morning. By noon, with the coffee and medicine kicking in, and realizing he was getting grumpy, he managed to edge his way into the shower and then, with a little difficulty, dress himself.

Invigorated from the shower, he negotiated the stairs without incident and entered the kitchen about twelve-thirty. Isobel was setting out plates for the men's lunch.

"You must be feeling better, Mr. David," said the housekeeper as her brother and Dougal Erskine walked in.

"Much better, thank you, Isobel—three on a scale of ten now, maybe even four."

"And what can I get for you?"

"I think I'm ready for a pot of tea."

"And to eat?"

"I'm not hungry just yet."

"I wish ye'd let me gie Hardy the thrashin' he deserves," interposed the gamekeeper.

"We'll let him be, Dougal."

"He doesna deserve yer kindness, David."

"I'm not thinking of what he deserves, but what we ought to do. God will take care of what Hardy deserves. We have to take care of what we're to do."

"An' he deserves a thrashin'!"

"Then we shall let God give it to him without standing in His way. Hardy's dangerous when angry. I wasn't paying attention and I drove him to anger. It was my own fault. Besides, intending no disparagement to your prowess with your fists, Hardy could likely whip you and me together with one hand tied behind his back. I want no stain of murder on Whales Reef during my watch— either yours or mine. So we will give Hardy a wide berth and let him bluster and rant as much as he likes. I intend to keep my distance until he simmers down. I would appreciate it if you would do the same. If you see him in town, follow the example of the Levite with the Samaritan and cross over to the other side of the street."

For the next few hours David busied himself by puttering about the house, walking outside a time or two for some fresh air, then spent another hour in bed. Finally he got up and tried to read, but by five o'clock and feeling noticeably better, he could stand the confinement no longer.

He donned his boots, bundled up, and with walking staff in hand set out from the house. He had scarcely left the outbuildings behind him before he knew where his steps would lead. After the magic of the previous evening, he wanted to see Loni.

Fondly replaying much of their conversation over in his mind, he slowly made his way over the moor to the Cottage.

The walk between the two houses took longer than usual. He made no attempt to hurry. At length the Cottage came into view. He approached and, after knocking several times, walked into the kitchen through the back door.

"Hello . . . Alonnah!" he called. "Hello, are you here?"

No answer came from within. David wandered through the kitchen and into the entry.

"Anybody home?" he called up the wide staircase.

Still only silence greeted him. He now made his way into the Great Room.

The room was cold. There had obviously been no fire in the fireplace all day. More and more curious, he left the room and walked out of the house, this time by the front door. The rental car was gone.

Disappointed not to have been able to accompany her into the city—presumably where she was attending to additional business with Jason—

David made his way back through the house. He made sure all the doors were closed and everything in order before returning across the island to the Auld Hoose.

He glanced at his watch as he went. He hoped she was home soon. Otherwise she would miss the last ferry of the day.

David was out early the following morning. He was still sore but able to resume his normal activities. He had missed his morning walk. Reviving the tradition he had enjoyed for so many years with his cousin and uncle, he stopped by the bakery for a bag of butteries. He deflected Coira MacNeill's barrage of questions about his black eye, which proved a challenge. But at least it kept her from too many questions pointing in other directions.

David continued on to the Cottage. Now that Alonnah was hooked on tea and oatcakes, it was time to introduce her to warm butteries topped with butter and jam.

As he came into the drive and approached the Cottage, again he saw no car parked out front. He nevertheless tried the doorbell. There was no response. She must indeed have missed the ferry, David thought, and had spent the night in Lerwick. He returned to the Auld Hoose.

He set out for yet one more trek across the misty moor about one o'clock. Clutching his favorite walking stick, wearing thick brown wool overcoat, rubber boots, and cap on his head, and with his sheepdog scampering to catch up behind him, he could not prevent an expression of concern on his face. Arriving at the Cottage, he was about to enter by the kitchen door, thought better of it, and walked around the house. Still there was no sign of the car.

David walked inside through the front door and slowly retraced his steps from the previous afternoon. The chill from yesterday was even more pronounced. The place felt like a tomb. It was obvious no one had been inside since his previous visit.

Realizing he was taking a liberty, David climbed the stairs. The door to the study stood open. Slowly he entered and glanced about. The leather book on the rolltop desk drew his eye. He turned back the cover, saw Loni's name, and closed it.

She *must* be around somewhere, he thought. She was never without her journal.

Still not worried, though curious and growing more concerned, he went to the kitchen to use the phone. A minute later he had Jason MacNaughton on the line.

"Jason, hello, it's David Tulloch. I assume you had a meeting with Miss Ford?"

"Yes, she was here yesterday."

"When did she leave?"

"About three."

"Really—that early?"

"Yes . . . why? You sound worried."

"She did not return to the Cottage yesterday evening. I assumed she probably missed the ferry and spent the night in the city. But she is still not back today."

"Right, she wasn't going back to Whales Reef."

"Where else would she have been going?" asked David.

"She was on her way to the airport."

"The airport?"

"She was on her way back to the States."

"What!" exclaimed David.

"I assumed you knew."

"I knew nothing about it!"

"I'm sorry, David. All she told me was that she would be flying to Aberdeen on yesterday's evening flight. She gave me the keys to her rental car, we signed the final documents, and that was it."

David stood there stunned. "I'm completely bewildered," he said at length. "Did she say why the sudden change of plans?"

"Only that she had to get home," replied Jason.

"What about the mill and all the rest of it? Will your office be handling everything? I hope the people will not be left hanging again."

"No worry of that. Miss Ford signed all the necessary papers to place the mill and the finances of the estate in your hands. She gave you complete charge of her affairs. She told me to decide on a salary amount for you that I felt was fair, then to pay you double that. She said you would not pay yourself enough."

"She said that?" said David, unable to keep from smiling.

"She was most insistent that you not set your own salary. As of yesterday, everything on Whales Reef is in your hands. I merely assumed you knew."

49

A LEGACY BEGINS— *THE SILENCE*

Whales Reef, 1924

Brogan Tulloch stood at the window of his room, gazing out on a quiet twilight over Whales Reef. It was sometime after eleven o'clock.

He had left Emily at the hotel a little over an hour ago. Returning home, he had lain down and tried to sleep. But it was too early. He rose from bed, threw on a robe, and paced the room. Eventually he came to rest at the window.

All he could think was how he might contrive to see the girl again. The dinner at the hotel and the walk in the gardens afterward had been the perfect end to the day. Yet once it was over and he had a chance to reflect on his peculiar behavior, he was wondering what was becoming of him.

The night wore on. What passed for darkness at this time of the year descended on the Shetlands. A gorgeous intermingled sunset and sunrise of brilliant reds, yellows, oranges, and purples rose in the south, shifting in that wonderfully imperceptible way gradually from southwest to southeast. He continued to stare into the dusky silence.

What was on his mind, twenty-three-year-old Brogan Tulloch could not have said. He was unaccustomed to soul-searching. He disdained the very idea that he was the sort of person requiring analysis. All this brooding . . . it signaled a change in the spiritual and moral atmosphere. He wanted no part of it. He liked who he was. He wanted no clouds of change blowing in off the horizon.

Funny how the silence felt different on this night. It was so quiet. He had never noticed it before. Usually at this hour he was either down at the hotel or staggering home after the revels had broken up. Once Emily had gone up to her room, however, he had had no interest in staying. He saw Craig at the bar watching him leave with an expression asking the unspoken question whether Brogan was ill to be going home so early.

When was the last time he had been so sane and sober at such an hour? He hadn't had a drop of alcohol all day. His senses felt keen, awake, invigorated.

Whatever was going on was obviously due to the presence on the island of the American girl Emily Hanson.

But why? The question had gnawed at him for two days now.

He and she were completely different. He had no interest in her, he tried to tell himself. Then why had she so thoroughly gotten under his skin from the first moment he laid eyes on her? She wasn't even that beautiful. She was religious, a Quaker of all things.

He was behaving like a ridiculous schoolboy!

Yet he couldn't stop thinking about her. When they were together he turned pensive. The kinds of things he had said to her tonight he had never admitted to another soul, not even himself.

Sleep eventually overtook him sometime between one and two in the morning.

Brogan awoke hours later with sunlight streaming through the window.

Gradual images of the previous night returned . . . dinner at the hotel . . . the walk with Emily in the gardens.

He rose from bed and again sought the window. What had come over him last night with all those pensive reflections? So this was what mornings without hangovers were like. Actually . . . he felt great! He drew in a deep breath and began to dress.

From somewhere in the house the Westminster chimes tolled the half hour. *Probably half past seven or eight,* thought Brogan. He picked up his pocket watch from the nightstand.

A minute after ten-thirty! How could he possibly have slept so late?

The words played themselves back in his brain: "Remember, we're leaving Whales Reef in the morning."

Seconds later he was galloping down the stairs. He hardly heard Sally asking where he was off to. Two minutes after that the Studebaker roared out of the garage, sending dirt and gravel spraying and chickens squawking.

Brogan slowed his father's car as he made his way through town, busy at this hour with women about their shopping and also with carts and horses and dogs, then accelerated again out of the village. Northward he sped toward the ferry landing.

Even as he half skidded to a stop in front of the deserted pier, he knew he was too late. Across the mile-and-a-half sound he saw the ferry chugging toward the opposite shore of mainland Shetland. Though the distance was too great to make out individuals, he could see the small boat's rails lined with members of the Northern Adventure Tour.

With a sinking feeling of more dismay than he would have thought possible, he got out of the car and walked onto the wooden deck. He stared after the retreating ferry until it disappeared in the morning mist.

The image of Emily Hanson rose in his mind's eye. She had been wearing the same dress on both evenings he had seen her at the hotel, a navy-blue wool that, while not perhaps the latest from Paris, had been attractive enough. Out on the moor, however, she had worn baggy trousers, a working man's plaid shirt, and hiking boots. Nothing in her appearance, or anything else about her, created the impression that she belonged to some fringe religious sect.

But it was not her clothes that drew him. It was the picture of her mouth, her laughter, her wit, her intelligence, and her eyes that filled his thoughts.

Brogan drew in a deep breath of the sea air and slowly walked back to the car.

The whole island felt deserted.

50

ABOVE THE ATLANTIC ... AGAIN

For the second time in seven months Loni Ford was seated in a 747 and looking down from six miles above the Atlantic Ocean on her way home from Scotland. On her lap was her great-grandmother's journal she had hastily grabbed from the coffee table in the Great Room in her madcap rush to pack before leaving the island. As much as she wanted to forget, she still found a comforting, sad, lonely solace in her great-grandmother's words.

She had cried twice since takeoff. Her wet handkerchief was still in her hand. She had used up two handkerchiefs during the short flight from Lerwick to Aberdeen yesterday, and half a box of tissues during the night at the hotel. She'd had almost nothing to eat since leaving the Cottage.

This trip home was unlike that of the previous November after the financial conference at Gleneagles. During that flight she had promised herself that she would never set foot in Scotland again.

She obviously hadn't kept that vow. How could she have known she was about to inherit an island?

She couldn't say such a thing to herself this time, though she would if she could. One part of her never wanted to set foot on Whales Reef again. She had asked Jason MacNaughton if it was too late to change her mind. Was there some way she could relinquish the inheritance? Not without enormous complications, he replied. The tax liability was already set in motion. She could not stop it.

She was a property owner, a millionaire if Jason MacNaughton was right. A reluctant millionaire.

What a disastrous trip. She had been a perfect idiot more than once—lashing out at David and Audney, falling head over heels over a flock of sheep, and then falling for the shepherd himself—a man who was already engaged.

What was she thinking, getting all decked out in her nicest dress? And why had she sprinkled on a dab of perfume at the last minute?

What an unbelievably stupid thing to do. He was engaged to Audney!

Right now she just wanted to get home, go to work as if nothing had happened, and eventually talk over the finances of the thing with Maddy.

The fairy tale was over. It was time to get back to her real life.

PART 4

PART 4

51
MOTHER OF ALL REENTRIES

Washington, D.C.

Animated cries ranging from joyous greetings to exclamations of surprise brought Madison Swift out of her office.

"Loni!" she exclaimed, stunned along with the rest of her staff. She ran forward, and the two embraced like teenage girlfriends.

"Hi, Maddy . . . I'm home," said Loni.

"I see that!" rejoined Maddy, stepping back and gazing up and down at her tall assistant. "What a surprise. The last time I heard from you it was all about monkey wrenches in the works and having to stay indefinitely and asking me about that obnoxious Texan—which, by the way, I got the lowdown on. Now, suddenly you're here! Come and fill me in."

Loni followed her boss into the familiar office.

"Why the change in plans?" asked Maddy.

"Let's just say," replied Loni as she eased into her usual chair opposite Maddy's desk, "that an unforeseen new monkey wrench made a hasty departure imperative."

"Sounds mysterious."

363

"By the way, how do you know that Jimmy Joe McLeod is obnoxious?" asked Loni.

"He was here. He walked straight into my office without knocking and started throwing his weight around looking for you."

"And he eventually found me," rejoined Loni. "He showed up at my door on Whales Reef. All six-and-a-half feet of him, boots and hat and twang to match."

"Well, I have the goods on him. It's all there in that tube in the corner waiting for you. You won't believe what I dug up."

"I don't want to think about him right now. Just put me to work. What's on the agenda? What new deals are cooking?"

"Hey, not so fast. When did you get in? What about jet lag?"

"An hour ago."

"An *hour?* Did you even go home?"

"Just to drop off my bags and change."

"Then you need some downtime."

"All I want is to get back to my routine."

"It's Friday. I'm not about to plunge you into something new on the last day of the week. Plenty of time for that on Monday."

Maddy paused, staring across her desk with a puzzled expression. Her eyes narrowed.

"What?" laughed Loni. "Why are you looking at me like that?"

"I'm not sure. Something's different about you."

"I'm just tired."

"No, it's a *good* different. Something . . . I don't know, a light in your eyes I've never seen before. You're happy, more exuberant, even tired."

"It must be finding out I own an island," said Loni. "Believe it or not, the solicitor over there told me—"

Loni glanced back at the open office door, rose to close it, and returned to the chair.

"He said I was a millionaire," she added.

"Whoa! That would put a sparkle into anyone's eyes. Congratulations, Loni!"

"Thanks . . . I guess. I'm still in a daze. That's what you see in my eyes—the deer-in-the-headlights look."

"I don't think so. Are you sure there isn't something you're not telling me?"

A serious expression came over Loni's face. "I *do* feel different," she admitted. "Knowing who I am, where I came from, the connection to roots, you can't know what a difference it makes. I can tell that changes are taking place inside me. And—"

Loni hesitated, her lips quivered, and she looked away. It was enough. Maddy pounced.

"I knew it! There's something more."

Whatever Loni's boss had expected, it was not for Loni to burst into tears.

"Oh, Maddy," she said, "I got myself into a terrible pickle."

Maddy jumped out of her chair and hurried around the desk. She laid a gentle hand on Loni's shoulder. "I'm sorry, I didn't mean to pry."

"No, actually it feels good to cry," said Loni, "though I've been crying on and off for two days."

"Care to tell a friend what's going on?"

"I'm not sure I'm ready."

"It has to do with a man, doesn't it?"

Tears filled Loni's eyes again. "I can't think about it. What am I saying? I can't think of anything else."

"One thing's sure, you are definitely in no shape for work." Maddy glanced at her watch. "Okay, here's the plan," she said. "I'm taking the rest of the day off. It's about lunchtime. I am going to treat you to something I discovered while you were gone—a genuine high tea right here in D.C. My treat. We will take all afternoon."

Loni could not help but laugh at Maddy's enthusiasm.

"After lunch," Maddy continued, "we'll go to a park, then have a salad or something for supper, and then catch a movie. I think *Da Vinci Code* is still playing. Do you like Tom Hanks?"

"He's okay," replied Loni, still smiling.

"Or," Maddy went on, "in keeping with my management philosophy of giving clients choices so they make the final decisions themselves, if you are too jet-lagged for a night out—Option

Two: after our high tea I will buy you some chocolate, then you go home, take a hot bath, make yourself a big bowl of popcorn, put on your pajamas, and watch *While You Were Sleeping*. If you aren't sound asleep by then, I don't know jet lag when I see it."

"Chocolate and popcorn!" laughed Loni. "You sound like my grandparents."

"They are the two essential ingredients in the Madison Swift blues-relief regimen!"

52

HIGH TEA STATESIDE

"You were actually thinking of *not* accepting the inheritance?" said Maddy as her conversation with Loni an hour later continued into the tea shop.

"I was uncertain what to do," replied Loni while glancing about for a table. "It was so complicated. At first I thought it ought to go to someone there."

"Just as you said when the letter came a month ago."

"Then I met my two cousins, who were both vying for the honor before I came along," Loni went on after they were seated. "That complicated everything all the more."

"How so?"

"Long story. Let's just say one of them turned on the charm and conned me."

"What did he do?"

"He tried to coerce me into turning my affairs over to him. When I realized what was going on, I knew I couldn't let the inheritance go to him."

"And the other?"

"That would be David, the shepherd-chief of Whales Reef."

"That sounds very bucolic. Are you saying there are actual sheep?"

Loni smiled. "Apparently I own a flock myself. But it's mostly the gamekeeper who—"

"Gamekeeper!"

"Yes. Believe it or not, I employ a gamekeeper . . . and a housekeeper and butler."

"Get out of town!"

"Really."

"This sounds more like a movie script every minute!"

"And even after the fiasco with Hardy, I was set to walk away again when I found out that the inheritance taxes could be as high as four million dollars."

"You've got to be kidding!" exclaimed Maddy. "And now they're on *your* head?"

"It may sound worse than it is. I nearly fainted when the estate's accountant told me. But I went over everything with her and our solicitor. They assured me the estate's assets and investments could absorb the taxes with relative ease, though I might have to sell off a few oil leases."

"Oil leases? Goodness, girl—you are a tycoon."

"Hardly," laughed Loni. I'm still trying to get my head around it. But the estate is worth a lot of money. I need to lay it out to you and have you help me figure out a financial game plan."

"That's what I do. How fun to do it for you."

"Who would have dreamed I would become one of your clients?"

A young lady came to their table and gave them a friendly greeting.

"We would like high tea for two," said Maddy. "My friend here just returned from Scotland. I want to show her that Americans know how to do this too. And two coffees."

"Actually," interjected Loni, "I would like a pot of tea, please. What do you have . . . PG Tips, Typhoo, Scottish Blend?"

"We have PG Tips," said the girl.

"That will be perfect. And with milk."

When the girl was gone, Maddy arched an eyebrow. "How many more surprises do you have up your sleeve?" she said. "I thought you hated tea."

"A lot of things changed for me over there, Maddy," said Loni as a faraway expression spread across her face. "I'm not the same person as when I left."

"That is obvious. But you're making me nervous. You're not yourself, girl. Where's my old Loni?"

Loni smiled wistfully. "I'm not sure, Maddy. Right now I think she's Alonnah."

"So when will Loni be back?"

Loni drew in a deep breath. "I'm not sure she will be."

"The old you was my best friend. I don't know if I want a new you."

Loni smiled again. "That is sweet of you. I hope I'm the same person, or will be after I get all this figured out."

"So you're a millionaire, you are drinking tea, you're going by Alonnah now, and you've got a strange new light in your eyes—that's a pretty topsy-turvy two weeks."

"Please, Maddy, I'm confused enough as it is."

"All I'm saying is that you're definitely different. All these years I've only known Loni. I guess I'm going to have to get to know Alonnah. But whichever one you are, the instant you mentioned that shepherd fellow, a glow came over you."

"It did not."

"I know you, Loni. I'm telling you that something is going on here."

"It's over, I tell you. I'll be back to work on Monday . . . as *Loni*."

"*Over?* What's over?"

"Nothing. There never was anything . . . and it's over anyway."

"Come on, girl—admit it, you're an emotional wreck. It's the man, isn't it, the shepherd?"

Again tears flooded Loni's eyes.

"What's the big deal?" Maddy added. "So you got smitten by some guy? There's nothing wrong with that."

"I'm not smitten."

"Even if you are, it happens all the time."

"Not to me."

"Point taken. Nor to me. But still . . . what haven't you told me that makes it so complicated?"

"Probably the fact that he's engaged."

"Whoa! Okay, I see now—that changes things."

"And then there's Hugh," Loni added. "That's another monkey wrench."

"I'm not interested in Hugh. Tell me about this Scottish guy."

"There's no point, Maddy. I just want to forget."

Loni was temporarily rescued by the arrival of their tea and coffee and first plate of goodies.

"Okay then," said Maddy when they were alone again, "give me the Wikipedia on this mysterious shepherd you're trying so hard not to tell me about."

Loni wiped at her eyes, drew in a breath, and poured milk into her tea. She proceeded to give Maddy as brief an account of David as she could, which went on longer than she intended.

"I made a complete fool of myself more than once," she said. "As I learned more about him, I soon realized he was no ordinary shepherd. He was well-spoken, articulate, educated, knowledge-able, a modernist in some ways yet traditional in others. He is unbelievably gentle, sensitive, chivalrous, yet progressive too. The passion that most deeply drives him is the duty he feels to his people. In that sense he is two centuries behind the times. The villagers all call him *Chief*."

Maddy stared across the table. "It's definitely the glow," she said. "It's obvious, Loni."

"What's obvious?"

"You are in love with the man."

This time Loni did not object. She merely glanced away. Telling Maddy everything, then hearing the words aloud . . . she knew Maddy was right.

"So may I ask you the obvious question?" said Maddy after a moment.

"Of course."

"Why did you leave?"

"I don't know!" wailed Loni. "Suddenly I realized what was happening. It wasn't just finding out he was engaged. I think what frightened me most were the feelings welling up inside me. I didn't know what to do. I panicked."

"So he's engaged?" said Maddy. "When did that ever stop a red-blooded American girl from going after a guy?"

"I'm not that kind of person, Maddy."

"You don't believe in fighting for something you want?"

"Not for a man. That's not how people are over there. I would never *fight* for someone like David. It would ruin everything. If he and Audney are supposed to be together, I wouldn't interfere with it. Maybe that's one of the reasons I left."

"You don't sound convinced."

"I'm more confused than anything."

"I think you hit the nail on the head a minute ago—you're afraid. Falling in love can be scary. I would think you would be used to it."

"Hardly," said Loni. "This is a first for me. I've never been so twisted up in knots. And yes . . . I'm terrified."

"What about Hugh? Didn't you feel this way when you met him?"

"Actually, no."

"Okay . . ." said Maddy slowly. "Bombshell time. Care to elaborate?"

"It's different with Hugh."

"How so?"

"I don't know . . . just different. We drifted into it, went on bland dates, talked about our work. After a while he started kissing me. He was a gentleman. He never tried anything. I just took it in stride, but I can't say, even the first time he kissed me, that it made my heart rush."

"Well, I certainly wouldn't know!" laughed

373

Maddy. "I've never been kissed by a guy in my life. And family doesn't count. So . . . what are you afraid of?"

"I don't know!" moaned Loni. "My feelings, I guess. When your brain and heart start doing cartwheels and you can't get a deep breath, you become vulnerable. I told you I hardly dated in college. The whole girl-guy thing passed me by. Hugh is the first boyfriend I've ever had. I thought I loved him. I had no reason to think otherwise. But then this!"

She paused and took a drink of tea. "A white panic came over me and I had to get out of there," Loni went on. "All my old self-doubts swept over me. Now I feel like an idiot. I wasn't thinking rationally. I threw my things in my suitcase, got in the car, drove to the city, took a cab to the airport, and put two of the most expensive flights I will ever take in my life on my credit card, which is probably maxed out, and now here I am. I left in such a rush I probably left half my things behind."

Loni paused. "As ridiculous as it sounds," she added, "maybe you're right. Maybe it is as simple as that I was afraid of falling in love."

"It may not be as ridiculous as it sounds," said Maddy. Her voice was more pensive than usual.

"Now it's my turn to ask about that expression in *your* eyes," said Loni.

Maddy smiled. "I think I might have been in love once," she said.

"You!" The instant the word left her mouth Loni regretted it. "Maddy, I'm sorry, I didn't mean . . ."

Maddy smiled. "Forget it. I know what you meant. I haven't given you the idea that I am the falling-in-love type."

"I wouldn't express it exactly like that, only that you have told me that you are not interested in marrying or dating and all that."

"Which I'm not. But now that we're doing true confessions here, some of that may be my own defense mechanism to keep from being hurt again."

Loni waited.

"Yeah," said Maddy, "I fell for a guy, and I was afraid of it too. I was afraid of the possible rejection. I was afraid of all the feelings bubbling up inside. I'd always tried to be stoic and in control. I got giddy, laughed all the time, talked too much, and behaved like a perfect imbecile . . . and my fears were well-founded."

"The guy dumped you?"

"Not really. Honestly, Loni, he never knew why I was acting so silly. I never told him. He never suspected. Eventually he left the firm I worked for and that was the end of it. I've always regretted I didn't say something, didn't somehow make my feelings known."

She sighed. "It's one of the bittersweet episodes of my life. Not even my mom knows. I wouldn't dare tell her. I would never hear the end of it."

It fell silent for a moment as they sipped from their cups and nibbled at the sweets from the tray in the middle of the table.

"What was his name?" asked Loni. "Or do you remember? How long ago was it?"

"Do I remember! Of course I remember. It was about twelve years ago. But I will remember him until the day I die."

Maddy smiled sadly.

"His name was Tennyson Stafford. Not the kind of name you forget. He was a financial whiz. He was destined to rise in the ranks faster than me."

"What became of him?"

"No idea. I tried to forget. So I know exactly what you're going through and why all those sudden feelings are frightening. But I look back now and wish I'd handled it differently."

"What would you have done?"

Maddy thought for several moments. "That's the sixty-four-thousand-dollar question. I don't suppose you ever know. But I worked *too* hard to convince myself that I didn't care . . . steeled myself against the hurt, adopted my macho feminist persona with pantsuits and short hair, and threw myself into the game of trying to make it in a man's world. I tried to convince myself that Tennyson was now forty pounds overweight and that I'd dodged a bullet. Of course, none of that did any good. You always wonder. But time passes and I got over it. Well, maybe not entirely. But it recedes into the past, and life goes on. You can't go back. So it's too late for me, but not for you."

"But, Maddy, it *is* too late! It so completely unhinged me that I ran away. Now I feel stupid. Yet I can't go back. There's no reason to go back. How would I explain myself? *Hi, David, I'm sorry I ran away, but I realized I was falling in love with you. So have a nice marriage with Audney.* How ridiculous would it be for me to show up again?"

"You don't think you should tell him how you feel?"

"That's the last thing I would do. It wouldn't be fair to either of them. I did the only thing I could have done. He's engaged to the island beauty, who really is a sweet girl. I would never do anything to get in their way."

"So what *are* you going to do? You own the island. You can't turn your back on it."

"I don't know—deal with it, get over it, and go on with my life. I have to put on my *Loni* persona and handle the island's business professionally and then probably sell it all to David. Why shouldn't he and Audney be lord and lady of the island? Nothing would make the people of Whales Reef happier."

"You know what I think?" said Maddy. "I think you need a few days to unwind and get your head together."

"I've been anxious to get back to work."

"All in good time. And I don't want to throw yet one more monkey wrench into your life . . . but speaking of decisions, you may have one to make sooner than later about Hugh."

"What do you mean?" asked Loni.

"I have the feeling he may be up to something . . . something involving you."

"Uh-oh—do you know something I don't?"

"Nothing specific, only that he called asking about you and was talking about big news and big decisions and wanting to talk over plans with you."

"Plans?"

"He didn't elaborate."

Loni sighed. "I suppose I am going to need to figure more out than I realized."

"Why don't you take all next week?" said Maddy.

Loni thought a moment. "You know what sounds really good? An extended visit to my grandparents. Maybe it's time I reconnected with those roots and forgot my Scottish roots for a while. I need to come to terms with my Pennsylvania past maybe even more than my Scottish. Thank you, Maddy. I will take you up on your offer."

"And Hugh?"

"I need to see him before I go. I just hope it's not what I think you think it is. I really can't deal with that right now."

"If it is, what *are* you going to do about Hugh?"

"I don't know, probably marry him. Who else am I going to marry? Just not right now. You know, Maddy, if I am going home for a few days, I think I'll skip the movie tonight."

"Sure, no problem."

"I need to relax and unwind and then repack."

"Don't forget the chocolate, popcorn, and a chick flick."

Loni laughed. "But I will have to call Hugh."

"Good luck!"

As soon as she reached home, Loni summoned the wherewithal to pick up the phone. A few seconds later Hugh's voice answered.

"Hello, Hugh," said Loni, "guess what, I'm home."

"What . . . when?"

"A few hours ago. I'm just getting unpacked. It was a last-minute decision. I didn't even have time to tell Maddy I was coming. I want to see you and catch up on everything, but I need to see my grandparents first. Could we get together tomorrow, and maybe you could take me to the train station?"

"The train station?" said Hugh in surprise.

"I decided to take the train up to Philly."

"Why the train?"

"I just felt like it. I don't want to drive up in my own car. Can you take me to the station?"

"Sure. But I've got big news about an important decision for our future. You free tonight?"

"I'm really bushed, Hugh. We'll have plenty of time when I get back."

"This is too big. I don't want to wait to spring it on you. How about I take you to the most expensive restaurant in D.C.? I'll pick you up—"

"Sorry, I just can't, Hugh. We'll catch up tomorrow."

Inwardly Loni sighed. Maybe the big news was that he'd lowered his golf handicap or had been invited to join one of Washington's prestigious country clubs. Though she doubted it.

She set down the phone and decided to attack her suitcase. She hoisted it onto her bed, opened it, and began to put away the contents or toss them into the laundry hamper. She'd reached the bottom of the case when an uneasy feeling came over her.

Quickly she grabbed her carry-on and threw it on the bed beside the other. She rifled through the contents, spewing them in every direction. A moment later a groan sounded.

Her journal and the letter box and all its contents were nowhere to be seen. They were still sitting on the desk in the upstairs study of the Cottage back on Whales Reef.

53
DISCONCERTING PROPOSITION

Loni was scarcely buckled into place the following morning in Hugh's BMW when, showing no curiosity about her trip, Hugh launched into the news he had been waiting a week to tell her.

"Something really big has come up, Loni," he said excitedly. "It's too good to believe. That chief of staff thing I wrote you about is off the table. It's much bigger. This is my chance, Loni! Everything's happening fast. Now that you're here, you can be part of it. We've got to get some plans in motion immediately."

"What kind of plans?"

"Everything—our future, Loni. Now I will definitely *not* take no for an answer like last Christmas. You *are* going to meet my parents. I'm trying to set something up next weekend. They need to be among the first to know."

Loni held her breath.

"You do know it's 2006?" Hugh went on.

"Uh, yes!" laughed Loni. "I was aware of that."

"And you realize the significance of it?"

"I'm not sure."

"Midterm elections this November. They're

only five months away. That's why we've got to jump on this quickly."

"Okay . . . move quickly on *what*, Hugh?"

"The election. Congressman Finney has decided not to run for reelection. He wants to put me up for the seat as his protégé!"

"Oh, I see . . . yes, that is certainly big news. But I thought you and your parents were from Connecticut. Isn't Finney from Wisconsin? Don't you have to run from your home state?"

"That's a second home. I was raised in the congressman's district. That's how I got the job on his staff. My dad knew some people he knew, and they pulled a few strings. The point is that Congressman Finney wants me to succeed him. So you see why time is of the essence. Everything has to be fast-tracked."

"That's fantastic, Hugh," said Loni, momentarily relieved. "I'm happy for you. Congratulations."

"Thanks, but you and I have to get everything in place. I'll have to reestablish residency, which should be no problem since I was raised there. But we should plan a trip to Wisconsin ASAP to look for a house. I'll need to file all the papers and then start speaking and revving up the campaign."

"Why can't you use your family home?"

"How would that look, a man running for Congress who is living with his folks? Image is everything. Besides, we'll want a place of our own."

"What exactly do you mean, Hugh? Who's *we?*"

"You and me of course, Loni. We're in this together. You know how I feel. This is our big chance. Congressman Finney thinks I may have a real future. He wants to mentor me. I'm young and you are every politician's dream. You know how it is in Washington—appearances are everything. The congressman thinks I could be a senator, even VP material someday. With you at my side, and with the mystique of your inheritance and that funny title you said the people called you—"

"Laird," said Loni.

"Whatever. Nobody will know what it means. It's the mystery of the British aristocracy, sort of a political Princess Grace. We'll make you a star, like American royalty."

"Hugh, it's not like that. It's an island of fishermen, not Monaco. The title is unofficial anyway."

"No one here will know. We'll play it up, publicize your rags-to-riches story. The tabloids will eat it up. We'll be an unstoppable combination!

"And speaking of your inheritance," Hugh continued before Loni could squeeze in a word. "I don't know how soon the funds from it will be available, but that would really help with the campaign. And like I say, we'll play up the aristocracy thing. It will be great!"

Loni's head was spinning. When she spoke,

hardly realizing what she was saying, her voice was soft.

"Do you realize, Hugh, that I own a woolen mill?" she said.

"What?"

"I own a woolen mill . . . on the island."

"Oh, okay—well, that shouldn't be a problem. It should be easy enough for us to sell off."

"Who said I wanted to sell it? I also own sheep and cattle and—"

Whatever else Loni had been about to say was interrupted by Hugh's laughter.

"Sheep . . . cattle! That's hilarious. We better not let *that* leak to the press. We want to present you as an aristocrat, not a farm girl!"

"You're right," said Loni, "this is moving fast. *Way* too fast. Aren't you getting a little ahead of yourself?"

"Do you really think so?" said Hugh in a perplexed tone. "I don't understand your hesitation. I've been planning everything we need to do. We'll have our official residence in Wisconsin, but we will maintain a house here in D.C. too. And we'll have to talk about when it would be best for you to quit your job. We might even want to work the wedding into the campaign, make it a society event emphasizing your long-lost inheritance. We won't want to make public your religious upbringing in Pennsylvania. People might think you were Amish or something—

that would conflict with the Princess Grace mystique."

At last it fell silent in the car.

"Uh . . . Hugh," said Loni after several long seconds, "please don't get me wrong—I am happy for you, but you are assuming a lot. I mean, am I missing something? Are you proposing to me?"

"Oh, right . . . of course. I guess I thought that was understood."

Keeping his right hand on the wheel, he rummaged through his coat pocket with his left. He pulled out a small box and handed it to her. "Sorry," he said. "I got so carried away I forgot one important detail."

Loni opened the box. Her eyes fell on an enormous diamond atop a platinum band.

"Put it on. I want to see how it looks."

Some inner sense made Loni hesitate. She picked it up with the fingers of her left hand and tentatively probed the fourth finger of her right hand.

"No, your left hand," said Hugh.

"It's too small, Hugh," she said. "I don't want to force it."

"I'll get it resized. Do you like it?"

"It looks expensive."

"It was!" laughed Hugh.

Loni replaced the ring in the box, closed the lid, and stared out the car window in silence.

"Hugh," she said at length, "why do you always give me chrysanthemums?"

"Huh—what kind of question is that?"

"Maybe an important one."

"What do chrysanthemums have to do with my running for office?"

"It has to do with us, Hugh."

"What about us?"

"Everything. Do you have an answer?"

"I don't know. I guess because I like them."

"Did you ever stop to think whether I do?"

"I don't suppose I did."

"Do you know that I'm allergic to them?"

"Actually, now that you mention it, I guess I remember. Okay, no big deal—no more chrysanthemums. Roses from now on. None of that matters. What matters, Loni, is that this is our ticket."

"To where, Hugh?"

"To *everything*—to the big time, the inner circle, the corridors of power, fame and fortune, Washington society. So . . . is it a go? *Will* you?"

"I can't give you an answer yet," said Loni. "I just got home. I'm tired. My life has been turned upside down in the last few weeks. I can't process all this right now. It's too sudden. I need to take a deep breath and think it all through."

"We've been talking about this for a year or more."

"We *haven't* talked about it. You assumed. I need to think about everything you've said."

"Sure, no problem. Just don't take too long. We need to go see my folks next weekend and then get moving on buying a house and making wedding plans. A week before the election would make dynamite press."

Silence hung in the air as Hugh pulled into Union Station.

"And once all this starts happening," said Loni softly, "you expect me to quit my job?"

"Of course. You will be a congressman's wife. Responsibilities, you know."

"Such as?"

"Cocktail parties, dinners, entertainments, travel, speaking. I want you to be a significant part of it all. You are smart, savvy, and beautiful besides. Your looks will be the greatest asset my political career could have. I mean, how far would John Kennedy have risen without Jackie?"

Loni felt her jaw drop as Hugh pulled into a parking space. He jumped out, grabbed her suitcase, and set it on the sidewalk.

"Well, I'm glad we got everything settled," he said. "Have a good visit with your grandparents. I'd walk you in, but I've got a meeting I can't be late for. We'll start making plans the second you're back."

Loni stood on the sidewalk a minute more, watching Hugh drive away. He had never once mentioned the word *love*.

54
THE GREEN FIELDS OF HOME

Southern Pennsylvania

In her intentionally nondescript rental car, Loni drove through town and into the farmland beyond without concern of attracting stares from the residents of the close-knit Quaker community of her upbringing. The train ride to Philadelphia, followed by the drive into rural southern Pennsylvania, had been full of so many thoughts and emotions that she could not have described her feelings had she tried. The excitement of Hugh's voice as he went on about his dreams had jarred with dissonance against everything she was feeling. Yet she knew it would be useless to explain it to him. He was on cloud nine. There was no reason to burst his bubble with realities—such as that she happened to like her work and had no intention of moving to Wisconsin.

Loni drove up to the familiar farm-style house where she had spent the first eighteen years of her life.

When her diminutive grandmother came to the door, this time it was Loni who broke into tears and sought Mrs. Ford's embrace as if she were a girl again.

Loni's request to stay a few days could not have struck more deeply into her grandparents' hearts. Hearing Loni say she needed to come *home* for a while brought tears to their aging eyes. She told them everything that had happened, repeating much she had written in her letter, then about recent developments and David and her hasty departure. She then showed them Hugh's ring and told them of the drive to the train station, before closing the small box and stuffing it back into the pocket of her jacket.

"My, but you have had a busy week!" said Mr. Ford.

"Did you give your young man an answer?" asked Loni's grandmother.

"No, Grandma," replied Loni. "It was so out of the blue and . . . well, it seemed more self-serving than romantic. I'm not sure I want to be his trophy wife."

"What is a trophy wife, dear?"

Loni smiled. "A poor choice of words, Grandma. Let's just say I haven't decided what to tell him."

"Do you love him, Alonnah?" asked Mr. Ford.

"I don't know, Grandpa. I guess that's what I have to find out."

The following morning Loni stunned her grandparents by asking if she could accompany them to Sunday Meeting. Overjoyed at the prospect, they were delighted at the ease and friendliness with which she greeted old family friends and relatives, even stooping down to give aging Betsy Schrock a warm hug. The dour woman had not grown a good deal sweeter over the years, but Loni greeted her as if they had been great friends. Most surprising to Loni was the warm reception given her from almost everyone there.

A feast followed at the home of Mr. Ford's brother, where Loni renewed connections witH her two childhood friends, cousins Jacob and Rilanda, and innumerable others—many first cousins, like her, now grown, but many seconds and thirds and variously cousin-removed youngsters who stared up at her with wide eyes.

Around the huge table they listened in rapt attention as she recounted the story of her discovery of her Shetland roots through Chad Ford's mysterious wife, Alison, and of the Tulloch family and its history. Even the children at the four card tables in the adjacent room strained to listen to the tall, striking blonde as if she were a Scandinavian princess of royal pedigree. And with half her bloodline originating in the Shetlands, perhaps she was exactly that.

Never again would Loni consider herself a stranger in the community. She had indeed come home again, and in the fullest sense.

By the time the day was over, Loni felt a quiet

sense of contentment, having reconnected to a past she now realized she treasured. As last she was able to apply Maddy's prescription as she and her grandparents revived their long-standing tradition that evening, enjoying hot chocolate and popcorn together. Loni told them more details about her recent trip, about the village and the remarkable inheritance.

Loni awoke on Monday to the sun shining through the familiar curtains of her room. She was at peace, though with no resolution presenting itself to the uncertainties looming on the horizon of her future.

By that afternoon she was ready to ask her grandparents' counsel. Again the three sat down in the living room. Expanding on what she had told them previously, Loni tried to lay out the options before her.

"I guess what it boils down to," she concluded, "is whether I should keep the inheritance at all."

"You can't just give it away, can you, dear?" asked Mrs. Ford.

"Not now that I have signed the papers. It's mine. Once the inheritance taxes are paid, however, I would be able to sell everything for a low price and let someone who is more deserving carry on as owner of the estate."

"You're thinking of selling to one of the two men you mentioned?" asked her grandfather.

Loni nodded. "I suppose I could sell it to

anybody, but it seems right that it go to one of the island's men."

"From what you have said, even if you sold at much lower than market value, it would still make you a rich lady."

A quizzical smile came over Loni's face. "I can't really think of it like that," she said. "I would happily sell it for a fraction of its value—I will have to ask Maddy about the legalities of that. Even that would give me far more than I will ever need, and I would be able to provide for you as well."

"Don't worry about us, Alonnah," said Mr. Ford. "We are well provided for. Our tastes are simple, and our needs are few."

"No Mediterranean cruises?" asked Loni with a smile.

Mrs. Ford chuckled. "We are happier under this roof together than anywhere in the world."

"Nevertheless, I need to know you will never want for anything. They are fond of talking about duty over there, and I have a duty to you. I've not paid enough attention to it up until now. That is going to change."

"We appreciate that more than you can know, Alonnah," said her grandfather.

"Anyway," Loni went on, "my other option is to retain my ownership and figure out some way to administer the estate. That's the difficult question—whether to put everything in someone else's hands, how much to be involved, how much I would have to be there. They have an old-fashioned term for what is called a *factor*. Essentially it means business manager. Back in the days of lords and ladies and dukes and earls, the rich landowners all had a factor who took care of their estates. That's more or less what I've already hired David Tulloch to do. On the other hand, the people of the island are accustomed to their lairds being one of them, someone they know. So you see how complicated it is. I need wisdom about what to do."

The room fell silent. When at length he spoke, her grandfather's voice was filled with careful thought and consideration of all the issues Loni had laid before them. Loni recognized the tone immediately from her childhood. She was about to drink from her grandfather's well of wisdom. She knew that no word would originate out of his own opinion or would offer counsel in accord with what *he* might wish. Rather, he would concern himself only with what was right, what was prudent, and what would be for Loni's long-term best interests.

His first words, however, surprised her. It was not the sort of analogy he often used.

"There is a saying in sports," said Mr. Ford. "Let the game come to you. In other words, don't push, don't press too hard. As the Word says, 'let patience have its effect.' Farmers must live by the same principle—let the seasons come, let the sun and rain, even the frost and snow each do their work in due course. Wait for the rain."

He paused thoughtfully.

"There are times," he went on, "when our own impatience urges us to act quickly, prematurely, impulsively. Yet often the urgency to act is counterproductive if one has not waited for the rain, so to speak. There are times to act decisively. There are other times when the best thing to do is nothing—to wait. I call it active, expectant waiting."

He smiled and looked Loni affectionately in the eyes. "I'm sure you remember the saying I am very fond of," he said.

Loni returned his smile. "I think so," she said. "That God is never in a hurry."

"You *were* listening!"

"Probably more than you realize, Grandpa. Actually, more than I realized either."

"My sense, Alonnah," Mr. Ford went on, "is that this is a time for you to wait, to rest, and to remember that in quietness and confidence God will be your strength. That waiting may be long or short—two years or two days. The duration of the season of waiting is not so important as that we release the grip of urgency, that we 'let go and let God,' as the old saying goes. To wait means to relinquish our *own* hold on the reins of destiny. Give God the reins. The time for decision will come. For now, let the peace of being at home enter your spirit and do its work. I'm sure you also know my favorite verse of Scripture."

Again Loni smiled. "Of course—Proverbs three."

"'Trust in the Lord with all your heart, and do not rely on your own insight. In all your ways acknowledge him, and he will direct your paths.'"

A long silence followed.

"He will make your way clear, Alonnah, in His time. Trust Him. Let God's game come to you."

Loni rose and gave her grandfather a warm embrace. "Thank you, Grandpa. That is true wisdom. I receive what you say. Now I know why I came to you."

55

THE BOULDER, THE CREEK, AND THE MEADOW

The next day, thinking that the following morning she would return to Washington, wearing running shoes, jeans, and a sweatshirt with its sleeves cut off, Loni left the house about eleven.

She walked through fields to the Quaker school and then sat a while on the front steps. She was coming to terms with many things.

At length she rose and continued on, walking briefly through the small town before returning to her grandparents' home. Reaching their mailbox, she turned and climbed a low wooden fence across the country road from the long driveway back to the house.

Soon she was making her way along a well-worn path between a fenced field of six-feet-high corn on her right and a lush green expanse on her left, where grazed fifty or more tan Jersey cows. Beyond that spread untold acres of golden wheat. This path was the shortest route to her uncle's house and had been used by generations of youngsters running back and forth between the two houses, cutting the three-quarters of a mile drive to just under half a mile. Loni's memory filled with images of scampering from one house to the other with her cousins Jacob and Rilanda who, even during the most painful days of childhood, had always been kind to her.

She had almost forgotten what fields of ripening corn and wheat smelled like. There was nothing like the fragrance of farmland, she thought, when the sun beat down on the earth, unless it was the smell of the woods after a spring rain.

Ahead, her uncle Herb and aunt Evelyn's tall house rose out of the fields like a landlocked lighthouse of white. Two other dwellings sat on the large family tract, homes for Jacob's family and that of his younger brother, Eli. A third unmarried brother lived in the main house with Herb and Evelyn and had by now, with nephews as his work crew, assumed most of the work of the dairy and crops. Jacob and his eldest son carried on the Ford family woodworking tradition in two modern workshops.

A thousand memories flitted through Loni's brain like the random flight of butterflies. Everything looked just the same . . . yet was also completely different to the eyes of her adulthood.

Had she waited too long to return to this place of childhood? Yet perhaps the fields of memory needed time to heal. Perhaps their soils required years to lie fallow to see what new flowers and trees might blossom from the long-buried roots of the past. For in coming to terms with one's past, timing is everything. Growth of new memories cannot be rushed.

This was the appointed time. The fallow fields were ready to blossom anew in her heart. Gratitude now came flourishing out of the purified soil of bygone years. The pains of the past can be transformed into happy memories for one determined to dwell in that re-creating miracle. Such a one Loni had become. The gray skies and gloomy horizons of former heartaches were slowly being imbued with all the colors of a newly radiant sunrise.

Such nostalgic seasons of renewal bring pain and happiness intermingling in an intricate dance, now one taking the lead, now the other. Every sight, every memory, thus brought a smile to Loni's lips as well as moisture to her eyes. Each in its own way was healing to her soul.

She reached a familiar fork in the path, paused, then turned to the right.

The course she now pursued led to a densely wooded grove of birch and pine three-quarters of a mile ahead that stretched east and west for several miles and gave way beyond it northward to hilly and, in places, rugged terrain.

She wondered if her grandfather still haunted their favorite fishing spot on the small river that came down out of the hills. At least it had seemed like a *river* to her young eyes. It was called Disappearing Creek for its propensity to disappear for stretches at a time in thick undergrowth, behind huge boulders, even occasionally underground before tumbling again into the light of day to widen and splash through its gravelly bed, forming here and there deep pools where, if one knew their ways and was patient and skilled in the fly-fishing art, decent-sized rainbow trout could be pulled from it. How the fish navigated the disappearing waters, no one knew, but the lively little stream, almost a true river during the spring snowmelt, was the favorite destination for the fishermen of their community.

Loni emerged from the trees some time later. There was the river in front of her, just as she remembered it. It *was* indeed a creek and not a river. Funny how much larger it had appeared all those years ago.

And there was their favorite fishing hole two hundred yards upstream.

She broke into a run. Why didn't she think to bring her rod? She had seen it hanging in the barn, probably where it had been gathering dust for fifteen years or more since she had last used it. Perhaps she and her grandfather could come back later in the afternoon. Dusk was always best for trout anyway.

She reached the hole and scrambled up the tall boulder with the creek winding around its base, creating the deep, dark pool where the fish lurked in the shadows.

From the high perch of this rock she used to sit for hours on end watching her grandfather wield his rod and line, manipulating his hand-tied flies with exquisite delicacy and patience, coaxing, luring, beguiling the trout to come closer and have a taste. She had learned everything she knew about fly-fishing from years of watching his every move, every flick of the wrist, every scarcely perceptible tug of the line, every glance of his eyes. She had watched it all from her perch on the overhanging boulder, not moving a muscle lest her reflection distract their quarry . . . watching until that magical moment at nine when her grandfather looked up from the bank of the stream and said, *"Climb down, Alonnah. I think it's time for you to try it."*

Her grandmother and grandfather had taught her far more than she had been capable of realizing when she was young. She was finally discovering how much their example had been instilled into her. She had gone to Scotland seeking her roots. Yet all along she had roots here too, deeper and closer and more personal roots. She had not appreciated them fully before now. But that was changing. Scotland opened her eyes to a legacy that had been right in front of her all along.

She sat for a long time reliving many happy times, remembering her first catch—only four inches but one her grandfather had praised as if it had been a thirty-pound Atlantic salmon.

Climbing down from the boulder, Loni struck out up the hill on the opposite side of the stream. Though she had come this way a hundred times, she always varied her route slightly so that no one would find her own special hideaway. The instant she had discovered it at eleven or twelve, it became her private place of solace and refuge.

A walk of ten more minutes, after squeezing between several tall boulders, brought her into a tiny secluded meadow about twenty feet from end to end with just one hole through the leafy canopy above that let a single shaft of sunlight down onto the grassy floor. She had come here to sit for hours, watching the irregular pattern of light slowly moving across the ground with the westward course of the sun.

So quiet, and enclosed by the dense surrounding wood, it was the only place in the world where she felt completely alone, and completely herself. She felt things here that she felt nowhere else.

As she sat down on this day, she no longer sensed herself alone. The eternal reality of God's ever-present accompanying Presence had begun to exert its healing pressure on her soul.

The tiny meadow, even after so many years, flooded Loni with memories. Feelings swirled inside that she could not have framed into words. When here, she had in some strange way been at peace with her girlish emotions and dawning self-perceptions. She would not have called it praying back then. Yet in her own way, in her attempt to make sense of who she was and where she fit into the big, wide, often painful world . . . perhaps even then she was learning to pray.

She lay down on the soft carpet of green and stared up through the blue overhead. She was at last formulating the questions in her adult mind that she had only *felt* as a child:

Who am I . . . who was I then . . . who am I now . . . who am I becoming . . . who is it that I want to be?

Was she Loni . . . or Alonnah . . . or both? Was she a Ford, or a Tulloch, or both?

Yes, she thought, even as a child whenever she

came here the chrysalis had been struggling to break free and come awake.

Loni let out a deep sigh, then began to pray.

God, help me know myself, she whispered. *Help me become who you want me to be . . . and do what you want me to do.*

Doubts again swept through her for having left Whales Reef so abruptly.

I see now, she prayed, *that I acted impulsively. I didn't stop to ask you what to do. This is all so new, trying to do what you want me to do rather than what I want to do. Help me learn to hear your voice. And if I did make a mistake, show me what you want me to do now. Help me, as my grandfather said, to wait for your answer.*

Loni's thoughts stilled. Growing drowsy and lost in her nostalgic reverie, a sound startled her upright.

It wasn't common, but she had grown up being warned by her grandfather that occasionally bears wandered out of the wilderness. More likely a raccoon or skunk, she thought, or a possum. Though they were nocturnal.

There it was again—steps creeping through the trees!

It wasn't crashing and chaotic like a bear, but soft like a deer stepping gingerly.

Loni sat motionless, trying to remember everything her grandfather had told her to do *if* she encountered a bear.

Again came a shuffling of leaves. Eyes riveted in the direction of the sound, Loni watched a shadow gradually begin to emerge. It was standing upright!

Panic sweeping through her, Loni rose to her feet and began to back away.

A man was coming through the trees . . . a hunter, it must be . . . or one of the local boys out with his air gun!

She must warn him so he didn't do something crazy and shoot without seeing who she was! Loni tried to call out, but her throat was dry. She couldn't manage so much as a croak.

The figure emerged into the clearing. Her eyes shot open, and her face went white. Head swirling, Loni's knees buckled.

Her surroundings went dark, and she collapsed into unconsciousness.

56

AN ANGRY FISHERMAN

Lerwick, Shetland Islands

It had not taken a fight with his cousin to tell Hardy Tulloch that the plans and schemes he had been cherishing were crumbling at his feet. His exchange with the American made that fact clear enough.

In his heart of hearts, the thought of encountering his cousin on some isolated bluff or coastline where he could give full vent to his lifelong animosity was so delicious that he had actually dreamed of it in his sleep. He knew he could kill David as easily as he could a twenty-pound cod, or toss him off a cliff without breaking a sweat.

But Hardy was no fool. He knew well enough that there would be unpleasant consequences if David just disappeared. Suspicion would naturally turn in his direction. And he was sufficiently wary of the Ford girl—who had shown herself possessed of more gumption than he had anticipated—and the American propensity for lawsuits, to attempt any hostile move against her. Talk around the village during the next several days was obviously favorable toward the do-gooder. Her touching little speech at the mill, and the evening with David at the Auld Hoose, were on the lips of all the auld wives as if she was suddenly their darling.

The fools! thought Hardy.

At present he deemed it the most prudent policy to lay low. For the moment it would be best to make no more enemies than he already had. Whatever he did from here on out, he would do in secret.

He did not learn until Saturday that the Ford woman was no longer even on the island. The consensus was that business had taken her back to the States.

Her absence was just what Hardy had been waiting for. What the current situation was, he did not know. It would behoove him to investigate and see what he might be able to do on his own.

On Monday morning, Hardy appeared at the offices of MacNaughton, Dalrymple, & MacNaughton, requesting to see the solicitor in charge of the Tulloch estate of Whales Reef. A few minutes later, with his secretary on her way to the supply cupboard for some air freshener, Hardy was seated in Jason MacNaughton's office. Introducing himself as one of the principle claimants in the business of Macgregor Tulloch's estate, to which Jason replied that he was aware of who he was, Hardy inquired whether the solicitor was aware of the private arrangement the American Miss Ford had concluded with him regarding the administration of her affairs until his pending suit contesting the inheritance was resolved.

"I was aware of no such agreement," replied Jason cautiously. "I'm sorry, did I hear you correctly, that you have filed a suit against the findings of the probate court?"

"Oh, aye!" replied Hardy expansively. " 'Tis weel enough kent that the lassie's grit-gran'father gave up his right tae the inheritance when he sailed til America. The inheritance'll be mine eventually, ye need hae nae doobt aboot that."

"I'm not so sure it is so simple, Mr. Tulloch," rejoined Jason with an indulgent smile. "Everything was thoroughly looked into by the court before they reached their decision."

"We shall see aboot that," said Hardy confidently. "What I want tae ken noo is hoo I'm tae take up my business as the lassie's factor."

"Her *factor,* you say?"

"Aye," said Hardy, "jist like she promised an' as she an' me agreed. I said I'd take care o' everything when she was gone."

"I see. Well, Mr. . . . uh, Mr. Tulloch," said Jason slowly, "I fear there is really nothing you will be able to do, nor do I see that there is anything I can do about the situation. Miss Ford indeed made arrangements for the management of her financial affairs in her absence. However, I am powerless to change them."

"So 'tis jist as I said."

"Unfortunately," Jason continued, "she made no mention of you. She left her affairs in the hands of another."

"An' who might that be?" Hardy shot back. "'Tis yersel', I suppose."

"Not at all," said Jason. "She left her affairs in the hands of Mr. David Tulloch. I'm afraid her arrangement is legally binding."

It is doubtful whether Jason MacNaughton visibly saw smoke coming out of Hardy's ears.

He was aware, however, of a sudden rise of temperature in his office.

Hardy rose with a silent expression of wrath on his face and strode from the room without another word.

It was well that Hardy did not encounter David for several days. The result could have been catastrophic for both men. As it was, he had to content himself, like the ancient Pharisees and Herodians, with holding counsel in his mind against him to see how he might destroy him.

57

STRANGER IN THE MEADOW

Southern Pennsylvania

When Loni began to come to herself, she thought herself dreaming . . . transported to a time and place far away.

She was gazing into sparkling eyes of cornflower blue, a wild crop of light brown hair falling over ears and forehead, a wide smile brightening a face, radiating light and life like the sun.

All she could do was stare. What a dream!

A great laugh rippled musically out of the sun face. The spell was broken. The dream had come to life.

Loni's heart skipped. *"David!"* she whispered in disbelief. "Is it . . . but how did you . . . is it really *you?*"

She reached up as if expecting her hand to pass through the image of a ghost. Instead her fingers touched his cheek and gently probed the sandpaper of his whiskers.

"It's me," he said brightly. "And I am glad to see you too! I just barely reached you before you dropped in a faint."

As her consciousness returned, Loni realized that she was lying in David's arms where he knelt beside her.

"I don't know what happened. I heard a noise in the trees, then I saw you. I thought I was hallucinating. How long have I been like this—an hour?"

"Only ten or fifteen seconds," laughed David.

Loni tried to sit up. David gently lifted her with an arm behind her shoulders, then sat back a few feet away.

"Whew, I think I am feeling better," she said, drawing in a deep breath. "Fainting is very strange. I'm not sure I want to make a practice of it. But what in the world are you doing here? Oh, and look—your eye is better!"

"Healing nicely, thank you."

"But what are you doing in America . . . how did you . . . I mean, how did you possibly find me? Out here . . . in the middle of the woods!"

"Your grandfather drew me a map. He thought I might find you here."

"You've met my grandparents?"

"A delightful man and woman."

"But I never told my grandfather about my special place."

"He told me you would probably say that."

"That crafty man. He was paying closer attention than I realized."

"He said he used to follow you here to make sure you were safe."

Loni smiled. "But how did you locate my grandparents?" she asked. "How did you know I would be with them?"

"It took a little sleuthing. Jason had some details, and the internet is amazing for tracking people down. And a phone call with your Madison Swift—"

"You talked to Maddy?"

David laughed. "Anyway, I left Shetland on Sunday, and here I am."

"But how did you get all the way out *here?*"

"I took a taxi from the airport. I didn't want to risk driving on unfamiliar roads."

"A taxi! That must have cost a fortune."

"Actually it *was* a little more than I had planned on."

Loni noticed the book lying beside David on the grass.

"It's my journal!" she exclaimed.

"You left it. I decided to return it to you in person."

At last Loni knew she wasn't dreaming. It *was* David! It was exactly the kind of thing the real David would do.

"Did you . . . ?" she began.

"Read it?"

Loni nodded.

"Do you need to ask?"

"No," she said, smiling. "I know you would never do such a thing."

"I confess I did open the cover. I walked about the Cottage trying to find some clue as to what had happened to you. The study upstairs was open. I saw the book. The instant I read your name I closed it. It has remained closed ever since. I knew it was not meant for anyone else's eyes."

"This book is *me,*" she said, "or at least my attempt to discover who I am. Maybe in a way this journal represents my quest to discover my true name. I have too many names to deal with—the *Emily* that was always my middle name and I had no idea why, the mysterious *Tulloch* that appeared in the letter from Jason MacNaughton. Most of all it's the confusion between *Alonnah* and *Loni*."

"Why confusion? Most people have nicknames."

"Loni is not just a nickname. It has been my identity until very recently, until the fateful letter from Jason began unraveling my well-ordered world."

She went on to explain how the name Loni had come about, and about her changing persona since being in the Shetlands.

"In a way I am feeling that the two halves of my identity may slowly be coming into harmony."

"All that's in this journal?"

"A lot of it, yes. But seriously, David—what are you doing here?"

"You left your journal," he replied with a twinkle in his eye. "I thought it the gentlemanly thing to do to get it back to its owner without delay."

Loni laughed. "*Really,* David . . . has something happened on the island?"

"Only your leaving without saying a word."

Loni glanced away. "I know," she said softly. "I'm embarrassed about that. I'm sorry."

"So it's my turn to ask *why*. Why did you leave so suddenly?"

"It's complicated," said Loni with a sigh. "There were things I was dealing with . . . personal things."

"Care to elaborate?"

Again Loni drew in a deep breath and let it out slowly.

"No, I don't want to elaborate," she replied. "But if I don't tell you it will gnaw at me until I do. Secrets, you know. Now that we've got this unofficial pact about openness, I don't suppose I have any choice."

"If you're uncomfortable, I hereby withdraw the pact."

"That is kind of you, David . . . really. But I will have to tell you eventually."

Loni paused briefly.

"In a nutshell, then," she began, "after our evening together at your house—and I hope you don't misunderstand . . . it was one of the most special evenings I've ever spent—but afterward I realized that it might not be fair to Audney, and you of course, for me . . . you know, if people talked about my being there alone so late with you . . . and what Audney might think."

"What does Audney have to do with it?" asked David.

"You and Audney . . . I didn't want to get in the middle of that and cause awkwardness for either of you."

"In the middle of what?"

"You and Audney."

David stared back with a bewildered expression. "I'm sorry," he said. "I'm totally confused. There is no Audney and me, except that she has been my best friend for years. I mean, I love Audney like a sister, but there's nothing that either of us would feel awkward about because you and I spent the evening together."

"Like a . . . *sister?*" repeated Loni.

David nodded. "Of course."

"What exactly do you mean, there is no you and Audney?"

"What do you mean what do I mean?" said David, growing still more confused.

"I'm talking about you and Audney. Your engagement."

"What engagement?"

"You and Audney being engaged to be married."

"Married!" exclaimed David.

"Yes. Aren't you and Audney engaged?"

"Where did you get an idea like that?"

"Didn't you propose to her?"

"Well . . . yes, I guess I sort of did," replied David.

"Sort of?"

"I mean . . . yes, I proposed to her."

"And that's why I left. I didn't want to get in the middle of it."

"But, Alonnah—that was eight, maybe ten years ago."

"Oh," said Loni in surprise. "That's, uh . . . a long engagement."

"That's what I've been trying to tell you—there is no engagement. She turned me down."

Loni stared back at him, wondering if she had heard him right.

"Audney turned me down," David repeated. "We have been the best of friends ever since, just as we were before."

"But I assumed . . . I heard two ladies in the

village talking about you and Audney. They were talking as if the two of you were engaged. Suddenly I thought I'd stumbled into the middle of something where I didn't belong."

"I should have suspected something like that," said David. "I knew there must be a misunderstanding." He laughed lightly. "I must say," he added, "if you are going to be part of the Whales Reef community, you should know that the gossiping old wives are not to be depended on. There are some who still think that Audney and I belong together."

"Are you still in love with her?"

"I was never in love with her."

"Now I am really confused! Why did you propose?"

"I knew she was in love with me. I wanted to make her happy. At the time I thought it was the right thing to do."

"And?"

"Audney was wise enough to know that I didn't love her in the same way she loved me. Her love was selfless enough to tell me so. She said that there was a woman somewhere I would fall in love with one day, and that she did not intend to steal affections that belonged to another. She loved me enough to turn me down."

"That is amazing. Nobody does that."

"Audney Kerr did. She said that there was also someone who would one day love *her* as a woman needed to be loved and that she would love him even more than she loved me. She said that she was willing to wait for that man, whoever he was."

"That man, I take it, is not Hardy?"

"Assuredly it is not Hardy! She is still waiting. She would rather not marry until fifty, or ever, than marry the wrong man. Being single is no disgrace in God's eyes. Marrying unwisely is."

Loni was struggling to get her head around this complete reversal of what she had been thinking since leaving the island.

"All right," she said at length. "That's why I left Whales Reef. It is obvious that I misunderstood the situation, and I feel stupid now for behaving rashly."

"It's not worth sackcloth and ashes."

"Just give me the luxury of wallowing in my foolishness. But that doesn't explain why you're here. And I *know* it wasn't just to bring me my journal, so don't try that one again. You may be a gentleman, but I don't buy that line for a second!"

David laughed, and then grew serious.

"I do owe you an explanation," he said. "The fact is, when it was clear you were gone, I realized I wasn't willing to lose what had become a special friendship. I wasn't willing not to see you again. I missed you."

He paused and drew in a thoughtful breath.

"When the uncertainty of the inheritance was

at its worst," he went on, "my aunt once accused me of being too passive. She said that as chief I should fight for it. I told her I wouldn't fight for something unless I knew it was right. I told her I hoped I had the courage to fight for what I believed in. But I also told her a man has to choose when and where to fight. After you left, I knew that such a moment had come. It was time to fight for a friendship I did not want to lose."

58
WHO AM I?

An hour later Loni and David were still seated cross-legged on the grass in the small meadow that, before that day, Loni had always considered her private discovery of solitude.

"I can still hardly believe my grandfather told you about this place," she said. "I am learning more about my grandparents than I ever dreamed."

"I don't suppose any of us know our parents—or in your case, your grandparents—as well as we think. Now that I am a man, there are so many things I wish I could ask my father. When you're young, you are too wrapped up in yourself to realize how important those memories will be later."

"I can't help feeling guilty for that. But then . . ." Loni added with a wistful smile as she paused.

"What is it?" asked David.

"I was just going to say that I didn't know myself either. I never really knew who I was. I'm still trying to figure it out. Going to Scotland, the inheritance, even meeting you—it's all helping me discover the answer to that all-important question."

"Why meeting me?"

"I don't know. After I got angry with you for not telling me you were the chief, I had to do some hard soul-searching. I realized you were not really as complicated as I had tried to make you. You *weren't* trying to hide anything from me—you were who you were. I mean, you are *David*. You aren't sometimes Dave, at other times a boyishly conflicted Davey. You are just David. You are *always* David, an integrated whole. You are at peace being David Tulloch. There are not two David Tullochs. There's just one, and he's you. You know who you are. You are comfortable in your own skin. I admire that. I probably envy it."

"And you?"

"It's different with me," replied Loni. "All of that is foreign. I'm *not* an integrated whole. My different selves are in conflict. At least that's been the case up until now. It's related to my lifelong uncertainty about my mother and my roots. Sometimes I'm Loni. Then I went to the Shetlands—and it all started with the letter from Jason MacNaughton addressed to *Alonnah Tulloch Ford*.

"Who is that? I wondered. The name on the envelope was a complete stranger. The unknown Alonnah of my childhood who had no mother became Alonnah *Tulloch,* and Loni didn't know who she was." She paused, smiled. "When I went to college and said to myself, and everyone else, 'From now on I'm going to be known as Loni,' I was only trying to fool myself into thinking I could stuff the *Alonnah* into a cupboard and pretend she didn't exist. But she was always there, always wondering who she really was and where she had come from, looking out from a crack in the cupboard, staring at me with her big childlike eyes of confusion and question: My name is Alonnah. Who am I?"

"I see what you mean," said David. "This hasn't just been about inheriting the property. Your entire sense of who you are has been at stake."

Loni nodded. "Self-knowing, I guess," she said with a smile. "The eternal question of humanity: Who am I?"

"There is a very perceptive line in one of George MacDonald's novels that pinpoints the universal question—*'I dinna ken whaur I come frae'* . . . I don't know where I come from. It is such an insightful cry of the human heart."

"That's me," said Loni. "All my life I haven't known where I came from. Then I landed on Whales Reef, and an entire family heritage overwhelmed me. Maybe that's partly why I left too. I suppose I needed time to absorb it all."

"And do you have it resolved?" asked David.

"Not yet," laughed Loni. "But I hope I'm getting there."

"Things are clarifying for you, then?"

"In some ways, but these things take time to sort themselves out in your depths. You don't just change your self-perception overnight. I realize that I'm *both* Loni and Alonnah. Now I just have to figure out how the two can live together, and how the *Tulloch* and *Ford* names fit into my new persona. And there's my middle name *Emily* in there too."

Loni climbed to her feet and glanced around the meadow. It was not just hers anymore. Henceforth her private world of solitude would always be shared with this gentle Scottish "chief" she had not even known existed two months ago.

"Maybe we should head back to the house," she said. "By the way, where are you . . . I mean, what are your plans? Are you staying—?"

"Your grandparents asked me if I would stay the night," said David.

"Oh, wonderful!" exclaimed Loni. "There's so much I want to show you—our church, where I went to school, the farms of some of my relatives."

"It sounds like you love it here."

"I am learning to. Yes, for the first time in my life, I think I do."

59

SPIRITUAL CONNECTIONS

Returning to the Ford home through fields of ripening corn, Loni gave David as complete an account of her past as she had verbalized to anyone.

"This terrain is certainly different from Whales Reef," David was saying. "It is so warm and humid. It's never like this in the Shetlands."

"It's nice here now. But winters can be long and cold."

"Do you get snow?"

"Sometimes a foot. That is rare, but it can build up to that and more."

They climbed over the fence, crossed the road, and started down the long drive toward the house. A white-haired figure stood watching their approach.

"The perfect image of the prodigal's waiting father," said David. "Not to suggest a comparison between you and the prodigal, it's the picture of the father in the distance that struck me."

"Perhaps there is more than a little truth in the parallel," said Loni. "Prodigality doesn't necessarily always mean drugs and crime or the life of a wastrel. I'm sure it takes as many forms as does home-going."

"You're right. I was merely reminded of the image of God's Fatherhood—always waiting expectantly for us, in the sense, as you say, that we are *all* prodigals in our own way."

They continued to the house. Returning her grandfather's smile, Loni went to him. He opened his arms and received her into his embrace.

"Grandpa," she whispered. "You knew about my special place all along."

Her grandfather merely held her close. David continued up the steps to the porch and inside.

For the rest of the afternoon David and William Ford talked like old friends. Their conversation ranged from theology to favorite books, from Studebakers and tractors to animal husbandry and crops and weather, even to woodwork, in which David, an admitted amateur, was full of questions for the man whose craftsmanship had been turning out handmade furnishings for half a century. With the eager humility of a son, David listened and absorbed the wisdom of the older man's years.

"Some of Alonnah's happiest memories are of this place," said Mr. Ford, smiling nostalgically as he and David walked through his workshop and the former showroom, filled with half-completed pieces he was working on. The aroma of oil and lacquer and sawdust filled David with reminders of another Carpenter's shop long ago, the very workshop and training ground of Saviorhood.

"This was where Alonnah got her first taste of the business world," said Mr. Ford. "Once she began interacting with customers, she was hooked. I should have seen then, like Scuffy the Tugboat, that she was meant for bigger things."

Loni saw from an occasional glance that her grandmother was in awe of the fact that David was chief of a Scottish clan, however small it might be. Mrs. Ford was also deliriously happy to have *two* guests to make up rooms and cook for. She and Loni kept busy in the kitchen all afternoon. The spread they set on the table for supper was a feast that could have fed a dozen hungry men—roast beef and mashed potatoes, gravy, biscuits with fresh honey, peas, green beans, coleslaw, with three pies waiting in readiness—apple, chess, and shoo-fly, the latter two completely new experiences for David.

The four talked all evening. Abundant stories from Loni's childhood kept the conversation animated. For the first time in her life Loni was able to appreciate her early years in new ways, aided by the fact that most of the stories were accompanied by David's infectious laughter. Popcorn and hot chocolate followed about nine, with no letup in the conversational flow.

David was momentarily taken off guard when Loni shifted the conversation in his direction.

"David, do you remember when we were on the way back from Lerwick and you said that your spiritual story was a long one? I am just as interested in yours as you are in mine."

"My turn to unburden the secrets of my past, eh?" said David.

"If I can, it shouldn't be so hard for you," said Loni with a grin.

"Touché!" laughed David. "But I would not want to bore your grandparents," he added.

"No fear of that, son," said Mr. Ford. "Nothing is more interesting, nor eternally important, than an individual's quest for truth, especially if that quest leads to God."

David became thoughtful. "There are more similarities in our stories than you might imagine," he began after a minute. "Both my parents are gone too."

"I am sorry to hear that," said Mr. Ford.

David nodded in appreciation. "My mother died only seven years ago. I knew both my parents, so I did not face the pain you did, Alonnah," he said, glancing toward Loni. "The loss of my father, however, was very traumatic. I was fourteen."

"What a devastating age to lose a father," said Mrs. Ford tenderly.

"He was a fisherman," David went on. "He went down at sea. The curse of Shetland life. I was so overwhelmed when I heard that his boat had gone down, I almost jumped off one of the island's cliffs."

"Goodness! I'm glad you didn't!" exclaimed Loni.

"Me too," said David. "That's where my quest to find God began, standing on the edge of the North Cliffs. I had just lost my father. Yet from out of the wind, swirling in the storm and the turbulence within my own soul, I heard the words, *I am your Father . . . find your Father.* It reminds me of what you told me, Alonnah, about how Quakers speak of God revealing himself inwardly."

"The Light Within," said Mr. Ford. "It sounds to me as if God's inner Light indeed revealed itself to you in that moment."

David smiled. "It saved my life," he said. "However the words or sensations came, they filled me with a sense of quiet, not exactly peace but calm enough to keep me from throwing myself over the side. Gradually I knew God had spoken to me. Over the years that followed, though I was young and the process lasted well into adulthood, I saw that we all have two fathers, and that our earthly fathers are given us so that ultimately we might discover our heavenly Father. Some, like you, Alonnah, face the challenge of discovering God's Fatherhood in the absence of earthly fatherhood altogether. I'm sure that isn't easy."

"No, it hasn't been easy," said Loni, "but I have had the best *grand*father in the world to demonstrate fatherhood to me." She gave her grandfather a childlike smile. "And I continue to see more of what I was unable to perceive as a child. But I have been curious, David, as you told me, why your experience turned you away from the church if it brought you closer to God."

"That is the other side to my struggle to find faith."

David paused, and the room remained quiet a few moments.

"We, too, would very much like to hear your story, son," said Mr. Ford.

David continued to gather his thoughts.

60

THE CANCER OF SPIRITUAL ELITISM

"I'm afraid one of my proclivities is always to start at the beginning of things," David began. "Every book I write begins with creation," he added, chuckling.

"Not a bad starting point," said Mr. Ford.

"My editors struggle with it a bit! They think I should get to the point quicker. In any event, my personal story is intrinsically tied to the religious history of Scotland. Many people are unaware of it, but Scotland was the second primary greenhouse, along with Geneva, where the Protestant Reformation flourished. Because of that, Scotland has been a deeply religious country for centuries. The Presbyterian Church of Scotland has dominated both religion and politics since the early 1600s."

"I was not aware of that," said Loni.

"Intrinsic to the whole reformational mentality," said David, "has been an emphasis on experiential outpourings of spiritual fervor."

"The same tendency exists in our history," said Mr. Ford. "In spite of our reputation of sitting silently in church, the followers of George Fox were so rowdy with jumping and stomping and shouting that they caused what was called 'quaking.' That's where the name came from. They were the original Pentecostals, you might say, though without the speaking in tongues."

David nodded. "I had occasion to learn some of that during my study of the history of British religious movements at Oxford."

"Oxford! So we are in the presence of the intelligentsia," chuckled Mr. Ford.

"Hardly that, I assure you."

"I don't know—Alonnah tells us you write books. That sounds like academia to me."

"A sideline," laughed David. "But I am fascinated by Quakerism, not only about George Fox and William Penn, but also your American John Woolman."

"Ah yes, our great antislavery advocate. Have you heard of Thomas Kelly?" asked Mr. Ford.

"The name rings a slight bell," replied David.

"He was a recent Quaker of the 1930s and '40s. He is a great favorite of mine."

"I think I mentioned him to you, David," said Loni. "I found one of his books out in the barn here and then discovered the same title in Ernest's study. Oh, Grandpa, I would love to show you that room in the Cottage!"

Mr. Ford shook his head. "I can hardly imagine myself gallivanting off to the wilds of Scotland! But continue with your story, son," he said to David.

David smiled. "I was making the point that emotional experientialism is deeply rooted in the reformational Protestantism of Scotland. One of the results has been a revivalist mentality. People are always on the lookout for new manifestations and enthusiastic outbreaks and mass conversions. Prophecy often also plays an important role in new movements. Swashbuckling new teachings promising the revelation that Jesus is coming back soon always attract great crowds."

"It has been exactly the same on this side of the Atlantic," said Mr. Ford.

"The effect is that periodic revivals have been part of evangelicalism's religious history for centuries. These are often led by evangelists, preachers, and prophets with the ability to stir the masses. Your George Fox is a perfect example, perhaps even a prototype of the evangelicals who followed—Jonathan Edwards, the Wesley brothers, Moody, Spurgeon, Whitfield, even Billy Graham in recent years. And the common thread is usually evident that such movements originate with a single dynamic individual whose teaching or preaching or writing attracts a following. Would you agree, Mr. Ford?"

Loni's grandfather nodded. "With the sad result that pride easily replaces humility, influence replaces truth, and division is the inevitable result."

"Exactly," rejoined David. "Obviously it doesn't always happen. Yet the danger is there nonetheless. With the best of motives, the lure of attracting a following seduces the best of men."

Both the young Scotsman and the aging Quaker were grieved by the words David had just spoken.

"What often ensues in large movements and small," he went on, "is that the leaders of movements become infected with a sense of their own power, of their ability to stir a crowd, to sway masses to embrace their teachings. Certainly many dynamic Christian leaders are humble and honorable, and no doubt usually the evangelistic motive is present. I'm sure it was with Fox, the desire to further God's kingdom. Yet I don't think the allure of the crowd to human vanity can be altogether discounted either."

"You have great insight into the dynamic of spiritual movements, son," said Mr. Ford. "That is exactly what took place with George Fox. I would say that pride in his oratory became his thorn in the flesh."

"Then the travel sets in. You have British preachers and evangelists traveling to America, bringing whatever new twist of revival or experiential Christianity defines their particular brand, going 'on tour,' as they used to say. And you have Americans doing exactly the same thing, going across to our side of the pond."

"Again, though you are speaking of Scotland's history, you have pinpointed one of Quakerism's historical tendencies as well. Our John Woolman died while on tour to Quaker fellowships in England."

"I had no idea," said David.

Mr. Ford nodded. "A sad story. He contracted smallpox while in England."

"From my limited knowledge, however," said David, "I don't think Quakers generally were traveling to draw crowds."

"You're right. Small home meetings of encouragement were the goal."

"Just the opposite has usually been the case in evangelicalism," said David. "The measure of success is always the size of the crowd. Yet revivals and faith healing shows often teach fringe doctrines, promising the faithful various manifestations and blessings if they practice the good Reverend So-and-So's particular methods and endorse his teachings. And of course contribute money to his ministry."

"That sounds cynical," said Loni.

"Don't be so sure, Alonnah," said her grandfather. "Your young Scotsman has great insight. I fear he has pinpointed a common thread. Go on," he said to David.

"I am not primarily speaking of the potential lure of financial opportunism," David continued, "though that is a legitimate problem. What concerns me more deeply is the division that results between the so-called haves and have-nots, between those who are part of the new revival and who make public displays of the new manifestations of spiritual gifts, and those who are *not* part of it. I call it the cancer of spiritual elitism.

"There have been several instances of such division in the historic denominations of Scotland, including splits that actually resulted in the identification of 'Exclusive' branches growing out of the parent tree."

David went on to outline some of this history in detail and how it related to his own spiritual journey. "You will scarcely believe it," he said, "when I tell you that to this day there are some exclusivist Christians who will not break bread with those from other denominations than their own."

61
PARTNERS OF NECESSITY

Whales Reef, Shetland Islands

Jimmy Joe McLeod had been cooling his heels in these frigid islands far longer than he'd planned. The whisky was good, but the coffee was terrible. And the weather was worse.

He'd waited around five days for the Ford girl to contact him. The driving rain all day Sunday kept him mostly inside. By the first of the week he was going stir-crazy. He'd visited all his holdings in the Shetlands and everything on Thorburn's list of possible sites that were for sale. Then the letter from the ungrateful minx giving him the brush-off had sent him into a tirade that had only partially moderated by the time he had Ross Thorburn on the phone. In a conversation replete with expletives, he filled in his second in command on the situation.

"I'm not about to just walk away with my tail between my legs," he barked. "We need to come up with a new angle. I want ideas, Thorburn. You're the one who has been handling this thing, so you find me a solution or I'll find someone who will."

"What is that intended to imply, Mr. McLeod?" asked Thorburn with edge in his tone.

"You know what it means, Thorburn! Don't make me spell it out."

Thorburn thought better of pursuing his growing annoyance with the overbearing Texan. "When you were on the island," he said, "did you have occasion to meet any of the other principal players—the two cousins?" he asked.

"Didn't have the pleasure," replied Jimmy Joe sarcastically.

"It might be worth our while to canvass the views of the fisherman at this stage. Our solicitors in Edinburgh tell me he is desirous of contesting the court's findings."

"What are his chances?"

"Slim to none. But it tells us that he is not willing to give up without a fight. That could work to our advantage."

"How's it gonna do that?"

"I am only suggesting, as his interests dovetail with our own, that he might be an ally in our attempt to gain control of the island. If you are willing to remain where you are another few days, I think this might be the time for you to meet our Mr. Tulloch face-to-face."

"Then let's get this ol' boy into town and rustle us up a plan!"

Ever the uncomplaining assistant, Ross Thorburn swallowed whatever might have been his reaction to his employer's demanding importunity and did what he always did—Jimmy Joe McLeod's bidding.

Hardy Tulloch walked into the Craigsmont Lounge in Lerwick, gratified again to find a full pitcher of beer awaiting him. He had not yet met the Texan, but the instant he walked into the room he knew who he was. Ross Thorburn, whom he had met previously, was a slender though unusually powerful man for his five-foot-nine frame and limp. But the huge man in boots and hat striding across the floor dwarfed Hardy by as much as Hardy did the diminutive Scotsman.

"How do, partner!" boomed Jimmy Joe. "Heard a heap about you, son—good to shake your hand at last . . . and a powerful hand it is!" he added as the two shook hands. "I like that—don't do business with a man whose handshake feels like a dead snake. If a man can't shake hands like he knows what he's about, he ain't got no backbone, that's what I always say."

Hardy had never been intimidated by another man in his life. He showed no sign of it now. The two titans of machismo were both accustomed to getting their own way. Fortunately, their meeting was based on a shared objective, and no clash of wills arose.

To one side Thorburn watched and listened to

the mutual bluster of the two men, keeping no counsel but his own.

"So if I got hold of what you're telling me," Jimmy Joe was saying, "for you to get your hands on the property, you gotta shake the Ford gal loose. But she's kin to the firstborn son a hundred years back or whenever it was."

"'Tis aboot the size o' it," said Hardy, nodding. "He went til America an' a'body said he gave up the inheritance, or was disinherited by his daddy."

"The boy didn't want it?"

"Some folk say the Auld Tulloch cut him off."

"If that's true, she'd have no right to it, if her granddaddy was cut off. Any proof of that?"

"None I ever heard aboot," replied Hardy.

"Then we gotta get us some proof. Who's living in the place now that the girl's here?"

"Nobody. An' she's gone hersel'."

"*Gone*—where'd she go?"

"I dinna ken. She left a couple days ago."

"Nobody else is there?"

"The housekeeper an' her brither's at the Auld Hoose."

"There's *nobody* at the big house?"

Hardy shook his head.

"Well, that's it, son!" Jimmy Joe boomed. "We'll go in and have us a look. Ain't a lock been built that I can't pick."

"The door won't be locked."

"So much the better!"

"But the auld man's study's been boarded up fifty years or more. They say it's got a deid body inside. That's likely where his records an' files an' sich like would be."

"Sounds fun to me! We'll bust it down and have a look for ourselves."

62

FOUNTAIN OF DARKNESS

Southern Pennsylvania

"All this is a long way around to get to the root of my own spiritual crisis," said David, "and I apologize for taking so long—"

"No. This is fascinating, and with many parallels to Quakerism," interrupted Mr. Ford. "We have suffered our own controversies, doctrinal disputes, leadership squabbles, and splits. Please, go on . . . we are extremely interested."

"You are very kind," laughed David. "Not everyone would be so gracious."

"No apologies needed, I assure you," said Mr. Ford. "I find your story fascinating."

"Well, then, to make a long story just a little longer . . . my life intersected with this history I have outlined when I was about ten. The American cousin of our school teacher came from the

United States with her husband preaching a corrupt form of experientialism in the extreme. Signs and wonders, healings, and speaking in tongues were all part of their bag of tricks to beguile and impress and sway the people."

"Were they affiliated with any of the denominations you mentioned earlier?"

"No, but their influence was even more exclusivist. I learned much later that the man was not a pastor at all. He had left his family, had an affair, subsequently married the young woman, and started a home Bible study where they honed their cultish ways. They called their little home church the Fountain of Light. As their appetite for influence grew, they expanded their horizons, until eventually the woman's cousin invited them for an extended visit to the Shetlands."

"What happened?"

"They turned the island of Whales Reef on its head. The gullible community was mesmerized. People flocked to their meetings and were putty in their hands. Speaking in tongues and the laying on of hands and exuberant singing and dancing and supposed healings and all manner of spiritual outpourings followed. Their meetings became emotional free-for-alls."

"Surely everybody on the island was not swept into it?" said Loni.

"Thankfully no," replied David. "But enough to

split the community between those who had seen the light and those who hadn't. This elitist mentality is deeply ingrained in the Scottish spiritual psyche dating back to the late 1500s when Calvinist reformer John Knox thundered against Catholic Mary Queen of Scots, when reformers burned at the stake heretics who did not endorse their intolerant form of Christianity. It has been part of our history right down to the Brethren exclusivists of forty and fifty years ago. Exclusivism is part and parcel of Scotland's religious heritage."

"What you are describing is simply a microcosm of the universal problem of judgmentalism within Christendom," said Mr. Ford.

"I suppose you're right, and our island was just a microcosm on a smaller scale of the same thing. In Whales Reef, the self-styled *Sister Grace* and *Brother Wisdom* found fertile soil to spread their cult-like teaching.

"The division was dreadful. Families were sundered. Neighbor refused to speak to neighbor. The church was taken over with the teaching. The Fountainites would literally cross the street and refuse to greet the reprobate non-Fountainites. Three deaths resulted directly from it."

"I can't believe it—that's horrible," said Loni.

David drew in a breath. "As you know, Loni, one of those was my best friend. It is little wonder that the experience scarred me deeply. I am sorry to say that it sowed seeds of bitterness in my heart toward my father for not stepping in and sending the two Americans away. Neither he nor my mother became Fountainites. But I could not understand why my father did not take a public stand against it. That's what made his death all the harder. I knew I had harbored resentments. Suddenly he was dead and I had guilt to add to the trauma of losing him.

"The whole experience turned me away from the church and organized Christian movements. The pastor of our kirk at the time allowed such division to reign in the community that I completely lost respect for the church and its clergy. I confess it also made me wary of Americans. I am embarrassed to say that I struggled when I learned about you," he said, turning to Loni. "I feared another American coming to upset and divide our community."

"I hope I will not do that," said Loni with a smile.

"I know you well enough to be sure you will not," rejoined David. "But all this explains why my spiritual quest has been an inward one. Over the years, of course, I had to take my resentments and guilt to the Lord for healing. And I grew capable of thinking about matters of spirituality on more profound levels than as a boy. The chieftainship came to matter to me more than my own life. I vowed that never again would any man or woman steal the legacy of my people or work division among them. And never again would a chief remain silent when its people were threatened by evil or falsehood."

"I think I am at last beginning to understand," said Loni. "Thank you for sharing all that, David. Much more makes sense now." She turned to her grandfather. "I told David last week, Grandpa, that you would like him. That was before I knew his story. But I sensed that the two of you would be kindred spirits."

"She also said he might make a Quaker of me," put in David. "What do you think, Mr. Ford?" said David with the hint of a smile.

"I would never try such a thing," replied Loni's grandfather seriously. "My days of thinking we Quakers have a corner on truth are long gone. Your father, Alonnah, in his own way, taught me that."

"How so, Grandpa?" asked Loni.

"His leaving the Fellowship made us realize how we had unknowingly allowed legalism to infiltrate our beliefs too. No one is immune. We must be constantly on guard. Legalism, experientialism, and elitism, as you point out, David, are cancers to which Christianity is almost abnormally susceptible."

"How can they be prevented, Grandpa?" asked Loni.

Mr. Ford looked at David. "Would you care to answer her?"

"I would rather hear your response. Loni is forever saying, 'My grandfather would say this,' or 'My grandfather would say that.' I am eager to know how you would answer her question."

Tears filled Mr. Ford's eyes at David's words. "I would say, then," he replied, blinking hard, "that if one is not actively living the principles inherent in the commands of Jesus, and seeking diligently to live life at the Center, the twin evils of doctrinal legalism and experientialism will almost always corrupt even the most vital expressions of our faith.

"From my limited vantage point I would say that the Quaker emphasis on quietude has provided a helpful antidote against the excesses of experientialism from which all of Christendom could learn. However, legalism lies in wait everywhere. Even the most radiant experience of the Light Within, if it leads not to obedience to Christ's commands, will become but one more spoiled blossom on the long history of experientialism in the church. To answer your question, Alonnah, the only preventative to legalism is obedience."

63

THE ROLLTOP DESK

The next morning after a farmer's breakfast of American pancakes with maple syrup, Loni led David outside toward the barn.

"I knew my grandfather would take to you," she said. "And my grandmother! I could not believe last night. They're always in bed by nine, but they were still going strong hours after that."

"They are a fascinating and energetic man and woman," said David. "How old are they?"

"They're both over eighty."

"That is hard to believe. They seem in their fifties."

They entered the dusky interior, where Loni proceeded to pull the chains for the bulbs hanging overhead. Each new burst of light brought exclamations from David as he took in the sights and smells of the huge building filled with old farm machinery and tools and bits of old furniture.

"I love this place!" said David. "What a heaven to grow up in."

"I want to show you where my recent saga began," said Loni as they continued into the depths of the barn. "It's where the remnants of my

441

Tulloch past were buried so far out of sight that no one knew about them."

She led the way to the far end of the building. They came to a stop in front of the rolltop desk.

"It looks just like the desk you showed me in the study at the Cottage," said David.

"It is an exact replica made by Brogan after he returned to the States following his father's funeral," said Loni. "Actually he made them both."

"He must have been quite a craftsman."

"That trait seems to run on both sides of the family. Brogan's son was Grant Tulloch, my other grandfather."

Loni opened a drawer and pulled out the box of business cards. She handed one to David.

He read aloud, *"Tulloch Fine Furnishings and Antiques—Old World Craftsmanship with Modern Functionality: Grant Tulloch, Philadelphia, Pennsylvania."*

"Grant's daughter was my mother, Alison, who married the Fords' son, Chad."

"So this is where your Scottish heritage merges with your American roots," said David, "in the back of a barn in an old forgotten desk in the farmland of Pennsylvania. An incredible story."

"Your being here, in its own way, adds to the completion of the circle," said Loni. "You are also related to these people—not directly like me, but tracing our parallel lineage back to old Ernest."

"All these years *you* didn't know about your mother's family, while over in the Shetlands *we* didn't know what became of Brogan. Suddenly both mysteries are solved."

"It is amazing when you think about it. The clues to both mysteries were in this desk, so intrinsically linked to its twin in the mysterious locked room of the Cottage. Everything converges here."

Loni began searching again, more meticulously than she had a month earlier. "When I was here before, I had no idea what I was looking for. I just rummaged about haphazardly. Now I am wondering if there is more we can discover about those years when the Tulloch name in America was lost sight of to its Shetland cousins."

After a few minutes, she withdrew an unlabeled manila envelope from one of the lower drawers. She lifted it out, peered inside, and took out a smaller envelope. She opened it and withdrew two sheets of thin parchment. Her eyes widened as she quickly scanned it.

"Oh, my goodness," she said. "How could I have missed this before?"

"What did you find?" asked David.

"It's a letter from my father to his parents . . . my grandparents!"

Loni sat down on a dusty chair and began to read.

"He must never have sent it," she murmured.

Her voice was scarcely audible. "It's dated 1975, the year after I was born."

After another minute she looked up to where David stood waiting. "This explains so much," she said, wiping her eyes with the back of her hand. "I don't know if I should show it to them. I am reading my own father's words when he was younger than I am now."

David listened attentively but offered no comment.

"It will break their hearts to see it," Loni said as if thinking aloud. "Though maybe in a good way. I have to show it to them."

With tears flowing freely, Loni handed David the letter.

> Dear Mother and Father, he read.
>
> I hardly know where to begin, so I will just say that I love you and am sorry for the heartache I have caused you. I honor and treasure my Quaker roots, and the training in spiritual values you gave me. I would not be the man I am without you. I am grateful beyond words.
>
> It was always my intention to work in the business and continue your tradition, Dad. I fully expected to marry in the Fellowship. When I started traveling to sell your work to stores and suppliers, I never imagined deviating from that

course. I certainly never expected to fall in love. But as much business as we did supplying Grant Tulloch of Philadelphia with your pieces, and being away from home as much as I was, this meant that occasionally I found myself invited to the Tulloch home. Grant was friendly to me and, knowing I was a Quaker, as was his family, and without a son of his own, I suppose he took me under his wing. Thus it was that I met his daughter Alison and unexpectedly I did fall in love.

At first it did not occur to me that this would cause division between us since Alison's family were faithful Quakers. I see how naïve I was and that I should have discussed it with you and sought your counsel ahead of time. But when it became clear that the more progressive leanings of Alison's family were not compatible with the beliefs of our Fellowship, I pulled away, and eventually, of course, we were married, not in secret exactly because her family was part of it, but in secret from you.

I am so sorry. I was wrong in how I handled it. I was young and so sure that Alison and I were meant for each other that I'm afraid the hubris of youth overpowered my good judgment. My parents-in-law, Grant and Mary, both urged me to talk to you and nearly withheld their blessing until I did. But I was headstrong. When they saw that we would probably elope if they made an issue of it, they reluctantly gave in.

That was four years ago. I now see the wisdom in what Grant and Mary advised. I am not a great deal older and wiser, but at least I am a little older and I hope becoming a little wiser. I want to see you and make amends. I am even hoping that a way might somehow open for us to work together again. At present I am assisting Grant in his business, but my dream is to bring the Ford and Tulloch businesses together.

Whatever may be your thoughts, however, and I know such may not be possible, mostly I simply want to see you. In fact, now that I have written this, I think I would rather tell you everything in person. I don't think I will mail this. I want to ask your forgiveness face-to-face. I want you to know Alison and learn to love her like I do.

And of course I want you to hold our dear little Alonnah in your arms, your granddaughter, the new light of our lives.

Your loving son,
Chad

The mood in the Ford home that evening after Loni's grandparents had read the unsent letter from their son was nothing like that of the previous night. They had leftovers for supper around a subdued and somber table. There was no popcorn later. Neither did David's laughter sound as they sat talking quietly and as Loni's grandmother wept softly.

"What happened when my parents were killed?" asked Loni.

"Black ice on the road," answered Mr. Ford. "A car from the opposite direction skidded and forced them off the road."

"How did I survive the crash?"

"The police said that the only explanation was a miracle, that an angel must have been in the back seat with you. The driver's and passenger seats were crushed beyond hope. But it was as though an invisible barrier went up between the front and back seats. They found you strapped in your car seat, crying but without a scratch. It happened not far from here. One of the policemen knew us, and when the identification was made, brought you to us. We contacted Grant with the news. He had lost his wife to cancer the year before you were born, and his mother only a few months after your birth. He was hit with too much grief all at once. Learning of his daughter's death sent him into a deep depression. By mutual consent we decided that we would raise you. Despondent and without a wife, poor Grant was in no position to care for a baby. He went into a long, slow decline after that and never really recovered. We contacted him a few times and tried to learn what we could about your mother and Chad. But he cut himself off, not only from us but from everyone."

David said little, feeling like an intruder in the deep personal griefs that had been hanging over the family since before Loni was born. By the end of the evening, however, though he had only known the Fords a day and Loni a month, he was forever bound up in the life of this dear family.

On this evening all four were in their rooms by nine.

Fifteen minutes later, Loni heard a light knock. The door opened a crack.

"Come in, Grandma," said Loni, who was seated in a chair opposite the bed and had just opened her great-grandmother's journal.

In her robe, Mrs. Ford walked in and sat down on the edge of the bed.

"I hope you won't feel me intruding, dear," she said. "I haven't really come to tuck you in like I used to."

"I could jump under the covers and let you," said Loni with a smile.

"That isn't what I wanted to talk to you about. Though it is tempting. Childhood always disappears much too fast for those watching from the outside. Children are anxious to escape it. Parents and grandparents never have enough of it."

Mrs. Ford paused. Her eyes were still red from the evening.

"I wanted to thank you for sharing Chad's letter with us," she said at length. "I'm sure you must have wondered if you should, knowing it would be painful."

Loni nodded. "I did. But I felt you would want to know."

"It was painful, of course, to be reminded of the tragedy. Yet I would not have wanted never to know how he felt. God bless the dear boy—it warmed my heart to hear his words, tears and all. Thank you again."

"Of course, Grandma."

Mrs. Ford rose to go, then turned. "Your David is one of the nicest young men I have ever met."

"He is something special," agreed Loni.

"When you and he are talking, you have the same look in your eyes you used to have in the showroom. He is good for you, Alonnah. I can see that you care for him."

Loni rose from the chair. She embraced her grandmother affectionately. "Thank you, Grandma, for everything you did for me. I love you."

"I love you too, dear. Good night, Alonnah."

"Good night, Grandma."

As soon as her grandmother was gone, Loni again opened the journal and returned her attention to her great-grandmother's story from ninety years before.

64
DUTY AND DESTINY

Without definite plans and having no idea what to expect when he arrived in the States, David had purchased a round-trip ticket and was scheduled to return on Friday. After two days at her grandparents', however, Loni was eager also to show him the capital. And she was anxious for David to meet Maddy.

They had not talked specifically about what Loni would do. It was clear that David hoped she would return to Whales Reef. His hints were more than obvious. Though *why* she would do so was ambiguous, and for Loni awkward and unclear. She knew that feelings for David were stirring within her. For his part, David gave no indication what he himself might be feeling. His story about Audney was unsettling to say the least. She was gorgeous. If Audney had not stirred David's blood, thought Loni, why would she? The most he had said was that he did not want to lose the friendship that had sprung up between them.

But what did that mean?

They departed early Friday morning in Loni's rental car, with many fond farewells and hugs and kisses from the Fords. Dressed in the same blue traveling suit she had worn on the train six days earlier, Loni carried the matching jacket to the car and laid it in the back seat, then took the wheel and they set out.

Loni had wanted to leave early to give them time to travel along some of the country roads so that David could see rural America up close and personal. As they drove along Highway 1 toward the Maryland border, David's eye was drawn to the red-brick buildings of a small college on their left.

"Lincoln University," he said as they passed the sign leading into the campus. "That's your most revered president, isn't it?"

"Yes, Abraham Lincoln," answered Loni. "He ended slavery and was then assassinated."

"Is this a famous school?"

"Not that I know of. I wasn't even aware it was here. There are hundreds of schools and buildings and streets named after Lincoln in the U.S. He and George Washington are the most famous names in our history."

"Yes, we are taught something about them along with our own notables."

"Which are?"

"Our history's famous personalities, you mean?" Loni nodded.

"That depends on whether you are asking a Scot or an Englishman!" laughed David.

"I'm asking a Scot."

"I would say Saint Columba, Kenneth MacAlpin, William Wallace, Robert the Bruce, Mary Queen of Scots, and Bonnie Prince Charlie. If you include men of letters, you would have to add Robbie Burns, Sir Walter Scott, Robert Louis Stevenson, and George MacDonald."

"A considerably longer list than ours."

"We have been at it longer."

The car fell silent. Both were silent.

"David," Loni said at length, "would it be too personal for me to ask . . ."

She hesitated.

"Go on," said David. "Nothing is too personal."

"I am embarrassed to ask, but . . . why didn't it work out with Audney? She seems like the sweetest girl in the world, and with such spunk."

"That *is* personal," laughed David.

"Sorry. I'll withdraw the question."

"No, it's okay."

He thought a moment.

"I don't know," he said slowly. "Who can say why love happens? You're right, Audney is sweet and has spunk. She'll take on anyone, including Hardy! As I said, I love her like a sister. But . . . and please understand I do not mean to disparage her in the least—Audney means the world to me—yet like many on the island, Whales Reef is all she knows. That brings with it an innocence that is wonderful, but there are things I can't talk about with Audney. If I can say it like this, her worldview is limited. Much of what interests me would be lost on her. She isn't curious about the wider world and the meaning of life. She takes things as they come and is satisfied with that."

"And you're not?" said Loni.

"No, I'm *not* satisfied to take things as they come. I want more. I want to know what they *mean*. I want to think about big things, to understand life and the world and God and myself more deeply. I'm fascinated and curious about everything life has to teach me. But if I said all that to Audney, she would laugh in her sweet way and say something like, 'Ah, David, ye make my heid spin wi' a' yer theories an' high thoughts.' She wouldn't be mentally hungry enough to try to understand. She knows I've written books but has never even asked to see them. She isn't curious about what makes me tick. It sounds like I am criticizing her, but—"

"No, not at all," said Loni. "I hear the love in your voice."

"I suppose what it boils down to is that our friendship is more superficial than I wish it were. But I take it for what it is and I'm grateful for it."

"I think I understand."

"When I met you, on the other hand, almost from the first moment we started talking about substantive things—"

"Until I got mad at you."

"Well, there is that!" he laughed. "But we won't

mention it. What I was going to say is that we *really* talked. You knew things about me in those first five minutes that Audney probably still doesn't know."

"Such as?"

"Nothing specific. I just have the feeling that you probably began to have a sense of what makes me tick."

Loni smiled. "I see. Yes, maybe I did at that."

"I hope it was mutual, that I began to sense what made you tick."

"But in my own way I'm provincial too," said Loni. "I haven't traveled like you. Until my trip to Scotland last November, I'd never been out of the U.S."

"Provincial—are you kidding?" exclaimed David. "You live in Washington, the center of the political world. That alone gives you a larger perspective than people on Whales Reef could fathom. It's more than that, of course—you are interested in things. You are a thinker. Immediately I felt a freedom with you to be myself, to say anything about anything—spiritually or about finances or travel or the world. I knew you were on the same wavelength. Not that you would agree with what I might say, but you would understand *how* I was thinking, and even *why* I was thinking what I was."

Again they drove on in silence, enjoying the countryside.

"May I ask you another question?" said Loni as they went.

"Of course."

"I'm grateful and flattered that you came all this way to see me, and for bringing my journal!" she added with a grin. "And for what you said about our friendship. But I'm still a little confused. I mean . . . really, David, *why* did you come? And why are you subtly urging me to return to Whales Reef?"

"You noticed!"

"I could hardly help it!" she laughed.

"You do have a way of going right to the heart of things. That question is as difficult to answer as the first."

David drew in a breath and thought again for a minute.

"I know you have much to think about," he began at length. "You've said that you do not plan to live in the Shetlands. That's fine—we all understand that. You are an American, you have a life and a job and friends and family here. No one is expecting you to be different than you are. I know this is a big change. It will take time for you to sort it all out. You need to make the decisions facing you slowly.

"However, when your great-grandfather came here to the United States and essentially relinquished his inheritance, I'm not sure he did the right thing. Maybe he did, I can't say. He followed his heart, they say. Yet some of the consequences that resulted from that decision may not have been the best for the people of the island. Now destiny has brought back his posterity at an important time in the island's history in the person of one Alonnah Emily Ford. We mustn't take that lightly. I know you think you can do what needs to be done from here, or that you can put things in my hands. Maybe that will be possible eventually. But I think it will take time, and I believe those are decisions you need to make *there*. God has somehow seen fit against all odds to bring the contents of the two rolltop desks and the key and the locked study all to light. You have been the instrument by which it happened. So again, I would say that destiny, fate, *God* . . . has appointed *you* with the responsibility of the future of the island, not me."

"Jason MacNaughton said something similar on the first day I met him," said Loni, nodding, "about my *duty*. It was a new idea. Most Americans today are not big on old-fashioned values like duty to God, family, country, and one's heritage. But Jason's words took root in my brain. I don't seem to be able to escape my duty. Maddy once called it my destiny. She said I *had* to go to Whales Reef."

"I'm glad you took her advice. What I would add is that, as you face decisions that will impact not only your future but the future of Whales

Reef, you first get to know the place, its people and culture. And as I said, those decisions would be best made on the island. You need to spend time among the people who love you before you decide what you are going to do."

"The people there don't love me."

"You would be surprised. There are some who do."

"They don't even know me."

"They are learning both to know you and love you. The laird's people are family. Even those who haven't yet learned to love you are devoted to you as their laird. I realize you have much to consider. I know you have your work. But if there is any way you could come back with me, I'm happy to help in any way I can. I'm just talking about spending more time there now, while the mill is getting up to full strength again, walking the lanes of the village, visiting with people. The villagers need to feel a connection with you, to know you care about them. In time, of course, your life here will resume. They will understand that. They will even take pride in the fact that their laird is a financial wheeler-dealer from America's capital."

Loni could not help but laugh.

"The point I am trying to make is that you need to give them time to get to know you as a friend as well as a laird. The island needs you for a while longer." David paused, then added,

"And in a way I haven't entirely figured out yet, maybe I need you too."

Loni was rescued from the dilemma of a reply by turning into the gas station she had been looking for. She pulled to a stop, and both got out to stretch and take a break while Loni filled the tank.

"It's chillier than I realized," she said as they returned to the car a few minutes later. "Unusual for July."

She took her blue tailored jacket from the back seat and slipped it on before climbing back behind the wheel. As she pulled the seat belt across her lap, something hard pinched against her side. She fished into the pocket of the jacket she had not worn since leaving Philadelphia days before.

Her eyes shot open as her hand closed around the small jewelry box.

Resuming their trip, Loni did not utter a word. The silence went on for more than ten minutes. Whether David sensed the change in atmosphere, Loni could not tell.

"Uh . . . David," she said, "there's something I have to tell you. I wish I didn't have to, but I can't keep such an important thing from you."

"You are under no obligation," said David.

"Maybe not to you, but I am to myself. I *have* to tell you."

David waited.

"Remember those flowers beside the door," said

Loni after another moment, "on the first day you came to the Cottage to see me?"

"I do," said David with a smile. "The big blooms with flags and the Statue of Liberty."

"That's it—tacky in the extreme. I was embarrassed for you to see it."

"We Scots occasionally do tacky as well."

"They were from . . . well, there's a guy in Washington—"

"Hugh, right—you mentioned him. Your boyfriend."

"Yes, the flowers were from Hugh. We've been seeing each other for about a year. And actually the flowers weren't all. When I got home last week, he . . . he gave me this." She pulled the box from her pocket and handed it to him.

David opened the box. "This looks like an engagement ring."

"That would be correct."

"You're not wearing it."

"No."

"So now I find myself asking the same question you asked me a few days ago: Are *you* engaged?"

"I'm more confused than engaged. No, I'm *not* engaged."

"Did this Hugh propose?"

"Sort of."

"Like Audney and me—a *sort of* proposal?"

"You had to be there!" said Loni with a sardonic smile. "Let's just say it wasn't Hugh's finest hour.

Not to put too fine a point on it, but he was a perfect nincompoop."

"What did you say?"

"That I had to think about it."

"But you kept the ring."

"I didn't want to make a fuss in front of the train station."

"And have you thought about your answer?"

"Probably not as much as I should have. I didn't know another man was going to show up that I would . . ." Loni stopped.

"Another man who would distract you with talk about duty and destiny and islands and villagers and an inheritance?" laughed David.

Loni exhaled a sigh of relief. *Saved by the bell.*

Had David sensed she was about to blurt out more than she had intended? Had he stepped in to protect her from saying something she would regret? Or had he intervened to keep from hearing what *he* was not ready to hear?

"Exactly!" said Loni quickly. "How could I think of Hugh and engagement rings with all that's on my plate, right?" She hoped her flippant response did not betray her sudden flurry of emotions.

David closed the box, handed the ring back to Loni, and they drove on. The subject of Hugh and the ring did not come up again.

65
GIRL TALK

Loni had telephoned Maddy and kept her abreast of events and that David was coming to Washington with her.

"I can't wait to meet him," Maddy had said. "He sounded so refined and courteous when he called to find out where you were. And not engaged after all! By the way, how did he get my number?"

"I don't know," replied Loni, "probably from the solicitor. Lawyers know everything, you know."

Arriving in Washington, after she had David situated at a hotel near her apartment building, and agreeing to return after checking in at work, Loni went straight to Capital Towers. Fortunately Maddy was in the middle of nothing urgent. The moment the door of her office closed behind them, the days of pent-up emotion poured out.

"Oh, Maddy," Loni wailed, "I've made a mess of everything!"

"Why? And by the way, your dashing Scotsman is very handsome."

"How do you know?"

"I looked him up on the internet. Educated at Oxford, writes books, a sought-after naturalist. You didn't tell me all that."

"I suppose he is a bit of a celebrity. At least in the Shetlands."

"And such a gentleman. I love his accent. Why didn't you bring him with you? The whole floor is dying to meet him."

"I had to talk to you. I've been so confused."

"What's there to be confused about? You've met what sounds like a great guy."

"But I'm a perfect idiot around him. I almost blabbed that I was falling in love with him. Then he got quiet after I showed him the ring from Hugh."

"What ring from Hugh?" asked Maddy slowly.

"Oops—did I forget to mention that?"

"Uh . . . I've heard nothing about it. Are you telling me I was right about those hints he was dropping?"

Loni nodded. "Hugh sort of proposed to me on the way to the train station last weekend."

Maddy stared back across her desk with her mouth open. "You've got to be kidding," she said after a moment.

"I'm afraid not."

"I hope you had the good sense to turn him down."

"I didn't give him an answer. But it was dreadfully awkward, with him telling me he plans to run for Congress and that I would look good on his arm at parties. I'm not sure that's what I'm looking for in a marriage."

All Maddy could do was shake her head as Loni pulled out the ring for the second time that day and held it across to her.

"He just handed it to me while we were driving, assuming I would know what it meant."

"He proposed to you while driving?"

"It was a strange proposal . . . if it even was a proposal."

"I always knew Hugh was a moron," said Maddy. "The guy is beyond belief. He will make a perfect congressman. It will serve the people right if they elect such a dolt."

"Let Hugh have his time in the limelight if that's what he wants. Now that I am waking up, I suppose is the best way to describe it, I can't believe what I saw in him. I guess you drift into relationships without thinking about it like you should. But what am I going to do?"

"Tell Hugh to take a long hike off a short pier is my advice. How can you even think about Hugh alongside a hunk like your chief?"

"Actually he is about the best-looking guy I have ever seen. But he's not like that. He's just . . . well, he's *David*. He's nice. I know that he would treat the poorest and most homely girl in the village with the same courtesy and respect as if he were mixing with royalty at Buckingham Palace. He is the *truest* man I have ever met."

"So what's the problem? What does he think about you? Is the feeling mutual?"

"I really don't know."

"You must have *some* idea."

"I'm not very good at reading what men are thinking."

"Give me thirty seconds with him and I'll tell you what he's thinking. But please tell me I misunderstood a minute ago—you didn't actually show David the ring?"

"I'm afraid I did."

"What would possess you to do such a thing, girl?"

"We have a pact not to keep secrets. But David clammed up afterward."

"You told him you turned Hugh down?"

"I didn't *exactly* turn Hugh down."

"But you're going to, right?"

"Probably . . . yes, of course. How could I accept such a ridiculous proposal? He was a dolt, just like you say. But—"

She paused almost sadly. "I thought I liked Hugh," she said. "How could I not have seen how different we are? Like I said, I suppose part of me was asleep. In any case, once David showed up at my grandparents', I quit thinking about Hugh altogether."

"How long is David staying? What are his plans?"

"He was scheduled to fly to England tomorrow. I told him I wanted to show him D.C. He's trying to reschedule. He wants me to go back with him.

But then the thing with Hugh came up and I put my foot in my mouth and he got quiet. Now I don't know what he's thinking."

"Who cares what he's thinking—if he wants you to go back with him, go."

"But nothing has changed since I left."

"Except that David came to get you! Men don't chase women five thousand miles for no reason. I tell you, girl—he's interested. Did he say why he wants you to go back?"

"He said it was my duty and destiny."

"Hogwash."

"He said I needed to be there to make the right decisions for the island. He did say that he missed me and that the people needed me."

"That's all code, Loni. Don't you get it? He's in love with you."

Loni sat stunned to hear Maddy speak so bluntly.

"He hasn't said a word to give that impression."

"Men don't say it. He came to America to find you. That's his way of showing you what he's feeling. I tell you, that man is in love with you. Now go to Scotland with him."

"I don't want you to get frustrated with my not being here."

"No chance of that. You can stay away six months. I've got a temp filling in. She's no Loni Ford, but she's adequate. Your job will be waiting for you. And don't forget, I'm taking you to New York with me!"

Loni let out a long sigh. "Whatever I do, I can't leave things hanging with Hugh. I have to resolve that before I do anything. I am not about to return to Scotland with Hugh's ring sitting on the night-stand in my apartment. I need to talk to him."

"Bad idea." Maddy thought a moment. "Miss Ford," she said, "take a letter."

Loni grabbed the blank legal pad and a pen from Maddy's desk.

"Dear Hugh," Maddy went on.

Loni chuckled to herself as she took down Maddy's businesslike dictation.

"Thank you very much for your recent offer to join in your political future. However, I've since realized that cocktail parties and fundraisers do not fit into the future direction I envision for my life. Thank you for the times we've shared. I wish you every success.

"You will find your ring enclosed. Alonnah 'Loni' Ford."

Loni set down the pen and glanced over what she had written. "Very succinct and courteous," she said pensively. "Actually, it's perfect. But it's sad in a way. I don't think Hugh will understand. I really should talk to him in person."

"Talking to him won't make him understand, Loni. He doesn't listen. Hugh is on a different wavelength . . . Mars, you know. No, Jupiter better captures his view of himself. He would just try to change your mind and twist you up in knots. Do you really want that while David is here?"

"No, actually I don't. You're right—that is exactly what Hugh would do. He is so confident in his ability to talk me into anything that he would try to browbeat me into accepting him."

"Talk to him later if you have to," said Maddy, "after the emotion of the moment has subsided. For now, put the ring and the letter in a courier packet. Then you and David make arrangements to fly to Scotland and do whatever you need to do to figure out what kind of future you have together. The moment your plane lifts off, I will have your packet delivered to Hugh."

Loni smiled. "That is very good advice, Maddy. For someone who isn't interested in men, you sure seem to know how relationships work. But promise me you won't fire me when I'm gone."

"Loni, I told you before that you and I belong together. I told you once that going to the Shetlands to find out about your inheritance was your destiny. Now that destiny has shifted. If you and David have a future together, just like he said, that's something you have to discover for yourself in Scotland, not here."

66

TWO ARE BETTER THAN ONE

Suddenly Loni's face brightened. "I just had a sensational idea," she said excitedly. "I *do* need to figure out what to do about the estate and finances and everything. You're totally right. I thought I could do it from here, but . . ."

"And?"

"I have a request to make."

"Go on," said Maddy.

"I've still only told you sketchy bits about this inheritance that has fallen in my lap—"

"Yeah, like your being a sudden millionaire who owes three million in taxes!"

"I know," laughed Loni. "It sounds like I'm talking about someone else. There are more details and complexities than I can begin to comprehend—mineral rights and land values . . . I own a hundred separate buildings from cottages to a hotel to a mill to the entire main street of a town. There is a thriving wool business. I am boss to thirty or forty employees, and landlord to several hundred. Then there is the matter of rents—are they too high or too low? And maintenance issues—are the roads on the island my responsibility?

"There are a million questions I have no answers for. When I was sitting in the lawyer's office last week, going over the chart of accounts and balance sheet, I thought I more or less understood what was going on, but my head was swimming. All I wanted to know was whether there would be assets and cash to cover the taxes. Most of the rest was beyond me. I'm in over my head."

"That's why you need to go back with David to sort all that out."

"That's just it—I don't know *how* to sort it all out. I need a strategy to deal with all this. I hardly know where to begin. I talked to my grandparents and I value their advice. My grandfather was a businessman, he knows what he's about. But I also need the counsel of someone with financial expertise. What should I keep, what should I sell? Mr. Tulloch had a huge portfolio of investments. That's where most of the tax money will come from. But selling off a portfolio of that size is not as easy as snapping your fingers. We need to go over the portfolio and decide how to handle it, perhaps keep some of the investments and raise cash elsewhere—from the oil leases or from selling some of the land. I would really like for your expertise to guide me through it all. Will you help me?"

"Of course," replied Maddy. "I would love nothing more."

"Then," Loni added slowly, "would you consider going to the Shetlands with me as my financial advisor? You know, a working vacation?"

"Whoa!" exclaimed Maddy.

"You could look over everything firsthand, sit down with the estate's solicitor and accountant and ask the questions I don't even know to ask."

Maddy stared at Loni from across the desk. "That is an idea that will take some getting used to!"

"You told me you've always wanted to visit Scotland . . . family roots and all. Maybe we're related."

"I know I said it. I'm just not sure if I *meant* it!"

"It would be so fun, Maddy! My house, the Cottage—it's so big you could have a whole wing to yourself."

"For once in my life I'm speechless."

"But you're not saying no."

"I promise I will think about it. But what about the rain?"

"Yes, it rains. And it's cold."

"You said you hated all that."

"You get used to it."

"And the tea!"

"Actually I've learned to like it. You get used to that too."

"I don't know if I *want* to!"

"And bring walking shoes and jeans and warm clothes."

"Wait a minute—I said I would *think* about it!

And after seeing you in that fisherman's getup, I'm not sure I want to go quite as far as you did in getting into the spirit of the place."

"What are you talking about?"

"The picture of you in the raincoat and hat and boots. It was hilarious."

"How do you know about that?"

"David told me about it when he called. He emailed it to me."

"That rogue!" laughed Loni.

"He said you wanted him to take it for me."

"I suppose I did say that. But stop changing the subject. Please, come with me, Maddy," begged Loni. "After all, two heads are better than one. We once took New York by storm, didn't we? Let's take Whales Reef by storm too."

Still shaking her head, a smile crept over Maddy's face. "You're on, girl!"

67

CLANDESTINE SEARCH

Lerwick, Shetland Islands

What the clerk at Shetland Outfitters thought of the large fisherman and even larger cowboy both asking for the cheapest athletic shoes they had—in sizes twelve and fourteen—it would be difficult to say. Jimmy Joe had to squeeze into a size thirteen, and was swearing under his breath as he tiptoed behind Hardy across the gravel entry toward the Cottage.

It was 1:20 a.m. and not dark enough to hide their movements. Their footsteps could not be said to be altogether silent, but the gravel beneath them presented far less a problem by virtue of their recent purchases than it would have otherwise.

Since his meeting with Jimmy Joe at the Craigsmont, Hardy had learned that Dougal Erskine was back in his quarters at the Cottage, a fact that changed their plans and would necessitate considerable caution, as the dogs would also be back in residence.

Accordingly, late that afternoon Hardy had driven to the Cottage, intentionally making enough noise as he knew would bring the surly gamekeeper to investigate. Dougal appeared around the side of the Cottage three minutes later with three dogs bounding and barking after him to see Hardy standing at the front door.

"Hey, Erskine!" said Hardy jovially.

"What is it ye're wantin', Hardy?" he said gruffly.

"Jist tae see the mistress o' the hoose."

"She's no here. She's gone home, a'body kens that."

"I guess word didna reach me."

"So ye can jist gae yer way," said Dougal.

Hardy turned from the door and took a few steps as if to accompany Dougal back in the direction of the barn.

"So what's goin' tae happen wi' the Cottage?" he asked. "The two Mathesons comin' back, are they?"

"Hoo should I ken?" rejoined Dougal. "The mistress didna share her plans wi' me. Noo I got work tae do," he added and strode off around the house toward the barn.

Hardy waited a few moments until he was out of sight. The dogs continued to run about and follow him as he walked back toward his car, just as he knew they would.

At length he stopped, pulled from his pocket a handful of dog biscuits. "Here ye be, lads," he said softly. "A wee snackie for ye. Winna hurt ye, but ye'll be sleeping sound tonight!"

Watching them hungrily gobble up his offerings, he went on his way and returned to the village.

With no cover of night to protect them, for night at this time of the year was a mere figure of speech, the two intruders crept stealthily toward the silent stone edifice known as the Cottage.

There had been no break-in reported on Whales Reef in a generation. Hardy knew the door would not be locked. He knew the dogs would hear nothing. If the cows and chickens and horses became restless, it would not be enough to blow the alarm. He also knew the old coot Erskine was a traditionalist, and that no gamekeeper in Scotland was worth the name without a gun at his side. Scarcity of burglaries and wild game notwithstanding, Dougal Erskine was known to sleep with a loaded shotgun leaning in a corner of his bedroom.

As Hardy had predicted, the front door of the Cottage was open, and not so much as a squeak came from the well-oiled hinges, nor a peep from the dogs sleeping off the effects of their afternoon snack.

Flashlights and crowbars in hand, the two crept in their sneakers up the main stairway. They would require no tools of demolition, however. Hardy was in for a surprise to find the mysterious study unlocked. They entered the room, shined their lights around, and a minute later were ransacking the desk and its drawers for anything that might prove Brogan Tulloch a disinherited heir.

Their job was rendered immeasurably easier from the file labeled *Letters to and from Brogan,* which Loni had discovered earlier sitting on the writing desk in the middle of the room.

"This is what we need!" said Jimmy Joe, rifling through the file. "Letters from the old man to his wayward boy. Ought to tell us what we want to know."

He eased his large frame into one of the chairs with the file in his hand. "You take half of 'em," he said, handing Hardy a stack. "See what you can find. You can read, can't you, son?"

"'Course I can read. What do ye think we are, illiterates? Public education got its start in Scotland."

"Don't get your dander up. Just asking."

After an hour, they had found nothing of value.

"Well, no matter," said Jimmy Joe. "I'll take a couple of these from the boy and the carbon the father left of his. I'll fly down to London and get one of my boys to work his magic. He could copy the *Mona Lisa* if he had to, and he's even better with handwriting. I'll be back in a week or less. You start spreading the news about the lady lying to the folks. When I show up, we'll have 'em right where we want 'em."

Meanwhile, in his Edinburgh office, Ross Thorburn was looking over some documents that had come to Mr. McLeod's personal attention from the corporate headquarters in Houston. They outlined the restructuring of the company's U.K. holdings whose details he had been reviewing earlier. This dossier came complete with a list of top personnel. His own name was nowhere to be seen.

The document one of his own men, with no allegiance to McLeod, had uncovered now made sense. He was being groomed to take the fall.

He seethed with silent fury. He had given the

big blowhard ten years and had made him millions. If he thought he could cut him adrift now, after promising him that he would head up the expanded Shetland operation, he could think again.

Carefully he resealed the envelope with the same skill he had used many times to lay eyes on Jimmy Joe's private correspondence.

In the meantime, he had to find a way to confront the man without divulging how much he knew.

PART 5

68
CRISIS IN WHALES REEF

Whales Reef

No one in Whales Reef knew what it was about.

David was gone. No one had heard from him in a week. Their new American laird had not been seen nor heard from since her sudden disappearance a week and a half ago.

Word had begun circulating through the village last week—the origin of the report was uncertain—that a major change coming to Whales Reef would be announced at three o'clock Monday afternoon on the last day of July in the town square. It was a development that would affect every resident on the island. When it was known, it would be cause for universal jubilation. Far from the tidings of gloom and doom that had hung over the island for the year of doubt about the inheritance of Macgregor Tulloch, the forthcoming announcement would bring good news for all.

Speculation ran rampant. Rumors hinted in the direction of untoward mischief on the part of their new laird, who was not what she appeared to be. But all would be resolved when her lies were exposed.

As far as David's role in the affair, speculation flew just as wild. Not that his work, especially in summer, did not regularly take him away from the island, sometimes for weeks. But someone always knew his whereabouts—either the Kerrs at the inn, or his aunt and uncle Tavis and Rinda Gunn, or the two Mathesons. On this occasion, however, they all professed themselves as bewildered by his sudden disappearance as everyone else. Theories ranged from despondency over not receiving the inheritance, to his being called upon to lead some tour at the last minute, to the more dubious notion that his disappearance and the laird's were somehow connected and that David was party to the deception being perpetrated by the money-grubbing American.

The one man who gave the impression of knowing more than he was telling was Hardy Tulloch. The smile on his face and resumption of his confident gait from a month earlier indicated clearly enough that whatever was going on must involve favorable developments concerning his claim to Macgregor Tulloch's inheritance. On the basis of the obvious pleasure he took watching the village work itself into a frenzy of perplexity, not a few were of the opinion that Hardy had started the rumor himself and that there was nothing to it whatsoever.

That did not stop every man, woman, and child on the island from being present when the fateful hour came. Fortunately there was no rain. Even the fishermen were on hand, their boats bobbing idly in the harbor.

The mill closed for the afternoon. The Whales Fin Inn emptied of patrons and owners, as did every shop and cottage on the island.

Even Saxe and Isobel Matheson, not known for participating in island affairs, were on hand, as much as anything to be able to give David a report upon his return. Dougal Erskine, however, remained out on the moor with the sheep.

As the crowd milled about in a buzz of anticipation, most, though for no tangible reason, expected David to appear. It was not their chief, however, but his braggart cousin and former claimant to the lairdship who jumped onto the bench at the foot of the monument when the appointed hour came.

"Welcome tae a' o' ye my frien's an' neighbors," boomed Hardy. The square quickly settled down. "Ye're wonderin' what this meetin' is a' aboot, so I winna haud ye in suspense longer than necessary. I'm here tae introduce ye tae a frien' o' mine who'll soon be a frien' tae yersel's as weel. He comes tae Whales Reef as the bearer o' good news."

As he was speaking, from behind the monument, hidden from most of the gathering where he had been waiting inside his rented SUV, a huge man walked around and stepped up beside Hardy. His hat and boots presented spectacle enough to send murmurs through the crowd. Those few residents who had previously encountered the man found themselves skeptical about the proceedings.

Hardy stepped down and again the throng quieted.

"How do, folks!" said Jimmy Joe effusively. "The name's McLeod . . . Jimmy Joe McLeod. I hail from Texas, which I reckon most of you've heard of. My hat probably gave me away anyway, if my accent don't!"

He paused, apparently waiting for laughter. None came.

"I'm a businessman," he continued. "*McLeod's the name and oil's my game* is how I like to put it. And that's what I'm doing in the Shetlands. I got some oil interests up north on the big island. What I'm mostly interested in is getting hold of land in these islands before the real boom hits, which it's sure to do. I've been trying to buy up some of the ground on this island of yours because it looks like a way that you and me and all of us could make a pile of money. But when I talked to this lady of yours—what you call your new laird, the American gal called Ford—she turned me down flatter'n a June bug on a railroad track, if you know what I mean. I told her it'd make her a small fortune, and all you folks too. But she didn't care about any of you. She must figure she's got her dough, so what do any of you matter to her. She just said no and that was that."

A few disgruntled murmurs spread about.

"Well, after I talked to my friend Hardy here, what did he tell me but that she ain't the true heir of old Mr. Tulloch's at all. He tells me that the court folks made a mistake and that's *he's* eventually going to be named the heir. He's got his solicitor filing appeals with them folks at the probate court. But all that's likely to take time to get sorted out, and meanwhile all you poor folks ain't getting what's coming to you and what you deserve. It don't seem right the Ford lady can treat you that way. She ain't been truthful to you good folks, and the way I hear it your own chief is in on it. They're out to swindle you. That's why I'm here, to try to help. So I figured why not tell you good people what's going on so that you can tell the lady you don't take kindly to her standing in your way of making a lot of money. You all need to tell her you don't think what she's doing is right."

By now everyone was talking at once.

"But she's the legal heir," called out Keith Kerr, who was standing near the front of the crowd and one of the village's acknowledged leaders in David's absence. "I dinna see that anyone can change it."

"I'll grant you, partner, that she's been named heir for the time being. But the question is whether it's *legal*. Turns out I got evidence here proving it ain't."

With the words, he withdrew the fruit of his labors in one of the seedier parts of London. He held up a yellowed envelope.

"This here's a letter," he said, "that's recently come to light and was written by Mr. Ernest Tulloch, dated almost eighty years ago. I reckon you all know the name."

"We ken who he is weel enouch," said Keith.

"Well then, partner, did you know that he cut off his son, Brogan, from all legal claims to any portion of his inheritance—and all his posterity with him?"

Jimmy Joe paused briefly to let his words sink in.

"In other words," he went on, "no inheritance coming through his oldest boy is legal. This here's proof that the Ford gal's claim is sure to be overturned. What I'm fixing to do is give this letter to Mr. Tulloch here, and his solicitors will present it to the court, and that will be the end of your American laird. She's nothing but an imposter."

The whole crowd of villagers erupted into bedlam.

"So what I aim to do," Jimmy Joe went on, raising his voice, "is get each of you who are occupants of property on the island to take one of these documents that Mr. Tulloch will distribute among you, and look 'em over and then sign 'em. I'll be picking 'em up in another day or two. These are what's called Letters of Intent, and they state your desire to lease your property from me and not her—once it's in Mr. Tulloch's and my hands, that is. These letters will show the Ford lady the will of the people, as we are fond of saying in America. By your signing these papers, she'll know you ain't pleased about her trying to take advantage of you behind your backs, and that you want her to do what's right and let me take over your affairs without waiting for it to be dragged through the court all over again. By then your mill would likely be bankrupt and a lot of your people out of work. You gotta convince her to quit playing around."

"If she owns oor places, like she does my hotel," objected Keith again, "what good's all yer papers?"

"It'll show her she has to listen to you all. People have rights. They got the right not to be taken advantage of. If she won't listen, and if you're all behind me, heck, we'll sue her pants off. Courts don't look kindly on people's rights getting taken advantage of. She's going to lose the inheritance anyway once Mr. Tulloch's solicitors get hold of this letter. Then he's going to sell to me. All I'm saying is that the longer you have to wait, the more likely it is that your mill has to close and you all don't get what's rightly coming to you."

By now the crowd was abuzz like a hive of angry wasps, still not sure what to make of what the big man was saying.

"What I got in mind," Jimmy Joe said, raising his voice, "is for you to sign these Letters of Intent. Then I've also had a petition drawn up nice and legal for you to sign as well. The petition demands that she relinquish the inheritance and lists your rights she's violating. She's going to lose it all anyway. This letter"—he held high the yellow envelope—"cuts her off from any claim to property on Whales Reef. Here it is signed in Ernest's own hand, saying no future son or daughter or great-granddaughter can come along later and claim any part of his inheritance. It's what they call legally binding. It's proof that the lady's inheritance ain't worth the paper it's printed on."

By now Jimmy Joe could hardly be heard over the hullabaloo.

"We gotta force her to give up the inheritance before she finds herself in court, where she's going to lose," he shouted over the din. "If it's signed by everyone in the community, this petition is the kind of thing the court looks at to see if people's rights are being violated."

"Why should we care who owns oor hooses?" asked Coira MacNeill, "or my bakery or Keith's hotel? Why should I sign a letter sayin' I want a lease wi' yersel'. I ken naethin' aboot ye?"

Nods and looks of confusion broke out in Coira's vicinity.

"Because I'm the one who's going to share the wealth of the island with you all."

"How ye goin' tae do that?" insisted Coira.

"The first thing you'll notice on that paper is that when the lease on that bakery of yours gets turned over to me, your rent will be lowered by twenty-five percent on the very first day. It ain't just an empty promise—you can see it right here in black and white. Show 'em the papers, Hardy. Let 'em see for themselves."

Those closest to Hardy clamored forward. He handed out several sheets. Keith Kerr stepped through the crowd and took one of the Letters of Intent. The crowd quieted and waited. They knew Keith was incapable of speaking an untrue word. A moment later he looked up and glanced around.

"He's right," said Keith. "It says it right here: 'twenty-five percent reduction in current rent.' "

Murmurs of approval spread through the crowd.

"You'll also notice that it calls it a lease of indefinite duration," said Jimmy Joe. "That means you got the right to stay in your places for as long as you want. I can't evict you or sell your places to anyone else who can evict you. So long as you pay your rent on time every month, nobody can do a thing to you."

"Every month? We pay six months at a time," interjected Coira again.

"I like to get these things taken care of monthly. Same amount—you just pay one month at a time instead of having to come up with a big chunk twice a year. Better for you that way. Ain't it worth the lower rent to pay me on the first of every month?"

A few nods went around.

"These letters also promise that I'll take care of all maintenance and upgrades needed. All you gotta do is come to ol' Jimmy Joe and he'll take care of you."

"The laird already did that," said Keith, still skeptical.

"And I'll keep doing it, partner! The best is that when you sign on the dotted line like we say, and sign this here petition, the minute your Ford lady transfers title to me, you'll get a personal check from me for five hundred pounds. I'll write you the check now—you just hang on to it. Sorta like a pledge between you and me. When the deal goes through, it's five hundred pounds cash in your pocket. Heck, you'd likely get your whole first year's rent for free! That's the kind of man I am."

At last arose shouts of approval.

"It's what in the business world we call a win-win deal—for you and for me."

"Why would ye do all this for us?" persisted Keith.

" 'Cause I've taken a mighty keen liking to your

little island, partner. I figure I'd like to help you folks. So you all take one of these letters from your friend Hardy and you look them over, and I'll be back in two days to collect them. Then we'll put it to the lady to see if she's really looking out for you or only for herself. Soon as I'm back I'll write every person whose name is on this list a check for five hundred pounds as a deposit on your house or land, payable when the Ford gal agrees to do the right thing by you all. You get her to agree, and you can put that cash in the bank."

69

ABORTED PLANS

London

Had David possessed an inkling of the chaotic turn of events erupting on Whales Reef during his absence, he would not have postponed his return flight and lingered in Washington, D.C., with Loni, touring the city and the Capitol building and visiting the presidential monuments. Nor would he have planned three days in London.

After touching down at Heathrow, David had lined up a full itinerary for the two American ladies, including *Les Miserables* and *Phantom of the Opera* in the West End, and as much of London as they could cram into three days. His plans were aborted, however, the moment they left airport customs. Activating his mobile phone for the first time since departing for the States, he found half a dozen frantic messages awaiting him from Jason MacNaughton. He immediately telephoned the solicitor in Lerwick.

"Jason . . . David Tulloch."

"David, am I glad to hear from you! Where are you calling from?"

"Heathrow—just got in."

"Did you manage to make contact with Miss Ford?"

"I did. Your help in locating her grandparents was spot-on. She's here with me, in fact."

"In London?"

"She and I flew over together."

"That is good news. The two of you need to get home immediately. There is mischief afoot on the island."

"What kind of mischief?"

"Your friend Hardy and a Texan by the name of McLeod are inciting the people against you and Miss Ford."

"What!" exclaimed David, motioning to Loni, where she and Maddy stood nearby looking into one of the airport shops. She came and stood beside him. David turned on the speaker of his small phone. They huddled closer so they could hear amid the surrounding hubbub.

"I would never have learned of it had it not

been for Dickie Sinclair," Jason was saying. "I believe you met him."

"Right, Alonnah's friend."

"It seems that he and your Rev. Yates are friends. Dickie was visiting him on Sunday afternoon two days ago, and Yates told him about disturbing rumors floating about. A town meeting was apparently planned for the next day—that was yesterday. A sixth sense told Dickie he should be there. So he returned to Whales Reef. That's when he called me."

"A meeting about what?"

"Hardy Tulloch and this Texan are stirring everyone up with promises of riches. They're telling people that you and Miss Ford are taking advantage of them. They are threatening a lawsuit claiming that Miss Ford has violated the people's rights."

"That's preposterous!"

"Perhaps, but he also claims to have new proof that Miss Ford's inheritance is invalid."

"Hardy has been playing that card for a year," said David, trying to stay calm, though his blood was rapidly reaching the boiling point. "What is this new proof?"

"Apparently," answered Jason, "the Texan has evidence—what he claims is ironclad proof—a letter from Ernest Tulloch cutting Brogan and his posterity off from all future claims to any part of the estate."

As they listened, David and Loni looked at each other in bewilderment.

"Whether he is right or not," Jason went on, "the whole island is in an uproar. There is a petition circulating demanding that Miss Ford relinquish her property ownership on the island or face legal action. The McLeod fellow has also promised five hundred pounds to every tenant of hers who signs whatever these papers are that he's circulating."

"That's bribery."

"Probably. But hard to prove."

"Are you saying there's more than the petition?"

"He has also drawn up actual lease agreements."

"That would seem to be getting the cart before the horse."

"I think his intent is to get people so prejudiced against Miss Ford and yourself that she will bow to the pressure and give in. I had hoped that Dickie could get his hands on one of the documents so that I could look it over. Unfortunately, we have not actually seen it. Meanwhile, Hardy Tulloch's lawsuit contesting the probate findings has been filed in Edinburgh. Another town meeting is scheduled for tomorrow afternoon. How soon can you get here?"

"It's too late to get a flight north tonight," said David. "We'll try to get the earliest possible flight to Aberdeen in the morning."

70

THE TOWN SQUARE AGAIN

Whales Reef

Jimmy Joe McLeod—tycoon, oil magnate, and wheeler-dealer extraordinaire—was not a man who relished life's simple rustic pleasures. He was a Ritz-Carlton and Four Seasons man. It was doubtful that he even knew what the *6* in Motel 6 originally stood for.

The notion of spending a night in the Whales Fin Inn was not one that filled him with anticipation. In his youth, before oil had gripped him, he had done a stint as a used-car salesman. The lot motto had been *We'll stand on our heads for a deal!* and Jimmy Joe never lost sight of the wisdom of that policy. It was in the same spirit of doing whatever he had to for the deal that he remained on the island after the tumultuous meeting in the town square on Monday. He was supremely confident in his down-home ability to win friends and influence people. If the promise of five hundred pounds was not enough, he would win the bumpkins over with good-ol'-boy backslapping joviality.

For the rest of the afternoon, therefore, he had

the fishermen at the harbor hanging on his every word for one story after another, giving them winks at his off-color jokes as if they had been friends for years. When an abrupt rain shower sent them running up the street to the inn about five, Jimmy Joe continued in his role of benefactor and *raconteur*, striding across the floor to Keith Kerr and calling out in a voice loud enough to be heard over the din, "Hey, partner—the beer and whisky and whatever else anyone hankers after for the rest of the afternoon and evening's on me. You just keep the spigots flowing and the bottles uncorked and you and me'll square up tomorrow."

Whoops and cheers spread through the common room. For the next hour Audney and Evanna could hardly keep up. The men of the village, most of whom were forced by constraints of finances to limit their intake to a pint every two or three days, seemed determined to make up for lost time and empty Keith's casks of special brew before the night was out. With the supper hour approaching, and the village in a festive mood, Audney slipped out the back and ran to the Gordons to enlist Rakel's help with the crowd at the pub.

By evening's end, Jimmy Joe was on a first-name basis with half the men of the village, and they were *all* on a first-name basis with him. Whatever reservations they might have had about the petition and Letters of Intent were washed away by the amber liquid flowing freely from the pub's four taps. When Jimmy Joe climbed slowly to his room a little after eleven, the ample fish supper and three quarts of beer he had enjoyed over the course of the afternoon and evening sent him into a sleep deeper than he had thought would be possible on a bed a foot shorter than his massive frame.

He awoke with the touch of a headache, came downstairs to a breakfast prepared at Audney's hand, and started the day off with an entire pot of coffee. He rose at length and announced to anyone who cared to listen that he would be in Lerwick for the rest of the day and Tuesday night but would return for the next day's meeting to collect the letters and petitions. He was shrewd enough to know when not to overplay his hand. He had created enough buzz already. It was time to let the leaven do its work, or as the fellow said, let the crawdad stew simmer a spell. His absence would create more talk, speculation, and increase yet further the groundswell of approbation in his favor.

Meanwhile, Hardy was laying low. He knew that not everyone on the island was his fan. He was also astute enough to realize that Jimmy Joe had done his work well. He was making a hit in the village. Hardy could see that it was time for him to take a backseat and let the Texan play out what he called their ace-high straight. He had urged Jimmy Joe to strike while the iron was hot and collect the petition and letters on Tuesday. They needed to get the thing done before David returned. Loyalty to the so-called chief was so high that David remained the wild card. They needed to move quickly before he could interfere.

The Texan insisted that the extra day's wait would tilt the island's mood from mere assent to eagerness. Allowing a hint of concern to spread lest Jimmy Joe withdraw his offer would create a stampede once he returned. "After forty-eight hours, son," he had said, "they'll be clamoring to give me whatever I want. I been ropin' cattle like this for more years than I can count. All part of the game. You gotta let all the parts of the sting play out. Trust me—they'll fall into our laps."

Jimmy Joe's words were prophetic. By Wednesday morning, when he did not appear on the first two ferries from the mainland, a restlessness began to spread through the village that maybe he had changed his mind. When he drove off the ferry in his huge black Range Rover shortly after one o'clock, the running, cheering crowd following him to the square was made up of more than two hundred people.

An hour and a half later, the entire village was gathered at the monument. Jimmy Joe and Hardy were still seated in the Whales Fin Inn with thirty or forty men clustered around them and crowding all the way to the four walls, drawn as much by the thought of more free beer as by any new information to be gained from what they were saying. At ten till the hour, Jimmy Joe drained what remained in his glass and rose.

Time to buy me an island! he said to himself.

For one of the few times in his life feeling dwarfed by another man, and also unaccustomed to someone other than himself occupying the limelight, Hardy followed the wide-brimmed white hat from the inn. Side by side the two Goliaths crossed the street through the boisterous throng to the center of the square.

Jimmy Joe jumped onto the bench, took off his hat, and waved effusively to the crowd. Thunderous applause and cheers told him all he needed to know.

"Howdy again!" he called. "Thanks for the welcome. You all's going to make a Shetlander out of me yet!"

If possible the cheering grew louder.

"All right, then," said Jimmy Joe as the noise gradually quieted. "I got my checkbook with me and I'm fixin' to write checks to anyone ready with their signed letters and who has signed the petition Hardy's been circulating. This here's going to take us a spell. So if you'll just bring your letters up, we'll let your friend Hardy collect them. Then I'll go back to the hotel yonder and start writing checks. But remember, they won't be any good until we got the Ford gal lassoed, as we say. And if anyone hasn't put your John Henry on your letter or the petition yet, Hardy's got 'em right here and there ain't no time like the present."

71

CONFRONTATION

As Jimmy Joe was still talking, a great bustling surged forward. Hardy was nearly overrun with outstretched hands holding the papers they had been given on Monday.

Hardy jumped down and had gathered perhaps the first fifty letters, villagers around him clamoring to sign the petition as well, which now ran to five pages of signatures, when from the rear of the crowd a gradual quiet began to spread from the street.

The throng split like the parting of the Red Sea. As the dividing of the crowd moved toward them, Jimmy Joe and Hardy looked up to see a man and a woman walking toward them through the sea of expectant faces. Whisperings now filled the square.

The four-seater plane David had chartered from Aberdeen to Sumburg had left Loni so sick she was still pale. The wind was fierce, and she was not only sick but terrified in the tiny plane from takeoff to touchdown. Maddy, on the other hand, enjoyed the rough-and-tumble flight immensely.

Minutes after landing they were speeding out of the airport in David's car. Except for two brief stops en route for Loni to gag beside the road, David drove from the airport to the ferry landing faster than he ever had in his life, making the three o'clock ferry by seconds. Now it was Maddy who was glad to get out and make the crossing on the deck of the small craft. The madcap drive through the Shetland capital on the wrong side of the road had proven more frightening for her than the hour-long flight.

None of the villagers saw them drive from the ferry into the village. Everyone was at the town square. They shared the ferry with one other car, however, whose driver David did not recognize. Caught up in the rush of the events that followed, he soon forgot the man altogether.

As they arrived at the center of town, few took notice of the second American woman climbing out of the backseat of David's car any more than they did the other stranger, who drove into their midst from the ferry shortly thereafter. Remaining beside David's car, Maddy was quickly swallowed by the crowd speaking in what to her ears sounded like gibberish.

Around the square, reactions to the sight of the two were mixed. So prejudiced against Loni by this time from Jimmy Joe's manipulative narrative, amid the exclamations of surprise were scattered boos and grumblings.

David and Loni stopped in front of the bench. They stared up at the two big men. Thunderlouds gathered across Hardy's brow. If Jimmy Joe was flummoxed by their unexpected appearance, he did not let it show.

The staring contest did not last long. Ignoring her queasy stomach, Loni was the first to speak. "What is all this?" she said.

"It ain't none o' yer—" began Hardy. He was instantly silenced by a grip from the Texan's massive hand on his arm like the bite of a horse.

"How do, Miss Ford," said Jimmy Joe. "Nice to see you again, though you're appearing a mite green around the gills."

"Never mind how I look," said Loni. "I want to know what's going on here."

Jimmy Joe's eyes flitted toward the cylindrical tube she carried in one hand with a slight premonition.

"What's going on is that these good folks don't much like the way you've been conducting things. They think they'll be better off renting their homes and businesses from me."

"That may be, but it is of no consequence. I already told you that I have no intention of selling."

"You might not have a say in the matter. When

this petition is presented to a judge, he's likely to agree with these poor folk that you are using your position to violate their rights. Judges don't take kindly to that sort of thing."

"What petition?"

"Show her, Hardy."

With a smirk of satisfaction, Hardy handed her the papers. Loni glanced over them briefly, then passed them to David.

"What lies have you been telling them, Mr. McLeod?" said Loni, her face slowly taking on a shade of crimson. "How did you coerce them to sign these?"

"Just the truth, Miss Ford. Most of them have also signed Letters of Intent to lease from me as soon as you either agree to sell or step down, or find your inheritance taken from you. And at far better terms than they are receiving at present."

As they were speaking, Odara Innes made her way forward. Approaching David, she quietly handed him one of the Letters of Intent . . . unsigned.

David looked it over and then walked back to his car, where Maddy still stood. "See what you can make of this," he said, handing her the paper.

"If you refuse to acknowledge the people's wishes," Jimmy Joe was saying to Loni, "we now have proof that invalidates your claim to the Tulloch title entirely. You can save the time and expense of a protracted court battle by stepping down, turning the estate over to the rightful heir, or selling the island to me. Those are your only choices, Miss Ford. It's what the people want . . . ain't it, folks?" he added loudly, turning and gesturing to the crowd.

A subdued clamor of nods and *yeas* and a few shouts acknowledged that he still had a good many people on his side. Seeing David and Loni in person, however, made it more difficult to believe that they would lie to them.

"What kind of proof?" asked Loni.

"This letter from old Ernest Tulloch himself," replied Jimmy Joe with swagger in his tone. "Have a look."

Loni took the letter from his hand, withdrew the single sheet from its envelope, and read it. David returned and stood beside her.

"This is very interesting," said Loni slowly. "If I might ask . . . how did you come by this? Did you break into the Cottage? Because that happens to be against the law."

"The door wasna locked," blundered Hardy.

"Shut up, Tulloch, you fool!" spat Jimmy Joe.

"More interesting than the fact that you broke into the Cottage," said Loni, "is that I happen to have a copy of a letter also from Ernest Tulloch that directly refutes everything in this one. David, would you mind getting my journal with that carbon of Ernest's letter in it from the car?"

David hurried through the crowd again and

quickly returned. Loni opened the book and withdrew a folded sheet.

"I have here a carbon copy of a *genuine* letter from Ernest Tulloch," she said, "the original of which he sent to the U.S. I found it in his study. Since the letters he sent to his son after his move to the United States would no longer be in the Shetlands at all after being sent, it is obvious to me, having read many letters from Ernest Tulloch to his firstborn, that you have produced a forgery."

"That's a mighty serious charge, Miss Ford. If you will just compare the handwriting—"

"And forgery with intent to defraud is a serious crime, Mr. McLeod. David, if you will take this letter and keep it safe as evidence," she said, handing him Jimmy Joe's suspicious letter.

"Hey, hold on a minute, little lady—that's mine!"

"*Yours,* Mr. McLeod? That seems rather an audacious claim for someone caught with his hand in the cookie jar. If you all would care to hear Ernest Tulloch's actual words to his son, Brogan—and I could produce several that express essentially the same thought—let me just read a brief portion. Let's see . . . yes, here it is." She turned to the crowd and raised her voice:

"Let me reiterate," she read loudly, "my abiding affection for you, dear son, and my promise that your inheritance or any part of it remains yours any time you wish it. I have spoken with your brother and can assure you that Wallace, too, is anxious to share the estate with you, even to relinquish the future lairdship to you at my death if such should become your wish. Though such a change would not go down well with his wife, we have already suffered enough from that quarter to include that in our considerations. Wallace and I both understand and respect your decision to remain where you are and to leave things as they presently stand. Know, however, that you will always be in my heart, as I know you are in Wallace's."

By now, as if hearing a voice from the grave, stone silence had settled over the crowded square of listeners. Ernest's own words instantly put to rest the myriad rumors regarding the relation-ship between the Auld Tulloch and his eldest son that had been fueling gossip on the island for three generations.

Loni's voice stopped. She glanced up and saw Maddy approaching.

Still standing on his perch, the Texan recog-nized her. He began to sense that things might be going south.

"Loni," said Maddy, "this Letter of Intent is one of the most devious documents I have ever seen.

The lower rent clause is binding only for three months, at which time the owner may set rent at any level he wishes. There are no limits or safeguards. Rents are payable on the first of every month with a grace period of three days. After that, tenants can be evicted without cause. These documents give the people no legal rights, no legal recourse against eviction. He could empty the island four months after taking ownership."

"Okay—thanks, Maddy."

72
SECRET PLANS

Loni took several steps toward the bench. "Get out of my way, Hardy," she said. "I need to talk to the people."

Steadying herself with David's hand, Loni jumped up beside Jimmy Joe.

"I don't know how many of you heard that," she said loudly, "but my associate has examined these letters you signed. Whatever Mr. McLeod told you was probably untrue. In fact, after three months, under the terms spelled out here, your rents could be doubled or tripled or more. I happen to know that this man is definitely lying to you and has very different plans for Whales Reef than whatever he has told you."

"Now just hold your horses, Miss Ford," began Jimmy Joe.

"Stop, James McLeod—just stop! Whatever deception you are foisting on these people stops here and now. You will not bully *me* again, as you did so many years ago in Mrs. Schrock's Quaker school. Nor will you bully these good people and take advantage of *them*. You will not tear down the mill and houses and destroy this village—" As she spoke, Loni slowly drew several large sheets from the tube in her hand.

"—nor build your oil refinery here," added Loni.

The deathly quiet among the crowd was broken by gasps at her words.

"That's absurd. I would never—"

"I said stop, James McLeod!" interrupted Loni. She paused and waited. The men and women were hanging on her every word.

Jimmy Joe stared back at the woman beside him, glancing briefly to the papers in her hand. Recognition dawned. An expression of shock spread over his face, to see the gangly girl he had made fun of more than twenty years ago suddenly turning the tables on him.

"Your lies must stop!" Loni repeated. "I have in my hand copies of your blueprints, which I have obtained, *legally* by the way, and which show your secret plans for Whales Reef."

"How did you get those?" cried Jimmy Joe.

Ignoring the question, Loni turned to the crowd.

"These are drawings and blueprints," she said loudly, "showing the oil refinery that your new friend Mr. McLeod has been scheming for years to build on Whales Reef. He tried to gain control of the island when your former laird was alive. He tried to persuade me to sell the island two weeks ago. When I refused, he and Hardy broke into the Cottage, and, I assume, when they could not find what they were looking for, concocted this scheme behind my back and David's to turn you against us. I don't know what he told you or promised, but these are his true plans."

As she spoke, Loni unrolled the blueprints.

"Come and look, all of you!" she said. "You will see these drawings are labeled *Whales Reef Oil Refinery, McLeod Enterprises.* You will also see that not a single house or building presently standing on this island remains. All your homes and businesses, the inn, the woolen factory—they're all gone. Only the church, the Auld Hoose, and the Cottage remain. Everything on this island except those three buildings is slated for demolition. You will also notice that the harbor has been replaced by an oil dock."

Pandemonium broke out. Loni handed David the blueprints. He was swarmed by Keith and Fergus and enough of the men to validate within seconds what she had said.

"I have tried to do my best for you, and I always will," said Loni, now having to shout to be heard. "I will protect and preserve your property, your way of life, your livelihood, and the mill. I would never do anything to hurt a single one of you."

"Hardy," she said, turning to her third cousin, "give me those petitions. I intend to burn them personally."

The square broke into riotous cheers for their laird. As goes the allegiance of all fickle crowds, suddenly Loni was their hero.

73
FALLING OUT

By now the blueprints were in Keith's hands and making their way slowly through the crowd. From where he watched, a slow smile spread over David's face as he witnessed the new laird coming into her own.

In the shadow of the stone monument, Jimmy Joe stepped down and was attempting to slink away, no mean feat in size fourteen boots and a huge white hat. An argument broke out as Hardy hurried after him.

"Ye lied tae me!" he growled, latching on to the Texan's arm.

Jimmy Joe correctly surmised the tone of his

erstwhile partner's voice. Being foiled by a woman in front of a crowd had put him in a foul mood. He was itching for someone to take it out on.

"I never promised you anything, Tulloch!" he shot back. "This is your fault for not keeping these yokels in line. I counted on you to hold up your end."

"An' I got a' the signatures. Ye ne'er told me ye intended tae destroy the village an' the fishin'!"

Those near enough recognized the look on Hardy's face. Everyone on the island knew to stand clear when his eyes flashed and his fists twitched. But Jimmy Joe McLeod stood at least two inches taller and probably outweighed Hardy by twenty pounds. Whether Hardy Tulloch was capable of fearing another man is doubtful. But the reputation of Texas was sufficiently ingrained in his image of the Wild West to make him wary of starting anything he wasn't sure of being able to finish. He had heard stories of large knives and small pistols hidden in tall leather boots. He thus limited himself to threats.

"What did you expect?" said Jimmy Joe. "I would have made you a rich man. You'd never have had to fish again in your life. Oil's where the money is."

"My mum an' my brithers has got hooses here, no tae mention my livelihood—ye was plannin' tae level it a' wi' oot tellin' me, ye bounder!"

"What did you think I was going to do? Looks like you're just as big a fool as the rest of them!"

"Who are ye callin' a fool!"

"I'm saying it to your face, Tulloch—you big lout!"

Jimmy Joe shoved Hardy aside and clomped through the crowd.

The shock of being manhandled, along with the Texan's surprising strength, left Hardy briefly speechless. A moment later he came to himself. He ran after Jimmy Joe in a rage.

"Wait jist a minute, ye blackguard!" cried Hardy. "I'll kill ye for that! Nobody talks tae Hardy Tulloch that way."

The crowd scrambled away to make room for the two angry men. Seconds later, Jimmy Joe's Range Rover roared to life. Its huge tires spun on the smooth cobbles and skidded away, Hardy shrieking obscenities after it and waving his fist in the air.

The sound of the racing engine sped toward the ferry landing, with Hardy galloping after it. Silence settled over the crowd.

A few glanced at their wrists or pulled out pocket watches. The next ferry wasn't scheduled for at least twenty minutes. Even slowing to a walk, Hardy would reach the landing in less than ten. A few of the men, anticipating a deliciously diverting brawl, began edging their way toward the street. It promised to be a rare entertainment, with the tantalizing possibility of seeing Hardy get whipped. A few also cast glances over the sea southward. Black clouds had been gathering on the horizon for several hours. The fishermen knew the signs and could smell rather than feel the wind about to kick up. They were mentally weighing the attraction of fisticuffs at the landing with a good chance of being caught in a deluge.

Gradually a few of the men started toward the landing. More followed, until a good-sized group of men was hurrying along the main street out of the village.

Watching the stormy departure of the two men, with a good many men on their heels, still standing on the bench where she had delivered her short but impassioned speech, Loni was overcome with exhaustion. She had been running on adrenaline for days. She and David and Maddy had rushed north frantically from London, driven across southern Shetland at breakneck speed, then had walked into the middle of a hornet's nest.

Confronting her childhood nemesis, the bully James McLeod, whose family had left the Fellowship when Loni was eleven, had sapped the last ounce of her emotional reserve. Fatigue rushed over her like a wave. She stepped down. From where he stood, David saw the sudden pallor come over Loni's face. He hurried quickly forward and offered his arm. Loni took it, and they walked slowly through the stupefied crowd.

The noise and din resumed. Everyone closed around them, asking a million questions at once with happy expressions of gratitude and hand-shakes.

David returned the greetings from his friends with characteristic good cheer.

"We will visit with you all very soon, I promise!" he said loudly. "Right now your laird and your chief need to get to our respective homes to shake the dust of travel from our feet. Perhaps I shall see you at the inn this evening."

Enthusiastic jubilation followed as they walked to the car, David carrying the documents and petitions and blueprints. Maddy stood waiting.

"Quite a performance, girl!" she exclaimed. "You told that big lummox where to get off."

"I guess I did at that," said Loni. "The infor-mation you gave me helped. Were the documents really so devious as all that?"

"Worse. If you care to go over the details, the fine print was like nothing I have ever seen."

"It is enough for now to have exposed the scheme for what it was."

They climbed into David's car.

"So . . . this is Whales Reef," said Maddy as they made their way along. "Is it always like this?"

"Hardly," laughed David. "You happen to have come during tumultuous times. I think you will find our island generally quiet and peaceful once this hubbub settles down. But now," he added, glancing toward Loni, then over his shoulder at Maddy, "I think it's time to get you ladies home."

Loni smiled. "*Home* . . . hmm, that does have a certain ring to it."

74
THE CLIFFS

During Jimmy Joe's reckless drive to the ferry, the same inconvenient reality occurred to him as had suggested itself to some of the village men, that he would likely have a longer-than-pleasant wait before he could get off this ridiculous rock.

He arrived at the landing, slowed, and looked out across the empty sound. He neither saw nor heard any sign of the rusting tub.

He was not a man who enjoyed the feeling of powerlessness. If he thought it would do any good he would probably have tried to swim the channel. The idea of spending another minute on the island only intensified his rage.

But he didn't have to sit doing nothing. He threw the SUV into reverse, half skidded off the wooden landing, then jammed his foot on the accelerator and sped off northward along the narrow western road. Might as well see where it went, he thought. He would keep an ear cocked for the boat's engine.

In less than a minute he found himself driving along a dirt track barely wide enough for the Range Rover. It was unlikely anything so large had ever been on this road that headed toward the isolated northwest part of the island. A small sign warned, *Extreme Danger, Peat Bogs Ahead.* He had no idea what a peat bog was, but he had the good sense to slow down.

The road soon came to an end. Jimmy Joe stopped and got out. He glanced back to where he could see the blue of the ocean in the distance and listened.

Still no sign of the ferry.

Looking around, he thought he had never seen a more desolate place in all his life, unless it was the desert of West Texas near Amarillo. He set off walking absently along the path leading away from the dirt road. Without knowing it, he was soon approaching the high cliffs that defined most of the northern extremity of the island. Five minutes later, he stood on a high bluff over-looking the sea.

Behind him, coming from the south, black clouds were approaching rapidly. Huge drops had already begun to fall on the town. By the time the curious men on their way to the landing reached the edge of the village, they found themselves under a downpour. All but one turned back. He eased his car through the villagers as they sprinted for their homes, along with those caught out in the town square.

Standing on the treacherous bluff, a gust of wind brought Jimmy Joe to himself. He was just thinking that it was time he returned to the landing when he heard a noise behind him. He turned.

"What the—?" he said irritably. "What in the heck are you doing here?"

"I'm here to ask you about these plans," said the other, holding up a sheaf of papers.

"How did you get those?" snarled Jimmy Joe.

"Never mind how I got them. You made promises, and it is clear you planned to cut me out."

"What . . . those? That proves nothing."

"I know what you planted against me. I won't go to jail for this."

"You've got no proof."

"I'll take you down with me."

"You'll do no such thing, boy! I'm still running this show. Now get out of my way. I'm through with this tomfool place!"

As the words left his mouth, a bolt of lightning flashed offshore. Unconsciously Jimmy Joe glanced toward it.

A deafening crash of thunder followed. Instantly rain began to pour down over the north end of the island.

75

GUEST AT THE COTTAGE

David carried Loni's and Maddy's bags into the Cottage just as the rainstorm hit. They all hurried inside.

"You warned me about the rain!" laughed Maddy as they bustled into the entryway. "Whoa!" she said, gazing about at the high ceiling, oak paneling, and circular stairway swooping down from the landing above into the center of the foyer. "Look at this place. Hey, girl—it's a mansion!"

The house was chilly. David quickly had a fire going and the central heat turned up. As they suspected, they found evidence of mischief in Ernest's study, though nothing appeared seriously amiss. Loni vowed to talk to Hardy, and sternly, to make sure nothing had been taken, or if it had, to get it back.

"I'll run home while you get settled," said David. "Do you think you would at last like to have Isobel and Saxe take up their apartments here? With two ladies to cook for, Isobel would be in heaven. I think she's sick of men."

Loni laughed. Maddy had a puzzled expression on her face.

"My housekeeper and butler," explained Loni. "I told you about them."

"Oh yeah—I am dying to see a real butler!"

"I'm afraid you might be in for a disappointment," said David. "He was more a handyman and valet to my late cousin. I'm afraid he is feeling out of sorts that I won't allow him to wait on me."

"He can come over and wait on me," said Maddy. "I'm on vacation!"

"Perhaps that can be arranged. What do you think, Alonnah?"

"It might be a good time for them to return," she replied. "There is still so much uncertainty about the future, but for now . . . yes."

"And didn't I hear something about a gamekeeper?" asked Maddy.

"Yes, Dougal Erskine," said David. "He's already moved back here to the Cottage—out in the barn, that is."

"You make him stay in the barn?"

"He has a small apartment attached to the barn. It's quite nice, actually. Uncle Gregor took good care of the three of them. Well . . . I guess I will see you later," David said, turning to Loni, then hesitated. "We've been together almost constantly recently. Seems a little strange to just say goodbye and walk out."

"Especially in that rain!" said Loni. "Listen to it—it sounds like hail."

"That could be. I've seen hail here when the

temperature is seventy degrees, a rarity in itself even without the hail."

"Are you sure you want to go out there right now? How about a cup of tea first?"

"I ought to get home and check in with Isobel and Saxe. But how about you two coming for supper tonight at the Auld Hoose?"

"Something simple," replied Loni. "No big deal that will set the village talking."

"I'll just have something here," said Maddy. "You two—"

"Nonsense," interrupted David. "The three of us are a team, right? I'll have Isobel whip up—no, wait, I've got it. Let's go to the inn for fish and chips. That may set people talking even more, but we need to be seen right now."

"Perfect," rejoined Loni. "Fish and chips sounds great. You will love it, Maddy—a genuine old-fashioned Scottish pub with fish and chips you have to eat with your fingers."

"If you're sure the two of you don't mind my tagging along."

"You're my honored guest," said Loni. "But first I would like to get you settled. We'll take showers and sit down in front of this nice fire with cups of tea to settle our stomachs—at least for me. I won't force the tea on you quite yet, Maddy."

Loni turned and looked deep into David's eyes.

"Thank you, David . . . thank you for coming to

find me. We got back in the nick of time. I still don't know how all this is going to work out." She paused and glanced about the Great Room. "But you're right in what you said. This does feel like home. So shall we meet you at the inn?"

"I will head over there after swinging by the Auld Hoose. People will have a lot of questions about what happened in the square. I need to be there. I'll walk the village, greet everyone again."

"In this rain!"

"I'll wait till the squall passes. But I need to assure everyone that life is back to normal."

"Spoken like a true chief."

"Why don't I come back for the two of you around six? By the way, Maddy," he added, "on behalf of this chief and his people . . . welcome to Whales Reef!"

"Thank you, kind sir!" replied Maddy with a nod and curtsey.

David turned and left the Cottage.

Loni had scarcely sipped at her tea before she was sound asleep in her favorite chair in the Great Room. In her guest quarters upstairs in the East Wing, notwithstanding the danger of napping so late in the day, Maddy flopped onto the bed and was likewise asleep within minutes. Her introduction to tea would have to wait.

With an energy boost from an hour's sleep, the evening at the Whales Fin Inn was more enjoyable for the two women than it might have been otherwise. Though the front of the storm passed, the rain lingered, coming down hard at times, yet did not prevent a steady stream of villagers dropping in, desiring, as they said, to pay their respects to the chief and the laird.

By ten o'clock, all three of the day's arrivals were in their beds in the Cottage and Auld Hoose and, in the case of the two Americans, slept soundly in spite of their late naps. The rain striking the roof was as mesmerizing to Loni as would have been the sea in the distance had she been able to hear it.

The next morning Loni treated Maddy to her favorite breakfast of oatcakes, jam, and tea—to which Maddy's "No comment" brought Loni's "It will grow on you!" in reply.

After acclimatizing Maddy to her surroundings and taking the opportunity provided by a three-hour respite from the rain for a walk through the village, and giving Maddy a tour of the mill, Loni spent a good part of the afternoon putting Ernest's study back in order. A more comprehensive search of Ernest's file cabinet revealed more than had her cursory inspection three weeks earlier, including an unexpected discovery that would once and for all put to rest the nonsense about Hardy's claim to the inheritance. She was excitedly on her way to the Auld Hoose immediately to show the document to David.

Rain engulfed the entire Shetlands almost without stop for the rest of the week. Even David, whose walks over the island were legendary, kept close to one or the other of the two family homes. Loni was disappointed to have to postpone her reacquaintance with the moors and beaches of the island.

Loni telephoned Jason MacNaughton to confirm personally that she was again in the Shetlands with a friend whom she wanted to look over the estate's legal and financial affairs. He was eager to learn the upshot of the McLeod affair. They arranged to get together for a preliminary meeting on Friday.

After returning from Lerwick the next day, Loni and Maddy joined David and braved the rain to enjoy evening "tea" at the Croft with Sandy and Odara Innes and widowed Eldora Gordon.

"You three probably don't know," said Maddy, turning to her hosts during the meal, "what a popular woman our Miss Ford is back in our nation's capital."

Loni looked across the table with an expression of perplexity. Maddy cast her a knowing glance, then returned her attention to the nods and questions from the two older women.

"Oh yes," Maddy went on matter-of-factly, "quite the hot ticket in town. In fact, a man who may be a congressman by the end of the year recently proposed to her. Bought her a huge diamond ring—the whole nine yards."

Wide-eyed looks and more questions went around the table. Loni shrunk back in mortification.

"Tell us aboot it, lassie!" said Sandy.

Again it was Maddy to the rescue. "She could have been an important lady . . . who knows, maybe even wife of the president someday."

Exclamations of wonder filled the small room as Loni tried unsuccessfully to shush her friend.

"But she turned him down," continued Maddy. "Gave him back his ring. That's our Alonnah—a mind of her own. Wasn't interested in the glamorous life. A simple girl, that's her."

When the meal was over, as they were adjourning to the sitting room and the two older women disappeared into the kitchen to prepare tea, Loni pulled Maddy to one side.

"What were you *doing?*" she whispered. "I nearly died of embarrassment!"

"I've been waiting for you to tell him," replied Maddy. "David had to know. For all he knew, you might still be thinking of marrying Hugh. So I decided to take the heat for you and get it out there. Believe me, you will thank me later."

"If you say so. But . . . wow, I wasn't ready for that!"

By the end of the evening, besides having

embarrassed Loni, Maddy was beginning to perfect her Scottish brogue and had the other five in stitches as well with her Elvis, Bostonian, Texan, and Minnesotan accents.

76

SATURDAY AT THE AULD HOOSE

David Tulloch awoke on Saturday morning as he had on thousands of previous mornings. He descended the stairs and proceeded through his long-established morning routine—filling and turning on the water boiler, then stoking the fire in the great room and adding fresh peats.

He rose from his knees in front of the hearth, glanced about the empty room, and shivered. The storm had indeed dumped several barrages of hail on the island, and not with a surface temperature of seventy degrees. This wintry blast had come straight from the Arctic. He doubted it was above forty-five. It went against his grain to use central heat during the summer months. On a day like this, however, the place would never warm up. Reluctantly, he walked across the room, turned on the thermostat, and upped it to sixty-five.

He returned to the kitchen and set out a pot for tea as the water came to a boil. The pounding on the roof most of the night told him that this might not be the best of days for an early walk. He opened the kitchen door to have a firsthand look. A gust of wind blew splatters of rain against his face and sent the papers on the table behind him flying. Rain was driving down in slanted sheets so thick he could hardly see the barn. With some effort he closed the door against the gale.

He poured water out for tea and waited for it to brew.

After several weeks with Isobel, Saxe, and Dougal under his roof, he had to admit that today's morning quiet was nice. Dougal was an early riser and constantly coming and going, and Isobel was such a fussbudget that she refused to let the chief brew his own tea.

She was a dear soul, David thought with a smile, with a heart of gold and hands of service . . . just a little *too* helpful for one such as him who was accustomed to fending for himself. He was a man for whom solitude had always been as necessary to his spirit as oxygen to his lungs.

He poured out a large mug of tea and wandered back into the great room, where his Bible and favorite devotional book sat waiting beside his reading chair.

He sat down in front of the fire and let out a sigh of satisfaction. This was his favorite time of day, whether he was out on the island with his sheep or inside in this room surrounded by memories of family and clan contemplating the timeless truths of Scripture.

An hour later David sat staring into the glowing embers of peat, lost in reflection. His Bible lay on his lap still unopened. He had long since emptied his cup but not refilled it. The silence seemed to be speaking. But he was not able to discern what it was saying.

At length he rose, brewed a fresh pot of tea, and made a concerted effort to read. Still he could not concentrate. Finally he gave up, bundled himself in rain gear, boots and hat, and left the house for the barn. He found the sheep and cows huddled under the protective over-hangs of their respective stables—the latter awaiting Dougal's appearance for the morning's milking, which must go on rain or shine. Not that they worried about a little rain. But this was a downpour and, all things being equal, they were not opposed to the idea of trying to stay dry. He greeted his woolly ovine laddies and lassies and their bovine cousins, and tossed a supply of oats and hay into their respective bins. On this day, however, his friends of the animal kingdom held little interest for him.

Sight of the empty garage reminded him, if the rain did not let up, that he was stuck where he was for the day. The American ladies had borrowed his car for another trip to the big island. Unless there was a change, he did not envision getting soaked to the skin on a cold and windy day like this by a walk into town.

He returned to the house, removed boots and mackintosh, and climbed the stairs to his office, where he sat down and tried to work. This last month had been so hectic it had put him behind on his book and two articles he had contracted for. He had a tour scheduled to begin in a week. He had not even begun preparations.

Two hours later David still sat staring at open texts and notes on his desk, but had not yet written a word. The sensations filling him on this day were new, unfamiliar, disconcerting. He was out of sorts. He had his solitude . . . yet something unknown was determined to intrude into his place of inner quiet.

Meanwhile, Loni awoke Saturday morning and discovered Maddy nowhere to be found. Even Isobel, busy in the kitchen, had seen nothing of her. Assuming she had gone out—though for a walk on the moor or along the wild shoreline or to the village, she had no idea—Loni could do nothing but wait until she reappeared. Returning with her basket from her morning visit to her hens some time later, Isobel was at last able to shed light on the mystery.

"Your friend is in the barn with Mr. Erskine," she said, poking her head into the Great Room, where Loni sat with her tea.

Curious, Loni rose, bundled up, and left the Cottage through the kitchen door. She found Maddy decked out in rubber boots, gloves, an old work jacket of Dougal's that came down to her knees, and with pitchfork in hand. She and the gamekeeper were engaged in animated conversation while cleaning out several horse stalls.

"Maddy!" exclaimed Loni. "This is a surprise!"

"I haven't had so much fun since I was a girl on my grandfather's farm," said Maddy. "How this takes me back!"

"The lassie's got the blood o' her Scots kin in her veins," said Dougal, "an' is a hard worker as weel."

"Good for you, Maddy!" laughed Loni. "Dougal hasn't yet privileged *me* with one of his pitchforks. Nor does he frivolously hand out praise. He must like you!"

"Aye, but ye're the laird, ye see," said Dougal. "Wouldna be fitting for the likes o' yersel' tae muck oot a stall."

Still laughing, Loni left the two, who quickly resumed their conversation, and returned to the house. After Maddy was cleaned up an hour and a half later, they took the ferry in David's car across to Shetland. Not surprising given the weather, they were joined by no villagers bound for Lerwick on such a day.

"Did your mother ever read to you the story about the three lost boys?" asked Maddy as they set off across the sound in the rain.

"My grandmother did," replied Loni.

"Oh . . . of course, I'm sorry, Loni—I forgot."

"It's okay, Maddy," said Loni. "What about it?"

"Rough stormy water like this always reminds me of it in a nostalgic sort of way," said Maddy almost dreamily. "No land behind us, nothing but open sea in front of us—we could be far out to sea just like the three boys who went out on a raft in the storm and were rescued by the ferry captain."

"Let's hope no one will have to rescue us!"

A good portion of the previous afternoon they had spent in Jason MacNaughton's office, familiarizing Maddy with the legal aspects of the estate and its holdings. They were scheduled to meet him again on Monday, along with Mrs. Bemiss, for an in-depth analysis of balance sheet, income, and expense accounts of the estate's properties and businesses, all the bank accounts, and a review of U.K. tax laws and their bearing on Loni's inheritance. Their plan on Saturday was to visit most of the sites in northern Shetland in which the estate held interest. Armed with a clearly marked map and accompanying notations in the solicitor's hand, they set out in the miserable weather, creeping along some of the narrow roads at thirty miles per hour, to locate several parcels of undeveloped land, one small refinery on land owned by the estate and rented to BP, and the sites of several oil fields where the estate maintained income-producing leases.

"I still can't believe it," Maddy said as they returned to the ferry late that afternoon. "You own all those places. Girl, you are a land baron!"

"It's all so detached from my real life," said Loni. "I suppose on an intellectual level I am aware that what you say is true. But it is in a dream world someplace. I'm just . . . *me,* and anxious to get back to work on the seventh floor of Capital Towers."

"Forget it, girl. If you think your life will ever be the same, no way. There's no going back. And you're forgetting the elephant in the room that will change your future more than being a tycoon."

"What are you talking about?"

"You know good and well what I'm talking about. Has *he* said anything?"

"I can't think about that . . . no, he hasn't."

"Give him time."

"Maddy!"

"Just sayin'," said Maddy with a knowing smile.

The remainder of David's day progressed much as it had begun—walks back and forth through the house broken by reflective silences in front of one window or another staring out into the rain, with three or four more inconclusive sojourns to the barn and back, and an attempted walk out onto the moor in the rain, which ended after less than ten minutes when he turned back and returned to the house.

As much as he had been looking forward to having the Auld Hoose to himself again, something felt wrong. Something was missing. The solitude that had always been such a refuge to his soul was disconcerting now.

And so the long, dreary, empty, monotonous, unproductive, lonely day wore on as if each minute were an hour.

By the time he banked the fire and covered the coals, turned out the lights, and climbed the stairs for the night, he was beginning to understand the message of the silence—that the season of solitude in his life was drawing to a close. It was time to share that innermost region of his self with another.

The realization, however, brought in its wake an inrush of quandaries, complications, and impracticalities.

Sleep did not renew its acquaintance with David until well after one in the morning.

77

KEEPER OF THE KEY

For several days David had let it be known that he and Loni would be in church on Sunday. When the day came, the rain eased somewhat. By 10:30 the church was packed.

Loni had asked Rev. Yates if she and David could say a few words. At the conclusion of the service, he was only too happy to turn the pulpit over to them. After a brief greeting from David to the villagers and his introduction of Loni, she rose and came forward.

"It is nice to see you all this morning," she said, smiling affectionately. "I realize you do not yet know me well, and I am still learning your names. I hope you will bear with me. I am also aware that the locked room at the Cottage has been a great mystery to you for many years. For those of you who have not yet heard, that room is now unlocked and open. Indeed, there was nothing dreadful inside, but rather evidence everywhere of the man of learning and study and wisdom that I am confident describes him whom you refer to as the Auld Tulloch.

"I hope to dispel what has been such a mystery among you for so long. To that end, I would like you to see it for yourselves. Therefore, you are all invited to the Cottage this afternoon at two o'clock, or anytime thereafter, for what we call in the States an open house. You will be able to walk through the Cottage and see the study of Ernest Tulloch for yourselves."

Murmurs of approval spread through the congregation.

"We will have tea and coffee on hand and as many oatcakes and sweets as Mrs. MacNeill has been able to bake in the last two days since I told her of my plan. I want to thank you personally, Mrs. MacNeill," said Loni, looking toward the village baker, "for keeping my invitation a secret. Isobel Matheson and I have been busy baking as well.

"As I said, I still do not know many of you. So please come so that I can meet you. At three o'clock I will share a little more about my plans, which I know you have all been anxious about. I will also make an important announcement concerning someone in your community. However, you will have to contain your curiosity until that time."

Loni glanced toward the minister and smiled. "Thank you, Rev. Yates," she said, then stepped down from behind the pulpit.

That afternoon most of the villagers turned out to walk through the Cottage and see the study and introduce themselves to Loni, everyone expressing their gratitude for what she had done to rescue the woolen mill and factory. Stirling Yates was on hand with the rest. During the two weeks since his announcement he had been enjoying himself immensely, meeting with and visiting the villagers on a more equal and less clerical footing than before. His friendly presence on this day at the Cottage in jeans and work shirt further deepened the increased regard in which he was held by those getting to know him in a true way for the first time.

Shortly after three, Loni took her place on the balcony above the entry foyer with David beside her. The villagers gathered below and on the stairs crowding in as best they could.

"I want to thank you all for being here today," Loni began as they quieted, "and for the welcome you have shown me in recent weeks. I know we had a bit of a rocky start, but I think we have weathered that at last. I almost feel that today represents a new beginning of a friendship between me and you that I hope is a good and happy one for us all."

She paused as she gazed down from the landing.

"Before I begin with what I want to say this afternoon, I want to formally introduce my friend Madison Swift," Loni continued, looking to where Maddy stood at the foot of the stairs. "If you haven't yet greeted her, I hope you will make her feel welcome as well. Maddy is not only my friend, she is also my boss and a renowned investment analyst. I asked her to return with me to help me make wise financial decisions that will be good for all of you, and that will secure the prosperity of Whales Reef for many years to come. Not only that, Maddy also has Scottish blood in her veins, from the MacGregor clan no less. So she is one of us!"

Whoops and cheers went up. Those nearby turned and spoke a few unintelligible words to Maddy.

"Listen to me," laughed Loni. "I am talking like *I'm* one of you!"

"Ye're aye one o' us noo, lassie!" cried Noak Muir from the back of the crowd. "An' we're a' prood o' ye for what ye done wi' the Texan bloke!"

More cheers and shouts joined Noak's.

"Thank you, Mr. Muir—" laughed Loni.

"Nae, nae, lassie," interrupted Noak again. "If ye're oor laird, there canna be this carryin' on wi' *misters* an' the like."

"All right, then, Noak," said Loni, smiling. "I shall take your admonishment to heart. The man you call the Texan was a handful all right. Coincidentally as I'm sure some of you realized from what I said, it turns out that I knew him as a child, though I knew he didn't remember me."

"Weel, ye stood up tae him, lassie—'tis a' that matters."

Once more the crowded entryway quieted.

"My friends," began Loni again, "and I think I may at last truly call you that, this study behind me which you have all now seen was locked fifty-three years ago with this key." She held up the dark iron key in her hand.

She went on to tell about her first day on the island and Sandy's visit. As she recounted his story of the funeral of Ernest Tulloch, many nods and comments punctuated her account from others who remembered the day.

"On that day Sandy saw Elizabeth and Ernest's

firstborn son, Brogan, and his wife disappear up these very stairs into the room behind me, where they shut themselves behind the closed door. Only now, from reading letters and a journal from those former times, am I now able to tell you of the danger to Ernest's legacy had Sally allowed control of the room to pass to Wallace's wife, whose hatred of Ernest was by then well known and was the reason she chose to lock the door behind me in order to preserve the memory of the Auld Tulloch. Not everyone values legacies, and indeed there are some who will do their best to destroy them. Sally was wise enough to protect against that danger. By mutual consent on that day, she named Ernest Tulloch the posthumous Bard of Whales Reef, and Sally designated Brogan as Keeper of the Key. The room was sealed and never opened again until three weeks ago.

"Incidentally, in my examination of some of the files in the study, I came across the marriage licence attesting to the marriage between Ernest and Sally. This will put to rest another untrue rumor that has been circulating for some time. It is on the sideboard just there," she added, pointing down across the foyer, "if you haven't had a chance to see it yet.

"However, I was speaking about how I came into possession of the key to the Auld Tulloch's study. Unbeknownst to any of us, this key made its way to America with Brogan and eventually into my hands through Brogan's son, my own grandfather Grant Tulloch. Last month the key returned here to the Cottage where I opened the mysterious locked door.

"So now I intend to follow Sally's example, as your laird—though I must admit I am still having difficulty getting used to your calling me that!"

Brief laugher went through the room below her.

"And now, in the tradition begun by Sally as the mistress of the Cottage, I am going to assume the right to designate a new Keeper of the Key to what they called the Bard's Chamber. I do not believe that it will be necessary for the room to be locked. I intend to keep it unlocked and available for use, yours as well as mine. The room represents a spiritual heritage left by Ernest Tulloch for the entire island. Its use, however, will be at the discretion of the new Keeper of the Key of the Bard's Chamber. It will be his duty, and also his honor, to keep the Auld Laird's legacy burning bright."

Everyone listening felt the solemnity in Loni's voice and the import of the moment. From below, Maddy watched with awe to see what stature and confidence the mantle of her position had given her protégé.

"I pray," Loni concluded, "that the legacy of this proud family of which I am privileged to be a part will live on into future generations through men and women of Ernest Tulloch's posterity and into the lives of everyone who calls this island of Whales Reef home."

Seeing David where he stood at Loni's side, everybody listening assumed that she was about to turn the key over to him. Gradual exclamations of astonishment therefore began to circulate as she started down the stairs.

"In that spirit, then," said Loni as her eyes came to rest on one of the oldest men present, "I am today presenting this key to a man who truly knew Ernest Tulloch as a friend better than any other man or woman still alive."

She slowly descended the staircase and approached Sandy. Tears were now flowing down his aged cheeks.

"Lassie . . . lassie," he whispered.

Loni held out both hands with the key in her palms.

"Alexander Innes, lifelong friend of the Auld Tulloch," said Loni, "I appoint you Keeper of the Key of the Bard's Chamber."

His eyes glistening, daughter and sister beaming proudly beside him, Sandy took the key from Loni's hand. Loni stooped down and kissed him on the cheek.

"Lassie," he said in a barely audible voice, "ye do an auld man prood."

78
THE REEFS

The lengthy onslaught of rain and wind abated on Monday, but the seas remained turbulent. Most of the island's fishermen went out, though some of the currents proved dangerous.

Noak Muir in the *Bonnie Muir* found the going more difficult than he had encountered since his search for the *Hardy Fire* earlier that spring. Leaving the harbor and setting a northerly course around the west of the island, he passed the North Cliffs and found the swell from nor'-nor'-east perilously strong. He turned into it and battled it for twenty or thirty minutes before realizing it was hopeless to fish in such conditions. He began to navigate a wide circle to return to the harbor.

Now the surging tide threatened to pull him straight into the rocky shoals at the base of the cliffs. He sent one of his men to the bow with binoculars to watch for the outlying reefs for which Whales Reef had been named. Noak powered with all the *Bonnie Muir*'s engine could give him to round the northwest corner of the island before the swell and the wind battered them to bits.

A cry rang out from his lookout. It was not the warning of danger Noak had expected.

"There's a man snagged again' the cliffs!" he cried. "Cor lumme, stone the crows! 'Tis a deid body, Noak!"

The rest of the crew hurried forward to look.

Whoever it was, they were powerless from where they were. Noak was doing his best to keep himself and his crew from joining the poor blighter. There was no sign of another boat gone aground anywhere on the reefs.

Ten minutes later they were safely around the point and heading for the harbor at full speed. Noak was already on his radio to the Coast Guard.

They reached the harbor. Within minutes, half the men of the village were piling into cars and the rest on foot making for the north end of the island in a swarm.

Reaching the Peat Fields and seeing the black SUV parked at the end of the road, no one had to be reminded who had been driving it.

Within the hour dozens of the village men were standing on the bluff north of the Peat Fields, staring straight down onto the rocky shoals below.

Someone thought they saw a white object hung up against the rocks. It might be a hat, some said. Nobody could see it clearly from so far away.

A police helicopter was first on the scene from Lerwick. Those in the village who had not made the trek to the cliffs turned out to watch it whirring overhead toward the north of the island. A Coast Guard rescue boat was not far behind.

The waters were treacherous. No diver could be sent to recover the body. The helicopter could not risk getting so close to the cliff. A rubber skiff was launched from the rescue boat. With the aid of ropes and daring maneuvering, it managed to get close enough to snag the body and pull it from the cliffs, which had unbelievably kept it from being washed out to sea. By all rights, the body should never have been found.

No one on Whales Reef needed to be told who it was. It took the police but an hour to identify the victim to the press as American James Joseph McLeod of Texas. The initial determination was either suicide—the man was obviously despondent, everyone in the village said, after his deception had been unmasked—or an accidental fall, though no one could imagine what he was doing on the North Cliffs.

A preliminary investigation, however, amid numerous lacerations and cuts and broken bones from the fall, and the obvious deterioration of the body from being so long at the mercy of the elements, revealed a gunshot wound just above the heart. The coroner stated it as his opinion that the man had been dead before toppling off the cliff. Several unidentified markings on his chest, as if he had been jabbed with some kind of pointed blunt instrument, remained a mystery.

79
QUIET EVENING

The brouhaha surrounding the discovery of the body off the northwest reefs kept David busy all day Monday. He traipsed out to the cliffs with the rest of the village men and was quickly swept into the investigation with the authorities. When the police helicopter set down a hundred feet inland from the cliffs shortly after the body had been recovered, the sheriff climbed out and ran toward the cluster of islanders to see if David was among them. Minutes later, the chopper rose and banked steeply around in the direction of Lerwick with David aboard in hopes of being able to identify the body.

Having done so and been questioned to see what he knew, David was returned to the Whales Reef harbor. A crowd was waiting for him. Having their chief whisked away from the north bluffs by helicopter, then deposited two hours later at the harbor by police escort was cause enough for excitement. David's confirmation of the dead man's identity—which they had all suspected—produced an uproar that spread over the island like wildfire.

The commotion did not die down all afternoon. A dead body set men's tongues talking as furiously as any women's gossip. Nothing was so delicious to speculate on as a suspicious death in their midst.

David remained in the thick of it all day, followed about and peppered with questions. The inn remained full all afternoon. The din in the common room was so loud that even Hardy Tulloch's voice at the table where he was holding court expounding his own theories about the Texan's demise could scarcely be heard ten feet away. It was only with the greatest difficulty that David managed to extricate himself, making a stop by the market before hurrying home about four. He had promised the island's two American guests dinner at the Auld Hoose after their day in the city. He was running out of time.

David quickly got out of his boots and muddy trousers, showered and donned more suitable informal evening attire, then set about preparations in his kitchen.

Loni and Maddy arrived about five-thirty straight from the ferry.

"I'm running behind with supper," said David. "We had considerable excitement here today. If you two want to take my car to the Cottage to change or rest up a bit, we won't be ready to eat until about seven."

"We saw people about everywhere in the village," said Loni. "What's the excitement about?"

"You won't believe it," said David, turning serious. "It's actually rather gruesome."

Loni and Maddy waited expectantly.

"A body was found on the northwest reefs," replied David. "Noak Muir's crew spotted it from Noak's boat."

"Oh, no!" exclaimed Loni as her hand went to her mouth.

"A . . . *dead* body?" said Maddy.

David nodded.

"One of the fishermen?" asked Loni with concern.

"Not exactly," replied David. "It was Jimmy Joe McLeod. He fell or was pushed off the bluff. He had been shot."

The two women stared back in disbelief.

"What happened?" asked Loni after a moment.

"No one knows. The police are looking into it. Not a very appealing subject for pre-dinner conversation."

"What a shock," said Loni. "Maybe we will go back over to the Cottage for some downtime at that."

With all the information she needed for her forensic analysis of the estate's holdings and finances, and armed with dozens of files and documents and financial reports, Maddy was scheduled to return to the States on Wednesday.

Loni had divulged nothing about her own

plans. Neither Maddy nor David wanted to ask. Throughout Monday evening at the Auld Hoose, as David engaged in friendly conversation with Maddy and asked about her work, Loni listened quietly but said little. Much was on her mind.

All three were silently wondering the same thing: Was there any reason for Loni to stay? Or was her business on Whales Reef completed?

As the evening wore on, David, too, became subdued. Both women sensed the change. Conversation lagged. By common consent the visit drew to a close. David drove the two back to the Cottage about nine-thirty.

He saw them to the door. Maddy went inside. Loni lingered. David was quiet.

"I know that Maddy will be leaving the day after tomorrow," he said at length. "I, uh . . . I assume you'll be going with her?"

The inflection of his voice hovered ambiguously between statement and question.

Loni stared at the ground but did not reply.

"I've been hoping you and I could spend some time together before then," said David.

"I would like that."

"Will you be meeting with Jason again?"

"No. Maddy has all she needs."

"You'll be around tomorrow?"

Loni nodded.

"Would you care to go for a walk? I would like to show you my version of your meadow. I want to return the favor of your showing me your special place."

"I would love to see it."

"Around one?"

"That sounds perfect," replied Loni.

"Good. I'll see you then. I'll walk over. And wear your island-exploring clothes," added David. "After the rain, it might be muddy."

80

THOUGHTFUL WALK

David appeared at the Cottage on Tuesday at one sharp.

"You'll be okay alone?" Loni said to Maddy as she and David walked toward the door.

"Hey, girl, if I can handle D.C. and New York, I can handle a village like Whales Reef. I may walk into town and have a pint of the best beer in the Shetlands. Meanwhile, I will canvass local opinion on their new laird."

"Don't you dare!" laughed Loni.

"I doubt you have a thing to worry about. These people are in love with you."

Loni smiled, then slowly nodded. "They have been unbelievably welcoming," she said. "I love them too. What a change a month can make. I felt like a foreigner and stranger. Now I feel that I belong."

She and David left the house. David led her past the barn and stables north into the center of the island.

"Have you been up the Muckle Hill?" he asked as their way steepened.

Loni shook her head. "I walked about its base several times and noticed the big stone on top. I intended to climb it, but then . . ."

She hesitated and smiled sheepishly. "I left sort of abruptly," she added.

"I noticed that!" rejoined David.

Fifteen minutes later, warm from the climb up the steep and soggy hill, they reached the summit. They stood a few moments looking at the ancient stone monument.

"What do all the markings signify?" asked Loni.

"No one knows," replied David. "They are Pictish or Norse, probably from the 600s to 800s, incredibly old and mostly worn away."

"You can see the whole island from here," said Loni, slowly turning about. "The entire coastline is visible. What a view. It's stunning. And there's Shetland . . . it's so close. From up here you see Whales Reef from such a different perspective."

"I come here as often as I am able and pray for the people of the island."

"What do you pray?"

David grew thoughtful a moment. "Many

things," he said. "But my father taught me what is called the Chief's Prayer as it was passed down to him."

"Would it be presumptuous for me to ask to hear it?"

"Not at all. The laird should know what the chief desires for the people. It goes like this: *A Dhe ar n-athraichean, cum agus dion do shluag anns an eilean seo le curam agus gradh. Gum biodh an aon eolas aca ort mar an Athair is a bha aig Criosda ort fhein. Agus gum biodh eolas agamsa oirbh, agus geill dhuibh, mar fhear-daimh umhail, fad mo re 'smo lo. Amen.*"

"That was beautiful, so lyrical and ancient-sounding. What does it mean?"

"It's Gaelic—a language that is nearly lost except in the western Scottish islands and Highlands. A rough translation would be something along the lines of, *God of our Fathers, keep and protect your people of this isle in your care and your love. May they know you as their own Father as Jesus knew you. And may I, their humble kinsman, know you, obey you, and be their faithful servant all my days. Amen.*"[1]

"That is as beautiful as the Gaelic," said Loni.

Loni looked at David and smiled. "You truly love these people and this island, don't you?"

"More than I can say," replied David softly.

---

1. Gaelic translation by John Angus Morrison.

"That is why this year of uncertainty over the inheritance has been such agony for me—I was unable to be all I wanted to be for the people. There was the threat of Hardy inheriting hanging over us, which would not have been good for the island, to say the least. Yet I could not openly contest it for fear of appearing self-seeking."

"That must have been hard."

David sighed. "There were many who misunderstood my silence. There were some," he added with a laugh, "who thought I ought to claim the inheritance by force, as if I could usurp legalities altogether. And when we learned that an American had been discovered who was the rightful heir, then indeed did speculation run rampant."

"I'm not surprised."

"I tried to put on a cheerful front and tell everyone that there was nothing to worry about and to give the unknown heir, whoever *she* was, the benefit of the doubt. And when they found out you were a woman, then did the island *really* erupt in a frenzy!"

Loni could not help but laugh.

"I could not help being concerned too. As I told you and your grandparents, my distrust of Americans went back to my boyhood. I was terrified that the island could be sold or changed or developed—all the things that our poor Texan friend planned to do. My concern for the future kept me awake many nights. Happily, shall we say, you turned out much differently than the evil specter of our overactive imaginations."

"I hope in a good way."

"In a *very* good way—from an opportunist bent on exploiting the island's resources for personal gain, you are a—" David stopped.

"Yes?" asked Loni slowly.

"I don't suppose I can call you a knight on a white horse riding in to save the mill and rescue the island from everyone's worst fears, but perhaps I shall call you a *princess* on a white horse."

Loni began to laugh again but caught herself. A strange look came over her face.

"I've never been called that before."

"A princess?"

Loni nodded.

"I meant it," said David. "That's how people think of you. What Maddy said earlier is true— everyone on the island loves you."

"After the way it began, that's hard to believe."

"You have won them over. They are very proud to have an *American* Tulloch as their laird."

They left the monument and continued down the north slope of the Muckle Hill. The turn of the conversation settled deep into their hearts. Both were quiet.

81
THE CHIEF'S CAVE

Twenty minutes later David and Loni were standing at the northeast corner of the island, gazing out over the treacherous North Cliffs to the blue of the sea that stretched toward Norway.

"What a terrifying height to be looking straight down," said Loni, taking a few steps back.

David nodded. "It's a dangerous place. The Shetlands are full of cliffs like this."

"Has anyone ever fallen?" asked Loni. "Any of the villagers, I mean—not, you know, visiting Texans," she added with a shudder.

"There are always stories. No one in my life-time. But this is where I came close myself after learning of my father's death. He is still out there ... somewhere," said David pensively. "It is a fear all fishing families live with."

Loni gently laid a hand on David's arm.

"David, I am sorry. I was only one when my parents were killed. I have no memory of it. But as a teen, I can't imagine the pain you must have gone through."

"It was a hard time."

"Especially for someone like you, who is . . ."

Loni's words trailed off. Unconsciously she withdrew her hand from his arm.

"You were about to say?"

"What I meant was that . . . well, you aren't like most men—tough and macho like Hardy. You're sensitive and gentle—you feel things deeply. Losing a father would be harder for you."

"You may be right," said David. "But enough of my reflections on the past. It's time to think of the future. Come, we're almost to the place I wanted to show you."

He led them a short way along the edge of the bluff. "It's been raining so much that it may be slippery," he said. He took her hand, then started down a steep path that led over the side.

"Is it safe?" said Loni.

"Probably not," laughed David. "But I could walk this path with my eyes closed. And I've already been out here today just to make sure. Stay close and hold on tight."

"You won't have to tell me twice." Loni's grip on his hand was already strong enough to alleviate any fears David might have had.

Gingerly he led down the steep trail that was beginning to dry out from the north wind following the storm. Halfway down, Loni's feet slipped and she slid into David's side. He stretched an arm around her to steady her. Keeping her close, they made it the rest of the way to the bottom without incident.

David released Loni and stepped back. Again he took her hand and led her under an outcropping of stone into the dark interior ahead.

"Oh, this is great!" exclaimed Loni. "Who would ever know it's here over the side of the cliff?"

"Everyone on the island knows it's here," laughed David, "though its use is supposed to be restricted."

"To whom?"

"Me."

"Just you?"

"It's called the Chief's Cave."

David released Loni's hand, and she peered about in the flickering light of the darkened little chamber.

"And with a small peat fire burning, it looks as though you thought of everything."

"I told you, I came out here earlier. And for your dining pleasure, m'lady, I have oatcakes and tea. You may take a seat on the tartan blanket. The water in the pot should be just right for tea."

"How fun—David, this is wonderful . . . it's so dry and cozy. Thank you for bringing me here."

Soon they were seated side by side, cups of tea in hand, staring out the mouth of the cave over the blue expanse of the sea. Cries of gulls and many varieties of seabirds filled the air. Otherwise they might have been completely alone in the world.

"It is so beautiful and peaceful," sighed Loni.

"I suppose this is like your meadow," said David. "It is my favorite place in the world. Did you see *Superman*?"

"Didn't everybody?"

"Probably not most of the people of Whales Reef," chuckled David. "I saw it in England when I was at university. This is *my* Fortress of Solitude. This is where I discovered God, and eventually came to terms with who I am and who I want to be. It has been my refuge ever since. This is where I feel most fully myself."

"I know exactly what you mean. That is how I feel in my meadow."

"I'm glad I was able to share that with you," he said. "I have wanted to share my special place with you ever since."

The silence that descended inside the cave was lengthy but not uncomfortable. The peats burned low and faded into dying orange embers. Both were enjoying the Eternal Now of the moment. It was a *Now* almost too full. Both were feeling many things.

It was David who broke the silence. His voice was soft, almost as if continuing a conversation already in progress. "Will you be going back with Maddy?"

"I, uh . . . I hadn't decided for certain," replied Loni hesitantly.

"Is there any way I could persuade you to stay?"

Loni did not answer.

"I don't want you to go," said David after another long minute.

Loni's throat was dry.

"I didn't just bring you out here for the view," David went on. "It was because . . . how do I say this? . . . because I wanted to invite you into my place of solitude . . . not merely the cave, this is just a symbol of something deeper inside *me* . . . inside my heart."

David let out a sigh. "This isn't as easy as I hoped it would be," he said. "I had it all planned and it made perfect sense. Now I'm fumbling over my words like a schoolboy."

Loni's heart was pounding.

"What I am trying to say," David went on, "is that I think I finally understand why Brogan left the island. What I mean is that I want to share my solitude with you, my life, everything. I want to share everything with you—every minute, every idea, everything I am thinking. Yes, you are a princess . . . *my* princess riding onto Whales Reef on her white horse to rescue me from my Fortress of Solitude."

Loni laughed lightly. The warmth creeping up the back of her neck began to engulf her whole body.

"Do you understand what I am trying to say?" asked David.

"I'm not completely sure, David," said Loni softly, a hint of fun in her tone. "Why don't you try to explain it to me just a *little* more clearly?"

David drew in a deep breath and let it out slowly. "You don't make it easy on a guy, do you?"

"That's not a girl's job!"

"All right, let me put it as simply as I can," began David again. "When we were in the States, I said the people needed you and that you needed to make your decisions here. What I really wanted to say is that I wanted you to come back more than the rest of them. I knew something was happening between us. But with all you had to cope with, I didn't want to put added pressure on you. Yet I suppose there is no way to keep such feelings hidden forever."

"I don't think so," rejoined Loni, smiling. "And knowing you, you probably already knew I was feeling the same way."

David smiled.

"I had a pretty good idea. At least I hoped so. But I could see you were unnerved by it. I didn't want to rush."

"Ever the gentleman."

"I don't know about that. But has this been clear enough for you?"

"It will do," replied Loni, slipping her hand through David's arm and snuggling close to his side. "And for my part I would just say I wasn't quite ready to go back to the States. So perhaps I might stay just a *few* more days."

They did not return to the Cottage for several

more hours. By then they had crisscrossed the northern half of the island several times and had been talking continuously since leaving the cave.

As they approached the Cottage, realizing that after this day life would no more be the same, their conversation gradually ceased. Leaving Loni at the door, David took her in his arms. She leaned her head against his chest for several long seconds.

Their respective places of solitude were now shared with the other. No words were needed.

At the same time that David and Loni were seated in the Chief's Cave, two detectives appeared on Whales Reef. They instituted intensive interrogations with all those willing to talk to them who had been present at the town square on the previous Wednesday. Everyone told exactly the same story. With so many eyewitnesses to the heated argument, there could be no doubt.

At five o'clock that afternoon, as he stepped off the *Hardy Fire* onto the quay at the harbor, Hardy found two men in suits, accompanied by two uniformed bobbies waiting to take him into custody.

It was all over the island within an hour that Hardy Tulloch had been taken to the jail in Lerwick, charged with the murder of Jimmy Joe McLeod.

82
CLOUDY FUTURE

Loni stood at the upstairs window of the Cottage's fabled study, staring out over Whales Reef. It was a crisp sunny day. The sea eastward was flecked with whitecaps. She remembered how empty and forlorn this view had seemed when she first arrived on the island. Now it was full of life.

Quiet life. Peaceful life.

Maddy had been gone four days now. She would be back in the office bright and early today, this Monday morning in the second week of August, ready to start the new week.

Loni glanced at her watch. Eleven-thirty . . . *hmm, that would make it six-thirty back home.* Maddy was probably already at her desk, thought Loni with a smile, with a tall cup of coffee—strong and black—beside her. Maddy would refuse to let a little jet lag slow her down.

Home . . .

The word repeated itself in Loni's mind. She was beginning to seriously wonder what that simple word meant.

A week ago she had assumed she would return with Maddy and be with her now, excitedly talking over the week's agenda, outlining her boss's speaking schedule, putting together prospectuses for potential clients as she had a year ago with the Midwest Investment Group—which, she was proud to say, was exceeding expectations. Not to mention that Maddy's long-delayed New York promotion was at last imminent. Maddy continued to talk about it as a partnership promotion, fully assuming that Loni would accompany her to the Big Apple.

That world of investments and high finance seemed remote and far away now, as if from another time, as if the Loni of that world were a different person.

She *was* a different person. Here she was standing contentedly with a cup of tea in her hand, looking out on the barren moor of a remote island in the North Atlantic she had never heard of two months ago, staring out on land that was hers from inside a huge, roomy, historic, wonderful "cottage" that everyone called the *haa*, the "laird's" home.

That laird was *her*. This was her cottage, her house. But was it also her *home?* She had not yet figured out the answer to that question.

Giving Maddy a final hug last Wednesday, with a few tears to match, watching her walk across the tarmac in gusty wind to the small waiting plane that would take her from Sumburgh on the southern tip of Shetland to Aberdeen, and from there to London and the U.S., watching her smile as she turned for a last wave . . . waiting for the plane to take off and disappear into the clouds above, then walking to David's car . . . it was obvious to Loni that *everything* had changed since her arrival with Maddy and David a little over a week earlier.

She had stayed. Maddy had returned to Washington without her.

How long would she stay this time?

The drive back to Whales Reef at David's side was quiet. Neither felt talkative. Their minds were busily reflecting on the same question.

What did the future hold?

Most of the legalities of the estate had been sorted out. The mill was flush with operating capital and again functioning at peak capacity.

The spirit on the island was full of enthusiasm and smiles. Even the fact of Hardy's arrest only dampened the spirits of a handful of his closest family and friends. Many secretly said to themselves that he had been bound for such a fate all his life. It was no more than he deserved.

The *business* aspects of the estate and village had been settled. But the *personal* scenario that had engulfed her was a different matter.

Business these days could be conducted anywhere. Oceans and time zones were no impediment to the internet.

Personally, however, it was a different story. Relationships could *not* be conducted long distance. She was in love with a man who lived in the middle of the North Sea five thousand miles from her home and career. On that front, the future was cloudy.

Loni took a satisfying swallow of tea and turned from the window in Ernest's study, the Bard's Chamber. She sat down at the rolltop desk whose contents she had tried to arrange as closely as possible to how she remembered them when she had first entered the mysterious room a month earlier. She had even managed to retrieve from Hardy prior to his arrest the letters between Brogan and his father that Jimmy Joe had pilfered.

She glanced at her left hand. The fourth finger was empty. The sight sent Loni's thoughts briefly toward Hugh.

For Hugh it was about appearance, influence, looks, glamour, impressing the right people. She wondered if Hugh had ever known her at all . . . or even wanted to. He would have received the ring back with her note by now. Could he possibly understand?

David's words had been with her continually since last Tuesday: *"I want to share everything with you—every minute, every idea, everything. . . ."*

It certainly hadn't been a classic American declaration of love. No fanfare. No brass band. No dropping to his knees to express some syrupy sentiment while she stood awkwardly waiting with red face and neck.

It was quiet, unpretentious, almost unemotional . . . though her heart had pounded like a bass drum as David poured out his thoughts and feelings. And when he had quietly taken her in his arms, she knew that at last she had found something she had been searching for without even knowing it.

She had found her *home* . . . the surrounding warmth of David's embrace.

Since that day she had learned the old-fashioned British term that perhaps described what had taken place better than most Americans could grasp.

Within two days it was all around the village that she and David had an "understanding."

Loni smiled. Ever since word began to circulate from cottage to cottage, across fences and gardens and beside clotheslines, from the bakery to the post office and everywhere up and down the main street, the village women had fussed over her and smiled and greeted her as if she were the personally adopted daughter of everyone. Having grown up without a mother, suddenly she had a hundred mothers.

Even Rinda Gunn, David's aunt, could occasionally be seen with the hint of a smile on her face, though whenever she saw David, it was still a curt, "Weel, yoong David," that greeted him.

Loni looked down again at her hand. She needed no symbol to know that she loved David, and that he loved her.

It was *understood*.

83
The Color of Love

Loni walked from the study downstairs, poured herself a fresh cup of tea, and returned to the Great Room.

Her eyes strayed to the mantel above the fireplace where she had set the tiny sprig of heather David handed her on the first day they met. She walked to the fireplace. Gingerly she picked it up. Though dry, the tiny blooms of heather still retained their color.

How fitting, she thought. It was just as true love should be. Though the newness fades in time, though the experience of age replaces the energy of youth, though perhaps the body weakens . . . the color of love never dies.

What an appropriate symbol to have been the first exchange passing between she and David before she even knew his name—a tiny heathery token of lasting and vibrant color.

Loni was reminded of another bouquet. She replaced the sprig of heather on the mantel and turned, set down her cup, left the room, walked across the entry and opened the front door. Several feet away still sat the storm-battered vaseful of tiny wet American flags and drooping brown chrysanthemums. How perfectly appropriate, she thought with a smile, were the two floral gifts from that day—the showy chrysanthemums full of glitz but no staying power, while the little sprig of heather was as full of color as ever.

She picked up the heavy vase with its dead blooms and tasteless ornaments, walked to the nearby garbage bin, and dumped them inside.

Half an hour later, again seated in front of the fire, the doorbell intruded into Loni's thoughts. She and David had planned to join each other for lunch at the inn and spend the afternoon in the village. It was time, David said, to let themselves be visible, to walk the lanes and streets, to let themselves be made over and questioned by the auld wives to their hearts' content.

Loni opened the door.

David smiled. "Do you remember the first day we met," he asked, "right here?"

"How could I forget? It seems like ten years ago. Has it really only been a few weeks?"

"Time has a way of playing tricks on the brain." David paused, then said, "I gave you something on that day—"

"I was just looking at it," said Loni, leading him inside. As they entered the Great Room, she walked to the mantel and brought back the little bouquet. "See—it still has its color."

"Heather is amazing that way," said David, nodding. "Remember my telling you that you would have to discover the mystery of the heather yourself?"

"Yes, and I think I may be beginning to."

"Retaining its color is but one of heather's many mysteries," David went on. "In hopes that you will continue discovering its secrets, and in recognition of a friendship that I hope will deepen through time as does the mystery of the heather . . . your hand, please."

Loni smiled and held out her two hands.

David reached into his pocket and withdrew a tiny circular object fashioned with intricate strands of heather interwoven and held tight with delicately thin white wool yarn.

Gently he slipped it on the fourth finger of her right hand.

"A beautiful heather ring—it fits perfectly!" exclaimed Loni. "How did you know the size of my finger?"

"A lucky guess. But I had Odara help me with it. She said she had personal experience in exactly this kind—though she wouldn't tell me what she meant. But somehow she knew the right size to make it. She and Sandy plucked the wool from your special sheep. They said you would know what that meant."

Loni smiled and nodded. "I do."

"Wherever you go, whenever you look at this ring, its heather will be a reminder that you belong to this island, and that you belong—"

He hesitated briefly—then added, "to its people."

David smiled, and it was a smile that went straight to Loni's heart.

"And now," he said, "shall we walk into town and give the ladies something to talk about?"

"With pleasure," replied Loni. "Let me grab my windbreaker. It's a beautiful day, but . . . well, it *is* the Shetlands!"

ABOUT THE AUTHOR

Michael Phillips is a bestselling author of a number of beloved novels, including such well-known series as Shenandoah Sisters, Carolina Cousins, Caledonia, and The Journals of Corrie Belle Hollister. He has also served as editor of many more titles, adapting the classic works of Victorian author George MacDonald (1824–1905) for today's reader, and his efforts have since generated a renewed interest in MacDonald. Phillips's love of MacDonald's Scotland has continued throughout his writing life.

In addition to his fifty published editions of MacDonald's work, Phillips has authored and coauthored over ninety books of fiction and nonfiction, ranging from historical novels to contemporary whodunits, from fantasy to biblical commentary.

Michael and his wife, Judy, spend time each year in Scotland but make their home in California. To learn more about the author and his books, visit *fatheroftheinklings.com*. He can be found on Facebook at MichaelPhillipsChristian Author@facebook.com. To contact the Phillipses or join their email family, please write to: macdonaldphillips@sbcglobal.net.

Center Point Large Print
600 Brooks Road / PO Box 1
Thorndike, ME 04986-0001 USA

(207) 568-3717

US & Canada:
1 800 929-9108
www.centerpointlargeprint.com